C000146596

Lucía and the Fates

ACCLAIM FOR WORKS BY NICHOLAS SHRADY

Sacred Roads: Adventures from the Pilgrimage Trail

"An ambitious undertaking…there is much here that is fascinating, and his pocket histories of the world religions are immaculate."

Edward Marriot, *The Times*

"Shrady unites incisive, often humorous writing with thoughts on the religious faiths he seeks to understand…wonderfully combining travelogues with spiritual ruminations."

Publishers Weekly

"In the six journeys that compose this travelogue, Nicholas Shrady approaches spirituality with that rare combination of faculties, a yearning heart and an open, discerning mind."

Dennis Drabelle, *The Washington Post*

Tilt: A Skewed History of the Tower of Pisa

"An absolutely fascinating look…at one of the most fascinating human-made structures in the world."

Chicago Tribune

"Charming history…delightful and educating at once."

The Washington Post

"Lively…informative and amusing."

The New York Review of Books

The Last Day: Wrath, Ruin, and Reason in the Great Lisbon Earthquake of 1755

"Shrady's vivid account…is exemplary popular history…a lively, completely approachable lesson in pre-earthquake Portuguese history."

Booklist

"Admirable and perfectly paced."

Simon Winchester, *The New York Sun*

"Shrady's account will find the same ready audience that delights not only in tales of catastrophes but in smart, stylishly written history."

Publishers Weekly

Lucía
and the
Fates

Nicholas
Shrady

Lucía and the Fates
Nicholas Shrady
nicholasshrady@hotmail.com

Copyright © 2020 by Nicholas Shrady

All rights reserved. No part of this book may be reproduced or used in any manner without written permission of the copyright owner except for the use of quotations in a book review.

FIRST EDITION

ISBN-13: 9798616281623

BISAC CODE: FICTION / GENERAL FIC000000

Cover art: "Girl with a Cigarette" by Frederick William Elwell, courtesy of Harris Museum and Art Gallery/ © The Estate of Frederick William Elwell/ Bridgeman Images.

Cover design and internal layout by Luca Funari, *lucafunari@hotmail.com*

Nicholas Shrady was born and raised in Connecticut. He received a degree in philosophy from Georgetown University. He is the author of *Sacred Roads: Adventures from the Pilgrimage Trail, Tilt: A Skewed History of the Tower of Pisa*, and *The Last Day: Wrath, Ruin, and Reason in the Great Lisbon Earthquake of 1755*. He lives in Barcelona, Spain, where he is a professor of literature.

Contents

Chapter One...17

Chapter Two...43

Chapter Three..71

Chapter Four...111

Chapter Five...133

Chapter Six..163

Chapter Seven..211

Chapter Eight..263

Chapter Nine...305

Epilogue...341

Other works by Nicholas Shrady..............347

For Eva,
Max, Juline,
Sebastian, *and*
Andrea

"Greater than the earth is light,
greater than man is the earth,
and man's existence avails him nothing
until he breathes his native air…"

Hermann Broch
The Death of Virgil

CHAPTER ONE

"PAQUITO, IS THAT YOU?"

The voice came down the telephone line hollow and diminished, as if it were traveling not only across a vast oceanic distance, but across a gulf in time. The ringing of the telephone hadn't startled him awake; he had been lying in bed, smoking a cigarette and watching the shadows of leafless trees skitter and sway like specters across the ceiling. He knew who the caller was from the first word. Paquito, the diminutive for Paco, itself the diminutive for Francisco, was confined to a close circle of Spanish aunts and uncles, cousins, nieces and nephews, the Vidals, his mother's people. It was the voice of his cousin Victor. He hadn't heard it for years, and while its timber had grown deeper, its resonance more measured, there was no mistaking it, like a rhyme never forgotten.

"Hello Victor."

"I'm sorry Paquito..." The caller hesitated, and then shifted to Spanish, thinking it perhaps better suited to the gravity of the moment. *"Es tu madre...ha muerto."*

He sat up in bed, taking up the ashtray that had been balancing on his chest. For a long time he said nothing, listening to his own shallow breathing and the random, intermittent sounds of the city in the plaintive hours before dawn. A siren struck up its wailing and grew fainter as it moved down the avenue. He recalled the last time he had seen his mother eight months before. He was seeing her off at JFK, an exile returning home to Spain after an absence of almost forty years. She had looked at once expectant and forlorn. Despite all the years living in New York she never appeared to belong in the city, something about her composure, the way she so often stood stock still like a figure in a painting while life unfolded around her.

The silence on the telephone grew awkward. Paco could sense his cousin's discomfort, his chafing at the role of the bearer of grim news. Somehow, this did not displease Paco. He heard muffled voices in the background, but he couldn't make out what was being said. Victor must have been covering the receiver with his hand. He imagined them, this clutch of relations, huddled around the telephone in the vast, chilled hall at Quinta Amelia, his grandmother already clad in black; aunts and uncles making an effort to look solemn, while silently calculating legacies; cousins looking put upon and imagining better things to do; assorted children playing unaware.

"How did she die?" he finally asked.

"In her sleep, it seems. She never woke from yesterday's siesta."

"Yesterday?"

"Well, that is, we think yesterday," Victor offered cautiously, "maybe before. We're waiting to hear from the coroner. Hilario, the caretaker, hadn't seen her for several days. We finally broke down the door this morning."

Alone and in bed, Paco thought, how alike they were. As her only child, the funeral arrangements would be left to him. He would have to rouse his father from his work in Brazil, of course, but he didn't see him attending to any details. Silence again, prolonged and interrupted only by an occasional wisp of static.

"Paco, are you still there?"

"Yes," he replied, but he wasn't, not really. His mind was reeling. If his mother had traveled to Spain to see her family, how was it that she was alone and no one had seen her for days? he wondered. He hadn't wanted her to go and now she was gone forever.

"We thought that Saturday would be an appropriate day for the memorial service. You should be able to get here by then, and the bishop is free."

The bishop, he thought. Good God, she loathed them, but this was clearly not the moment to argue. He couldn't imagine what to say next. All he wanted was for the call to end. "Thank you, Victor, I will call you when I arrive in Barcelona." And he hung up the phone.

It was the 11th of December, 1976. What had begun as just another gloomy Monday was now a day forever etched in his life's calendar.

Paco Fates woke at noon to the dull light of a leaden autumn sky seeping through the Venetian blinds. For a moment he nearly forgot that he was motherless. An empty whiskey bottle standing accusingly on the bedside table, a rank taste in his mouth, and a relentless pulse somewhere deep behind his eyes reminded him that he had drunk himself to sleep after the call from his cousin Victor. He soon recalled having wallowed in the dark until the break of dawn, periodically lifting his glass to the memory of Lucía Vidal his dead mother. He could not, however, remember having shed a single tear. It wasn't that he didn't love her, in fact, he adored her. The tears just didn't come. He rose from bed, put on a worn silk robe, and shuffled barefoot to the bathroom. He stood before the sink, stooping slightly to see himself. He had never much liked observing his own countenance reflected in the glass, but this morning the image staring back at him was especially dismaying. His skin had a grey pallor as if his blood and vital fluids had somehow been drained from him. The only color in his face was the scarlet tracery of his blood-shot eyes and the raw pink of his swollen lips. Perhaps he had been crying after all, but more likely it was simply the effects of the whiskey. The pounding in his head had traveled to his temples. He felt old suddenly, although he was not yet forty. He splashed cold water on his face and passed a comb through his thick hair. At least he still had that, the healthy mane of a Vidal, black as pitch with a mere trace of grey at his throbbing temples. All his other physical attributes—the straight, narrow nose, prominent jaw, and untarnished hazel eyes—were harder to place. From his father he had only his long, slightly unwieldy limbs.

Paco left his room and made his way down the long hall, past empty bedrooms and a series of Old Masters of questionable provenance, the latter acquired by his grandparents on annual jaunts to Europe, where the art dealers of London, Naples, and Amsterdam had made illicit fortunes at their expense. He crossed the checkerboard marble floor of the entrance hall and entered the kitchen. The air in the apartment was close and the temperature stifling. Management kept the building's furnace perpetually stoked to placate the thin-skinned dowager neighbors who were forever complaining of the cold. He opened the window above the sink, closed his eyes, and let the piercing winter air caress his face.

"A fine hour to be rising," a voice scolded.

Paco turned to find Margaret the maid entering the kitchen from the servants' wing while tying an apron behind her back. "Good morning Margaret."

"Good afternoon to *you* sir. I imagine it's coffee you'll be wanting." It was a gentle reproach, as much as she would allow, no matter how many years of dedicated service to the Fates family.

"Yes, thank you."

She filled the coffee maker and set about preparing a tray with a silver pot and creamer and a gold-rimmed china cup. Paco watched her with silent admiration. He couldn't help but imagine how satisfying it must be to always know precisely what to do. He knew that she was growing old, she had turned seventy-two only a few weeks before, but he marveled at her seeming immutability. Her hair, worn in a tight, severe bun, had long ago turned as white as bleached cotton and gave her a kind of timeless appearance. True, her face had grown jowly, but she still had a fine aquiline nose and eyes of a luminous, azure blue. Paco loved her unwaveringly. Now, he was approaching middle-age and she should have been happily retired, but here she was still dutifully preparing his breakfast. Poor Margaret, he thought, he would have to break the news to her, but he hadn't the wherewithal just yet. She would shed tears all right, buckets of them. Now there was an unlikely pair, Paco thought, the Irish domestic and the Spanish lady, the devout Catholic and the determined anti-cleric, and yet the women had been devoted to one another. His mother had always treated her maid with uncommon consideration, something which the city's upper-class matrons had forever been warned by *their* mothers to staunchly avoid lest the help grow too familiar. For her part, Margaret had helped his mother to avoid the innumerable traps and pitfalls with which New York society was strewn, allowing her a modicum of assimilation in a foreign land, a land that she was in, but not of.

"Where will you be taking your breakfast sir?"

"What?" replied Paco blankly, roused suddenly from his reflections and almost forgetting where he was. He could feel the sluggishness of the whiskey still lumbering through his veins.

"Your breakfast sir."

"Ah yes, thank you, Margaret." Paco took the tray from her out-stretched arms, avoiding her eyes and what he knew would be a disparaging look. He made his way gingerly out of the kitchen, crossed the entrance hall, and entered the library, setting the tray down on the large oak desk and settled into the chair with a sigh. Before him lay the scattered pages, random notes, and secondary sources scarcely thumbed that together comprised his creative efforts, such as they were, in the conception of *Antonio Gaudí: The Lord's Master Builder.* His publisher had already billed the work as "the definitive opus on the Spanish genius," but he was woefully behind schedule and the book's publication date had already been once delayed. His stomach felt queasy, he wasn't sure whether from drink, or the sight of such half-hearted scholarship. He managed to eat a bit of buttered toast with his coffee, but left an egg untouched. Paco gazed out the tall sashed window on the familiar view down Park Avenue with its succession of uninspired stately piles that housed the city's titan class and buffered them from the grim realities of the place. He did not like New York, didn't like its air of perpetual menace, the way it impinged on one's freedom of movement, one's sense of security. He liked his club, a few friends, the Morgan Library, MOMA, Books and Co., a bar or two, but were those reasons enough to remain? He wasn't sure. He wondered why he stayed. Inertia, he supposed. His father had inherited the cavernous eighteen-room apartment and in due course it would be his, but he had never coveted the place and was attached to little in it.

It had begun to snow, the first flakes spiraling slowly down and melting instantly on the pavement. The avenue was a snarl of traffic and horns and sirens were blaring their accustomed chorus. A file of young boys appeared, turned out uniformly in blue blazers, crimson ties, and grey flannel trousers, marching behind their school master like so many goslings. They were from the Billings School around the corner, likely bound for Central Park or one of the museums. How Paco had wanted to be one of them as a boy. They always appeared so knowing and self-assured; as well they should, for the world would be theirs for the taking. His mother, however, had insisted on a public school, much to his grandparents' horror, but his father had backed her up and she had her way. So it was Stuyvesant High School for Paco, where the hard knocks came *because* he was from Park Avenue. One could do worse, he recalled with a wan smile, than growing up privileged.

It began to snow harder and harder until the flakes grew so dense that the world vanished as if a curtain had fallen. The sky gave off a piercing white light that made Paco's eyes ache. He turned from the window and reached a slightly trembling hand for his cup, but the coffee had grown cold and he cursed himself silently for gazing too long on the avenue. He rose from the desk and made his way to the fireplace, where he took a cigarette from the silver box on the mantelpiece and lit it with one of the long wooden matches used to light the fire. He inhaled deeply, relishing the warm, sweet smoke that only seemed to accompany the day's first cigarette. Arranged along the mantelpiece were framed photographs capturing the family in various scenes and guises—on the beach in Southampton, in front of the Christmas tree in the drawing room in New York, descending the Spanish Steps in Rome—snapshots from a charmed life. Paco found himself observing his mother in a new, strangely penetrating light, as if he were contemplating a stranger. In each of the photographs, he noticed, as if for the first time, his mother appeared like an uninvited guest in her own family. Only in one faded, sepia-tinged image could she be seen smiling broadly. It was a photograph from the Spanish Civil War. His mother is standing between his father and another man, her arms hooked in theirs. They are all dressed in fatigues and sporting berets. A camera hangs around his father's neck. Rising in the background are parched rocky mountains and at their foot a gentle bend of the Ebro with poplars skirting the far bank. The men are looking straight on, smiling at the camera, but his mother is captured in profile, looking up and appearing to say something to the other man. The photograph, Paco had always been told, was taken by his father's friend and colleague Eugene Wright, the renowned photographer who later died covering the war in Algeria. His mother had been an interpreter for the Republican forces, guiding and translating for foreign journalists in an attempt to promote the loyalist cause in the international press. That is how his parents had met. But who was the other man? Paco remembered asking his mother once when he was a teenager and studying the war. She had stared at the image intently for a long time as if trying to call up a dim memory from another life.

"Just a comrade," she finally replied.

What was his name? he had wanted to know. But she only shook her head and silently looked away.

It was late afternoon before Paco Fates could get up the energy to shower and dress. He chose a charcoal grey suit in a discreet sign of mourning, but dispensed with a tie. It had stopped snowing. He wanted to walk and needed some fresh air to clear his head. As he emerged from the elevator into the lobby, Patrick the doorman opened the weighty wrought-iron door with a tip of his hat. "Afternoon Mr. Fates."

Christ, thought Paco, how would New York society get on without the Irish? "Afternoon Paddy." Paco stepped out the door and onto the freshly shoveled sidewalk. The air was bitter cold and wet. He buttoned his overcoat, and took out a pack of Dunhills from a side pocket. Patrick was waiting with a lighter in his cupped hands. Paco stooped to the flame and raised his eyes to look at Patrick's ruddy, red-cheeked face as he lit his cigarette. He offered the pack to the doorman and Patrick tapped out a cigarette and pocketed it before returning the pack. "Thank you sir, I'll save it for the end of my shift."

"You're welcome Paddy. Tell me, how's the family?

"Fine sir, thank you for asking."

"And your mother, any word from her of late over there in sunny Spain?"

The question caught Paco unaware and he felt his throat suddenly contract. He turned away quickly to hide his grimace. "Not a word," he said over his shoulder, and briskly set off down the avenue.

The streetlights came blinking on, and at each side street Paco looked west to see the sky ablaze in lurid shades of orange and pink. People were emerging from the office buildings along Park, looking up briefly to glimpse the narrow sky, before hurrying off to catch subways, buses and trains that would carry them falteringly home. Paco was content to walk aimlessly, thinking scattered thoughts of his mother and his own solitary existence. He felt a pang of self-pity, walking alone and bereaved, but it was a false sentiment he knew at once. The truth was, he prized his loneliness and always had. Besides, his father was still alive, if far off, at least temporarily, which reminded him that he had to make that dreaded call to Brazil. Somehow, it didn't seem quite fair. It should have been the father who was breaking the news to the son; the father who would have to console the son. He felt vaguely cheated, as if some fundamental rite were being violated.

Night had fully fallen in a rush. Under ordinary circumstances, Paco would have made straight for the bar at the Carlyle, the Pierre, or perhaps Elaine's his habitual bars of choice, but he was feeling decidedly morose and didn't wish to see anyone he knew, neither barmen nor habitués, lest he begin to shed tears and blubber and make a fool of himself. He walked east. It had begun to snow again. The swirling flakes were illuminated in the skirts of light cast by a succession of street lamps. The snow creaked beneath his feet with a sharp, metallic sound. The city always seemed less sullied with a mantle of snow, its inhabitants friendlier, uncharacteristically forthcoming. Children were out on the stoops of their buildings, hurling snowballs at passing trucks and taxis. Groups of young people, their arms locked together to keep them from slipping, were bound for bars and restaurants and a night on the town.

Their shouts and laughter crossed the frigid air and sent up their breath in great billowing plumes. He came upon a movie theater and considered going in to lose himself in the dark, in some mindless fiction, but the feature film playing was *Rocky*. No, he thought, a boxing movie would not do, he felt beat up enough. What he needed was a drink. At Second Avenue Paco turned into the first bar he came upon, McSomething or other, he couldn't quite make out the name on the snow-covered awning. In the entrance he brushed a dusting of snow from his head and overcoat. The place smelled of beer gone sour, wet wool, and decline. There were a few men at the bar, regulars, he guessed, tradesmen, doormen, the odd broker, all nursing their drinks to soothe the day's bruises and put off their return home to wives and children and the certainties of domestic life. A group of young people were sitting at a table in the corner playing a drinking game, the boys and girls alternately shouting and screeching. The grinning face of Jimmy Carter, the president-elect, appeared on the television screen above the bar, but the sound was off, and no one seemed to pay much attention. Paco hung up his coat on a hook on the wall and took a stool at the bar. He lit a cigarette, raised his head, and blew a trumpet of smoke toward the ceiling. The bartender shuffled over as if shackled with some ancient weight to which he had wearily grown accustomed. He had the swollen face and flat nose of a former boxer. He stood before Paco speechless, waiting for his order behind watery eyes. Paco felt like a dry martini, but looked around and thought better of it. "Whiskey," he said "neat."

The bartender reached behind him blindly and unerringly grasped a bottle a Jameson's. With his other hand he produced a shot glass from beneath the bar, placed it in front of Paco, and filled it to the lip. Then he waited motionless, instinctively poised to repeat the gesture. Paco picked up the glass, tilted his head back, and downed the whiskey in one seamless movement. The liquid descended like something molten, but was soon sending a soothing, balmy sensation that rose from his chest to the base of his skull. He placed the glass on the bar and pushed it forward, giving the bartender a look of quiet supplication. The glass was refilled and Paco nodded in thanks.

The assorted men at the bar were all sitting separately, hovering over their drinks. Still, they carried on a ceaseless banter among themselves, commenting variously on the weather, real estate, crime, and sports, in short, bar talk, inoffensive and congenial. Paco could never manage to properly engage in this manner of chatter. When he had tried as a boy at school, as a young man at Georgetown, or even lately among his fellow members of the Century Club, his contributions always managed to sound somehow contrived. Never mind, he didn't feel like conversation, however innocuous. He preferred to go unnoticed, to focus on the vagaries of the dim tawny light reflecting in his whiskey glass. He drank it down, sucked the air through his teeth, and motioned to the bartender for another. He supposed that he wanted to not think about his mother, but it was no use, he could think of little else. *Tu madre ha muerto,* Victor had said. Such an irrefutable phrase that, nothing to argue about there. Dead and alone, that's how they had found her. But who were they, he wondered? Victor had mentioned Hilario, the caretaker, but who else? And how had they found her? Sprawled on the floor with furniture toppled and objects strewn about and, as some hard-boiled detective would say, signs of a struggle; or slumped in a chair with a book open on her lap—Lorca perhaps, or her beloved Machado—and her mouth gaping; or simply stretched out stiffly in her bed like a corpse in some antiquated wake? He didn't know. He didn't know because her only child hadn't been there. But it was she who had left. Perhaps she had returned home to Spain knowingly to die, wanting to be alone, intent on not being a burden. That would be just like her.

The bartender was watching Paco with a look of spent tolerance, his eyebrows raised and his mouth twisted into a scowl. A silence had come over the place, and the other men at the bar were peering at him sideways with their heads hung low. Had he been muttering to himself? What did he care? It wasn't every day, after all, that a man loses his mother. Paco kept at the whiskey until the bartender stated simply, categorically "enough is enough." He thought to dispute this—wasn't that the man's job, to keep the anesthetic flowing?—but he lost interest. He *was* drunk. He could feel himself drooping on his stool like something invertebrate.

His stomach was churning and he realized that he hadn't eaten anything since breakfast. "Fine," Paco countered, struggling to enunciate the single syllable in an exaggerated huff. He rose unsteadily from his seat, reached into his pockets for some money, and scattered a few bills haphazardly on the bar. He turned and weaved his way to the wall, reached for his coat and struggled into it. Then he steadied himself, took a deep breath, and made for the door. As he cleared the threshold, he heard a burst of collective laughter at his back, and felt the cold air slap his face like a chastening.

"Steady now Mr. Fates."

Suddenly Paco was being helped out of a taxi, a taxi he didn't recall hailing. He looked up blearily, widened his eyes and saw Juan, the night doorman. Or was it Jorge, he wondered? "*Gracias, buen hombre*," he managed to slur. Paco allowed himself to be guided by the arm into his building, across the foyer, and into the elevator, where he drooped heavily against the wall and waited passively. The doorman pushed the button for the second floor and withdrew, bidding Paco good night. Paco saluted, but couldn't think why, except perhaps for those preposterous uniforms which made every doorman look like an admiral of the fleet. When the elevator door opened, Paco found Margaret standing in the threshold, shaking her fine, white-haired head in reproach. The doorman must have called up and alerted her. Paco advanced to the center of the entrance hall and looked around him warily.

"The sight of you," she said. "It's a good thing your mother isn't here to see you."

Paco stiffened suddenly and squared his shoulders, but he was teetering on his heels and squinting from the glare of the crystal chandelier hanging above his head. He shook off his coat, almost letting it fall to the floor, but snatched it up just before Margaret could get a hold of it, and threw it on the settee in the corner.

"Miss Katherine is waiting for you in the drawing room," Margaret announced curtly.

Katia, Paco suddenly remembered. Oh dear, had they agreed to meet for dinner? He couldn't recall; everything was a jumble. He felt unmoored, or worse, sunken like a shipwreck. He took a deep breath, trying to compose himself, and walked with careful, deliberate steps into the drawing room. Katia was sitting on the sofa in front of the fireplace, feigning interest in a magazine, which she was flipping through with crisp, rapid movements of her hand. She did not look up. Even in his muddled state, Paco could see that she was fuming, an impression compounded by the reflection of the fire's flames which played across the silk of her black dress and caused the string of pearls around her neck to shimmer.

"My darling, I'm so terribly sorry to…" He didn't finish the sentiment, having walked into a side table and nearly toppling it.

"Good Lord, you're in your cups!"

How he loved the way she spoke, but where *did* she learn these turns of phrase? Paco wondered. Perhaps from one of her roles in Wilde or Shaw. "Yes, I'm afraid I am, most" he replied meekly.

Well, I'm leaving," Katia said, rising from the sofa, "I've been waiting here long enough."

"No, please" he pleaded. "There's something I must tell you."

Katia stopped at once, she could hear the uncommon note of desperation in his voice, see the anguish in his face. She stared at him, waiting, utterly still. "What is it? What's happened?"

Paco gestured for her to sit and sunk into the sofa beside her, letting out a heavy, whiskey-laden breath as if all the life were being sucked out of him. "It's my mother," said Paco. "She's died."

There was a sudden crash, a high-pitched clatter of metal and shattering porcelain. Paco and Katia looked up startled to see Margaret in the center of the drawing room, the coffee service at her feet. She stood there motionless, her eyes shut tight and her mouth moving soundlessly. It was then that Paco began to weep, the tears streaming down his face unheeded, like a river breaching a levee.

Katia stayed up with Paco listening obligingly to his pent-up laments and scattered memories of a lost mother until the ashes had grown cold in the hearth. It wasn't easy to make sense of his train of thought, muddled as it was with liquor and tears, but he kept coming back to his mother's return to Spain.

"Why?" he asked repeatedly. "Why would she go back after so many years to a country she hardly knew? And alone no less. My father had desperately wanted to accompany her, but she had insisted on going on her own. What did she expect to find there? What was the point?"

Katia did her best to console him, but she could not answer the questions any more than Paco could. Katia knew that Lucía had been forced to flee Spain during the Civil War and for years had been barred from returning. She had left a mother and siblings behind, family that she hadn't seen in decades. The woman certainly wasn't neglecting her wifely duties, Adam Fates, Paco's father, was off in Brazil working on some photo project or another. In any case, the two of them had always struck Katia as more akin to a brother and sister than a married couple. Theirs was a curious union. She wasn't sure why, but it had always seemed to her that Adam was more devoted to Lucía than she to him. That left Paco, a grown man; and his mother wasn't compelled to stay in New York for his benefit.

"Forgive me," said Katia "but I don't find it inexplicable that your mother should wish to return home to see her family after so many years. Surely she must have missed them and they her."

"Missed them?" Paco asked, incredulous. He chuckled, but there was no joy in it.

"Well, yes, why wouldn't she?"

"I know I've told you that I spent a summer with my mother's family. I was sixteen or seventeen, too young to understand many things, but old enough to grasp a good deal. You can't imagine how they all spoke of her, and in front of me, her son, no less. They vilified her. For them, she was a pariah. I was so taken aback because so much time had passed since she was last among them. I couldn't believe how unforgiving they all were."

"Oh," said Katia "I wasn't aware of any of that. So, what had she done that her family couldn't forgive?"

Paco exhaled loudly, shaking his head. "Fuck if I know. Excuse me. I know that politics and class had a lot to do with it, that's for sure. My mother was a real radical back in the war. She even had a radio program;

a kind of propaganda show in which she tried to raise the soldiers' moral. Evidently it was a great success. They called her *Lucía the Red.* Can you believe it? I can't imagine that the family was too thrilled about that, they're a highly conservative bunch, hanging on to their ancient privileges and all that. I think she was lucky to have gotten out, she probably would have been shot. And then…" Paco's voice trailed off.

"What?"

"Something about a brother who was murdered during the war."

"You mean killed in battle."

"No, that would have been easier to confront. He was murdered by some death squad or something and left on the side of the road. It was in reprisal for something."

"God, how ghastly."

"Yes, I know, a lot of that went on, evidently," Paco said. He stared off thinking of conversations that he and his mother had had, or the lack of them. "The thing is, all these memories of the war were like an open wound for her, even after all these years, and one never wanted to press too much, insist that she explain things. And now it's too late."

"You could always confront her siblings, ask them."

"Yes, I could do, but I wish it had come from her. I wish I had her side of things. I don't know if I want their take on it all. I don't want my memory of my mother to be poisoned by them."

"Yes, I see what you mean. They really sound vile."

"Oh, they are. I've never told anyone about this, but I have long had this recurring dream, or rather nightmare. My mother is bound to the bannister of the staircase in the entrance hall at Quinta Amelia, the family seat, and a very impressive pile. I can only see her bare back. She is surrounded by her siblings, each of whom holds a switch, and they take turns whipping her. It all takes place in silence. I cannot hear the sound of the blows or my mother crying out, but I can see the blood-streaked wounds on her back. Outside the circle of siblings stands my grandmother stoically looking on, and Rose, the maid and great childhood friend of my mother, who is weeping copiously, but also in silence."

A shiver ran through Paco.

"You see...that nightmare has never lost its power for me. Every time it visits me I wake up in a panic, a cold sweat on my brow and at my temples, the sheets tangled. I think...no, I'm convinced, that when I objected so strenuously to my mother returning to Spain, much of my misgiving stemmed from the persistence of that dream. Does that make sense?"

Katia did not answer right away. Maybe, Paco thought, she was lost in painful memories of her own.

"Perhaps," Katia suggested finally "your mother wished to return home to die, to be buried in native ground."

"*This* was her home," Paco answered, his tone a bit too adamant, he realized at once.

It wasn't entirely true, Katia thought, but she did not wish to contradict him. Katia had been close to Lucía Vidal, and she knew that Paco's mother had always considered herself an exile, one of the vanquished. For her, New York was a refuge, a gilded one on Park Avenue to be sure, but a refuge just the same. It had always seemed to Katia that Lucía was merely biding her time in America, waiting for her life to resume back in Spain at some indeterminate, but ineluctable date. Katia recalled having once come across Lucía's address book alongside the telephone in the library and she couldn't help but peek inside to see who this woman actually knew. What she found were mostly blank pages, as if Lucía maintained little contact with people apart from the florist, her hairdresser, or the odd tradesmen. Even the fact that the woman had always maintained her surname in the Spanish manner and refused to be known as "Mrs. Fates" was indicative of her seemingly transient condition in America.

It was well past midnight when Katia led Paco to his room, undressed him with calm precision, and put him to bed, kissing the crown of his head like a child. Paco muttered something incomprehensible into the pillow and fell asleep instantly. She stood over him for a moment, listening to his fitful breathing. In the nearly ten years that they had been together, never had she seen him so vulnerable and bruised, and for the first time in as long as she could remember Katia felt that he truly needed her. For how long she did not know. She turned from the bed and left the room, switching off the light and gently closing the door behind her. She wasn't sure that she would return.

Katia was putting on her coat in the entrance hall when she noticed a light on in the kitchen. She went in to find Margaret sitting silently in her nightgown, her hair down and spilling over her shoulders. She was red-eyed and had a handkerchief pressed to her mouth, before her on the kitchen table lay the shattered remains of the two china cups.

"In all my years of service I never broke a thing," she said without looking up.

"It's nothing that can't be replaced," Katia replied.

"Unlike the Mrs." said Margaret.

"Yes, unlike the Mrs."

Katia took a seat beside Margaret and reached out to take a hand in hers, feeling the paper-thin texture of the old woman's skin and the boundaries of brittle bones that lay beneath it. The two women sat in silence for a long time, lost in thought. Then Margaret withdrew her hand, set both on her thighs, and looked about blinking. She seemed to have forgotten suddenly where she was or with whom.

"I must be on my way," said Katia.

"You will do no such thing. It is much too late for a woman to be out walking the streets alone," Margaret admonished. "This is no time for you to leave," she added, her tone milder. "Go to him."

* * *

Paco woke late after a dreamless sleep. Everything was silent, nothing stirring, but he knew that he was not alone. He saw that the other side of the bed had been slept in. Katia's black dress was laid carefully over the back of the armchair. And he smelled her, that delicious mixture of perfume, powder and a woman's skin. Sunlight was streaming through the blinds and at the top of the window a streak of sky, cerulean blue and cloudless, was visible. Paco rose and peered out; the light reflected from the snow was blinding and made him squint. There was scarcely any traffic. The sidewalks were still laden with snow.

He found Katia in the kitchen. For a long time he stood just outside the threshold unannounced, watching her move about the room as she prepared breakfast. She was wearing his robe; the silk had slipped down to reveal a shoulder as smooth as polished marble. Her feet were bare. There was something almost liquid about the way she moved. He wasn't surprised that the theater was her life. She was born for the stage. Had it not been for the theater, he recalled, they would never have met.

It was the winter of '67. He had been to the New York première of Pinter's *The Homecoming* at the Music Box Theater. For some reason he had gone alone, whether out of choice or because a date or a friend had cancelled, he could no longer remember. After the performance he went around to Joe Allen's for dinner and Katia, or rather Katie as she was known then, Katie Caraway, was his waitress. He had never seen anyone with such exquisite posture. She carried herself like a priestess, her tray like some sort of offering to the Gods. Everything about her was luminous, from her hazel eyes to her auburn hair, her skin. Every man in the dining room was watching her. He could tell at once that she wasn't from New York, even before she asked him, "How are you tonight?" in a sultry southern drawl.

"I would say that things are looking up."

Her eyes wandered over him and she managed a lazy smile. "Is it as depressing as they say?"

"What, eating alone in New York?"

"No silly," she said, "the play, *The Homecoming,*" she was looking at his playbill on top of the table.

"Ah, well, yes, also puzzling, claustrophobic, emotionally draining, and one of the most important plays I've ever seen."

"I'd kill to see it," she said in a tone that made Paco think that she just might.

She then proceeded to ignore him for the rest of the night, serving his dinner with mild disinterest and avoiding all conversation. He left her an inordinate tip and his card with a note:

*In an attempt to dissuade you from committing murder, would
you accompany me to another performance of The Homecoming.
If not, I shall visit you in jail. Either way, please call me.*

And she did, the very next morning. "My, my, you surely know how to
get this girl's attention." He was elated. When they met in front of the
theater she seemed to have grown more beautiful. During the performance she sat on the edge of her seat, leaning forward with her chin resting on her hands, and watched the action without once shifting or fidget-
ing or yawning. He had never seen such concentration. When the curtain
came down she was exhausted, as if she had been up on stage, which in a
sense she had. "One day I will play Ruth," she said with utter assurance.

They walked to Café des Artistes for dinner. She took his arm as if
they had known each other for years. When they entered the dining
room, conversation seemed to cease as men and women both watched
her with a kind of animal yearning. She wore a short white dress with a
clean geometrical cut—Courréges he thought it was—and high white
boots with a black stripe running up the sides. "It seems I've overdressed,"
she said, looking at the wood nymphs in the Howard Chandler Christy
mural under which they sat. When their dinner arrived she ate with undisguised relish and drank the Chateau Margaux as if she were knocking
back shots of bourbon. Paco hardly touched his food, content to simply
watch her and to listen to that low, smoldering drawl.

She was from West Texas, Midland, a desolate place made habitable
by oil and the staggering wealth it begot. Her daddy, as she called him,
was clearly one of the haves, but that hadn't stopped her mother running off with a roughneck from the oil fields. Like Paco she was an only
child. Not six months before she had been enrolled as a drama student
at the University of Texas. She didn't last a week. "Stifling" was all she
said by way of explanation. By the time her father found out she was
already settled in an apartment in the East Village with de Kooning and
the Hell's Angels as neighbors. He threatened to cut her off, but she
feigned indifference and he backed down. He had no one else.

Not long after that first dinner, Katia, as she was now called, began to land minor roles, which didn't remain minor for long. She may have lacked the formal training for Shakespeare, but she thrived in modern work by Williams, O'Neill, Miller, and the like. Everyone loved her, directors, critics, audiences, and, of course, Paco, madly.

* * *

It was the smell of coffee that drew Paco out of the deep pool of memory. He crossed the threshold, "Good morning," he said.

Katia started and let out a yelp. "Well, look who's risen from the dead." As soon as she uttered the words she regretted the choice of phrase, but he took no offense. Paco came up to her from behind, put his arms around her, and leaned down and gave her a kiss on the cheek. Katia slipped from his embrace, rather too abruptly, he thought.

"Where's Margaret?" he asked.

"Resting. She too has had a terrible shock."

"Yes, of course."

They took breakfast trays back to bed and ate side by side without uttering a word. Every sound—a knife spreading butter on toast, a spoon stirring, a cup set down on its saucer—seemed amplified, as if they occupied some bare, sequestered chamber shut off from the world and themselves. Finally, it was Paco who broke the silence. "Forgive me for last night, I…"

"No need to apologize," she said, before he could finish, "not for last night."

And then she rolled swiftly out of bed before he could ask, *if not for last night, then what?*

The sun was high in the sky, but it gave no warmth, and when the wind rose it burned one's cheeks. Paco and Katia walked arm in arm pressed tight against the cold. They were dressed for a winter outing. Paco had rummaged through his mother's closet looking for something for Katia. He had been momentarily shaken by the lingering smell of her; something of his mother hung on there, disembodied, but unmistakable. He found some old ski wear—sleek black pants, a heavy crimson woolen sweater, shaggy white fur boots—and when Katia was dressed, she looked as if she had stepped from St. Moritz circa 1965. Paco wore an old, threadbare duffle coat, a remnant of his days at Georgetown, and brown, thick-ribbed corduroys stuffed into high rubber boots. Despite his age, he always managed to look vaguely collegiate. They entered Central Park at 66th Street, skirting the diminutive children's zoo. There were no animals out, but one could smell their rankness invading the frozen air. A vast whiteness enveloped the landscape. In some places they were the first to tread the virgin snow, their steps made a crisp crunching sound as they went. Overhead, the dark, leafless trees rose in sharp contrast against the luminous sky; their shadows were pale blue in the snow. Dogs, momentarily unleashed as if on reprieve, were running wildly, leaping, burrowing, rolling in celebration. At the Wollman rink, Paco cleared a bench of snow with his sleeve and they sat and watched the skaters. The air was shot through with shouts and laughter and the sound of skates scraping the grey ice. Since they had entered the park Paco and Katia had hardly exchanged a word. He could sense that she was smarting. Had he said something cruel in his stupor the night before, something insensitive? He couldn't be sure. "Darling, if I've done or said something stupid or hurtful, I'm sorry, truly. As you can imagine, I'm not at all myself."

A young black man, tall, athletic, was skating expertly through the crowd, unleashing an occasional axel jump, spinning, gliding. Paco watched him in awe. "He makes it look so effortless," he muttered half to himself. His scrutiny was interrupted when Katia began to sob. "What is it?" he pleaded.

"Tell me Paco," she asked, her voice quavering, "what am I exactly to you? Am I a lover, a mistress, a companion, a partner, and do *not* say girlfriend for fuck's sake, this is not high school!"

He had been mistaken, she wasn't smarting, she was furious. Seldom did she use profanity, or as she would say, *cuss*. He hesitated, not quite sure what to say, she had taken up all of the most apt titles. "Well, all those things really and a great deal more," he finally offered, aware at once that it sounded half-hearted. "You mean everything to me Katia, you know that."

"Do I?"

"Is this about marriage, tell me, because…"

"No Paco, this is not about marriage, God forbid, this is simply about being more than an afterthought in your life. You know very well how I loved Lucía, how she was something of a mother to me as well. Did you not think for a moment that I would wish to attend her funeral, that I would want to be at your side at such a time?"

Paco closed his eyes and slowly shook his head, aware all at once of the depth of his own thoughtlessness.

"And for that matter," Katia continued, seeming to gain momentum, "did you not consider that Margaret would want to pay her last respects to the woman she spent most of her life serving? Really Paco, never have I known someone quite so self-consumed, and I work in the bloody theater!"

When Paco finally opened his eyes, the flawless skater had vanished. He felt like one of the young flailing children whose ankles were weak and gave way like rubber. "You are absolutely right," he said, straightening up. "I will book the additional tickets immediately."

"It's too late," Katia said, looking away, "at least for me." It was not something that she ever imagined she would say. They sounded like the very first words of an ending.

"What do you mean it's too late? What are you saying?"

She turned to him, her eyes red and flooded like swollen pools. "I'm leaving Paco. I've accepted a role in London. I had wanted to tell you last night, but for obvious reasons it wasn't the moment."

He sunk back on the bench reeling as if he had taken a blow to the head. "What role? When?" he asked incredulous, his voice barely more than a whisper.

"Oh, does it really matter?" Katia's voice was cracked, she sounded to Paco like a different person entirely. He had never seen or heard her like this before.

"Yes...no...I mean..." Paco didn't know what he meant, he was groping. "Must you go?"

"It's *The Cherry Orchard* at the Old Vic. I am to play Varya. It's a wonderful opportunity." She was trying her utmost to sound convincing, but
Katia could feel her determination waning.

"But must you go?" Paco repeated.

"Don't you understand?" she asked, shaking her head in disbelief.
"I sought out the role. I *want* to get away!"

"I never imagined that you were so unhappy," said Paco, dumbstruck.

"I hadn't been until now."

They sat in stunned silence, the two of them gazing into the distance,
but focusing on nothing. They might have been strangers sharing the
park bench, but maintaining a polite remove. Clouds slowly enveloped
the sun, and the blanched landscape grew bleak. Katia suddenly sat up
straight and insisted on returning to her apartment, "alone," she added
unequivocally. They rose and embraced. Paco tried to hold her tighter,
as if to somehow retain her in his clutches, but she pushed back gently.
He looked down at her face, blotched and sodden, and she looked off
in profile to avoid his eyes.

"Chekhov, how apt," said Katia finally. "Do you know the play?" she
asked, neither expecting nor waiting for him to answer. "Varya is perpetually in tears on account of her powerlessness. With neither money
nor a husband, she has no control over her fate." She laughed, but it was
a mirthless laugh, full of derision and defeat. "It will be the role of my
life." And with that she broke away and began walking briskly toward
the park exit. Paco called after her, but she didn't stop, she only cried
out without turning, "Come and see me at the Old Vic!"

* * *

Paco sat at his desk staring at the telephone and trying to compose
in his mind the words which he would utter to inform a man that
he had lost his wife. He had been putting off the call, fearful of his
father's reaction, dreading the agony that he would unleash, but it

was getting late. How he wished that his father was there with him, not only so that they could mourn together, but so that he could seek advice regarding Katia. His father was so resolutely charming, had such a way with women, as they say. Katia adored him. She confessed to Paco once that she couldn't quite understand why Lucía wasn't more smitten with her husband. Paco recalled being put off by the observation, miffed that someone was questioning his parents' love for one another. But it was true. He didn't know why. He told Katia that he thought his parents had a very solid relationship, but he immediately realized how paltry that sounded, as if he were describing some arranged Victorian union. Perhaps that was Paco's problem, that his lack of commitment and resolution with Katia had somehow been conditioned by the diffidence of his parents' marriage. Jesus, he realized suddenly, he was too old to blame his parents for the shortcomings in his love life. He had to focus. He had to make the call. There was no more time to spare, not if he wanted to allow his father to get to Spain in time for the funeral. Paco suddenly sensed that he was not alone and looked up to see Margaret standing in the threshold. She seemed to him to have grown smaller as if the loss of his mother had diminished her physically.

"Ah, Margaret, I'm glad you're here, I wanted to speak with you."

"And I with you sir."

"Yes, of course, please come in and sit down," he said, motioning with an outstretched arm to a chair in front of his desk. She took several steps into the library, but chose not to sit. She looked at him with a stricken expression and waited unmoving. Paco cleared his throat. He was thinking of what Katia had said hours before: *Really Paco, never have I known someone quite so self-consumed...* Was this the way Margaret regarded him as well, he wondered?

"Margaret, I wanted to know if you would care to accompany me to Spain for my mother's funeral. Forgive me for not having asked you sooner. The fact is, I haven't been myself since I learned of my mother's death, as I'm sure you've noticed. I know how much you loved her and how much she loved you. You would do me a great service, that is, you would do me a great honor if…" He was beginning to babble, he knew, but he wanted nothing so much as to put things right with at least one woman who he truly loved. Luckily, Margaret seemed to sense his unease and interrupted.

"That is most generous of you sir, truly it is, but what would I be doing there not understanding a word they're saying and being nothing but a burden to you? No, but thank you sir. I have asked Father McTyhe at St. Thomas More to say a Mass for her on Sunday. She knows that I am praying for her."

"Are you quite sure?"

"I am sir."

"Very well Margaret. Now, what is it that you wanted to talk to me about?" Margaret looked at him uneasily and began to wring her hands. She looked like a child who had been caught in a lie.

"Oh that," she exclaimed nervously, "nothing really sir, nothing that can't wait." She said good night and began to sidle out of the room, but stopped suddenly and turned again to Paco. "No one ever treated me as decently as your mum did, not even my own mum," she said, her voice fragile and distant, as if she were somewhere else, in her childhood perhaps. "I feel as if I've lost a sister, a daughter even." And then she backed out without another word.

Paco had the distinct sensation that he had come very close to losing the third woman in his life. He glanced at his watch; it was nearly midnight, an hour later in Rio. He dialed the number on the old rotary phone and listened as the distant connection clicked improbably down the line. As the telephone began to ring he prepared his most soothing voice, hoping to rouse his father gently from his sleep.

"*Boa noite, quem deseja?*" came a female voice as soft and inviting as slumber. There was music playing in the background, something brassy with a bossa nova beat, and the sound of raucous laughter. Paco was taken aback; he had not expected Brazilian revelry.

"*Senhor Fates por favor.*"

"*Momento.*"

Paco waited, hoping that his father would be coherent. There was a loud clatter, as if the telephone had fallen to the floor. Finally he heard his father's voice, boozy and resolutely jovial. It was a voice he had heard before.

"Adam Fates here…alooo…alooo…"

Paco cringed, but said nothing, only slowly and gently hung up the phone. For a long time he sat in silence, wondering if he should call back. In the end he settled for a telegram, laconic and aloof:

```
PAPA TRIED TO CALL YOU BUT COULD NOT GET THROUGH STOP
DEEPLY SORRY TO INFORM YOU MOTHER HAS DIED STOP
VIDAL CLAN HAS ARRANGED FUNERAL IN TORTOSA CATHEDRAL
SATURDAY NOON STOP
I WILL BE AT THE RITZ BARCELONA STOP HOPE
TO SEE YOU THERE

PACO
```

CHAPTER TWO

Paco tried to sleep during the flight, aided by generous quantities of complimentary wine, but to no avail; behind him, a group of zealous pilgrims bound for Santiago de Compostela sang folk songs to the accompaniment of a guitar out of tune. When turbulence hit they murmured prayers and clutched rosaries. Just his luck, thought Paco. He rose and made his way to the back of the plane to smoke, taking a seat in an empty row beside the lavatory. The plane's engines produced a relentless din.

For Paco, there had always been something peremptory about his journeys. When he was sixteen, he was packed off to Spain for the summer. His mother had insisted that he know his Spanish relations, even though she herself refused to return until Franco was dead and buried, or so she was fond of repeating. Only later did he discover that, in fact, she had tried to return on several occasions, but her visa applications had always come back stamped: *denegado*. Paco reached into a breast pocket of his suit jacket and withdrew an envelope, worn and discolored, on which he read, as he had innumerable times before, his name and the request *To be read on route*, in a neat flowing script. Although he could have recited verbatim the contents of the letter which the envelope enclosed, Paco removed the brittle writing paper with care and read anew.

May 27th, 1955
New York

My Dearest Paco,

For the first time you are traveling alone to an unknown land that is nonetheless a part of your heritage. Do not be afraid. You are a young man now, strong, intelligent and capable, and you will make your way. Trust your instincts. I know that a great deal of what I am writing we have discussed before, but there is something about seeing things in writing that makes a more lasting impression.

It is high time that you get acquainted with the Vidals. They are immediate family, however distant geographically, and you must know that they are a part of you and you of them. There is much about the family that will seem new to you, and strange, and perhaps incomprehensible. If ever you feel lost or lonely, turn to your uncle Francisco, after whom you were named, he will help to guide you through the labyrinth of the Vidals' world. Please send him my love and tell him how I miss him every day. Tell him too that there is no excuse for him not visiting us in New York, and that he is welcome always and forever. Be always courteous and attentive with your grandmother, but do not let her bully you. She is head of the family and is accustomed to getting her way. Hold fast to your principles if ever they are challenged. Of your aunt Inés there is little that I can say as we have not spoken since I fled my home at the end of the war. As children we were inseparable, but as we grew older our differences about life and the world divided us. Of her husband Javier I can recall little more than his penchant for tennis, and that he was a lovely dancer. Their son Victor is, I suspect, the one you will be seeing the most of. He is a year or so older than you and exceedingly bright from what I understand from mother. If you two do not "hit it off", as you say here, well, do your best to get on. He is your cousin and will be your link to the Vidals for the rest of your days. That leaves you uncle Borja, and here, forgive me, but I must be very plain—tread carefully. I don't know how to fully explain it, except to say that in life one sometimes meets people whose intentions are not always good. There was always something

*hard and dark about Borja and I fear that that has not changed.
I scarcely know his wife Paulina or their twin girls, whose names
I don't even recall. I have been absent and detached for so long that
when you return to New York, it will be you who will be informing
me of the family. Ah yes, I must not forget Rosa! I believe that she
is now the cook, but when I was a girl, she was a young chamber
maid and one of my closest companions. God does not often create
children so kind and selfless. You will love her as I did and still do,
for I am sure that she has not changed. Tell her that she is forever
in my thoughts.*

*So, beloved Paco, keep your mind alert and your eyes and heart
open, Spain awaits you, and I will count the days until your return!*

With all my love,

Mamá

*P.S. Please make good use of the beautiful camera that Papa gave
you. I want to see pictures of everyone and everything! And again,
Papa was devastated not to be able to see you off, but he got stuck on
assignment in Cuba. He loves you more than life itself!*

Paco folded the letter carefully, slid it into the envelope, and returned
it to his breast pocket. He could remember the details of that first
journey to Spain with uncanny clarity. He had traveled in a sleek
Lockheed Super Constellation, seated beside a mild seminarian who
politely introduced himself and then proceeded to spend the entire
flight immersed in the verses of St. John of the Cross. At Barcelona airport a chauffeur smartly turned out in grey with gleaming black boots
and a peaked cap collected him in an antiquated Hispano-Suiza. No
one from the Vidal family came to meet him. The chauffeur's name,
he said, when Paco asked, was Sebastián. He smelled of tobacco and
cheap cologne. His hair gleamed with pomade. They drove south in

silence while Paco gazed out at the placid sea and the ragged figures working the vineyards, groves and fields. When they passed through the half-ruined villages trailing dust, old men crowded into slices of shade stared at the big car with the single boy occupying the back seat. The journey to Tortosa seemed interminable. He fell asleep lulled by the heat and woke up soaked in sweat with the car idling before a high, spiked gate with the name Quinta Amelia wrought in looping iron letters across the bars. The chauffeur tooted the horn and waited expressionless until a stooped figure appeared and opened the gate with slow, deliberate movements, doffing his straw hat, but lowering his eyes as they drove passed. The gravel drive was flanked by cypress trees that stood like uniformed sentinels and led past olive groves and orchards and towering palms. When the house came into view Paco gasped, and his eyes, wide with amazement, caught those of Sebastián observing him in the rear-view mirror. Before them rose an imposing brick edifice with a many-gabled roof from which rose towers encrusted with variegated tiles. There were crenelated parapets, balconies fashioned from what seemed a tangle of iron, and colored glass filling irregularly shaped windows. The whole effect was at once fantastical and slightly sinister, as if the house had somehow grown out of the landscape like something organic rather than having been built upon it.

The front door did not swing open to release a multitude of Vidals spilling down the steps to greet him, a scene that Paco had imagined again and again in his mind's eye. The car proceeded past the grand entrance and crept around the back of the house, parking in a courtyard that gave on to what looked to be the servant's wing and the garage. Sebastián did not come around to open his door. Paco stepped out of the car and into a withering heat. Above him a penitential sun hung in a white sky. It was four o'clock, siesta time, and everything seemed suspended in a kind of shuttered stupor. There were no human sounds, only the humming of bees, the mechanical drone of cicadas, and the distant howling of dogs penned up somewhere in the near distance.

"Welcome traveler!" a woman called as she came out the back door and rushed toward him, drying her hands on her apron. She reached up and grasped his shoulders in her hands and looked him up and down. "So this is Paquito, at last! But you are a man, my God, and handsome!"

Paco smiled tentatively, but could think of nothing to say but *"gracias."*

She could see that he was at a loss. "Forgive me, I am Rosa."

"Ah, of course," said Paco, smiling broadly. "My mother sends all her love. She says that you are always in her thoughts."

"Seeing you, it is as if your mother had returned." Her eyes welled up and she quickly brushed back a tear.

Sebastián had removed Paco's bag from the trunk of the car and placed it at his feet with an air of finality as if his duty were done.

"Take that up to his room," Rosa demanded.

Sebastián looked at Rosa with surprise and then at Paco with a grimace, and slowly reached down and picked up the bag and led the way into the house.

His room was perched on the attic floor beneath the gables. It wasn't in the servant's quarters exactly, but it wasn't a proper guest room on the second floor either. There was nothing lacking, nothing superfluous, just a narrow bed, a side table, an armoire, a desk and chair, and a wash stand. A crucifix hung above the bed, otherwise the walls were bare. A single window provided a view over countless olive trees that stretched in immaculate rows to the foot of distant mountains the color of tarnished silver.

Paco sat down wearily on the bed. The house was silent around him. On his bedside table he noticed a photograph propped against the lamp. He reached over and picked it up and saw a cracked and faded image of his mother, perhaps at the age that he was now, standing alone in a garden bathed in dappled light. He could not imagine her childhood here. From time to time she spoke to him of her siblings, his uncle Francisco and aunt Inés, of her late father, and her mother with whom she kept up a steady if strained correspondence, but who she hadn't seen for nearly twenty years, not since the Civil War had separated them and rendered them irreconcilable. Paco had never met any of the Vidals. They had never come to New York to visit. They were a mystery to him, inhabitants not so much of another country as another world, archaic and uncharted, like a lost civilization, and he had been set down amongst the ruins. He was not quite sure what to do or what was expected of him. He laid his head down, exhausted from the journey and the heat, and slept.

When he woke, the light had changed; the air was cooler. He looked at his watch, but realized that he had neglected to set it to Spanish time and was unsure how long he had been asleep. He heard a tapping and raised his head from the pillow to see a boy sitting in the corner, drumming his fingers on the desk top.

"Well, it's about time. You've been out for hours."

Paco sat up, bleary eyed and sluggish. "You must be Victor."

"Yes, how astute. And you are *tia* Lucía's boy, Paquito."

"It's Paco."

"No. In this house Paco is our uncle, *tio* Francisco. You are Paquito, little Paco." His tone was at once mocking and haughty.

"I must have been in a deep sleep, I didn't hear you knock," said Paco.

"That's because I didn't. I'm not in the habit of knocking on the doors in my own house."

Paco supposed that this is what his mother meant by "not hitting it off." He disliked his cousin instantly and knew that it was going to be a long, trying summer.

"So how old are you Paquito?"

"Sixteen."

Victor groaned, *"joder"* he said. "Well, I'm eighteen, two years your senior, so you will address me always with reverence."

"When is your birthday?" Paco asked.

"In July" he said, looking away.

"In July you will be nineteen?"

"No, eighteen."

"Ah, so you're not eighteen quite yet. Actually you're just one year and one month older."

"Oh, you are astute. Just the same, I'm your elder. Don't forget it, *maricón.*"

"What was that?" said Paco, standing up from the bed and approaching Victor. He was tall for his age, and although Victor was seated, Paco could tell that he was small for his. When he was looming over Victor, he said, "I dare you to repeat that."

"*Tranquilo*," Victor stammered, and he rose and slipped past Paco and made for the door. "Follow me," he said over his shoulder. "Everyone is in the garden waiting to meet Lucía's boy."

"Lucía's boy," Paco muttered to himself and sighed.

* * *

"Excuse me?" came a voice, rousing Paco from his reverie.

Suddenly he realized that he wasn't alone. There was a man smoking in the seat next to him. Paco looked at him, blinking. He was of indeterminate age with thinning, pale red hair and milky blue eyes. His cheeks were rosy and rather too well shaved. A failed priest, Paco thought immediately. "Oh, nothing," said Paco as he lit another cigarette and gazed out the window at the oceanic darkness.

At Barcelona airport Paco and his fellow passengers descended from the plane and were obliged to walk across an expanse of tarmac to the terminal. The Mediterranean light was blinding, and compared to the chill of New York the temperature was positively balmy. Paco felt an odd contentment, the circumstances of the journey notwithstanding. He always loved coming to Barcelona, although he always dreaded the possibility of encountering one of the Vidals. It was a city at once familiar and foreign, like a dream in which certain details are recognizable, but the contexts are skewed. As Paco made his way through Customs, he was stopped by a member of the Civil Guard, who saluted Paco briskly, raising his hand to touch the crown of his gleaming patent leather tricorn. Paco wondered how long they would go on wearing those slightly comical hats. On the wall behind the guard he noticed an official portrait of a uniformed prince Juan Carlos where until not long ago Franco's image would have hung. It was the first sign of the new times. Nearly forty years of autocratic rule, how long the country had had to wait for the dictator to die, Paco reflected. The guard, whose gut was straining the buttons on his shirt, motioned for Paco to place his suitcase on the table. Without uttering a word he looked Paco in the eye and then jerked his head toward the bag, indicating that he should open it. Paco did so, revealing a duty-free bag which he had stashed in the suitcase. Inside the bag were two bottles of exceptional single malt whiskey and two cartons of Dunhills. When the guard looked inside his expression turned from reticence to one of longing. Paco thought he heard him sigh. He reached inside his jacket, withdrew a pack of Dunhills, tapped out a cigarette and offered it to the guard. "*Por favor,*" said Paco. The guard took the offering, never shifting his gaze from Paco, who took a cigarette as well. Paco produced his silver lighter and lit both their cigarettes. The guard inhaled deeply, raising his head with his eyes now closed, and exhaled languorously. When he lowered his head and fixed his eyes on Paco once again he was almost smiling. "*Adelante, señor,*" he said, and sauntered off smoking as Paco closed his suitcase and made his way out of the terminal.

It was Thursday. He had two days before the funeral and no one knew where he would be, no one but his father.

* * *

He was startled awake by an angry, persistent knocking. The room was dark, the curtains drawn, and for a moment Paco forgot where he was. Then, widening his eyes and blinking, he propped himself up on his elbows and looked around to take in the faux Louis XV furniture, the embossed floral wallpaper, the gilded mirror, the fruit basket and split of champagne, and remembered that he was in a room at the Ritz. He had wanted to lay down for a brief siesta after his long flight, but the rank taste in his mouth and the heaviness of his limbs told him that he must have been out for hours. He peered at his watch, it was nearly seven o'clock. The knocking resumed. He got up from the bed, walked to the door in his stocking feet, opened it a crack, and peeked out to see who it was. His father was standing in the hallway looking slightly annoyed.

"Well, are you going to let me in, or have you got someone in there with you?"

Paco swung the door open and stepped into the hallway to embrace his father. "Papa, you made it!"

"Of course I made it."

They broke off, but held each other at arm's length for a moment of scrutiny. They hadn't seen one another for more than eight months, since just before his mother returned to Spain.

"You look well," said Paco. His father had his perpetual tan. He was wearing a midnight-blue pin stripe suit, a white shirt, and a pale green silk tie, the color of his eyes. He may have been a photographer, but he was always impeccably turned out. The only thing that distinguished him from an investment banker or the like was his silver hair, which was swept back from a high forehead and almost reached his shoulders.

"I wish I could say the same. You look a bit…disheveled."

"Yes, I know, I overslept my siesta. Come in." Paco stepped aside and let his father pass. He turned on the lights and went to the window and drew open the curtains. There was a last blush of pink light in the sky and the street lamps on Gran Via were already on. When he turned around he found his father standing in the middle of the room, looking around with a smirk.

"So what's with the Ritz?" his father asked. "I booked here as well when I got your telegram. I'm just down the hall. But I would have preferred something a bit more authentic, the Oriente, say."

"Where would you stay if you didn't want any of the Vidals to track you down?"

"I take your point."

Suddenly the banter stopped.

"I'm in shock; I still can't quite believe it," said Adam Fates, shaking his head and sighing. "All of this seems so unreal, as if it might be some monumental misunderstanding and Lucía is alive somewhere, waiting for us."

"I feel as if a light had been extinguished and I can't quite find my way," said Paco.

They fell silent, as if out of respect for Lucía. A light had been snuffed out, they both knew it, and henceforth they would be groping, each in his own way, in the land of the shadows.

"Who called you?" asked Adam finally.

"Victor. It was odd because I haven't spoken to him since I was sixteen, but I recognized his voice instantly. Funny the things that one remembers."

"How did she die, of what?"

"Her heart I was told. I don't know much more than that, I'm afraid."

Adam muttered a curse. "She was always so indifferent to her health, so reluctant to ever visit a doctor."

"I can scarcely believe she's left this world," said Paco, before he began to sob quietly.

His father put an arm around his shoulder. "If it's any consolation, never forget that you were a wonderful son to her…a wonderful son to both of us."

Paco wiped away the tears with the back of his hand and smiled faintly, nodding. "Let me have a shower. Then let's get some dinner, I'm famished after the journey."

"I've booked a table at *La Punyalada* for eight o'clock."

"We'll be eating with the waiters at that hour."

"That suits me just fine. By the way," his father added as he sat down in an armchair to wait, "why did you send me that terse telegram? Why didn't you call?"

Paco didn't wish to tell the truth, but he was still groggy and at a loss as to what to say. "I was rather out of sorts," he replied apologetically "wasn't thinking clearly." And he retreated into the bathroom.

* * *

They walked up Paseo de Gràcia in the fading light, two smartly dressed, exceeding tall foreigners—*guiris* as they call all non-natives—towering above the crowds. A wind was blowing from the north, the *tramontana*, and it was cold, colder than many visitors realize the Mediterranean can get in the late autumn and winter. Neither of them had thought to take an overcoat when they left the hotel, and they both turned up their suit collars and walked with their hands thrust into their trouser pockets. As they approached Calle Aragon, they stopped to look across the avenue at Gaudí's Casa Batlló. The façade was illuminated and the light casting shadows among the building's sinuous forms and reflecting off its multi-colored tiles created an otherworldly air.

"So how is the book coming along?" Adam Fates asked.

Paco had to check himself from asking what book he was referring to. The truth was that *Antonio Gaudí: The Lord's Master Builder* was stalled and had been for some time, and both his agent and his editor had grown increasingly strident in their pleas to see a manuscript. "Slowly," said Paco finally, which was not a lie strictly speaking, but rather less than the truth. His father turned to look at him; he must have sensed this bit of calculated ambiguity. Paco kept looking straight ahead.

"In a bit of a rut are you?"

"Nothing I haven't been through and worked out before."

"Anything I can do apart from taking your portrait for the back cover?"

Paco smiled weakly. "Alas, no, not unless you'd like to write the book."

"Not a chance, I'm strictly an image man."

They continued walking, the crowds parting before them. Shops were closing and there was sporadic racket as metallic shutters came down with a crash. Young shop girls were rushing off to meet friends and *novios*. Paco had always been acutely attracted to the young women in Barcelona. They were so unlike those in New York, although he was unable to determine just how. Perhaps it was a certain Latin allure, something innately coquettish. His father must have been ruminating on the women as well.

"Tell me, how is Katia?" he asked.

It was an innocent enough question asked in passing, and Paco had been expecting it, but it was jarring nonetheless. *How is the book coming along? How is Katia?* Both questions seemed to point to his present failures. Paco remained silent just long enough for his father to stop, sensing that something was amiss. "What?" he asked. "What's the matter?"

"Nothing," said Paco. "She's in London rehearsing Chekhov."

"I'm surprised she isn't here."

"So is she."

"What do you mean?"

"I hadn't thought to ask her and she didn't take it well."

"I'm not surprised."

"Really, I've never known you, that is, knew you to be exceedingly considerate where mama was concerned. You were forever disappearing on assignment." He saw his father's face go taut. "I'm sorry Papa, I'm just trying to cope with the loss of one woman at a time." Paco took his father by the arm and they continued walking in silence.

The restaurant dining room was empty but for a table at the rear near the kitchen where the staff were having their dinner before the shift began, just as Paco had anticipated. One of the waiters, an elderly man with a generous paunch and short fat legs rose wearily from the table when they came in, struggled into his too-tight jacket, and was fixing a black, clip-on bow tie to his collar as he approached them. His father insisted that they be seated in the front at a table by the window with a view onto Paseo de Gracia. They ordered dry martinis—up with a twist, olives on the side—as his father always insisted. Paco took out his cigarettes and offered one to his father, but he declined, raising a hand and shaking his head.

"Have you quit?" Paco asked surprised as he lit up.

"No, but I'm trying to cut down. Even my Brazilian doctor is advising moderation."

His father reached into his jacket pocket and withdrew eye glasses, which he set on the end of his nose and cocked his head back to read the menu. Paco looked at his father's rope-veined hands with their liver spots that no Brazilian tan could hide, and realized all at once how much he had aged since they last saw one another. He was far from feeble to be sure, but twilight was descending sedately, inexorably. Suddenly Paco felt himself awash in a current of remorse. He didn't want his father to die without him and in a far-off place as his mother had done. When the time came, he wanted to be at his side, providing succor, bearing witness, consoling. In his mind he saw himself at his father's sick bed accompanied by a troupe of teary-eyed Brazilian beauties who would strike up wailing when *senhor* Adam finally expired. Paco laughed inwardly. There were worse ways to go, he thought.

The waiter returned with their dry martinis, olives sunken in the depths of the frosty glasses. Adam Fates let out a sigh of exasperation, and brusquely plucked the fruit out of his glass with his fingers while the waiter looked on perplexed by the strange ways of foreigners. Paco told his father to order for them both, knowing that this would placate him since fine food was among the few rich things that he truly coveted, along with Leica cameras and fine suits and shoes. In thoroughly correct, if halting Spanish, his father ordered sautéed artichokes with *serrano* ham, roast duck with pears, a green salad, Manchego cheese, and an exorbitantly expensive Rioja Gran Reserva, 1964. He looked pleased with himself. When the waiter shuffled off, his father raised his martini glass: "I would like to propose a toast," he said, suddenly looking uncharacteristically solemn, "to Lucía Vidal, a very great lady who we very much loved, even if some of us weren't always as considerate as we could have been. Lucía my darling you will be dearly missed. *Salud!*"

"*Salud,*" echoed Paco, and father and son sipped the cool gin. Neither spoke for a moment, both silently remembering a wife and a mother. Then Paco said:

"Forgive me for that earlier comment. The truth is I never saw you be inconsiderate to mama, on the contrary. No offense intended."

"None taken."

Adam looked out the window, but he wasn't looking at anything; his eyes had a blurred look, as if he was no longer fully there. When he spoke again, his voice seemed to come from some far-off place.

"How I loved her, and how sorry I now am that I was so often absent. This latest stint in Brazil especially. What a fool I've been."

"I never heard her complain."

"No, you wouldn't have. Still, I should never have allowed her to go off alone."

"From what I know, she didn't give you much of a choice."

"No, no, she didn't," said Adam almost in a whisper, shaking his head, his eyes fixed in that distant, unblinking gaze.

The waiter brought the wine, just in time to rescue them from excessive mournfulness. All at once, the elaborate ritual began: the pouring, the swirling, the examining, the tasting, and finally the delivering of the verdict. Paco always loved to watch his father go through these prescribed motions. There aren't many instances in life in which one can decide something, anything so summarily, his father had once told him when he was a boy, and Paco had never forgotten it. His father had his eyes closed. Clearly, he was relishing the moment. Then he blinked, looked at the waiter, and pronounced the wine *ex-tra-ordi-nario,* his tongue working hard to caress the syllables. The waiter bowed slightly and retreated muttering to himself under his breath. Some other customers trickled in, a party of Catalan businessmen, a golden-aged dandy with his impossibly young mistress, but no other foreigners. In fact, few foreigners ever set foot in Barcelona, and certainly not in December. It was one of the things that Paco liked most about the city. It hadn't been tainted by tourism, not yet. He noticed his father looking around the dining room, registering everything, the furniture, the pictures on the walls, the cutlery, like an appraiser.

"*La Punyalada*...The Stabbing, rather a sanguinary name for a restaurant, don't you think?" said Paco.

"It used to be called the *Olimpic,* but one day a man was stabbed in the middle of the dining room, and everyone began to call it *La Punyalada.* The name stuck and the owners finally adopted it, officially."

"My lord, where did you come up with that bit of trivia?"

"I used to come here during the war. It was a very popular spot with journalists, writers, photographers. I had dinner here once with your mother. We sat, as fate would have it, at this very table. Or perhaps fate has nothing to do with it. I insisted on the table after all."

Paco looked stunned. He placed his hands flat on the tablecloth as if he might somehow soak up something from that distant evening. "Tell me about it," he murmured, almost in a whisper.

"Actually, very little has changed in the place…"

"No, no, I don't mean the restaurant. I want to know how you two came to be here."

"Well, it was our wedding day, the 12th of December, 1938. Tomorrow would have been our 38th anniversary. We were married in the town hall in Gracia, a short walk from here. Didn't your mother or I ever tell you about this?"

"Vaguely, I knew that you two were married in Barcelona during the war, but I never heard the details. Go on."

"As I was saying, the ceremony—a civil ceremony, of course—took place in the town hall in Gracia, which is now a barrio, but was then a village on the edge of the city center. We were married by the local magistrate or justice of the peace, I can't recall. I do remember that he was an anarchist and rushed through the ceremony; he didn't seem to think much of ceremony of any kind. Robert Capa and Martha Gellhorn were our witnesses. He took scores of photographs, but we never saw them. What a pity. That would have been something to treasure, wedding photographs by Robert Capa. Anyway, we all walked down here after the ceremony, but it wasn't a very cheery celebration."

"Why was that?"

His father said nothing for a long time, but his mind, Paco could see, was working unsparingly, deciding perhaps what to reveal and what to keep for another occasion, or no occasion at all. It wasn't the first time that Paco sensed this sort of selective narrative from his father, it had always been like that between them, especially when certain subjects were broached, like the war, or Paco's lack of siblings. This vagueness had always left him ill at ease. Weren't families supposed to share everything? Wasn't there information, even delicate, compromising, slightly scandalous information that could be revealed in a family's inner circle? What was so unspeakable about the Fates family? Paco's mother had been even less forthcoming about the past than his father, although he could understand her reticence more readily. She had had to leave everything behind, her family, her friends, her country, her language. For her, exile was like a scar that never quite healed, like stigmata. But what of him? Why should he be privy to everything? Perhaps the idea of utter disclosure was a chimera. Perhaps a life without secrets would be insufferable.

"Look," his father said, but he was cut short by the waiter, who arrived with their plates of artichokes and ham. He didn't go on, but took up his fork and knife and began eating. "Ah," he said, his head tilted to one side, his eyes closed, "this is *pre-cisely* as I remember it."

"From the cheerless celebration?" asked Paco, his tone sardonic.

"I didn't say 'cheerless', I said not terribly cheery. Paco, for Christ's sake, there was a war on. Barcelona was being bombed. For the Republicans, the war was lost and had been for months. People were hungry, and the great rush for the French frontier had begun. Everything was utter chaos. The Fascists were closing in on the city and we had to get out. An American passport for your mother was the fastest and safest way to do that."

"So, it was a marriage of convenience then, is that what you're saying?" Paco asked, shocked.

"No, of course not, I loved your mother. Let's just say that events precipitated the wedding."

"Forgive me, but you said 'I loved your mother' rather than 'we loved each other.' Was the feeling not mutual?"

Paco saw his father straighten in his chair, and turn his face to the window, peering hard, as if the answer to the question might be found somewhere out on the avenue, but all that could be seen was his own reflection, ghostly and slightly distorted. After a moment, he turned back to Paco. He was smiling slightly, resignedly, his eyebrows raised. "Not entirely, I suppose. But not every successful marriage is brimming with passion. What does it matter now?"

"So you considered it a successful marriage?"

"What is this some sort of tribunal?" his father asked, not waiting for a reply. "Yes, I considered it a successful marriage, far more than most. Lucía and I respected one another, and helped one another, and yes, loved one another on a very profound level. Perhaps you imagine that without passion love is somehow wanting. I don't know. I can't answer that, but I do know this: sometimes life is a question of mucking along as best we can. Not very eloquent, I grant you, but there you have it." And then he added by way of an afterthought, "by the way, before you begin to question a thirty-eight-year marriage, perhaps you should examine your prolonged relationship with Katia, or is that utterly beyond reproach?"

Paco did not reply. Now it was his turn to look at his mute reflection in the window. His father, he knew, was right to respond as he did. Who was he to question anyone on the depths of their love? Perhaps Paco's problem was that he only truly loved himself, but the truth was that he *did* adore Katia, and realized at that moment how much he missed her and wished that she was there with them now. What a fool he had been not to have asked her along from the start. "Well," he said to his father in a contrite tone, "you're absolutely right. I'm sorry. I didn't intend to turn this into another cheerless dinner at The Stabbing," he added, smiling now.

"It wasn't cheerless then, and it isn't cheerless now. Sometimes these things need to be said. But remember, we are here to pay tribute to your mother, not question her life." And then, taking up his wine glass, he repeated, "To Lucía Vidal, *salud!*"

The duck was superb, and so too the cheese, and the second bottle of Rioja was even better than the first. They talked about Lucía Vidal, her singular beauty, her steely character, her notorious inability or refusal to adapt to New York society, and her sometimes comic grasp of American English and slang. And they laughed great belly-aching, tear-inducing laughter that they hadn't shared in years. By the end of the dinner they were tipsy and exhausted and as happy as a father and son could be in spite of their loss. Finally, they asked for the bill and a brandy for the road. When the waiter returned he was balancing a tray bearing their snifters in one hand and a weighty book in the other. He put the book down on an adjacent table and served their brandies. Then he apologized for the intrusion and said to Adam Fates: "I thought that

I recognized you sir, but I wasn't sure. It was your height that first set me remembering, but your face, well, I never forget a face."

Adam Fates looked on stunned, not quite sure what to say. And then the waiter retrieved the book from the other table. It was a kind of photo album or scrap book, and he opened it and turned several pages full of yellowed clippings and former menus and sepia-tinged photographs and drawings and caricatures of what must have been former illustrious customers. And then he stopped on a page and nodded his head and turned the book for Adam to see, pointing a pudgy finger at a bygone snapshot. "That is you, is it not, sir?"

Adam Fates reached for his glasses and peered at the image and seemed to sober up in an instant. "For the love of God, where on earth..." he exclaimed.

"Señor Sabaté, the late maître, he was forever taking photographs, perhaps you remember him?"

"Yes, I think I do now. We talked shop about cameras and such on a few occasions."

Paco craned his neck and looked on too, and there they were, Adam Fates and Lucía Vidal flanked by Martha Gellhorn and Robert Capa, sitting at the same table that they occupied now. Their glasses are raised in a toast and they are beaming, all of them, as cheerful as anyone could seem.

"Imagine," said Adam Fates in a hushed tone, speaking more to himself, it seemed, than to Paco or the waiter, "after forty years and on the eve of my wife's funeral I am seeing the first photograph of my wedding day."

"My condolences, sir," said the waiter, suddenly appearing ill at ease.

"I would like to acquire this photograph," said Adam Fates. Then, removing his glasses and looking up at the waiter, he added: "Name your price."

"Oh, I'm afraid I couldn't do that, sir, some things are priceless, no? Not everything can be bought...or sold."

Adam Fates sighed and seemed to sink into his chair. "Yes, of course, thank you for showing this to me." And he carefully closed the scrap book and handed it back to the waiter, smiling wanly. When the waiter was out of earshot, Paco said:

"How extraordinary, I can't quite believe the old guy recognized you."

"Yes," said his father, looking dazed, lost in thought. He put his glasses back on, examined the bill, and reached into his jacket for his wallet. He took out twenty thousand *pesetas*, left it on the silver plate, and rose to go.

"Don't you need change," asked Paco.

"No."

They were already out the door and on the avenue when the waiter came rushing out to stop them. "Your change, sir," he said, extending the silver plate laden with coins and several bills.

"No, no, that is for you."

"It is far too much."

"It is not enough," replied his father.

"Thank you, sir, but what of this?" And he handed his father an envelope.

Both Adam Fates and Paco looked inside and saw the photograph, which had been carefully cut from the scrap book.

"To sell such a thing would be shameful," said the waiter. "Good night, gentlemen."

"*Buenas noches y gracias buen hombre,*" said Adam Fates.

They walked down Paseo de Gracia arm in arm, weaving slightly from the drink. "I almost forgot why I loved Spain so much," said father to son. "What wonderful people."

* * *

Sleep was impossible, what with the jet lag, the alcohol, and the evening's conversation, which had left his mind racing away to places unknown and unexplored. They had stumbled up the broad, sweeping stairs of the hotel he and his father, propping each other up and stopping periodically on a step to laugh, or insist on some arcane point, or catch their breath. A few hotel guests had passed them and looked away nervously when his father greeted them rather too boisterously. They had bid each other good night in the hall, all embraces and back slapping, and his father had said without prompting: "There is so much that Lucía should have told you poor Paco," before weaving off down the hall, muttering as he went. What precisely had his father meant by that? Paco wondered now as he lay on his bed still dressed, smoking in the near dark. The more that he thought of his mother, the more mysterious she grew until he began to question whether or not he had known her at all. Really known her, that is, the essence of her, Lucía Vidal the woman rather than the woman that was his mother. Or were these all just alcohol-fueled ruminations, conjectures that would not stand the scrutiny of light the next morning when, or rather if, he woke refreshed? His mind wandered to the rest of the Vidal clan. Tomorrow he would be among them after years of deliberate remove. The thought filled him with dread. Kin or no kin, he loathed the lot of them with the exception of his *tio* Francisco, at least when he was sober. What would they all look like now, he wondered? He could only conjure them up as they had been during that strained summer of '55. Their first encounter is what always stuck indelibly in his mind like a childhood trauma slow to heal.

* * *

Paco had followed Victor down the silent, empty halls of Quinta Amelia, although he had had the unnerving sensation that they were not alone, but were being watched, spied upon from behind doors and curtains by beings just waiting for him to trip so that they could pounce upon him. The whole atmosphere had been hostile. The place seemed irked by his very presence, and when they descended the carved wooden staircase polished to a luster, the squeaking of their steps sounded like a sort of snickering. They crossed the library steeped in shadow and came to some thick, blood-red velvet curtains, which Victor parted to reveal a broad brick terrace baking in the afternoon heat. They stepped out squinting and it took a moment for Paco's eyes to grow accustomed to the glare. Then he saw them, the Vidals, seated as if arranged for a portrait beneath a towering pine in the garden below the terrace, waiting for him and wearing expressions of practiced indifference. When Paco and Victor approached, all conversation and movement abruptly ceased. He felt the collective gaze of the Vidals on him, measuring him up, taking stock of him. The first thing that he noticed about them, oddly enough, was the outmoded look of their clothes. He couldn't quite put a finger on it, but somehow the women's hemlines were passé, the cut of the men's suits no longer the fashion; even the dresses of the young girls seemed to belong to another era. In New York they would have all been taken for what they were, well-to-do provincials. Paco made straight for his grandmother, who was seated on a cushioned wrought-iron chair alongside a marble-topped table set with an elaborate tea service and plates of sandwiches and cakes. He was struck at once by the size of her. She was far heftier than he imagined. She was clad entirely in black, a black silk dress with a high collar and long sleeves that revealed nothing but her head and her hands, which were surprisingly slender and fine given the rest of her. She wore her hair up in a chignon. Her eyes were nearly as black as her dress. She wore rouge carelessly applied. Paco could not quite believe that this woman had produced his mother.

"So, at last, Lucía's boy," she proclaimed without emotion, fixing Paco with a stare that seemed to go right through him. Paco bristled; there was that *Lucía's boy* again. She drew him toward her and he kissed both her rouge-smeared cheeks. He remembered what his mother had written in her letter: *Don't let her bully you.*

"Actually, my name is Francisco, but everyone calls me Paco," he said, smiling and watching her gaze for a reaction, but she ignored this bit of impertinence.

"You are named after me!" came a voice, obviously that of his uncle Francisco.

Paco turned and saw him sitting slightly apart from the others, a cane propped on the edge of his chair. In his right hand he held a tall glass not quite upright. He looked insubstantial inside a baggy cream-colored linen suit. His swollen ankles were bare.

"Let us pray that he takes after you in name only," said another man, making a low sound resembling a chuckle and showing his teeth and gums in a surly smile.

Uncle Borja, thought Paco.

"Oh, do shut up," said Francisco. He placed his drink at the foot of his chair, took up his cane, and began to struggle to his feet. Everyone looked elsewhere in silence. His legs were as thin as twigs, the result of a bout of childhood polio, and buckled slightly. He bumped his chair, causing his glass to topple. "*Joder!*" he hissed. He regained his balance and stood upright, sweating profusely. "Come," he said to Paco, recovering his composure, "let's have a look at you."

Paco approached him and offered his hand, but his uncle grasped his shoulders, hugged him close, and held him swaying. He reeked of booze. "How we have been looking forward to this moment my boy."

At this Victor let out a derisive laugh, more like a sneer, and drew a withering look from his grandmother, which quieted him instantly.

Francisco released Paco and fell back into his chair with a whimper. Paco proceeded with the introductions, making his way to his uncle Borja, who extended a moist hand, and held Paco's for what seemed just an instant too long. "You have inherited your father's good looks," he said, leering.

"Such a discerning eye you have," interrupted the woman at his uncle's side. "I am Borja's wife, your aunt Paulina, and these are your cousins Antonia and Alejandra," she said, shifting her gaze to her twin daughters, who scarcely looked his way and in unison offered the remotest of smiles. They must have been slightly older than Victor, twenty or twenty-one, he guessed, and gave the distinct impression of wanting to be elsewhere. They were identical twins and mildly unattractive on account of narrow eyes set too close together, a trait that made them appear irremediably dull. They wore identical blue and white checked dresses, a pretense of twins that Paco thought they would have outgrown long ago.

"Come, come, don't ignore your *tia* Inés." Paco turned to his aunt reclining in a deck chair in a swath of sun light. She removed her sunglasses as Paco approached, and he was slightly startled to behold what looked like his mother in ten years' time. She offered her cheeks, and as Paco kissed her, he thought he smelled his mother too.

They ate the sandwiches and cakes, and drank the tea and lemonade in near silence, and when the Vidals did speak, commenting vacantly on the heat, the help, or a thread of local gossip, they did so among themselves. No one addressed Paco, or asked his opinion of anything, or bothered to explain what, if anything, they had in store for him over the summer. It was as if he wasn't there. What especially upset him, however, what struck him as not so much odd as downright inexplicable, was that not once did anyone ask after his mother. Before him sat his mother's mother and a host of her siblings and in-laws and nieces and nephew, and no one thought to inquire after Lucía Vidal. *If ever you feel lost or lonely, turn to your uncle Francisco,* his mother had written. But did she know that he was a drunk? He had fallen asleep in his chair, his head lolling back, his mouth agape, his lifeless legs collapsed in front of him. And no one paid him any heed. Turn to your uncle Francisco indeed, thought Paco.

"Don't tell me I'm late!" a voice shouted from the terrace above the garden. Paco looked up to see a man come bounding down the stone stairs three steps at a time. He was impeccably dressed in a white polo shirt, white trousers, and white canvas sneakers. In his right hand he carried a tennis racquet which he twirled intermittently. Paco rose from his chair to be introduced, but the man swaggered past and made straight for the sandwiches. It was immediately clear to Paco that this must be his uncle Javier, and that it was the food that he feared missing rather than the introduction to his nephew.

"My lord, I'm famished," he announced, filling his plate.

"Did you have a good game my dear?" asked Inés.

"What?" he responded, his mouth already full. "Oh, yes, of course."

"Really?" she replied. "I ask because your shoes are so pristine, not a trace of red clay on them. You must verily float above the court."

Her husband looked down at his sneakers as if to confirm this, and momentarily stopped chewing. There was a long pause, and finally he said, "How odd," and shrugged.

"Yes," said his wife, "quite."

Paco was still standing and his uncle's gaze fell on him. He looked relieved to change the subject. "I'm sorry, who are you."

"I'm Paco Fates."

"Ah, of course, Lucía's boy."

"Yes," said Paco, no longer caring, "Lucía's boy."

* * *

A chill, tenuous light was creeping up Gran Via from the east when Paco rose from his bed at the Ritz. He had dosed off fitfully in the early morning hours, but true sleep had eluded him. His eyes scalded. There was no need to look into the mirror to know that they were blood-shot and sunken. He showered and dressed, and made his way down the empty corridor and grand staircase, across the still lobby with its outlandish potted palms, and past the doorman, who was sitting just inside the entrance, his chin on his chest, quietly snoring. How was it that some people could sleep anywhere, Paco wondered enviously, and he hardly at all. When he stepped out onto the sidewalk he was taken aback by the wet winter cold of the Mediterranean, a cold that seemed to seep into his very bones. He put on his overcoat and reached into a pocket for his cigarettes, lighting one and savoring the day's first warm lung full of smoke. Then he coughed, producing a hollow clatter from somewhere deep in his chest. No one was about and there was an eerie silence, as if he were the only one alive in all the city. He proceeded to Paseo San Juan, then up to Avenida del Generalísimo Francisco Franco and across to Calle Mallorca, where he got the first glimpse of the soaring spires of the Sagrada Familia with their ceramic-sheathed finials rising above the roofs of the surrounding apartment blocks. As he drew nearer to the temple, the great half-finished mass of the edifice came fully into view. Everywhere there were cranes and scaffolding, piles of rough-hewn stone and mounds of sand, scattered tiles and steel bars, dust and debris. It had been more than five years since Paco had last visited the site when he was engaged in the preliminary research for *Antonio Gaudí: The Lord's Master Builder,* and he couldn't help but notice that the works had progressed as little as his book. Somewhere from inside the building site came the sharp striking of a solitary chisel on stone. The temple seemed to loom above him like an ill-disguised monument to dogma, and it reminded him, he suddenly realized, of Quinta Amelia, where the too-patent images drawn from nature, the absence of straight lines and clean angles, and the relentless religious symbols somehow managed to become obliquely unnatural and vaguely menacing. Paco's head began to spin at the whole grotesque, overwrought mess, so that he had to sit down on a nearby bench. He was in a cold sweat, his heart racing. All at once he grasped unequivocally what he had only timidly suspected previously, that is, that he found Gaudí oppressive and his architecture little more than glorified kitsch. No, he now knew that he could not go on, that *Antonio Gaudí: The Lord's Master Builder* would never see the light of day, not by him anyway. He would have to return the publisher's advance, of course, but what of it, he had savings enough. His agent would kick and scream, and warn him that he would never publish again, but it wasn't true. He would write something else, something from the heart, something that he believed in. Suddenly, Paco felt giddy and unburdened. He stood up, turned, and strolled leisurely back toward the Ritz, leaving Gaudí and his unfinished, misbegotten pile behind.

He found his father in the dining room delicately peeling the shell from a soft-boiled egg, a copy of *La Vanguardia* spread on the table at his elbow. As always, he was flawlessly dressed, at least what Paco could see of him, in a pearl-grey turtleneck and a blue blazer. He didn't look like a man who had been out late the night before and—what was it that Katia had said, oh yes—in his cups. How did he do it? Paco wondered.

"Ah, there you are," his father said, as Paco approached the table. Then, examining him more closely: "Christ, you look a bit rough. How'd you sleep?"

"Barely a wink."

"Well, I slept like a baby in swaddling clothes," he said, looking proud of himself. "I suggest that you get something in you, we've got a long day ahead, and who knows when we'll get something decent to eat."

Paco gestured to a waiter, a tall bald man in a tailcoat and a face devoid of all expression. He could have been made of wax. Paco ordered *tortilla de patatas, pan con tomate, jamón,* and *café con leche,* and the waiter glided off wordlessly.

"So where were you earlier? I went to your room before coming down to breakfast, but you didn't answer the door."

"I went for a walk."

"Where to?"

"The Sagrada Familia."

"How's the work progressing?"

"No noticeable change since I was last there five years ago."

"They're never going to finish that bloody thing." Then he added, grinning: "Or perhaps they'll finish in time for your book launch."

"I've decided to abandon the Gaudí book," Paco said matter-of-factly.

At this his father stopped eating, wiped his mouth with his linen napkin, removed his glasses, and looked at Paco perplexed. "Really, why? You've worked so hard on that book."

Paco couldn't imagine where his father got that impression, but he didn't wish to dispel it either. "I've come to the irreversible conclusion that I can't bear the architect or his work."

"When did you decide that?"

"This morning, although I've suspected as much for a long time."

"Well, I never thought much of his work myself, all a bit over the top, if you ask me." He went back to eating his egg, but asked, chewing: "Have you got another book in mind?"

"I thought I might try my hand at a novel."

"Splendid, what about?"

"That depends on how things go down in Tortosa."

"Oh dear," his father said with mock gravity "a saga about the Vidals. That should be a gothic tale."

They were silent for a time. Then the waiter appeared as if from nowhere with Paco's breakfast, laying the plates in front of him with a kind of unctuous solemnity. Paco was about to start eating, but suddenly laid down his fork and looked at his father squarely, "Papa."

His father stopped eating and looked at Paco over his glasses, sensing that his son had something important on his mind. "What is it Paco?"

"Papa, last night when we were saying good night in the hallway in front of my door, you said: 'There is so much that Lucía should have told you, poor Paco.' What exactly did you mean by that?" Paco watched his father turn his face away, looking at nothing.

"Did I say that?" his father answered after a prolonged pause.

"Those very words."

"Funny, I don't recall. Anyway, we had quite a lot to drink, didn't we?"

"Yes," said Paco, "yes, we did."

CHAPTER THREE

THE 20TH OF NOVEMBER. They call it autumn here in New York, Lucía thought, but it was colder than any winter in Tortosa, a remorseless cold that penetrated everything and left one brittle, as if the slightest blow would cause one to shatter like crystal. She had been in New York for more than 35 years and still she could not grow accustomed to it. She stood at the window glad to be inside looking out. The morning light was dull and flat. On the avenue below, she could see people holding onto their hats, walking stooped and headlong into the wind. Above, the sky was the color of milk, and low. The tops of the buildings were lost in mists, everything looked stunted. Soon it would be Thanksgiving. She loved the Americans for celebrating so secular a holiday. No saints or martyrs or Virgins or priests to intercede, just a day of thanks. She would spend the day with Adam and Paco and Katia in the land of plenty, and she would be ever so thankful.

During her first years in New York everything seemed to Lucía so oddly provisional, as if she should have kept a suitcase packed and been ready to return in an instant to the world from which she had been forced to flee. She marked the passing of days, etched them in her mind like a castaway scratching successive lines in stone. With Adam forever being sent off to godforsaken places to cover the latest war, revolution, famine or disaster, only her son Paco and devoted Margaret kept her grounded in that perpetually shifting terrain that was America, where it seemed that everything—a profession, a home, a marriage, a life— could be shed like a change of skin. How utterly different it was from

Spain, where one's past was inescapable and followed one everywhere like an elongated shadow, dark and distorted. But to lament what she had left behind, even though it was nothing short of everything, struck Lucía as an unpardonable lack of gratitude. After all, Adam was a considerate husband and a dedicated father, as well as a photographer of considerable renown, and, as her female friends never tired of reminding her, one of the most attractive men in New York. Paco was a bright and healthy young man. Like her, he was somewhat taciturn, and she did wish that he would get on with it and marry Katia, but otherwise he caused her little worry. Certainly she was well provided for, living in patrician splendor on Park Avenue and summering in Southampton. She had friends, longtime acquaintances of Adam's mostly, but they had accepted her from the outset, and she was grateful to them and to him for having provided a place for her in a new world. She had even found work teaching Spanish to proper young ladies at the Lindley School, something which provided her with a modest income and a routine. No, she would not allow herself to lament, at least not out loud for all to hear. What crowded her thoughts and dreams, however, was something else altogether. For all the blessings that Adam Fates and America had bestowed upon her, despite all the time that had transpired since her arrival, Lucía Vidal could not escape the sensation, persistent and irreparable, of feeling somehow adrift. Detached from one's country, one's language, one's family…one's world! How weary it left her, how full of longing, and something more, what was it? Dread, that was it, a dread born not merely of the obligation to flee homeland and abandon family, that was every immigrant's predicament, but of country and kin turning their backs on her. That an unjust regime had forced her into exile was at least an indignity that Lucía could suffer collectively, knowing that thousands more shared her condition, but to be cast out by family, how that cut to the very bone.

The sound of a key in the lock, the front door slamming, and then Paco's voice urgent, jubilant, *mamá!*

"In here," she cried out, turning away from the window and looking toward the front door in expectation. Her son came bounding into the drawing room, a newspaper held high as if in triumph. "The bastard is dead!" he shouted, the words pronounced with more glee perhaps than a mother wishes to hear. "The 20th of November, 1975, we'll have to make this day a family holiday!" Lucía stood motionless. Paco approached and thrust the newspaper into her hands. At first she did not look, but only stared blankly at her son. Somehow, she had never imagined this day. The man had seemed immortal. Slowly she lowered her gaze and read the headline, her lips moving soundlessly: *Franco Is Dead in Madrid at 82.* Atop the column was a photograph of a ghostly old man, his sunken chest bedecked in medals and ribbons, his cheeks hollow, his neck shrunken within a gaping collar. Lucía turned back toward the window, her mouth slack, her head tilted slightly to one side, as if she were trying to hear some distant, far-off sound just out of earshot. Seeing her reaction, Paco took a step back, coughed mildly into his fist, and retreated quietly, closing the double doors of the drawing room behind him as he went. Lucía remained there, still, expressionless, gazing absently at nothing, oblivious to the strident sounds of the city drifting up from the avenue. She did not weep or cry out or damn the dead man. She thought only of the previous fallen. All at once faces came into focus in her mind's eye, bearing expressions and uttering words and phrases from a lost time and place. She watched this phantom procession drift past: a revered tutor, dear friends, neighbors, laborers from Quinta Amelia, and more heartbreaking still, an innocent brother, and finally, a lover. A faint shudder went through her.

What world would have emerged had they all prevailed? Lucía asked herself. What life would she have led?

* * *

Lucía did not believe that death was a suitable cause for celebration, no matter how monstrous the deceased. Adam, however, had insisted, Paco agreed, and so she relented. Her husband called to make a reservation at Casa Carmelo, their favorite Spanish restaurant, but he was told that they were fully booked, at which point he put Lucía on the phone, and after an animated chat with Oscar, the Spanish maître, she booked a table for three at nine o'clock.

"How *do* you do that?" Adam asked her after she hung up the telephone.

"One would have thought that after all these years you would have learned how to speak properly to a Spaniard."

"What? I suppose that I should have asked after his mother."

"Something like that," she replied, smiling. Suddenly, she was glad to be going out, despite the occasion.

They took the #6 train to Astor Place and walked west on 8th Street. The wind had died and the sky had mostly cleared, leaving a smattering of clouds illuminated from below by the lights of the city. The trees along the street were bare, their silhouettes twisted in the lamplight. It was still bitterly cold, but Lucía was wedged between the twin towers of Paco and Adam; she felt secure, immune even. They heard the intimations of celebration flooding the evening air a good block before they reached the restaurant. The sound was an agreeable blend of laughter, Spanish song, the clinking of glasses. As they drew nearer, they saw that people were drinking and chatting on the sidewalk and on the stoops flanking the building, oblivious to the cold. They entered through the swinging glass doors and plunged into the crowd. The room, long and narrow with a fine marble-topped bar, a stamped tin ceiling, worn white-tile floors, and walls adorned with a generous, if undiscriminating collection of art, was teeming. The air hung heavy with smoke and the slightly rank odor of too-tight quarters, as in a crowded dormitory or a lowly rooming house. It was, Lucía could see at once, a gathering of exiles. They had that look, not overtly shabby, but nothing too prosperous either, although they had done their best. There were men with frayed collars, stains on their too-narrow ties; women wearing cheap perfume and abundant makeup, the better to mask the lines of disappointment. They were shopkeepers and clerks, mechanics and teachers, waitresses and seamstresses, a few bohemians, artists. Back in Spain they had all possessed a place, fit into a complex, connective geography. Here, however, they gave off a transient air, an impression of people just passing through. Lucía saw people that she knew or recognized, others whose faces looked vaguely familiar, but she could not say from where exactly. A striking woman, her black hair pulled tight and arranged in a bun, her lips a lush red, squeezed past wearing a matador's crimson *traje de luces*. A few men were sporting capes. Everyone was shouting in Spanish and kissing one another. It was bedlam. Lucía and Adam looked at one another and smirked in dismay. Paco was beaming. A bottle of champagne, floating above the crowd, was weaving and bobbing its way toward them, and they soon saw that it was held aloft by Oscar, the maître, followed by a white-jacketed waiter bearing glasses and more champagne. Oscar halted before them and kissed Lucía on both cheeks. His eyes were welled up, his round face flush. He scarcely acknowledged Adam and Paco.

"My darling Lucía," he sputtered, while managing to fill three glasses and another for himself "I can't believe it. What emotion, *que bárbaro!*"

"I feel as if we were back in Spain," said Lucía.

"Soon we will be, *ojalá!*"

They raised their glasses. "*Viva España! Viva la Republica!*" cried Oscar, his chin held high, his chest thrust forward.

"*Viva!*" they replied and drained their glasses.

Lucía had not heard that particular toast for nearly forty years, and it transposed her instantly to another time, another man. Quim had been fond of that precise wording: *Viva España! Viva la Republica!* he would say, and drink down that heady red wine, the color of ink, that they somehow managed to procure at the front no matter how dire the circumstances.

"Are you all right darling?"

Lucía looked up at Adam absently. "What? Oh, yes, yes I'm fine," she managed.

"You were squeezing my arm as if your life depended on it."

"Come," said Oscar "I have saved you a table in back." And he led them through the throng, bestowing kisses and filling glasses as he went.

They were seated at a quiet table in the dining room's hinterland far from the din at the bar. When they sat down they all turned their heads and looked back longingly at the revelers. It felt as if they had been marooned. The cooks had emerged from the kitchen, their aprons soiled.

The waiters had loosened their ties. They were Spaniards to a man, and all staggeringly drunk. It didn't matter. They were beyond reproach. This was the night that they had all been waiting for, year after year, lost in exile, making their way in a new country, but dreaming of the day that they might return to theirs. Adam grew impatient, then resigned. They had been forgotten. They drank champagne and ate olives and waited.

"Spaniards never seem to really adapt to life in the States, not like the Irish, say, or even the Italians," Paco observed as he took in the celebration from afar. "Why is that?"

"They are anarchists by nature," offered Adam.

"Is that so?" said Lucía, looking mildly offended.

"I'm sorry, I didn't mean you darling, but it's true, they have trouble adapting to anything."

"Rubbish," she replied, then directing herself to Paco, added: "It's different somehow when one is forced into exile."

Adam got up and went in search of a waiter.

"But immigrants are always fleeing something—famine, poverty, persecution," Paco added.

"Still, that's a choice, a desperate choice, but a choice all the same. War is different."

"Do you long to return?"

Lucía didn't answer immediately; she was looking at her hands, playing with the rings on her fingers. "I did once," she said finally "but I haven't considered it for years, that is, until tonight." Then almost in a whisper: "Suddenly, it seems possible."

"But your life is here and has been for years. What would there be for you to go back to?"

"Family."

"Oh, that bunch."

Lucía shot him a look of reproach.

"Sorry," said Paco "it's just that..."

"You don't need to explain. I know very well what they're like, but they are my family. I love them still, I suppose, or some of them anyway. Who knows, it's been so many years since I've seen them."

"I don't think I ever really told you, but the summer that I spent in Tortosa was the unhappiest time of my life. They all treated me like a poor relation, an outcast. Uncle Borja and little Victor, father and son, they were my tormentors. For years they crowded my nightmares. But the worst was the way they spoke of you with such undisguised disdain, such loathing. I have always hated them for that."

"You never told me as much."

"No, I didn't want to offend you."

"I'm sorry; I thought it was important that you get to know your family."

"Well, you certainly achieved that. Still, I can't fathom why they hate you so."

Lucía couldn't help noting a hint of reproach in his voice. Perhaps she had been wrong to leave so much unsaid for so long. "I renounced them," she said plainly "them and everything they believe in, their class, their religion, their politics, all of it, and for that they cannot forgive me."

They resumed gazing at the general mayhem, but their spirits had been dampened. Her family never failed to cast a pall over everything, Lucía thought, but there was something more, something troubling Paco, she could sense it.

"About getting to know the family..." Paco continued, but then stopped short, as if not sure whether or not to press on. He wasn't looking at her.

"Yes?"

"It's just that you seem to have been so selective in what you've always told me... about the family and your past, I mean, selective and at the same time secretive."

"Oh, how is that?"

She should have known something was coming, a compromising question, an unsavory revelation, an accusation, perhaps. She should have braced herself, but she didn't think that she needed to, not with an adult son.

"Why have you never really told me about the circumstances of your brother Carlitos' death?"

Now he was looking at her, examining her, gauging her reaction. She winced, perhaps unperceptively, she wasn't sure. She closed her eyes, as if not wanting to bear her own son's scrutiny, but it was no use. She bowed her head and looked down, gazing with unseeing eyes upon the spotless linen tablecloth.

"What do you wish to know?" she whispered.

"I don't know, really. Why he has been such a dirty secret, I suppose?"

"He is *not* a dirty secret!" Lucía replied, almost shouting, surprising Paco, but also herself. Why such vehemence for a sibling so long gone? she wondered. She tried to compose herself. Her son was silent, waiting for her to go on.

"Did the family talk about him that summer at Quinta Amelia?" she asked, tentatively.

"Yes, they did, or rather grandmother did."

"Go on."

"Well, one day I was sitting with her on the sofa in the drawing room, looking at the family photo album. I kept on seeing a young boy in all the group portraits. I asked who he was?"

"And what did she reply exactly?"

"That he was my uncle Carlitos. I thought it rather odd that I had never heard of this uncle of mine. 'And, where is he?' I asked innocently."

"'Dead' she replied, icily, before abruptly turning the page, but there he was again, gazing out at us from another photograph. I remember thinking that he looked so angelic, so utterly happy. He seemed to possess something that the rest of you lacked. I knew I was being tactless, but I couldn't keep myself from asking how he had died. And you know what she said? 'Ask your mother.' Not without spite, I might add. And then she left me there on the sofa with the album open in my lap and this mystery turning in my head."

Lucía could well imagine her mother acting so. She could hear the tone of simmering reproach in her voice, grasp her resolve to continue blaming her daughter for Carlitos' death. It only confirmed why Lucía considered a possible homecoming with such trepidation.

"When I returned home, of course, I asked after this uncle Carlitos, and I remember vividly you turning white as a ghost and replying simply that he had died in the war. You looked so shaken, so wounded. There have been other times when I broached the subject, and your response has always been the same. It's no longer enough. Now I'm asking. How did he die exactly?"

Lucía looked at her son intently. She would tell him, tell him in a manner that she hoped he would never forget. "It was malice and ignorance and envy that killed Carlitos," she said, her voice trembling. "And he didn't die on the battlefield or in a bombing raid; he was murdered in cold blood, like untold numbers of others." She might have gone on, might have revealed much more, other details that deserved to be revealed from a past buried, but never forgotten. She wasn't sure she had the wherewithal. When she spied Adam approaching, she knew she was spared. Another time, she thought.

Her husband had a waiter in tow, a stout figure who lurched abruptly as he approached and almost crashed into the table. He had the gnarled, swollen hands of someone who had spent years at sea. They ordered snails, salad, lamb chops, and a bottle of Vega Sicilia. Adam repeated the order slowly, as if speaking to a child, not quite sure that the waiter had taken it in. He hadn't written anything down. When the man staggered off, they all raised their eyebrows.

"It's anyone's guess what we'll actually be served," said Paco.

"Tonight, everything is forgiven," Lucía insisted.

"As long as he doesn't forget the wine," said Adam.

Lucía excused herself and rose to go to the lady's room. She had to make her way past the bar, pressing through the crowd, waving and nodding to people she knew. She saw Pablo, her hairdresser from Elizabeth Arden, but he was caught in the crush and she could not catch his eye. Suddenly, she saw another man, his face somber, unfamiliar, staring at her intently from across the room. She smiled weakly and quickly looked away. The bathrooms were in the basement and Lucía had to wait in line on the stairs. Bits of boozy conversation floated around her:

not just Franco…bloody regime…I'll stay here, thank you…America. Lucía listened halfheartedly, uncomprehending. The champagne had gone to her head. Her mind wandered.

Had she ever felt a kindred spirit with these fellow exiles? She wasn't sure. Certainly she had never deliberately sought out other members of the Spanish exile community in New York, or marched in front of the consulate in shrill protests against the Franco regime as she was sometimes urged to do. Not that she was indifferent to the plight of the fallen precisely. She had always contributed unfailingly to the Fund for Republican Veterans of the Civil War, albeit anonymously. But there her activism stopped. She knew very well what she had never wished to become, and that was an object of pity. She had met exiles who positively wallowed in it, who seemed to cherish their vaunted place among the vanquished, and repeated their oft-told tales of struggle, idealism, and defeat to anyone who would listen until their monologues became a kind of performance, a parody even. Over the years, of course, the subject of the war would sometimes come up in social situations in New York, when someone, upon hearing the irrepressible Spanish inflections in her English—the rolling of the *r*, for example, or the *i* pronounced as *ee*—discovered that she was Spanish. They couldn't seem to resist making some hackneyed pronouncement about the war—*civil wars are always the most tragic,* was a favorite, or *it was the last great romantic struggle* another—and she would nod her head obligingly, and furrow her brow, and adopt a suitably stricken expression, and more often than not, there the subject would mercifully come to a halt. Some assumed that she was a Francoist on account of her comfortable circumstances, and she did little to dissuade them; she hadn't the energy. Call it resignation. The political feuding that she had endured during the war had left her ideologically spent. Eventually, however, word got around that she had fought with the Loyalist—*fought,* in fact, was an almost laughable exaggeration since she had never so much as touched a gun, or fired one anyway—and had only escaped Spain thanks to Adam Fates, and only then by the skin of her teeth.

When she emerged from the lady's room and was returning to the table, the stranger who had fixed her with his stare as she crossed the bar was waiting at the top of the stairs. She tried to move past him, but he stepped sideways to block her path.

"Lucía Vidal, well, I knew it was you."

Lucía looked up to a narrow face as white as bone, the jaws almost blue. His eyes, dark and sunken, had the reckless look of a man who had lost everything. Nothing about him registered. "Do we know one another?"

"It's Santi Trias."

Still she drew a blank.

"From Quim's column... you remember Quim," he added, his voice biting.

"Yes, of course," she stammered, her heart began to race. "Still, I can't place you, forgive me."

"Ah, well, years of forced labor do tend to take their toll."

"I'm sorry."

"You, on the other hand, have hardly changed; you're as beautiful as ever. I could have picked you out of a crowd. What am I saying? I *did* pick you out of a crowd."

"That's very kind of you to say," she said, but she didn't mean it. There was something threatening about his manner, his tone. He was leaning in very close. His breath was fetid, tainted with whiskey. She wanted to flee. "Well, uh, Salva, I..."

"Santi," he corrected her. "Santi Trias."

"Forgive me, of course, Santi." She looked off across the bar, hoping that Adam or Paco would come along and rescue her.

"Perhaps you would allow me to buy you a drink," he offered, leering, "for old times' sake."

"I'm afraid that I have to get back to my table." She offered her hand. "Good luck Santi."

He took it in his. She could feel his bones, as stiff as wire, gripping her like talons.

"Tell me, are you still working in radio?" he asked

"What? No! That was all long ago, another time. I have nothing to do with any of that anymore."

"What a pity. I can still hear your voice, so melodious and clear, as it came to us through the airwaves. I learned a good bit of English thanks to you. All those broadcasts so full of fervor and camaraderie. You were quite something. *Lucía the Red*, that's what we called you! Ah, those were the days when people still believed in something, don't you think?"

"I don't know I..."

"I'm not at all sure what we would have done without you," he said, talking right over her.

"Thank you," Lucía stammered. "Now I really must..."

But he wasn't having it. "It's just that I feel I have come to know you... intimately."

"I don't see how that could possibly be." She was trying to wrest her hand from his, but he would not let go.

"Well, you see, Quim spoke of you every day, all day, really."

"Did he?" She managed to free her hand finally and turned to go.

"There was so much time to talk in prison," he called after her.

His words took a moment to register, but Lucía suddenly halted and wheeled around abruptly. "Prison...what do you mean to say?"

"We were cell mates Quim and me, and a number of others, of course. Very crowded it was. One learns a lot about other men in such close quarters, more than one would like sometimes."

"Is this some sort of joke? Quim died in the battle of the Ebro."

"Who, Quim? Oh no, many thousands of men, yes, but not our Quim."

All around them was the high-pitched noise of merriment, but Lucía heard none of it. Her mind was reeling. She forced herself to focus. Her face grew hard, her eyes narrowed. "You're lying, I don't believe you. Quim is dead!" she shouted. A few people around them turned to look, but Lucía didn't care. "Dead!"

"Come, come, Lucía, let's not make a scene," he said coolly. "I have no reason to lie." He reached into the breast pocket of his jacket and withdrew a wallet. His slender fingers searched the folds and brought out a yellowed newspaper clipping, which he unfolded with exceeding care and handed to Lucía. "See for yourself."

She took it, looking at him warily, and shifting several paces until she was beneath the light cast by a wall lamp. The image that she saw was faded, but clear enough: a group of ragged men, bearing picks and shovels and assorted tools, and surrounded by rubble, were posing stiffly, unsmiling for the camera. Behind them rose a towering cross in the landscape. Lucía had to squint, but there was no doubt; there was Quim standing among them. It was an attenuated Quim, a Quim with crudely shorn hair, a Quim gaunt and aged, but it was him, unequivocally…alive.

"That shot was taken in the Valley of the Fallen. I can't remember the year, one dissolved into the next. Dates were irrelevant," said Santi Trias. "But can you believe it?" he added, taking back the tattered keepsake, holding it at arm's length and peering at the image. "We had to build the son of a bitch's tomb."

"Where is he?" murmured Lucía.

"Quim? He was released some years ago. He headed back to the family farm in El Perelló, or so I heard."

Without a word, Lucía turned and departed. Santi was saying something at her back, but she did not care to listen. She disappeared into crowd, jostled this way and that, oblivious to the life around her, like a somnambulist. When she reached the table, Adam and Paco were both intently digging snails from their shells.

"Ah, there you are darling," said Adam, rising from his chair. "We thought you might have gotten lost."

Lucía smiled wanly. "There was an enormous line for the lady's room."

"*Mamá*, you don't look too well."

"Paco's right, darling, you look rather pale. Are you all right?"

"What? Yes, I'm fine, just a bit overwhelmed that's all."

"I'm sorry; I shouldn't have insisted that we come."

"No, no, I'm glad that we came," she managed "very glad indeed."

* * *

For days she did not sleep. The nights seemed interminable, as if dawn had been banished, never to return. The face of Santi Trias with its ghostly pallor kept intruding in her mind, leaning in close, crowding her thoughts. His words echoed in the darkness: *Quim spoke of you every day...so much time to talk in prison...one learns a lot about other men in such closed quarters...* How was it possible, she asked herself again and again? She tried to think back, but it was all so impossibly remote. Forty years had passed, the better part of a lifetime. It wasn't just the memory of Quim that had slowly faded and grown ill-defined, but so many of the details of Spain and her early life, or her *other* life, as she thought of it. She had long ago ceased to dream in Spanish, which did not really surprise her, but left her with a queer unease as if her subconscious had been not so much eclipsed as irrevocably erased. They say that memories of childhood stay with one always, but it wasn't true she had discovered. Her memory had become like something liquid that spilled through her fingers and seeped into the ground and was gone, never to be recovered. She was alarmed to realize that the images of her own family, the family that she had left behind, had grown dim and ill-defined. She could no longer readily conjure up their faces in her mind, but only vague approximations devoid of telling details, like those of distant relatives rarely seen. She was losing an earlier self, and no matter how much she groped frantically for the contours and textures of her youth, darkness was closing behind her and obscuring all that had been familiar.

It did not help that the world of Quinta Amelia and Tortosa and the Mediterranean was so astonishingly different from anything that Lucía knew or had seen in America. Nothing seemed to bear association, not the landscape or the light or the very air even. She recalled how relieved she had been to discover that Adam's family had a summer house near the sea and she would not be landlocked in some sprawling continental expanse. When Adam first drove her out to Southampton one spring day in 1939, not long after their arrival in the States, however, it wasn't a sedate sea akin to the Mediterranean that she found, but an ocean vast and menacing. The mere sight of its grey mass swelling and receding under a bruised sky filled her with dismay. She was pregnant with Paco at the time and she was reluctant to approach the water's edge for fear of being swept away and sucked into its unfathomable depths. She had longed then for the Mediterranean and the more measured world that it defined. Now she could hardly recall with any degree of clarity that placid, tide-less sea of her youth.

What little news of her family Lucía did receive came from the strained correspondence which she kept up with her mother. A sporadic letter written in a feverish scrawl would sometimes arrive from her brother Francisco as well, but more often than not they were maudlin texts full of self-reproach and descended quickly into gin-induced incoherence. They were a torture to read those letters from a brother lame and lush, but so too were her mother's, worse even, for their subtle spite. If Lucía wrote desperate for news and details of her siblings and the goings on at Quinta Amelia, the replies from her mother were almost cruelly quotidian, touching upon little more than the weather, tedious local gossip, unwavering praise for Franco *el Caudillo*, and assiduous descriptions of assorted religious feasts—*Yesterday was Corpus Christi and we all partook in the procession... The bishop came to lunch after Mass on the Feast of the Annunciation...* For all their lifelessness her mother's letters—written on shabby paper, Lucía couldn't help but notice, as if to compound the disregard—might have been written by a clerk; they contained nothing revealing in sentiment, nothing to console a daughter cut off from family in a strange, distant land. Lucía had been banished, deemed anathema, like a heretic. There were times when she suspected that she might never return, that in the life given to her to live, and which had seemed to hurtle past at an alarming pace, Spain and her family were lost to her forever.

That is, until the 20th of November, 1975, the day she learned that Franco was dead at last and Quim alive. Suddenly, Lucía found herself reaching back and recovering memories that had been all but forgotten, or deliberately cast out, she wasn't sure which. It was as if a hidden chamber filled with relics from the past had been unlocked, and as she rummaged about, removing the dust and patina of ages, these tokens from another time took on a new life. She suddenly recalled a photograph that Francisco had taken of her in the garden at Quinta Amelia. What had become of that photograph? she wondered. It was from an age when photography had not yet lost its magical, wonderous quality; not like the present, when snapshots were taken hastily and without a certain scrupulousness. She remembered the white linen dress that she had worn, the mottled light of spring, the jacaranda in bloom. And as these images grew sharper in her mind's eye, all at once the entire day came into focus with a host of details that astonished her, as if she were not so much remembering the past as reliving it, wholly and faithfully.

* * *

There had been a call in the morning to inform her mother that officers of the Army of the Republic would be paying a visit to Quinta Amelia *to inspect the house's suitability to billet troops.* Those were the actual words that they had used or, at least, that was how her mother had repeated them again and again, incredulous at their impudence. The house had been graced by King Alfonso XIII, the Papal Nuncio, Antonio Gaudí, and Albéniz, she shouted. How would it not be *suitable* for a band of Republican rabble? She refused to receive them. Lucía was to go in her place, but before she did so, Francisco had insisted that she put on her most flattering dress. We cannot disappoint the loyal troops of the Republic, he had said drolly. She changed into a sleeveless white linen dress, and they had gone to the garden, where Francisco took her picture and others with Carlitos beneath the jacaranda. Later, when the officers arrived to the house and were shown into the entrance hall, she remembered descending the staircase to greet them and the way they watched her unfalteringly as she approached. Until then, she had had little experience with men, but at that moment, perhaps for the first time, she understood the power that women could wield. The officers were transfixed and she liked it.

As it happened, it wasn't the strapping coronel from Madrid with his almost comic swagger and air of a *macho ibérico* who Lucía was attracted to, but the rather timid junior officer with the shock of pitch-black hair and hazel eyes. She was surprised to learn that Lieutenant Quim Soler was a local boy, born and raised just a few valleys over in El Perelló. She had never seen him before, but that wasn't surprising; he was a country boy, a farmer. She knew it the moment she shook his callused hand. Their paths would never have crossed were it not for the uniform and the official visit. During the tour of the public rooms, she could see the expression of wonder on Quim's face. Neither man said much, but the coronel strutted about as if he were to the manor born. Quim lagged behind, taking everything in. Occasionally, Lucía heard him gasp. In the end, the coronel found the house most *suitable*, he said, matter-of-factly. He regretted that he would have to remain living at the regimental headquarters, he added, but Lieutenant Soler and his men would occupy the third floor, part of the servant's quarters, and the stables. She never did see the coronel again. As for Lieutenant Quim Soler, who moved into Quinta Amelia the very next day with a handful of troops, she scarcely left his side that whole spring and summer of 1938.

* * *

Adam and Lucía planned to drive out to Southampton a few days before Thanksgiving to prepare for the holiday weekend. Paco and Katia would come out later on the train along with Lorenzo di Marco, a filmmaker and long-time friend of Adam's. "I might bring someone along if that's alright," he had told Adam. It's what he always said, and then never failed to appear with an almost indecently young woman at his side. Lucía always wondered where he found these last-minute companions, but she never got the chance to ask. They never lasted long.

They set off on Tuesday morning. Patrick the doorman helped them out of the elevator with their bags and boxes of assorted groceries, wine, and bottles of gin and whiskey. Adam walked to the garage on Second Avenue to pick up the car while Lucía waited in the entrance. Shafts of pale autumn light slanted through the glass of the front door and caught Lucía where she sat waiting, her eyes closed and her head tilted back to catch the rays.

"A fine day," announced Patrick, peering through the glass and up toward a cloudless sky.

"Yes," replied Lucía, keeping her eyes closed. "It could be spring."

Patrick rocked on his heels. "Bad weather on the way though."

"Oh?"

"A chance of snow for Thanksgiving Day, or so they say."

"Will you be off on Thanksgiving Patrick?"

"Yes indeed, Mrs. Fates. One of the young lads will be on the door."

Patrick was the only person who called Lucía "Mrs. Fates" and whom she never bothered to correct. He could not fathom that a woman would keep her family name.

"And what are your plans?"

"Oh, the usual," said Patrick "dinner with the missus and Liam, then a bit of football on the television, perhaps a stroll in the park."

"That sounds lovely."

A few neighbors came and went, but Lucía kept her eyes closed, her face trained to the sun.

"Here comes Mr. Fates now."

Adam pulled up to the curb in front of the building. Patrick opened the front door for Lucía and then scurried around to the passenger door on the left side of the car and opened that too. As she slid into the front seat she was immediately taken by that rarefied smell, a combination of leather, wood and wax that reminded her of a gentleman's club. It was a Bentley, a 1956 Continental S1 Fastback Coupé, she knew, having heard Adam explain it countless times to strangers who stopped to ask after it. It was a beautiful thing, silver with red leather upholstery. The dashboard was made of some exquisite, exotic wood. The motor did not sound like those of conventional cars; it purred ominously. Adam often complained that the machine cost a small fortune to maintain, but he could not part with it, it had been a legacy from his father, and while he loved the car as he loved few things, Lucía suspected that he also secretly feared it. He was not a natural driver, did not seem at ease driving. He gripped the steering wheel until his knuckles went white and held it at arm's length, his back pressed firmly against the seat. He concentrated on the road with an uncanny intensity, rarely speaking.

And that is how they drove out of Manhattan, crossed the Triborough Bridge, and began the long journey out to the eastern end of Long Island. They had made the trip countless times, but somehow the ride never failed to fill Lucía with a peculiar angst. She could not recall a landscape so profoundly dull; one gazed alternately at little more than scrub forest and mean suburban sprawl. They spoke little. The radio, tuned to WQXR, crackled Mahler. The reception was seldom good, static and white noise were forever interrupting the programming. Adam never seemed to notice; he only drove on unperturbed.

For Lucía, the sound of the radio never failed to awaken her own associations with the air waves, when it was she who leaned into the microphone in the ghostly silence and let her voice drift out into the night, bound for unseen villages and battlefields, barracks and cities under siege. She could recall those monologues virtually verbatim. Perhaps it was the ardor of those distant words that made them so indelible. She still uttered them from time to time, just to recall the weight that words once possessed, when they seemed a matter of life or death...

Good evening brave comrades wherever the war may find you. This is Lucía speaking to you from Tortosa, Catalonia, the Republic of Spain. I address you in English so that many of you valiant volunteers who have come from far-off corners of the globe to join the struggle to save Spain from the Fascists understand the gratitude that all freedom-loving Spaniards feel toward you. How we admire you for your noble sacrifice! Many of you have come to fight for a cause and a people without even knowing the language of the land, but that hasn't stopped you, because you speak a universal language, that of freedom and liberty and solidarity...

It had been Adam who first suggested that Lucía "give the radio a try", as he put it. He and a few of his journalist colleagues said that her English was excellent and her voice like velvet. All those English-speaking *brigadistas* from the U.K. and the States, Ireland and Australia, Canada and South Africa could use a bit of morale boosting, they insisted. "Yes," Adam had said "give the boys something to dream about."

Quim had been against the idea from the start. He knew that there would be trouble. "You will be a marked woman," he said. Why had she not listened to him? Instead, she was drawn by vanity and the glamour of the radio and the thought of a captive audience, but also a desire to be a part of the struggle, that too. Women were contributing to the war effort in myriad ways, working in factories and hospitals and canteens. They were even fighting at the front! Why should she not do her part?

And so, once a week, under the cover of darkness, she allowed herself to be led by an information commissar, rail-thin and soft-spoken, to that narrow attic in the ancient quarter of Tortosa, where all was quiet but for the gentle hum of the transmitter. At first, she was self-conscious and unsure of herself and read the prepared scripts in a dull tone without inflection. How odd it was to speak into a microphone with nobody before one! But soon enough, she got the knack of it, grew confident, bold even, and cast aside the scripts and chose her own words, words from the heart, words that no propagandist from the Ministry of Information could have composed. She would talk on and on, seduced by her own rambling soliloquies, carrying on a one-sided conversation with her unseen audience. She found herself revealing things about her own life and world and Spanish society and the injustices that she had seen and been a part of even. And therein lay her power, her credibility. She was someone from the ruling class, the landed gentry, the well-to-do, who had decided to publicly renounce her privilege. And they loved her for it, oh how they loved her! They dubbed her *Lucía the Red*, and waited eagerly for her weekly broadcasts as if they were letters from loved ones...

I have a brother, Carlitos is his name. He is the Benjamin of the family, the youngest of my siblings, and while he is too young to fight, he is not too young to know the difference between right and wrong, justice and injustice, a noble cause and the travesty of the murderous fascist crusade. How proud he makes me when I hear him cry: Viva la República! How he stirs my heart, and how my other siblings, still lost in their delusions of class and power, how they fill me with sorrow and shame.

She had thought her words so genuine and above censure, until, that is, they led to the death of an innocent. And how her voice was silenced then.

* * *

"Did you say something, darling?"

Adam's voice cut her musings short, she must have mumbled something audibly.

"Oh, no, nothing, just thinking out loud, I suppose."

Someplace around mid-island, Adam turned off the highway and began looking for Sunset Farms, where they bought their Thanksgiving turkey each and every year. It was a Fates family tradition. So too was their inability to find the place. How could one, thought Lucía? Everything looked the same, the stunted trees, the low non-descript shops selling carpeting and liqueur, tires and pets, the gas stations, the hideous houses. She never saw any people, no one out walking. Where were they? she wondered.

They found the place at last. The sign for the farm was partially obscured by a billboard announcing Sunset Estates. They turned into the unpaved road and passed a progression of building sites. Everywhere there were mounds of weed riddled earth, piles of lumber and cinder blocks, lamp posts lying on the margins, waiting to be erected, a few cars and trucks parked about. A tiny shed bore a sign with OFFICE printed in bold red letters.

"Good Lord," said Adam, "old man Mosley must be selling out."

At the end of the road they came to the farm. The house looked weary, all peeling paint and the roof sagging, but there was still a fenced-in muddy patch brimming with fowl. Even with the windows closed the stench was overpowering. Adam honked the horn, and an old man in overalls and a soiled olive-green army jacket emerged from a barn alongside the house. Adam got out and waved and made his way toward the man, gingerly avoiding puddles and patches of mud as he went. Lucía stayed put. She watched them shake hands and talk, the man waving his arms at the construction all around them. Adam nodded his head, listening. Lucía looked out at the turkeys and watched their erratic movements and panic-stricken eyes. She could hear their low, collective gobbling. "It won't be long now," she said to them under her breath. Adam and the man disappeared into the barn. Soon her husband returned to the car bearing a large brown paper bag, which he put in the trunk. She could feel the weight of it.

"Well," proclaimed Adam when he got back into the car, "that's the last bird we buy from farmer Mosley."

"What's happened?"

"He's sold the family farm, subdivided, and made a bundle. They're moving to Florida, says he can't stand the cold."

"So we won't ever have to come back here?" Lucía asked, smirking.

Adam feigned shock. "I for one will miss it dearly. I've been coming here since I was a boy. Best turkeys in the tri-state area."

It's what he said every year. As they drove away, Lucía turned back to look at the doomed birds for the last time and wondered how that could be so.

They arrived as the light was beginning to wane. Towering hedges cast blocks of shadow over the lawn. The flower beds were cropped. The pool was drained. Dorothy and Archie Candee, the house's caretakers, had turned on the lights, got the furnace going, and lit the hearths throughout the house. They had been hired by Adam's parents and were the house's most impervious feature. They were childless. They occupied the servants' wing, but no one doubted that they were the true lords of the place. Adam called it Candeeland, but not in front of Dorothy and Archie. The house had been Adam's father's wedding present to his mother. A department store fortune allowed for such munificence. It was built by Stanford White in the Shingle Style. The interior consisted of vast, exquisitely proportioned spaces. Once, astonishingly drunk, they had ridden bicycles in the drawing room. In the summer, light flooded the rooms. There was always beach sand on the floor; it ground beneath the soles of one's shoes, scratched the floorboards, but no one cared too much. The furniture was overstuffed and slightly worn, the fabrics faded from the sunlight and the years. Adam was forever getting offers to sell the place, astronomical offers from bankers and Hollywood producers and pop stars, but he always politely said no. It wasn't a question of the money, he insisted. The Park Avenue apartment left him cold, Lucía knew, but he loved the Southampton house, so too did Paco. And while Lucía had learned to be happy in the house, on occasion it also distressed her, for it reminded her of everything that Quinta Amelia had never been, that is, warm, inviting, relaxed.

They took their dinner on trays and sat in front of the fire in the library. Adam had gone down to the cellar and found a dusty bottle of claret. "We're still drinking wine that my father put down," he said. "God bless the man and his nose." The wine was extraordinary, smooth as velvet, in the fire light it glowed like a ruby. "Don't mention this to Lorenzo," Adam insisted, swirling the wine in his glass. "He'll drink it all."

"When is he arriving?" Lucía asked.

"Tomorrow afternoon, he's coming, or rather they're coming—we'll see who's on his arm—on the 6:50, the same train as Paco and Katia."

"I like having outsiders at the feast," she said.

"Lorenzo's practically family."

"I meant his surprise date."

"I wish he would marry one of them. I'm growing tired of being introduced to them, getting to know them, and then having them disappear."

"He's never going to marry. He's not the marrying type. That's why he has a new woman every time he turns up. He doesn't *want* them to last."

"Well, all I know is that no man wants to grow old alone."

"How romantic of you."

"It's true."

"I wish that Paco would hurry up and marry Katia. He's going to lose her if he's not careful. She's going to grow weary of waiting."

"They're as good as married."

"That's not enough for a woman."

"Listen to you, *que conservadora,*" mocked Adam.

Lucía did not smile. They fell silent and stared into the fire, sipping their wine and biting into toasts of cheese and paté with a desultory air.

No man wants to grow old alone, the phrase stuck in Lucía's head. So, what then had become of Quim? she wondered. Was he alone, alone and half mad after years of forced labor and deprivation, his teeth gone and his spirit broken? If there was no one to see to his needs, was he ill-shaven and shabbily dressed, under nourished and uncaring? Was he the butt of village jokes, jeered at by young boys, pitied by a few, but otherwise overlooked, invisible? Or had he married some black-clad spinster from the village upon his return? Lucía tried to imagine her. A woman who had always loved him; a woman who had waited and would have gone on waiting however long, not like that aloof Lucía Vidal, who had run off with some American when the going got rough. Lucía saw this phantom wife fulfilling her myriad domestic duties: preparing Quim's meals, hauling water from the well so that he could wash, ironing his single white shirt for the village feasts in El Perelló, warming his bed with her thick and barren spinster body. All at once, Lucía felt consumed by a sentiment that she had never known in all her years, namely, jealousy, directed at an imaginary woman, no less.

She heard herself groan audibly and inadvertently click her tongue. Adam turned to her. "Oh darling, don't worry so much about Paco and Katia, they'll be fine."

Lucía looked at him blankly, at a loss as to what to say. "Yes...yes, you're right," she offered finally. "No need to worry about something that we can't control."

"Precisely," he replied, as he reached for the claret. "More wine?" He filled her glass without waiting for her to reply, and then stood to stoke the fire.

In another year he would be sixty-five, thought Lucía as she watched him move. He was still so handsome, so agile in everything he did. How could she be thinking of Quim, a love from another world, a passion long ago spent, when she had Adam Fates? She couldn't fathom it.

And yet.

There was a screeching of metal and a dull, rhythmic thumping as the train rolled in late to Southampton station. Lucía and Adam were waiting on the platform beneath a bleached, florescent light. Faces looked out vacantly from the car windows. A handful of passengers got off the train and made their way toward cars idling in the parking lot. It wasn't before a shrill whistle blew, signaling the train's imminent departure, that Paco, Katia, Lorenzo and a young woman descended unhurriedly from the bar car. Although she and Adam were out of earshot, Lucía could see Lorenzo saying something to the others, and then all of them laughing in unison.

"It appears that Lorenzo's in fine form," said Adam, smirking.

They all walked toward one another and converged on the platform as the train pulled away. There were hugs and kisses all around, and Lorenzo introduced Lucía and Adam to Gabriela. She was from Argentina, and immediately launched into Spanish with Lucía. Her accent was like music. She couldn't have been much older than Katia, and beautiful. A mane of black hair spilled over her shoulders, her eyes were almost oriental. She must have had Indian blood. Lucía thought that she saw Adam wink at Lorenzo. They gathered their bags and made their way to the car.

"Ah, how good of you to fetch us in the Bentley," Lorenzo said haughtily.

"You know very well that it's the only car we own," Adam replied.

"Among other reasons that's why I love you," proclaimed Lorenzo, as he took the front seat and Lucía, Katia, Gabriela and Paco squeezed into the back.

"And how does that square precisely with your ideology?" Adam scolded, knowing that Lorenzo was a committed Marxist, but also a lover of fine food and wine, beautiful women, and rich friends with elegant cars. Only his clothes were habitually shabby. He was famously indifferent to his appearance.

"Perfectly," he shot back, "I believe that everyone should be able to drive a Bentley."

"Then it wouldn't be the same."

"And that is why you are a bourgeois, my favorite bourgeois."

From the back seat came a flourish of giggling.

They drove to Bridgehampton to have dinner at Bobby Van's. Bobby loved to see them because Adam parked the Bentley in front of the restaurant. He said that it lent his place panache, which he pronounced *panash*. The restaurant was a watering hole for a group of prominent writers and artists –James Jones, Frank Stella, John Knowles, a few others—who sometimes played poker in the back room while Bobby played the piano in the front. It was not uncommon to find Truman Capote drinking alone at the bar before lunch.

They sat at a table by the fireplace. There were a few other patrons, locals mostly, but it was out of season and the place was quiet, like a club. They ordered steak and Saint-Émilion. "The meat will be inferior to what you are used to, but still," Adam said to Gabriela smiling. She did not understand until Lucía translated and then Gabriela smiled too. "Thank you," she said.

Lorenzo began to talk about his latest documentary, *Painters at Work*, the film consisted of interviews and studio scenes of all the New York artists that he thought worthy of his attention. They were all his pals, his contemporaries. The competition to be in the film was furious. More than a few offered him canvases in exchange for a part in the production. Lorenzo, however, would have none of it. He had his own criteria.

"Everyone believes that artists are incorruptible, that their work is sacrosanct," he said, snorting. "They are worse whores than bankers, less scrupulous than arms merchants."

Listening to Lorenzo was like attending to a king at court. The pronouncements, the aesthetic judgements, the gossip even, were somehow irrefutable. Lucía, alas, had heard it all before. She began to tune it all out. Once Lorenzo got started, there was no stopping him. Gabriela, she could see, was lost to it, unable to follow the art talk. The language was beyond her. When Lorenzo paused to take a breath, Lucía asked Paco to change places with her. Gabriela looked relieved. The two women carried on a hushed conversation of their own, a conversation of exile, loss and longing. Gabriela had only recently been forced to flee the military junta in Argentina; displacement was still new to her. For Lucía, it was the tenor of her life. Still, their common status as exiles was like an instant bond. They listened to one another. Lucía explained the recent revelation about Quim, she wasn't sure why. She felt compelled to speak with someone, to unburden herself, and Gabriela, a virtual stranger, understood her in a way that her friends and family would not. She would not betray her.

When they returned to the house, Lucía showed Lorenzo and Gabriela to one of the principal guest rooms. Gabriela thanked Lucía again for a lovely evening and for having her to stay. She then said goodnight to Lorenzo, stepped across the threshold, and shut the door behind her. Lucía and Lorenzo stood in the hallway, Lucía smiling and Lorenzo speechless. There was a sound of a lock turning.

"I believe that there's another room made up on the third floor," said Lucía.

"Undoubtedly," said Lorenzo. "No need to show me, I'll find my way." And off he went alone, sulking.

Adam laughed when Lucía recounted the incident as they were getting ready for bed. After a pause, he grew more serious.

"What were you and Gabriela's talking so intently about? The two of you scarcely touched your food."

Lucía froze. Had Adam heard her mention Quim? she wondered in a panic. She didn't think that she had mentioned his name, but she couldn't be sure. Anyway, Adam had been across the table, listening intently to Lorenzo, and she and Gabriela had been whispering in rapid Spanish. No, it was impossible.

"Didn't Lorenzo tell you anything about her?" she asked.

"No, not a word, why?"

"Her father was kidnapped and murdered recently."

"Christ! Lorenzo didn't say anything about that."

"He was a judge in some provincial capital. A right-wing death squad came in the night and hauled him off. A few days later they found him in the trunk of a car with a bullet in his head."

"I never would have guessed that she'd recently been through anything traumatic, poor woman."

"You know, she's a journalist. She's gotten death threats of her own. That's why she's here. I have the sense that she doesn't know anyone in New York. Would you help her out, introduce her around?"

"Yes, of course, but she's going to have to work on her English."

Lucía had been getting undressed, but she stopped suddenly, and stared motionless at the floor. "They came in the night and then left him for dead...It reminds me so much of the civil war—*llevarse a alguien a dar un paseo,* to take someone for a walk, that's what they called it. That's how they murdered Carlitos. That's how they murdered Lorca."

"I know, darling," said Adam, sounding slightly weary, as if he'd heard it all before, "I was there, remember, but that's all a part of the distant past."

"Not for me it isn't."

* * *

In the morning the sky was alive with ashen clouds racing overhead. Occasionally, great beams of biblical sunlight burst through the cover and turned the heavens a pearly grey. Dorothy Candee had been up early baking and the house smelled deliciously. Lucía was having coffee at the kitchen table when Lorenzo appeared, looking slightly wounded.

"Good morning, sleep well?" asked Lucía, peering over her cup.

"What else was there to do?"

Here was a man accustomed to getting what he wanted, thought Lucía, and suddenly he hadn't. "Help yourself to coffee."

Lorenzo was well acquainted with the house. He opened the correct cupboard to reach for a cup, knew where the sugar was. He served himself coffee and stood looking out the window. Lucía watched him slyly, half-pretending to read yesterday's newspaper.

He was not an attractive man, not physically. His legs were short, his girth too considerable. If one saw him in the street with his boots, his workman shirts and unironed trousers, one would have said that he was a plumber, an electrician, or some other tradesman. His wide face was ruddy from too much drink, although in all the years that she'd known him, Lucía had never seen him drunk. Only his eyes, blue like gentians, were beautiful. Still, women loved him; Lucía loved him. If it were anyone else I would be wildly jealous, Adam had told her more than once. After a conversation with Lorenzo one wanted to rush off and attempt to write it all down. Everything he said had weight, even his humor.

"Any Indians coming to share our table?" he asked, without shifting his gaze from the window.

"Paul Weems, the writer, is coming alone."

"Terrific. I haven't read anything of his for years, but I am very fond of him."

"And Jeremy Branch."

Lorenzo was silent.

"What?" asked Lucía.

"Nothing…He's just so, how should I put it? Chiseled, that's it, so proud of himself and all the money he's made. How can someone so dim succeed like that? Can making piles of money be that easy?"

"He's bringing Cecilia Cousins."

"The actress?"

"Yes."

"Well, well, she's a real beauty. Things are looking up."

"It seems to me that you have beauty enough in Gabriela."

"Evidently, I don't *have* anything."

"Patience, you've only just met her."

Adam appeared in the threshold wearing a tattered silk bathrobe and thick woolen socks on slipperless feet. "Happy Thanksgiving," he said wearily. He padded into the room, bent to give Lucía a kiss, and joined Lorenzo staring out the window. "Sleep soundly did we?" he asked Lorenzo, but there was no reply. "What's out there that's engrossing you so?"

"The light…it really is extraordinary out here."

"I must take some pictures when I wake up."

"It won't last."

"It never does."

Adam got a cup of coffee and sat down beside Lucía. "It smells divine in here."

"Dorothy's been baking pumpkin pie and fresh bread," said Lucía.

Gabriela came through the kitchen door from outside. Her cheeks were red, her eyes tearing from the wind. "*Buenos días,*" she said, stomping her feet and rubbing her hands together.

"*Buenos días,*" Lucía replied.

Gabriela approached the kitchen table and leaned down to kiss Lucía on both cheeks. "*Hola,*" she said to Lorenzo and Adam, smiling.

"No kisses for us," said Lorenzo to Adam, pouting.

"*Feliz día de acción de gracias,*" said Adam, haltingly pronouncing the Spanish term for Thanksgiving.

"We thought you were still sleeping," said Lorenzo.

"I wake early for *paseo.*"

"A walk," Lorenzo corrected.

"Yes. The beach is very beautiful and the houses very big."

"This is where the capitalists vacation," said Lorenzo.

"And unscrupulous Marxists," Adam sighed. "Don't pay attention to him," he added, waving toward Lorenzo.

"I think this is not so easy," said Gabriela.

Lucía gave a low, mischievous laugh.

"You seem to be doing quite well," Lorenzo replied in a tone of mock offense.

"Oh *cariño,*" murmured Gabriela and went to Lorenzo and kissed him on a jowly cheek.

"That's better," he said.

They heard footsteps coming from the back stairwell. Dorothy entered the kitchen looking stolidly determined.

"Happy Thanksgiving," said Adam.

"Anyone who stays in the kitchen is welcome to help," she pronounced without preamble, "otherwise kindly be on your way."

Only Lucía stayed behind.

At two o'clock precisely, Lucía, who had never been inclined to abandon a Spaniard's peculiar notion of time, entered the drawing room and announced that lunch was served. She was taking off an apron, a dish towel still draped over one shoulder. She wore a pale gray cashmere turtleneck, a double string of pearls, and wide, charcoal flannel trousers. She was no longer young, but still she was beautiful, more beautiful than women half her age, at least to the sort of men who knew the real thing. Guests and family hastily finished their cocktails and made their way to the adjoining dining room, where Lucía indicated where everyone should sit. She placed everyone just so, none of the couples sitting together, Lorenzo far from Jeremy Branch, Cecilia Cousins ensconced between men, Gabriela between Spanish speakers. It was a gift.

The long, damask-covered table was crowded with an array of plates, bowls and platters brimming with the *tapas* which Lucía prepared every year. They were her contribution to Thanksgiving. She would not have known what to do with a turkey. There were gleaming, marinated olives, wedges of Manchego cheese, fried squid, sautéed clams, *tortilla de patatas, pimientos de Padrón,* and best of all, Spanish *jamón de bellota.* No one knew where she got it, and she would not let on; not even Zabar's carried it, but Lucía had her sources. "What is life without secrets?" she would insist.

"Oh darling, this is wonderful, as always," said Adam.

"*Fantástico!*" Gabriela agreed.

They ate with gusto, noisily, determined, passing plates to and fro, filling their glasses with Albariño, talking with their mouths half full.

"Absolutely delicious," Paul Weems pronounced "even if it is not altogether orthodox fare for Thanksgiving."

"Nonsense," Lucía shot back playfully "the Spaniards were eating these dishes with the natives long before the pilgrims arrived."

"Is that true?" asked Cecilia Cousins. She had been exceedingly quiet, intent perhaps on not coming across as the celebrity that she was. It was no use.

"Everything that Lucía says is true," said Lorenzo with a knowing grin, trying to establish a rapport with the actress, who was sitting on his right.

"For Anglos, the history of America begins at Jamestown," Paco added, before turning to translate for Gabriela.

"Where *did* the Spaniards settle?" asked Jeremy Branch. He likely knew the answer to the question, but he didn't want to be left out of the conversation. Lorenzo's interest in Cecilia was plain to see.

"All over the South," said Katia "Florida, Texas, New Mexico, and then California, but that was later."

"Had they prevailed we'd all be speaking Spanish," said Adam.

"*Ojalá,*" Gabriela whispered to Paco.

"Do you get back to Spain often?" Cecilia Cousins asked Lucía.

For a moment Lucía was taken aback, and it was Lorenzo who answered. "No she does not."

"I'm afraid I've not been allowed to go back," said Lucía finally.

"Oh, I'm sorry."

"There is no need to be," said Lucía graciously. "Everything is changing very rapidly. Soon anything may be possible."

Paco and Katia cleared the plates from the first course, and Dorothy pushed through the swinging doors from the kitchen bearing the turkey on an enormous platter of polished silver. Everyone gasped at the sight of the bird and greeted Dorothy fondly. She nodded and smiled almost imperceptibly. Had Adam's parents still been alive, she would have been wearing a dove grey uniform with a white apron and headpiece, but the tone of the house had grown more egalitarian, more relaxed under their son. She wore a green tweed skirt and a beige twinset. Archie, her husband, did not appear, but waited in the kitchen for his dinner.

In lieu of grace, they made their way around the table, everyone obliged to identify something for which they were genuinely thankful. Weems began, professing profound thanks that his daughter Jennifer, or "Jezebel" as she had insisted on calling herself the last three years, had finally abandoned an Oregon commune. Cecilia Cousins mentioned an upcoming role and apologized rather too emphatically that she was bound by contract not to reveal the project or the director by name. Lorenzo cited a clinical test which, much to his surprise, had come back negative. Paco was infinitely grateful that the deadline for his biography of Gaudí had been extended, again. Katia announced that she would be Meryl Streep's understudy in the Broadway production of Williams' *27 Wagons Full of Cotton.*

"Who's Meryl Streep?" Cecilia Cousins asked.

"You'll discover soon enough," Katia replied.

Adam was relieved that *Life* was *not* sending him to cover the latest fighting in Beirut; he had grown too old for war, he admitted. Jeremy Branch gloated something about a dividend windfall (to which Lorenzo snorted).

Lucía was thankful…no, thankful was too tame a notion to express just what she felt, infinitely grateful came closer. She was infinitely grateful to know that Quim Soler was alive, that he had survived the war and the camps and all the horrors that she had been spared. She could not say so, of course. She glanced at Gabriela and caught her eye and a knowing stare and an almost imperceptible nod. Meanwhile, the others were waiting for her to reveal the object of her thanks. Finally, she uttered something about the hope for Spain's young king Juan Carlos. Gabriela came last. One could see that she was thinking hard, perhaps more about how to express what she wished to say than the sentiment itself.

"You can tell me in Spanish and I'll translate," Paco offered.

"No," she replied, and after a short pause added: "I am thankful that I am not dead."

"Well, I think we can all say that," joked Jeremy Branch, who must have been unaware of Gabriela's circumstances.

"For some it means more than it does for others," chided Lorenzo.

A hush fell over the table.

"What?" Branch insisted.

"Later," said Lucía, gently putting a hand over his on top of the table.

At last Adam, who had been diligently carving the bird, changed the subject, turning to Cecilia Cousins, his eyebrows raised, and asking "breast or leg?"

After the feast they rose from the table and returned to the drawing room for coffee and brandy. Paco laid a fire. The conversation grew oblique, the speech slightly slurred, but everyone was happy, satiated. The house had been built for moments like these.

"Look!" someone exclaimed, "it's snowing."

All conversation stopped and everyone turned or craned or stood to look through the windows that gave onto the back garden. The flakes were fat and coming down with a certain languor, as if they were in no rush. It was the first snowfall of the season.

"Time for a walk," Paco announced, breaking the lethargy.

Everyone gathered in the front hall, where Lucía and Adam rummaged in a closet and emerged with an assortment of coats and scarves, boots and hats, odd gloves and mittens. When everyone was bundled up they looked like a pack of peasants on the steppe.

They walked along the deserted beach. The great houses on the oceanfront were shuttered and silent behind the dunes. The sand was dotted with miscellaneous debris washed up by the tide: plastic bottles, a shriveled boot, driftwood, pieces of Styrofoam and cork, a garden chair; somehow, it all looked less sullied with a dusting of snow. As the group advanced it divided into smaller conversations, distinct strides. They walked for miles. The snow accumulated on their hats and shoulders, it stung their cheeks, and settled on their eyebrows and lashes. When the light grew dim they turned back, trudging through the sand like soldiers in retreat.

Lucía and Adam lagged behind, walking arm in arm. Bits of conversation and laughter from the others came their way borne by the wind. "This is not a Thanksgiving we're likely to forget," said Adam.

"No, I shouldn't think so." Lucía had begun to cry, but Adam didn't notice; her tears could have been produced by the wind and the cold. The surf thundered on their left, but the water was all but invisible behind a veil of snow. On their right the houses were swallowed up in shadow. "I can't stop thinking about Gabriela. 'I am thankful that I am not dead.' The way she said it; the way she looked. It was spooky and at the same time so familiar, at least to me. I felt the very same thing when I first arrived here." Adam did not respond except to squeeze her arm tighter to him. It was enough. After a pause he changed the thread of the conversation.

"I was shocked when Cecilia asked if you got back to Spain often, really, what a question."

"Yes, well, she's a true Hollywood type, not much concerned with world affairs, I suppose."

"But your response…" he stopped and faced Lucía, and only then did he see that she was crying. "Darling, why are you crying?"

"Oh Adam, forgive me, it's been a wonderful Thanksgiving, but Gabriela's plight, and then Cecilia's comment just got me thinking so of my own situation, my long exile, my distant family. Suddenly everything has come rushing back." The tears were falling freely now and Lucía pressed her face into Adam's chest, sobbing. He drew his arms around her, held her close, and whispered, "Don't worry, we put all that behind us. You mustn't dwell on the past."

"For years I did put it out of my mind," she said, brushing away her tears with a gloved hand. "I put it out of my mind because it was impossible to go back. Now, everything has changed."

"Well, why don't we plan a trip for the spring? We can make a grand tour of it, see Madrid too, and Seville," suggested Adam, suddenly sounding buoyant.

Lucía was quiet, weighing her words, not quite sure how to gracefully say what she knew she must.

"How about it?" he persisted. "Lucía and Adam make their long-awaited return!"

"Adam, darling, listen, this is something that I must do alone." She had never lied to him before, never deceived him, but she convinced herself that what she said was not strictly untrue. She did need to see her family, among others.

"Alone?" he repeated, alarmed. "Franco's still warm in his grave. It could be dangerous, and your family, they're even more dangerous. I would fear for you being amongst them." And then he added: "I won't have it. I forbid it!" but it didn't sound convincing.

Lucía smiled up at him. "But darling, you've never forbid me anything."

"Yes, I know, perhaps that's been my problem," Adam said in a bitter tone that Lucía had rarely heard him use.

He strode ahead of her, just a pace or two, enough to leave her alone at the rear.

When they got back to the house, darkness was falling fast, like the lights dimming in a theater. Everything lay silent beneath the season's first snow, the expansive potato fields and preened lawns, the cars parked in driveways, the still unplowed roads. The guests who were not staying the night promised to drive carefully. The men brushed snow from the cars' windshields, started the engines, turned the heat to full. Lucía and Adam, Paco and Katia, and Lorenzo and Gabriela stood in the drive stomping their feet and bidding farewell. Paul Weems rolled down his window.

"I give thanks to having friends like you," he said.

Then the cars drove off slowly in a file, forming a kind of caravan, their horns honking playfully, their headlights illuminating the whiteness.

Inside the house, they stoked the fire in the drawing room fireplace and talked quietly about the day, the perfect meal, the glamour of Celia Cousins, the snow which seemed to cleanse everything. Only Adam was quiet, uncommonly so. He was brooding, Lucía could see it. When the two of them went up to bed, leaving the others to linger, Lucía expected a row, but none came, only an unnerving silence, which was worse. He hadn't uttered a word to her, hadn't looked at her, since their fraught exchange on the beach. In the master bedroom, Adam sat on the bed, his back to her, as he slowly and deliberately undressed. Lucía stood in the middle of the room, watching him from behind.

"What is all this about?" she asked, although she instantly regretted the question for its fatuity.

"I don't believe that I have to explain that," Adam replied, without turning to address her.

No, she supposed he didn't. "You won't allow me to travel alone to Spain to see my family. Is that it?"

Adam turned then, frowning, a look of confusion in his eyes. "Allow?" he said, sounding incredulous. "I am not forbidding you anything. I never have."

"Yes, I know. I believe we've established that."

"Then why are you posing the question in that manner?"

She couldn't answer that. Adam turned away and continued undressing. There was an awkward silence. Lucía could hear laughter coming from downstairs, Lorenzo's booming voice.

"I am tired," Adam said, after a time.

"Me too, it's been a long day." Lucía was relieved that the talk had veered to something mundane. There would be time enough to argue about her journey home at another moment.

"I wasn't referring to the day."

"Oh," said Lucía, suddenly taken aback, "what then?"

"It's our life, our marriage, that I find exhausting."

Adam's voice had grown hard and strangely detached. He wasn't being merely dramatic, Lucía knew that. Adam didn't behave for effect. A flicker of panic rose up inside her. Something was about to change, perhaps forever. Outside, a wind had risen and flakes of fallen snow beat against the window panes, making a hissing sound.

"What do you mean to say?" she asked, her voice breaking. In truth, she knew precisely what her husband was saying, but she had always tried to avoid broaching the subject of their life together for fear of the fraud that would invariably come to light. They had long been living—always lived, if she were being honest—a kind of charmed pantomime. Theirs was a marriage of convenience that had somehow survived thirty-five years. She had thought it somehow invulnerable.

Adam turned toward her squarely and in his gaze Lucía saw something new, a pained look, as if something inside him had broken or cracked or gone awry. She sensed at once that she had pushed him too far. Lucía approached the bed and sat down at Adam's side.

"Perhaps if…" Lucía began, but Adam stopped her, shaking his head, his eyes closed tight, as if wishing to neither hear nor see.

"No, let me speak," he pleaded.

"Of course," said Lucía. She could feel herself growing pallid, bled of purpose.

He did not look at her. He sat with his head bowed, looking at his hands, the tips of his fingers touching, the gesture of someone contemplating what to say.

"Tell me," Adam said quietly. "What have I ever asked of you?"

Lucía was about to respond, *nothing*, but Adam wasn't expecting a response, he continued without pause.

"I know very well that you do not resent me or merely tolerate me. I know that we get on in our own way, but I know too something that has never changed, not in all these years, and that is that you do not love me, never have. Why is that? I so often asked myself. Many women are drawn to me, I can see it, sense it, but I have never sensed that from you, the only woman that matters. I cannot begin to tell you how frustrating that is. It's not your fault. I cannot blame you. I am well aware of the peculiar circumstances of our marriage, but still, I always hoped that you would come around, learn to love me. It's true that I never asked anything of you, but that doesn't mean that I didn't desire it. The single thing that I've desired more than anything else in life is that you love me. But it is the one thing that I cannot bring about. I cannot will it or buy it or scheme to make it happen. It is out of my hands and this afternoon on the beach I finally realized the futility of it all. I know now that it will never happen. I am exhausted, spent. I give up."

He fell silent then, as if he had uttered some final words at a trial, the verdict all but decided. They were facing a window that gave onto the road and further off the ocean, but all was black, the sky moonless. All Lucía could see was their reflection in the glass. Adam sat half dressed, suspended, she at his side, but not with him really. He wore an expression of utter defeat, as if beyond rage or struggle. They looked to her like something out of a scene from Hopper, a picture of loneliness despite their physical proximity. Suddenly, she grasped the breach between them, the unspeakable sadness of it after a life together. She didn't know what to say, where to begin.

"I…" she began, but stopped. The words didn't come, not even the thoughts that would have led to the words. She felt a kind of shame for having taken so much and given so little. She almost said: *You married the wrong woman*, but thought better of it.

"What are we to do?" Lucía asked, finally.

"Do? Oh, nothing, I suppose. I can't imagine us divorced. I suspect that little will change, really, except that I will be going away for a time, not just an assignment, something more prolonged. I need something new in my life, something to stir me. I would like to go off somewhere and photograph on my own, not for a magazine or a newspaper, just for me. I was thinking of Brazil perhaps."

"Brazil?"

"Yes, it's beautiful and miserable all at once."

* * *

In the weeks after Thanksgiving they continued to share the Park Avenue apartment. Adam was right, little changed. Lucía tried to be affectionate, to show her appreciation for everything, but they did not touch. It was too late. Slowly, Adam gathered his things, packed his bags, made his arrangements. And then one afternoon, a week before Christmas, the holiday lights on the avenues already illuminating the early darkness, Lucía came back to the apartment to find the rooms strangely quiet and a note on her bedside table.

Lucía my darling:

Forgive me for slipping off like a thief into the night, but it is better this way. Good luck to you in Spain. I hope you find what you are looking for. Perhaps I have never fully understood the pain of your exile. Still, remember that this too is your home, where you are welcome always.

Adam

Chapter Four

Lucía could feel the taxi driver's eyes watching her in the mirror. She imagined him wondering who this lady was with the fine, if slightly halting, Spanish accent and the expensive American clothes and luggage.

"Donde vamos, señora?" he had asked, when she got into the taxi, a rather comical car, square and compact, like something a child would draw.

Where to, indeed, Lucía thought. She wasn't sure. The plan had been to simply get to Barcelona, where everything would somehow fall into place, or so she had imagined. Now that she had arrived, however, after decades of excruciating longing, all she felt was unmitigated panic, like a child who has swum too far out to sea and suddenly turns to find the shore diminished and the people shrunken. She had no reservations, no immediate destination; she had come unannounced. She was free, but it did not feel like freedom, it felt like something else altogether, a combination of aimlessness and paralysis. *Donde vamos, señora?* Adam would have known what to say, where to go, what to do, but it was she who had insisted that he not join her. There were family affairs that she had to attend to, Lucía insisted, matters from the past that only she could address. Well, that much was true. Still, he hadn't taken it lightly. Why would he? He had every right to storm off to Brazil wounded and despondent. Even Paco, who had seen her off dutifully at JFK, had been perplexed. Why? He kept asking her. She couldn't answer, or wouldn't. Not everything bears scrutiny.

The driver cut the engine, but he left the meter running. He was in no rush. There was the periodic roar of planes taking off and landing, and the steady ticking of the meter and the flipping of numerals as the *pesetas* accumulated. He reached for the dashboard and turned on the radio. The car filled with the hectic rhythms of a rumba and a male voice whining:

Acércate nena, un poco más.

Acércate nena, más, más, máaaaaaas!

What she needed, Lucía decided, was time, time to acclimatize to this old-new world, to gather her thoughts, to reckon why, indeed, she had come at all. "Take me to the Ritz...no, better the Hotel Oriente on Las Ramblas, that is, if it still exists."

"It does, Madam, but are you sure that you wouldn't prefer the Ritz?"

"Quite sure."

They drove away from the airport and onto the highway that led toward the city center. Lucía peered out the window, searching for familiar landmarks but finding none. It had been nearly forty years since she'd last been here; it might as well have been a hundred. She had the sensation not of returning home but rather of arriving to an alien place, or a place where she had only been briefly, in passing. The highway was packed with trucks and cars and motorcycles, and flanked by towering apartment blocks. There were factories, office parks, warehouses, and schools, and train tracks leading every which way. Between the buildings she caught glimpses of cultivated fields and plots with neat rows of green lettuces and clusters of stakes around which tomato plants wound. Once, this had all been agricultural land, Lucía recalled, the city's orchard and garden. The astonishment must have been etched on her face.

"It has been some time since you have been here, no?" the taxi driver asked, glancing intermittently from the road to the rear view mirror.

"Yes, a very long time. It seems like a different place."

"Much has changed," he admitted with a sigh. "Much has changed and nothing has changed."

Here was the old fatalism, thought Lucía. It was such a Spanish sentiment, so ingrained and abiding. No American would ever make such a statement.

"What of the New Spain I've been reading so much about?"

"The New Spain?" he repeated, shaking his head dismissively. "There is no New Spain, just the Spain of always, a country run by priests, police, and politicians."

Lucía was silent. She had hoped to find a new spirit, not just the physical transformation of the landscape that was rushing past.

"Forgive me if I sound cynical, *señora.*"

"Why didn't you leave like so many others to France or Germany or Switzerland?" she asked.

"My wife asks me the same question every day!" he exclaimed drolly. He soon grew serious, however, and after a pause continued: "I don't know. This is my country, my place. I have many friends who left and found work in the factories in northern Europe. They come back for holidays driving Mercedes and boasting of their comfortable lives, but beneath the surface they are changed. Something inside them is gone. I can't tell you what it is, but I can see it."

Would they say that of her, Lucía wondered, that she had changed? How could she not have after decades in a foreign culture? What the driver was saying was true, something inside her was gone, something vital had been leeched from her. She couldn't say what it was either; perhaps it was ineffable.

"Don't listen to me, *señora!*" he insisted. "I meant no offense."

"Don't worry," Lucía assured him.

They were now on the Gran Via heading toward the center of town. It was mid-May and files of plane trees provided a lush canopy which contrasted with the soot gray buildings lining both sides of the avenue. The streets were crowded with shoppers and students and mothers pushing prams and elderly men leaning on canes and people sitting at outdoor cafes and on benches talking and smoking and whiling away the afternoon. Lucía's spirits rose, as she observed the animated street life that she had almost forgotten. How different it was from New York, where one was so rarely idle. When they drew up to the Hotel Oriente, the driver parked in front of the entrance and went in to make sure there was a room available. Lucía stayed put, watching the strollers on Las Ramblas.

She couldn't help but notice that everyone appeared slightly threadbare, their clothes out of date. It was like watching a decades-old movie. And then there was the sameness of everyone. Where were the Blacks and the Asians, the Latinos and the Nordic types, the Arabs? After New York, she was taken aback by the lack of variety. The driver returned accompanied by a bell hop, who opened the backdoor and offered Lucía a hand as she got out of the taxi. She paid the driver, tipping him excessively.

"Welcome home, *señora*," he said. Lucía smiled and was turning away to enter the hotel when he added: "Pay no attention to my blather. If people like you are returning, perhaps there is hope."

The hotel lobby was all marble and mirrors with dark heavy furniture and weak light. The air was heavy, as if it hadn't stirred for decades. There was a smell of damp, fried food, and black tobacco that came rushing back to her from some long-sequestered place. A few men were sitting about reading the sports pages, but they lowered their papers and stared brashly when Lucía entered, alerted by the clicking of her heels on the marble floor. The concierge, dressed as if for a funeral in a black suit and tie, stood behind the front desk, tapping a pen nervously on the counter, scanning the register, pursing his lips, waiting. He was thin as a whippet, with a long neck protruding from his white shirt collar, and delicate, womanly hands. Only when Lucía stood squarely before him did he raise his eyes above his half-moon glasses and acknowledge her presence. "Good afternoon, madam."

"Good afternoon, I would like a room please."

"A room," he repeated, as if she had asked for something unexpectedly extravagant. He began to flip through the register briskly, clicking his tongue. Lucía had the impression that it was all for show, a kind of pantomime of efficiency.

"I believe that my taxi driver already confirmed that there was a room available."

The concierge looked up and over Lucía's shoulder, as if searching for the driver, but found only the bell hop, a pimply youth with jug ears, waiting listlessly with her suitcase. He then dropped his gaze to her hand resting on the counter. "Will your husband be joining you?"

"No," she replied, then, "yes...yes, he will."

He looked up at her with the sort of patronizing half-smile reserved for a child or the feeble. Why had she said that, Lucía wondered? She felt inexplicably intimidated. "That is, later...perhaps."

The concierge sighed and turned the register with a practiced motion toward Lucía for her to sign. He then reached into a drawer and withdrew an official form from the *Ministerio del Interior,* obliging her to provide all of her personal details, as well as the length of her stay in Barcelona, the reason for her visit, and any subsequent destinations and contact information in Spain. As the concierge silently watched, Lucía filled out the form with a slightly trembling hand, pausing at the boxes indicating "business" or "pleasure" before checking the latter. As for her subsequent destinations, she left that space blank.

* * *

Lucía woke in the late afternoon with a faint light seeping through the blinds that did little to illuminate a spacious room cast in shadow. She lay in bed, the top sheet pushed aside, clad only in a slip, listening to the sounds which rose up from Las Ramblas. They were different from the street sounds of New York. The car horns blared at an odd pitch, the police sirens wailed in a different cadence. There was a jeering of sea gulls, the chilling shrieks of children at play, and an incessant, collective hum of human voices that she never heard on Park Avenue. She could smell the nearby sea, briny and slightly foul.

She got out of bed, showered, and dressed slowly, deliberately. She was dawdling from fear, Lucía realized with a twinge of embarrassment. How could it be that she had come all this way and instead of exhilaration she felt a kind of dread at the mere thought of descending to the street? All at once she became aware of how rarely she had ever been alone, truly alone, unaccompanied by Adam or Paco or friends or Margaret or even her family when she was a child. But other people traveled alone, in fact, many seemed to revel in their solitary journeys. Katia was often off on her own, traveling to auditions in strange cities where she knew no one, and she always seemed to come back somehow emboldened. Just as she was dismissing her temerity as ridiculous in a grown woman, the telephone made a noise, startling her. It didn't so much ring as produce a prolonged rattle; another noise, thought Lucía, that did not sound as it did in New York. She wondered who could possibly be calling her. No one knew where she was. She picked up the receiver warily, as if it might do her some harm. "Hello."

"Señora Vidal?"

Lucía recognized the smug voice of the concierge.

"International call for you, shall I put it through?"

"Yes, of course," she replied. Did he imagine that she was in hiding? There was some clicking on the line and then a hollow silence. Finally, a far-off voice came through enveloped in static. *"Mamá?"*

"Paco," she said brightly. "How on earth did you know where I was?"

"You are not a complete mystery to me *mamá*. I thought that you might lay up in Barcelona for a night before heading to Tortosa. I had to try a few different hotels, but I'm glad I finally reached you. How are you getting on?"

"Oh, everything is so strange, so changed, but I'm fine," she assured her son, trying to sound buoyant, although even she was aware of something fraudulent in her voice. Paco must have sensed it too; for a long time he said nothing.

"You know, *mamá*," he offered finally, "I still have some research to do on the Gaudí book; I could be there in a few days if you could stand the company."

"No," she replied, perhaps too quickly, too forcefully, and then, more calmly, "I mean, thank you for the offer, but I'm fine, really. I think that this is good for me. I need to be more assertive. It's one of the things that I so admire in Katia."

They were both silent for a time, contemplating the bond between a mother and a child, thinking the things that needn't be said, or did they?

"Paco."

"Yes, *mamá?*"

"Marry her." Lucía could hear her son sigh. It was not the first time she had proffered this advice, but who could tell whether or not it might be the last. "Soon, the years will begin to rush by."

"You're talking like you need a drink. Go to Boadas and have one on me. It's close by the hotel. Ask at reception."

"Yes, I think I will."

"*Mamá,*" there came another prolonged silence, the telephone line crackled. Finally, "oh, never mind, I just hope that you find whatever it is you're looking for."

"Thank you Paco, and please, stop worrying so, your mother is stronger than you imagine."

When she stepped out of the hotel and onto Las Ramblas, the early evening air was torpid, the sun still high in the sky, and Lucía knew at once that she had overdressed. For a moment she thought of going back upstairs to change into something less, well, splendid, but she resisted. The suit of pale blue silk that she had chosen to wear gave her confidence, and confidence was what she was determined to exude. She crossed over to the central promenade that ran up from the port to the Plaza de Cataluña. Under the plane trees the light was diffuse, the heat less oppressive. Lucía headed north toward the square, slipping in amongst the sea of strollers. The way was lined with kiosks, flower stalls spilling with blooms, and terrace cafes, where white-jacketed waiters stood waiting lazily, waving away the flies with languid motions of their hands. Pairs of gray-uniformed policemen, their eyes hidden behind dark glasses, their expressions inscrutable, walked slowly along, projecting a silent menace. In front of the opera house a crowd was gathering for the evening performance; it was still early and the patrons looked uncomfortable in their formal attire and out of sorts in the glaring light. How different the scene was from the last time Lucía had been on Las Ramblas, when the cobblestones had been pried up to help build barricades, the buildings flanking the boulevard were pock-marked or burnt out, ragged militias patrolled the way, and stooped civilians crossed hurriedly to and fro lest they get caught in a burst of random crossfire. How far-off and futile those days now seemed.

At the top of Las Ramblas she came to the Plaza de Cataluña, where everything was enveloped in a sultry stickiness and the people milled about looking dazed and exhausted. As Lucía crossed the square she was set upon by a black-clad gypsy woman and her sniveling child. At last, she thought, here was something that hadn't changed. The woman pressed a bunch of rosemary into Lucía's breast with one hand and offered a cupped, tawny palm with the other, all the while wailing softly, calling her *guapa... reina.* Lucía opened her handbag, but found that she had no coins and was obliged to extract a hundred *peseta* note, which the woman snatched away and quickly buried in the folds of her skirt. "Shall we see what the future has in store?" she cooed, taking hold of Lucía's hand. No sooner had the woman begun to trace the lines in Lucía's palm, however, then she abruptly dropped her hand and turned away without a word, grabbing the little girl by the arm and fleeing across the square. Lucía was left staring at her tainted, luckless palm, wondering what grave portents could possibly be etched there—a violent death perhaps, an incurable disease, a visit from a hostile stranger—what nonsense. She took no stock in omens or soothsaying, divination or the zodiac, never had. She raised her other hand, which bore the sprigs of rosemary with their delicate blue flowers, brought it to her nose and inhaled deeply. What came to her all at once was the smell of childhood, of the wild, perfumed terrain of Quinta Amelia, at first sweet and delicate, then hanging heavy.

Lucía tried to assure herself that she was merely ambling aimlessly, registering the changes which had transformed Barcelona in her decades-long absence—the new shops, the ghastly modern buildings of concrete and glass, the sheer volume and din of the traffic, the televisions blaring from every bar—but after an hour or so of this joyless strolling, she found that she had arrived to the place that she had been silently seeking. On the calle Ausias March, just off the Plaza Urquinaona, Lucía stood on the sidewalk looking across the street at the façade of the building at number 16. It was smaller than she remembered it, as are so many of the things that one hasn't encountered since childhood. The five-storey, neo-classical house looked not so much ruinous as suffering from a determined neglect. Soot had turned the once luminous, honey-colored stone of the façade a uniform gray. The delft-blue paint of the shutters was peeling. The iron balconies were rusted and cluttered with weathered furniture, butane canisters, and the odd potted plant. How it had all gleamed a long time ago. And how well-tended the garden, which extended behind the house out of sight from the street, but was vivid still in Lucía's memory. She conjured up the flower-filled parterres and borders; the palm trees, cypress, magnolias and lemon trees; the statues of Diana and her nymphs spied by Acteon, which rose from the central fountain; and the crisp sound of one's steps on the gravel-strewn footpaths that made their labyrinthine way through the lush enclosure. Lucía knew all these things and so much more because it was the house in which she had grown up, her home until the age of nine, when, from one day to the next it suddenly wasn't. Unlike so many of the receding details of a life, it took no effort for Lucía to recall with uncanny lucidity the day her childhood in Barcelona came to a swift, inexplicable end.

* * *

She remembered a grim November day with rain murmuring against the window panes and the garden sodden and off limits. Her parents had shut themselves in the library in the morning and Lucía and her siblings had been confined to the third floor nursery, where they played unsuspectingly for hours under the scrupulous gaze of Theresa their German governess. The hours passed and the house grew deeply silent and still, as if someone dear had been lost and the house was keeping mourning. Odd how a sense of calm can grow too prolonged and suddenly become unnerving. When Theresa excused herself to inquire about lunch—did she too feel that something was amiss?—it was Borja, the eldest, who spoke up: "Something is wrong," he announced, "the house is entirely too quiet. Lucía, go put your ear to the library door and find out what's happening."

"Why me?"

"Well, I could hardly send Francisco, could I."

"I can make it up and down the stairs," Francisco insisted.

"Yes, but you would make too much of a racket with those crutches of yours."

"What about Inés?" asked Lucía.

"I'm not going, I don't want to get into trouble," said Inés.

"Neither do I," Lucía pleaded.

"If you don't go, you'll get into trouble anyway. I'll tell *mamá* and *papi* that you were spying on them."

"We'll tell them that you're lying," Lucía said.

"No you won't, or at least Inés and Francisco won't, and baby Carlitos can't speak."

Lucía looked at her sister and lame brother, but they only looked away in silence.

"You see," said Borja, knowingly, "now go."

Lucía rose from her chair, where she had been reading, and made for the door. As she passed Inés and Francisco sitting on the floor she muttered "traitors" and left the room. At the top of the marble staircase she removed her shoes, silently padded down the two flights to the entrance hall, and advanced on tiptoes to the double doors opposite the salon which led to the library. Gently, she put her ear to a middle panel of the door and tried to listen. It took a moment for her to take in more than the sound of her own labored breathing and the pounding of her heart, but then from the closeted silence beyond the door she could suddenly make out the sound of sustained sobbing, no words or shouts or murmurs, just her mother weeping unrelentingly. Lucía wanted to open the door and rush in and fall into her mother's lap and do her best to comfort her, but something held her back, a vague realization that what was transpiring inside the library belonged to some adult province where she dare not intrude. She was about to turn and retreat up the stairs to the children's precinct where she belonged, when the library doors flung open and her mother stood frozen in the threshold, her face distorted and wet with tears. She did not reprimand Lucía or address her at all; she merely looked at her daughter blankly, as if she didn't really see her. Then she brushed past and climbed the stairs silently. Lucía took a step forward, craned her neck, and peered into the library, where she saw her father seated in an armchair by the window, gazing out at the garden, his face pale and expressionless, like some ancient bust of a fallen hero.

The next morning, Lucía and her siblings were packed into the Hispano-Suiza with their mother, bound for Tortosa. It was a journey that they ordinarily made only in summer, but it was not a season in the country that they were embarking upon, but rather a new life, although they hardly knew it then. Among the things and people that they would never see again were the house in Barcelona and all its fine trappings, the garden, a slew of upstairs and downstairs servants, Theresa their governess, and most agonizing of all, their father.

The truth was, she could scarcely recall anything about the man, save that stoic profile staring out at the garden. When Lucía and her siblings were whisked off to Tortosa, that was the end of it. There hadn't been any final leave taking, no cloying farewell with promises to be reunited. None of them would ever see him again. Their mother never spoke of him, at least not of her own accord, and if the children asked after him, wondering where he had disappeared to or what he was doing, her reply was invariably the same: "Attending to his business," she would say in a splenetic tone that did not invite further inquiry. Eventually, they stopped asking. Of course, among the children there was speculation. When Borja was intent on being especially cruel he would invent every manner of scenario—their father had run off with Theresa; he had been consumed by cannibals in Africa; had drowned himself in the Ebro; had lost his way and was forever searching for them—reducing his brothers and sisters to tears before taking it all back and proclaiming in a high-pitched, mocking tone in imitation of their mother: "He's attending to his business!"

It would be years before Lucía learned the truth. She was sixteen, old enough to hear what life could dole out to the unsuspecting, her mother had said. At first what her mother recounted in the manner of a cautionary tale on how not to gamble one's life away seemed too improbable a story, too ridiculous even, to account for the traumatic uprooting from their home and their life in Barcelona and the disappearance of their father. But there was something about the flat matter-of-fact tone of her mother's voice and her utter composure in the telling that made Lucía realize that what she was hearing was no fabrication. Her mother would never again allude to her father's undoing, once was enough:

Teodor Vidal i Llimona, one of the wealthiest men in Catalonia, lord of the sumptuous Casa Vidal in Barcelona; Can Xal·lida, the family's country house on the coast in Arenys de Mar; a townhouse in Madrid; paper, textile, and sugar mills both in Spain and Cuba; vineyards and agricultural tracts; a steamship line that plied the Mediterranean coast from Genoa to Marseilles to Alicante; as well as stocks, shares, interests, and bonds in myriad banks and industries too numerous to mention, had lost it all, the entire family fortune, all but the proverbial shirt off his back, at the roulette table.

And that was what Teodor Vidal was at last admitting to his incredulous wife that bleak, sodden November day when Lucía pressed her ear to the library door and heard only sobbing.

Of course, it was a scandal of the sort that consumed the idle and intentional gossip of the city for months. A pillar of bourgeois society, a figure of vast wealth and seemingly irreproachable social standing had been brought low by vice. The fall was debated in the cafes, whispered in the clubs, babbled in the streets, dissected in the newspapers, and railed against from the pulpit. For a time, the case even entered the local lexicon: *hacer un Vidal* (to do a Vidal) was synonymous with losing everything.

Her mother was right to take the children to Tortosa, not that she had much of a choice; the house was no longer theirs to live in. Her father, incapable of bearing the humiliation of life in Barcelona without all the luxuries to which he was accustomed, fled to the south of

France in search of anonymity and new gaming tables. He would win it all back, he wrote to his wife, his luck would change. It never did. Almost five years after the unraveling, as the disgrace came to be known in family circles, Teodor Vidal i Llimona died penniless and alone in a boarding house in Nice. His wife was obliged to pay for the body to be transported back to Barcelona. The funeral was kept secret. The casket was closed. What, Lucía often wondered, would they have seen but a man wasted and spent, dead from nothing but a lack of luck. Although he was buried in the rather imposing family crypt on Montjuic, his tombstone was exceedingly simple and bore an admonishing epitaph chosen by a wife who knew no forgiveness:

"For the fool, it is but a pastime to make mischief…" (Proverbs 10:23)

* * *

A wife who knew no forgiveness…would her mother forgive her? Lucía wondered. She hadn't in nearly forty years. Given the chance, she'd probably choose the same epitaph for her daughter. What was it about the Grau-Vidals that made it so hard for them to forgive? What did they gain by saddling her with such a debilitating burden of guilt? Yet again, she wondered why she had come.

When Lucía smelled the rain, she thought for a moment that the power of her recollections was playing with her mind, but then she looked up to find a low, livid sky and the air eerily calm. How long had she been standing there mired in the past? She wasn't sure. She looked around self-consciously, but the people walking past seemed not to pay her any mind. Anyway, what did it matter? Who would remember her here? Lucía was about to turn to leave and forget the site that only aroused the long-repressed memory of childhood loss and anguish, when the entrance door to her former house opened and a small middle-aged woman emerged carrying a pail of trash. Lucía watched her scurry to the end of the street to empty her garbage in the bin on the corner. The first drops of rain, scattered but swollen, began to fall, and Lucía instinctively rushed across the street to seek shelter in what had once been her front door. She stood in the threshold, peering up to see the heavens open and the rain begin to sluice down with a clamor. The woman made it back just in time to avoid the deluge.

"Mother of God," the woman shrieked, "what a tempest!"

"I don't seem to have dressed for the weather," said Lucía.

"At this time of year, one never knows what it will do from one hour to the next."

A wind suddenly picked up and the rain began to reach them in the doorway. "Come inside," said the woman, "you don't want to ruin your lovely suit." They ducked in the small door that had been cut into one of the weighty double doors that marked the entrance. It was a feature new to Lucía. Inside, she noticed a row of letter boxes along the wall. The house, she suddenly realized, had been divided into apartments, and this woman must be the *portera* in charge of attending the front door, sorting the mail, cleaning the stairwell, and the like. From her accent, Lucía gathered that she was from the south, Andalucía most likely, perhaps Extremadura.

"Have you come to see the apartment?" the woman asked.

It took a moment for Lucía to grasp this odd twist of fate, but once she did, she couldn't resist going along with the ruse. What better way to see what had become of the place? "Yes I have," she said.

The *portera* fetched the key, and they rode up in the elevator that had been installed in the stairwell, getting off on the third floor. Ah, the children's domain, thought Lucía, how apt. "How many apartments are in the building?" she asked.

"Twelve, not including my apartment and the notary's office on the ground floor."

So many families living where only one had once sprawled; Lucía didn't object, it seemed to her a far better use of space.

The *portera* unlocked one of the doors on the third-floor landing and handed Lucía the key. "I've got to get back to the entrance. Please lock up when you're finished and be sure to return the key."

Lucía crossed the threshold tentatively, as if she might encounter some horrific defilement. The air felt colder than it had outside and smelled of...what? She couldn't identify it, but it was a down-at-heel smell, the whiff of old clothes, shabbiness, decay. She wondered who had lived here last and when? She walked through the rooms, peering into corners and behind doors, sizing things up. Her heels clicked and echoed on the tile floors of the empty rooms. Lucía recognized the spaces, but only imperfectly. The apartment had been fashioned from Borja's and Francisco's rooms and a portion of the nursery. Walls had been put up to divide the once spacious rooms and she could see where the patterns of the crown molding above and the tile floors below abruptly stopped. What a pity, thought Lucía, that the fine proportions had been lost, the architectural details truncated, the spaces diminished. The overall effect was like encountering someone who had lost a limb; one had to make an effort not to turn away in revulsion. She walked to one of the rooms at the back of the apartment and approached a window, eager for a view of the garden, but when she looked down she gasped in horror. There below was not the finely-wrought green enclosure of palms and parterres, rose beds and serpentine paths, but a parking lot with cars squeezed where trees once towered and flowers bloomed. The only water in the litter-filled fountain was a murky puddle created by the rain. Lucía turned away and left the apartment, locking the door behind her. It had been a mistake to come, she realized. What on earth had she expected to gain by chasing after memories of days that were dead and gone? There was nothing for her here but a sense of baleful disappointment. She wondered if this would be the general upshot of things during her visit to Spain, the logical outcome. One can never go home again. Before she left New York, Paco had said as much to her, quoting some American writer, she couldn't recall who. Such an American attitude, she remembered having thought. Perhaps there was something in it.

Lucía dropped the key off with the *portera* as she was leaving and thanked her for allowing her to see the apartment.

"So you're not interested in the place then?" the woman asked.

"No, I'm afraid not."

"No, of course not, what would a lady like you want with such a place? It must have been grand in its day though."

"Yes," said Lucía "yes it was."

* * *

She had not had to ask the concierge at the Oriente the way to bar Boadas, as Paco had suggested. Why did young people always assume that there was no life until they came onto the scene? Lucía knew the bar well, and after her ungratifying brush with the past she rather needed a drink. She walked back toward Las Ramblas. The storm had passed and the city glistened in its wake. The rain had given an edge to the evening air that made Lucía shiver. In the west, a radiant violet blush was fading in a darkening sky. When she turned onto the calle Tallers from Las Ramblas and saw the familiar façade of Boadas with its neon "cocktails" sign glowing in the waning light. Lucía quickened her step. Not everything changes, she thought, but how is it that time leaves certain things be? Inside, nearly everything was just as she remembered it. The place had been altered ever so slightly with lamps illuminating the bar and framed photographs of celebrities hanging on the walls, but otherwise it was largely unchanged. For a bar, the space was diminutive, almost laughably so—with a few dozen patrons it felt positively teeming—but therein lay its appeal. Tonight, there were only a handful of customers, a few suited men slouched over cocktails, some young bohemians stewing in the vintage ambience. She took a stool at the bar. The suits looked her over and proceeded to straighten their backs. A blond middle-aged barmaid, attractive in a tarnished sort of way, approached and Lucía ordered a gimlet. There was no sign of Miguel, the owner who had once mixed her drinks, and come to think of it, Adam's and Quim's too. Perhaps he'd moved on; perhaps he was dead. Funny that she had been here with both Adam and Quim, although separately. Each man's reaction to the place had been telling. She recalled bringing Quim one oppressively hot summer night. He was on leave from the front, but didn't know the city, and she had agreed to show him the town. From the moment they entered the bar she could see that he was ill at ease. He was a country boy. He had done his best to dust off his uniform, but he still looked irremediably disheveled. He reminded her of a tradesman who suddenly finds himself in the drawing room and can't decide where to put his hands or quite how to stand. When Miguel came over to take their order, placing a delicate linen napkin on the bar in front of each of them, Quim hadn't known what to ask for; he had never seen a cocktail. Lucía ordered *caipirinhas* for both of them, and Quim watched silently, intently, as lime quarters were cut and placed in their glasses, sugar added and muddled with the lime using a pestle, crushed ice added, *cachaça* poured, and the drink vigorously stirred. When he tasted his first cocktail, he proclaimed—and she adored him for this—that it was "the finest thing that had ever touched his lips." And he meant it. Adam, on the other hand, who was no stranger to cocktails, took to the place instantly. She knew that he would. Boadas was a favorite haunt for foreign journalists, spies, diplomats and commissars. As soon as she and Adam had arrived, he stood in the doorway, scanned the room, and exclaimed: "Well, now we're talking" or something like that, one of those American expressions she so loved. He strode up to the bar and ordered a dry martini "up with a twist, olive on the side," as if he were at the Knickerbocker in New York. Lucía began to translate for Miguel, but the barman told her that he understood perfectly and proceeded to mix what Adam would deem "the best dry martini in Iberia." If Lucía remembered correctly, Miguel blushed.

"Your gimlet," announced the barmaid, setting down an old-fashioned glass filled with a bilious green liquid and a wedge of lime astride the rim.

"Tell me," said Lucía "is Miguel still around?"

"I'm afraid he's no longer with us," replied the barmaid, growing still and looking at Lucía curiously.

"How so?"

"No longer of this world."

"Oh dear."

"I'm his daughter."

"My condolences…here's to him," said Lucía, lifting her glass and sipping her drink. "Ah…perfect, he taught you well."

"Thank you. Know him, did you?"

"Yes."

"I don't recognize you."

"It was a long time ago, during the war."

"That would be before my time."

"Yes, of course."

The place was filling up. A group of three couples came through the door. "You're gonna love this place," one of the men was saying. They were all fortyish, but the women were wearing miniskirts and those mock-peasant blouses, the men sporting exuberant sideburns and platform shoes. How frustrating to be already getting on in years just when the winds of change had begun to blow, thought Lucía. The barmaid excused herself to attend to them. Lucía sipped her gimlet. The drink helped her to feel less self-conscious, but only just. If she had a cigarette, she'd smoke it, even though she wasn't a habitual smoker. She would have liked to have something to do with her hands. It wasn't easy being alone, she was discovering. No one had ever told her how to do it precisely. Now there's something her father could have taught her, she reflected bitterly, but quickly regretted the thought. *Your mother is stronger than you imagine,* she had said to Paco over the telephone only a few hours before. Was she really? She had her doubts. Lucía tried to focus on the moment, but she knew it was merely a means to avoid thinking of what lay ahead of her. This sudden homecoming was entirely her doing, and she suddenly realized with a mixture of regret and burgeoning panic that she had no idea what she would find in Tortosa, or how she would be received after so long an absence. They didn't even know that she was coming. Was this supposed to be her idea of a surprise? She resolved to call in the morning. No use lingering any further in Barcelona. And then, of course, there was Quim. What did she propose to do with him exactly, simply knock on his door? She tried to imagine the scene, what she would say: *Greetings Quim! Remember me? It's Lucía. We were in love once, but I thought you were dead—they told me you were* *dead—so I married Adam. You remember Adam, don't you? Yes? Splendid. We have a son named Paco…*Good Lord, what in God's name was she doing here in Boadas, in Barcelona, in Spain? She drained her gimlet. Presently the blond appeared, right on cue.

"Compliments of the young gentleman in the blue suit," said the barmaid, tilting her head back and to the side and winking approvingly, as she placed another gimlet on the bar. Lucía looked to the far end of the bar and saw a man raise his glass. The light was dim and her eyes weren't what they used to be, but she had the impression that he wasn't much older than Paco.

"I've never seen him in here before, but I'll give him this," the barmaid whispered, leaning in close, "he knows class when he sees it." She winked again before moving off.

It didn't take the stranger long to suddenly appear, hovering at Lucía's side. "May I?" he said, gesturing to the stool beside her. Lucía nodded, not really sure why. The gimlet stood as yet untouched. "You haven't touched your drink."

"I'm not sure that I will."

"Why is that?"

For a moment Lucía remained silent. She turned and glanced at him briefly and then looked back toward the bar. She was lonely, it was true, but was she this lonely? He was handsome in a swarthy sort of way, typically Latin, shorter than Adam, of course, but nearly every man was shorter than Adam. She couldn't make out the color of his eyes in the weak light, but there was something exceedingly steady, almost omnivorous about his gaze. He was younger than Adam, older than Paco. "Well, among other things, I'm a married woman."

"So where's the husband?" He made it sound more like a challenge than a question. She didn't respond. "You're not from here are you?" he continued undaunted.

"Yes and no," she replied coyly. It was just a bit of harmless banter, she told herself, and she needed some attention after all her solitary musings.

"Let me guess. Your Spanish is perfect, so if you weren't born here at least your parents are from here, or one of them anyway. But your style, the way you hold yourself, that's the giveaway. I'd say you live in Paris, perhaps Rio or Buenos Aires, even the States." There was a long pause during which he offered her a cigarette, which she declined, and then lit up himself, flourishing his lighter and snapping it shut showily. "Well?"

"Not bad," admitted Lucía, turning to him and allowing herself a trace of a smile. "I was born nearby, but I live in New York."

"I knew it!" he exclaimed, clearly pleased with himself. "I'm Nacho, by the way," extending his hand on top of the bar. Lucía hesitated, but then grasped it, surprised at how soft and insubstantial it felt. "Lucía," she said, as she withdrew her hand and took up the gimlet.

"So, come back often...Lucía?"

"No."

"No, why would you? This place is overrun with fascists and priests," he said sourly, puffing on his cigarette with grim determination, as if it were an inescapable obligation rather than a pleasure. "But New York," he continued, suddenly animated, "now there's a place I'd kill to go." Lucía shot him a look. "Relax," he assured her, "it's just a figure of speech."

"I would think that this is a very advantageous time to be here. Everything is changing."

"Everything is changing and nothing will change."

It was the second time that she had heard that sentiment. Her taxi driver had said the same thing almost word for word. "But don't you think..." Lucía began, but he cut her off.

"Let's skip the politics, you mind?"

No, she didn't mind. In fact, she was feeling a bit light headed and found it hard to concentrate, a combination of the alcohol and jet lag, surely. "I think I've had quite enough for one evening. I'm going to head back to my hotel."

"But it's so early."

"Not for me it isn't. I've been traveling and I'm exhausted."

"Just one more round and then I'll walk you home. You don't want to be out alone on Las Ramblas after dark."

"Very well," Lucía conceded, but she did so reluctantly.

Another round came and went, and then another. After that, she had only the vaguest of recollections: smoking hashish in a dark alley; watching municipal workers hose down Las Ramblas in the moonlight; a ghastly meal in a brightly-lit bar; and finally, Nacho trying to press her up against some dank wall in the shadows off the avenue. It took all the strength she could muster to push him away and manage a scream.

"*Zorra*," he spat, and slapped her for good measure, before hurrying off.

She made her way back to the hotel. The night clerk looked her up and down, alarmed, and asked her if she needed help getting to her room. Lucía didn't answer, just took the key and teetered to the elevator. In her room, she rushed to the toilet and retched until there was nothing left inside her but a vast emptiness.

In the morning she took a shower and scrubbed herself violently, trying to rid herself of any hint of the loathsome Nacho. Never had she felt such a fool or so sullied and bruised. Christ, the man had almost raped her, she thought with alarm. Being alone was more treacherous than she had ever imagined. She was too old for such adventures. What was she thinking trying to strike out on her own? Lucía wanted to weep, but the tears wouldn't come. She remained in the room all morning. When the maid knocked on the door, Lucía let her in, and took the desk chair onto the balcony and sat in the sun in an attempt to rid herself of the ashen pallor that was the mildest symptom of her hangover. She did her best not to think since it only led to self-loathing. When the maid left, Lucía went back inside. The room was spotless, the bed tautly remade, the stale air refreshed. She sat on the bed and picked up the telephone and dialed the number for Quinta Amelia, not knowing precisely what she intended to say. She was startled when someone picked up after the first ring and the voice stated dutifully: "Vidal residence." Her first impulse was to hang up immediately, but she stayed on the line, the telephone pressed to her ear, listening to her own anxious breathing. It was Rosa who had answered. She was lucky it was not Borja, say, or one of the nieces or nephews to whom she was an utter stranger. "Hola," the voice said.

"Rosa…it's Lucía." There was a silence. "Rosa?" Lucía said again.

"Oh, Good Lord, it *is* you. I could never forget your voice. Lucía! You sound so close. Where are you?"

"I'm calling from Barcelona."

"You're back! If only you knew how I have prayed for your return."

"Yes, I'm back."

"When are you coming? You are coming, no?"

"Yes, of course, soon, today perhaps. Tell me, how is *mamá*? Again there was silence. "Rosa, what's the matter?"

"Your mother, she is not well. She has had a stroke."

"When?"

"Three days ago. She is in the hospital, but they say that she is coming home today or tomorrow."

"How bad was it?"

"Lucía, she has lost her tongue."

"What? What do you mean to say?"

"Your mother, she cannot speak."

Chapter Five

IT WAS THE RATTLING THAT KEPT HIM FROM SLEEP, not that from the unhinged shutter or the loose panes of glass set off by the winds that howled down the Ebro river valley like some sort of mythological hex, but rather the one that rose up from deep inside him, from the hollows of his sunken chest, from his rickety lungs. Just when he felt himself drifting into slumber's voluptuous embrace the rattling would begin anew, the spell would be broken, and the urge to sleep would slip away. This was what his nights were like now, endless and unvarying, full of wheezing and gasping for breath as he lay in the ink-black darkness, in the bed where he had been born, and more than likely conceived, waiting for dawn and another day of, what precisely, life? Is that what this was? Is this why he had struggled so relentlessly to survive the years of hard labor in the camps? It seemed a bad decision now, he thought. *Work will redeem you,* the victors had never ceased to proclaim. He almost wanted to laugh, but restrained himself for fear of provoking a fit of coughing that might well do him in. Now, that would be something. After surviving twenty-two years of toil, hollowing out a mountain of granite to make room for the tombs of the Fascist fallen, he, Quim Soler i Masoliver, would die in his ancestral bed of…laughter. No, on second thought, that wouldn't do, not at all, it was too comic an exit to what had long been a tragedy. It sounded as if he had gone mad. He was tired and withered and lonely, but he was not crazy, no.

He hauled himself upright with a grunt and swung his legs over the side of the bed. The earthenware floor tiles felt cool on his feet as he poked his toes about until he found his slippers. He reached out with his right hand and groped for a box of matches on his bedside table. He struck a match, squinting as the sulfur flared in the darkness, and lit a candle stub. The flickering light revealed a sloping ceiling of white-washed beams, bare white walls, a large mirror-front armoire, a wash-stand and cabinet, and a cane-seated chair over which some clothes were draped. Quim stood and shuffled to the washstand, where he poured water from a ceramic pitcher into the basin and stooped to wash his face and hands. As he turned to reach for a towel, he caught a glimpse of himself full on in the armoire mirror and started, as if at the sight of an intruder. "Christ," he said out loud "what a sight." He stood there motionless, staring at the specter that he had become, an image made even more ghostly by the shifting shadows cast by the candle light. He was not yet sixty, yet already he had an ancient cast. His face had a sunken appearance and his eyes, like dark pools, seemed to have retreated into his skull. He stood hunched, teetering slightly on uncertain legs. Quim took as deep a wheezy breath as he could manage, straightened his back, and tried to recall the younger version of himself.

His shoulders had been strong, so too his arms and hands. How else could he have withstood the toil and the misery? He remembered the morning at the prison in Teruel, where he and other Republican ex-combatants had been confined after the war. They were in formation for roll call, several hundred of them—it was hard to keep track of the precise number since almost every day prisoners would drop dead of famine or disease and new captives would arrive at odd hours to swell the ranks of the vanquished—and the prison warden announced that they had important visitors who wished to address them. *Wished to address them*, that was the phrase the warden had used; Quim would never forget it. And the door from the administrative offices opened and a file of officials of some sort, along with a few military officers, and, of course, a cassocked priest, always a cassocked priest, emerged and formed a line on the dais in front of them. Then one of the officials stepped forward—a corpulent sort with dark glasses and a thin mustache just like Franco's—and launched into an impassioned speech, his

rather too strident voice filling the courtyard, about the vital recon-
struction work that needed to be done; and the Spain that would
arise like a phoenix from the ashes; and how their "red" souls needed
redeeming; and how God and Franco, the beloved *caudillo,* were offering them the chance to return to the Christian fold from which they
had been led astray through the false promises and trickery perpe-
trated by Bolsheviks and Jews, Masons and foreigners; and how they
were seeking volunteers from among the prison population to assist
in the glorious task of building the New State, like a shining citadel,
a New Jerusalem, that would be the pride of all the Christian world.
Then the warden came forward again and told the prisoners that if any
of them wished to partake in this noble enterprise that they should
take one pace forward. There was a moment of silence, followed by
scattered murmuring, and the sound of footfalls, at first isolated but
soon growing to a common shuffle. In truth, neither Quim nor any
of the inmates had had to dwell long on the logic of the proposition.
It wasn't redemption that they were seeking but sustenance. Because
in prison they were getting next to nothing, and the weaker among
them, the wounded, those who had lost all hope, were dying of star-
vation or thirst, or malaria, or typhoid, and that would be their fate
too if they remained much longer in that hellhole. A doctor in a white
gown appeared, accompanied by an officer bearing a clipboard, and
they proceeded to make their way among the men, stopping before
each in turn, and poking and squeezing them, and peering inside their
gaping mouths as if they were horses or beasts of burden at a country
fair, and summarily pronouncing them fit or unfit for the task, which
was the same as proclaiming whether they would live or die.

Well, thought Quim, if they had seen him as he was now, they would
surely have passed him by and he would never have lived past his twen-
ty-fourth year. As it was, he would labor and live and eventually become
the phantom figure whose reflection stared back at him now.

He descended the stairs slowly in the candlelight and entered the
kitchen. It was early still and all was silent, not even birdsong could be
heard. He prepared coffee, carried his cup to the window, snuffed the

candle, and stood waiting for the day to begin. At first there was only a dim magenta glow in the east, but no true light to speak of. Stars still filled the sky and there was a faint sickle moon hanging barely discernable like an afterthought over the darkened silhouette of the ridge to the south. There was a benign stillness to the landscape at this early hour that he treasured. These moments of silent calm on the cusp of day enabled him to forget the torments of the night. He loathed the night. There were times when he believed that his life consisted of more nights than days. All those years laboring deep inside the mountain they had rarely glimpsed the full light of day. Now, as a new day dawned, the past retreated in his mind to some dormant hollow and he could take his place again among the living. He watched the first amber light touch the rocky summit of the ridge and descend as slowly as spilled honey among the olive trees, casting elongated shadows over the terrain that were like the last throes of the nocturnal world. Quim lingered there at the window, knowing that in a matter of hours a blistering sun would be high in the sky and all the landscape would be blanched and shadowless. He thought of nothing, allowing himself only to stand suspended in the morning stillness, scarcely breathing. It was only when he became aware of a cautious knocking at the door that he noticed, blinking, that the gentle light of dawn had grown to a glare, and the cicadas were droning at a fever pitch.

Quim opened the front door to find Estela, the youngest daughter of the Curto family, who owned the adjacent farm, sitting in the threshold, a basket laden with fresh produce and sundries at her side. For a moment he thought of an allegorical figure in an engraving, illustrating a rich bounty or the salubriousness of rural life. He had forgotten that it was Saturday, and that this child would come around as was customary to deliver his weekly provisions. It was an arrangement that had arisen a decade before when he came back from his internment to find his mother dead and buried and himself, a bachelor, at a loss as to how to get on alone. He paid a modest fee, of course, but it had never been about the money. It was a benevolent act by kindly neighbors who could ill afford an extra mouth to feed. All told, the Curtos were an expansive clan, consisting of Estela's parents, Ezequiel and Elvira, seven children, a spinster aunt, a widowed uncle, ailing grandparents, and assorted livestock, including a much-prized mule. Still, they would never have allowed a neighbor to go wanting. It had been Elvira Curto who, unbidden, had cared for Quim's mother when she was alone and no longer capable of fending for herself. Quim owed these people everything. In the city, a man or woman alone and without sufficient means could starve and die a solitary death.

"Good morning, Estela, I hope you have not been waiting long."

The girl rose and brushed past him silently bound for the kitchen, where she would deposit the basket on the table and then pull out a chair and sit still and impassive with a kind of sidelong look and her mouth open as if she had just uttered something, although she never did. It was always thus. Quim had known the child for all of her ten years, and he had never heard her say anything intelligible. On occasion, she produced a sound—a grunt or a whimper or a whine, but never a word. Sometimes, Quim would spy her mouthing something silently and he wondered if she didn't perhaps have the power of speech after all, but chose to conceal it from the world. In truth, he cherished her company, as far as it went, although he couldn't say the same of her siblings, who came around now and again, snooping about and asking questions about the war and the camps which he did not welcome, and giving each other mocking glances behind his back as if he were a fool.

Quim prepared fried eggs and bread and sliced some dried sausage and set out some plums for Estela and himself. They sat across from one another; light poured in a south-facing window and formed a warm streak like a knife blade that seemed to cut the table in two. The sight of rather too many motes floating in the light reminded Quim that he had to be more thorough in his cleaning. Although he never expected a reply, he always spoke with Estela. She was a mute, but hardly feeble-minded, he knew.

"Well, we make quite a pair the two of us," he said drolly. "Still, I think you should try and find a younger man."

To this, the girl gave a lopsided smile and kicked him beneath the table with a bare foot.

"The hills are full of wildflowers. Shall we pick some for your *mamá* after breakfast?"

Estela's eyes grew bright and she squealed and nodded her approval.

"And afterwards we will wash your hair, which, my dear, looks filthy."

She shrugged and looked askance.

* * *

It was an ancient farm of venerable olive trees whose gnarly trunks were as broad as a bus and had been planted, by all reckoning, by the Moors, who for centuries had ruled over this corner of Iberia from their stronghold in nearby Tortosa, or *Turtusah,* as they called it. Olives were being harvested in the valley since before the advent of the printed word, before the discovery of the true movements of the heavens. The property had been in Quim's father's family for nine generations, and while there were no written family records, his father had been able to unfalteringly recite the names of the succession of long-suffering Solers and their brides and kin who had lived, worked, and died on the place. It was hard scrabble land, consisting of twenty-three hectares of olive groves scattered with almond trees and carob, walnuts and pecans, as well as a smattering of figs, apricots, apples, plums, pomegranate, medlar, and grape vines. Cal Soler, as the farm was called, spread out along the south facing slope of a narrow valley divided by a dry river bed. To the west rose the peaks of the Sierra de Cardó, and from the highest elevations on the property there was an expansive view east to the rice paddies of the Ebro delta and the shimmering silver waters of the Mediterranean Sea stretching to the horizon. There was no irrigation, they had always had to rely on the rains, which came mostly in winter and sometimes in great spring torrents that swelled the dry river bed with runoff from the surrounding hills that came rushing down the valley with a force that could carry off a car or a mule if anyone was foolish and disdainful enough to drive or ride down the track and attempt to forge the gully. Alas, there were years when it scarcely rained at all and the olive trees would wither and bear no fruit and the land became so hard and sunbaked that you would have thought it was cement. It was not a prosperous farm, but it was enough to keep a family alive provided that the weather complied, the blights didn't prove too resistant, and there were enough hands to work the place, but not too many mouths to feed. When Quim's father and brothers were alive they worked the place as it should be worked and all was well. They sold their olives and nuts to the local miller, and gathered and jarred their fruit, and cultivated a kitchen garden, and kept chickens and pigs, and sometimes took a day to hunt boar or fish for sea bass and bream and eels. And then the war broke out and the henchmen came for his father in the night because of something he had uttered in a bar, something anti-clerical perhaps, or against the oligarchy—they never needed much—and led him off to be shot in the dark. Later, his brothers were killed at the front, and after Quim survived the fighting he was sent to work in the mountain, and so for years the farm stood abandoned and the trees grew unruly and for a time the locals even stopped calling it Cal Soler.

They left the house after breakfast and began to ascend the terraces buttressed by dry stone walls rising in an orderly progression to the very top of the ridge behind the house. Quim moved slowly, hindered by his labored breathing, while Estela would run ahead but immediately double back, never venturing too far from him. Quim loved to walk among the great olive trees, as he and Estela were doing now, imagining the original Moorish farmers clad in *jellabas* and giving praise to Allah for an abundant harvest or an opportune rain.

"Did you know that the Arabs wear delicate slippers with pointed toes?" he asked Estela, who looked up at him with her mouth agape. "They are called *babouches.*" The strange new word caused her to squeal with delight.

The whole hillside was awash in a yellow sea of helichrysum, and the air was tinged with the scent of thyme and rosemary, lavender and olive blossom. The only sustained sound was that of bees, untold numbers of them, and their collective buzzing filled the landscape with an air of frenzy that suddenly struck Quim with a vague sense of dread. He could not help but recall the din that arose in the Valley of the Fallen from hundreds of men working in unison with grim, mindless determination. How was it that memory always managed to unsettle even moments of simple contentment like these? Was there no escape, no respite even, he wondered? Out of the corner of his eye Quim glimpsed something slithering fast and he turned to catch sight of a viper disappear into a cleft in the trunk of an olive tree. Estela saw it too, but she did not start; like him, she was a child of the valley. They stopped here and there to cut great bunches of helichrysum. Quim sat on a wall to rest and watched Estela skip about, and stop to peer at a bee, and pick up a stone to balance on her head, and cut a sprig of rosemary to wear behind her ear. A shadow passed on the ground in front of him like a specter and Quim looked up to see an eagle gliding in a cloudless sky, searching for prey. There was always something slithering or wheeling or hopping about in the valley. He and his brothers Pere and Xavi had always set snares for rabbits, or gone out with the shotgun in search of partridge and woodcock, or when they were old enough, wild boar. He had loved to hunt, loved the stalking and the stillness, and the senses all keenly focused on the kill. Now, he had neither the reflexes nor the heart for it. The last thing that he had killed, he recalled, as his throat tightened and his stomach turned, was a man. Quim closed his eyes, trying to block out the recollection, but it didn't work, in fact, it only made it worse. The absence of light had the same effect of heightened expectation that comes when darkness descends in a theater before the curtain is raised on the first act. And, as if on cue, he saw himself there again, playing out the scene in his mind's eye as he had countless times before.

* * *

They were marching fast, he and his column, or what remained of it, toward the river on a mid-November morning. All forms, colors and contours were dampened by a heavy mist. Everything was muted and ill-defined. It was like walking in a dream. A stench of spent munitions, human excrement, and the war-sullied river hung in the air. There was hardly a sound. The birds had fled months before when the battle began. Not a wisp of wind stirred the dry fallen leaves or the reeds along the riverbank. No one spoke. The only sound was the harried, uneven tempo of footfall in retreat, and then, somewhere in the middle distance, shots being fired. They had been defeated in the last desperate battle that would decide the war and they knew that all was lost. There would be pontoon bridges and boats waiting to ferry them across the river to safety, they had been assured by their commanders, but when they scoured the riverbank they found neither bridges nor boats. What they did find was a rope that had been strung across the surface of the river; it was not much, but it was their only means of escape. The enemy was just behind them, or all around them, it was hard to tell. Quim ordered his men to remove their boots and sling them around their necks, to try to keep their weapons and munitions above water, and to begin pulling themselves across to the safety of the far shore. He himself stayed behind, doubling back along their route in search of anyone who might have fallen behind. It was cold, but Quim worried that the sun was rising and with it the mist that was their only cover. He heard movement among the reeds and whispered urgently, "*Por aqui, rápido!*" But what emerged from the thicket was a Nationalist soldier, his rifle aimed at Quim. Neither man said a word. They were not ten meters apart. Quim did not move, but he saw that the man was shaking, that one side of his face was twitching intractably, and that the barrel of his rifle was swaying this way and that. Quim was carrying a pistol in his hand, but it was not aimed at the soldier. He wondered why the soldier did not shoot. Perhaps he was a new recruit and was unaccustomed to firing his weapon. Perhaps he had only shot at men from afar, but had never confronted the enemy face to face. It was not the same to kill a man whose face one can see, Quim knew. He was thinking these things when at last the soldier did shoot and he felt the bullet enter his left side just beneath his ribs. He was shocked. He had never been wounded, but was astonished by the absence of pain. All he felt was a warm, growing dampness as blood flowed from the wound. The soldier lowered his rifle. He appeared shocked, like a child who has unknowingly committed a terrible blunder. Quim looked at him blankly, without rancor. He did not want to kill this young man, not now that he was in retreat, and the war was lost, and no more men needed to die. But the soldier began to lift his rifle again and Quim had little choice. He raised his revolver in one swift, resolute movement and shot the soldier through the heart, and watched him buckle and almost shimmy, before hitting the ground with a dull thud. At once there was shouting close by and shots being fired and Quim turned and ducked and hobbled off, holding his side, making for the rope crossing. When he arrived at the riverbank his men were gone. He saw them making their way across the river and saw that they were being fired upon by enemy soldiers hidden along the near shore. Quim fired off the remaining bullets in his revolver in the vague direction of the enemy, unable to take aim, but hoping to momentarily silence their fire. Then he pulled off his boots and waded into the river. Still holding his left hand to his now sodden wound, he grasped the rope with his right hand, plunged his head underwater, and began to pull himself across, lifting his head sporadically to take in air. Soon he heard the water around him fill with the muffled whirring of bullets penetrating the surface of the water. He wanted to move faster, but the pain in his side was now excruciating. When he came up for air he could see that the opposite shore was still far off. He could see too that some of his men, those who had already made it across, were now returning the enemy fire and shouting at him, urging him on, cheering. He thought that he would make it. As he reached the middle of the river, however, the current was stronger, and when he extended his arm to pull himself further, the force of the water pushed him from the rope and suddenly he was groping at nothing, the rope was out of reach, and he was being swept downstream, adrift. He took a deep breath and put his head underwater and allowed the current to carry him off. There was no sense struggling. On he went, sporadically lifting his head and gasping for air and floating toward what he was sure would be his watery grave. And then all was a blank.

When next he came to, he was on his back, floating, but no longer in the water. He was on a boat or a barge or a raft, he wasn't sure. There was a smell of the sea and the river too, a sharp brackish stench. Above, the sky was cast in half darkness, and clouds, great livid, billowing masses, were moving fast. He heard the wind and something being plunged into the water, followed by a swish, and finally a lifting from the water before the routine began anew. Rowing, there was someone there rowing, but he could not see them, they were not in his field of vision, and he was unable to raise his head; he hadn't the strength. Suddenly he grasped where he was. This was the netherworld, Quim realized, the kingdom of Hades, and the unseen figure must be Charon, ferrying him across the river Styx. He was dead. And yet he still felt the pain in his side. How could that be if he was dead? he wondered. And then he knew. In Hell, pain was eternal, ever-lasting, just as the priests had always claimed, and he would always bear the pain in his side like a stigma. And what had he done to be Hell-bound? he asked himself. But he knew well enough. It was hardly the occasional lie, or the blasphemy, or the estrangement from God, or the fits of lust or pride, venial sins all. No, his offense was far graver, the gravest. He had killed men, many men, the last one that very morning on the riverbank back in the place that was life. Hell, Quim supposed, was nothing less than his due.

But he was not dead, and he had not gone to Hell. He had lost consciousness on the boat while floating on what he had imagined to be the Styx, and when he came to he was still lying on his back, but this time on a straw mat on the floor of a small white-washed room. Light was entering a single window; it was a cold, thin light, an autumnal light, a morning light. He was wearing clothes that were not his own—a collarless white shirt and trousers that were too big in the waist and too short in the leg—and he was clean, cleaner than he had been in many weeks. The wound in his side had been dressed. There was a broad bandage wrapped snugly, expertly around his girth. The pain was still there, but tolerable. He wanted to look out the window, to get his bearings, to discover where he was. The sea was close by, of that he was certain. The salty air was heavy with it, and he could hear the gulls making their staccato clamor. They seemed to have their nest on the roof. He tried to lift himself onto his elbows, but the sudden pain was like that of a knife being thrust into his side, and he dropped down wincing. There was a sound of a curtain being drawn, and Quim lifted his head to see a woman standing in the threshold. She was a thin, severe looking woman of indeterminate age—40 or 60, he could not tell—with crow-black hair gathered high in a bun and wisps hanging carelessly around her face. He could not see her eyes. Her lips were dry and thin as the Host. She was dressed uniformly in black—black smock, long black skirt, black apron. Her feet, tiny and brown, were bare. She held a pitcher and a basin. She did not smile or utter a word. They looked at each other in silence; even the gulls had quit their squawking.

"Where am I?" Quim finally asked.

She did not answer. She approached him, set down the pitcher and basin, and knelt at Quim's side. She poured water into the basin, took up a sponge, and reached for Quim's hand. He withdrew it, and repeated the question. Still, she ignored him and reached out again and took his hand firmly in hers and began to wash him. He was astonished by her strength. Then she raised her eyes to his, and without interrupting her task, she answered him in a tone of dull resignation: "You are in the delta, between the river and the sea."

The delta, Quim repeated to himself. All his life he had looked down on the flat marshland from the highest points on the farm in El Perelló, and he could have reached it on foot in half a day, although as a boy he never had, or rather had never dared. It was not a place where outsiders ventured, but something of a world unto itself. The boggish terrain had been given over to rice production, indeed it was suitable for little else; the only other things that thrived there were malaria and typhoid, violence and ignorance, or so he had always been told. Not even the Civil Guard patrolled the marshy expanse. There were few roads or paths, but a veritable maze of water channels that could only be navigated in small flat-bottomed skiffs. Fugitives from the law and escaped convicts often tried to make it there, it was said, for in the delta one could disappear; whether or not one would ever emerge again was another matter.

She told him to open his shirt and Quim complied. Only his mother had washed him like this when he was a small boy. There was something blissful about the water sluicing over his shoulders and down his chest. He looked at the woman sidelong and regretted that it was not Lucía who was doing the washing.

"Who brought me here?" Quim asked, weakly.

"Ximo, the fisherman…he said that he found you on the riverbank, thought that you were dead, but then you weren't. You should be dead," she added matter-of-factly, "you lost much blood, enough to fill a pot."

"How long have I been here?"

"Three days, going on four," she replied. "You have been drifting in and out of consciousness, feverish, delirious."

"What is your name?"

"Purificación, they call me Puri. I am a *curandera,* a healer. There is no doctor here."

"Well, Puri, you certainly know how to dress a wound," he said, looking down at his bandaged torso.

"That is child's play."

"To me, you are an angel."

"Oh, you would have lived regardless. You are like a bull that refuses to die. Perhaps there is something or someone you have to live for… Lucía, say."

Quim tried to grasped the woman's wrist, but an excruciating pain shot through him and his hand dropped to clutch his side. "I thought you were a healer, not a witch," he managed with a grimace. "What do you know of Lucía?"

"*Tranquilo,*" she hissed, "I know nothing of her. You were calling out her name in your fevered dreams."

He looked away, too exhausted to go on speaking.

Lucía. He wasn't surprised that he was uttering her name in his dreams. There was hardly a waking moment when he did not think of her. He longed for her touch, longed to hear the sonorous well-bred timber of her voice, longed to find himself enveloped in the luscious perfumed scent of her. There had been moments during his soldiering when he had thought of nothing so much as to desert, to steal off and seek her out and disappear with her to some sequestered place far from the killing and the misery. But these were mere delusions of the front. Now he simply wondered where she was, if she was out of harm's way, and whether or not they would ever see each other again. Wounded and far-removed as he was, Quim resolved to hold fast to the only part of Lucía that was currently within his reach and that was the indelible memory of her. He closed his eyes to lose himself in recollections before death snuffed them out or madness rendered them feeble and confused.

* * *

Quim had always maintained to everyone but himself that his first encounter with Lucía Vidal was due to nothing more than happenstance, a random act, like a hand of cards scrupulously dealt. It was nothing of the sort. Even as he recalled the circumstances now he still felt a faint blush of embarrassment.

It was a luminous day in late March, sumptuous billowing clouds racing across a pale blue sky, the almond trees beginning to flower, spring emerging, Holy Week a few days off. Quim had been summoned to regimental headquarters in Tortosa, for what he did not know. A dull-faced corporal met him in the entrance, saluted him with a weary air, and silently led him down a progression of empty corridors to a nondescript office with gunmetal walls and sparse light, where a coronel stood pouring over maps spread across a grand carved-oak desk, a desk fit for a notary, a bishop. Quim was told to sit. His name was Zuloaga or Zulorga, Quim could not remember; it was one of those peculiar Basque names, although the coronel was quick to point out that he was from Madrid. He was not a young man, but he appeared exceedingly fit. His barrel chest strained at his tunic. Probably a career officer, Quim remembered thinking. The regiment needed houses in the vicinity in which to billet soldiers, the coronel explained, and being from the area, he wanted Quim to recommend some large, comfortable houses of the local gentry where a detachment of troops wouldn't constitute too heavy a burden. The first place to come to Quim's mind was Quinta

Amelia. It was the grandest house thereabouts. He had passed it often, looming and whimsical, like something out of a fairy tale, whenever he walked to Tortosa from Cal Soler. The Graus were the largest landowners in the area, Quim explained to the coronel; they could well afford to put up troops. It wouldn't surprise him, he thought to himself, if they could have fed the entire army.

The family had always been the stuff of local gossip and speculation, as the rich often are for their less fortunate neighbors. The mother had a reputation for being something of a tyrant with her tenant farmers. She had a reckoning of all her lands, every rice paddy and olive grove, wheat field and orchard. It was impossible to cheat her, they said. Of the absent father, who no one had ever set eyes on, there were only rumors: he gambled, he drank, he had run off. Quim had heard of the Vidal twins, Inés and Lucía, and the three brothers, one a bully, another lame, and the youngest as tender as a cherub. The girls were said to be inseparable and identically beautiful, although one was more outgoing, the other silent and taciturn. Quim had never had any contact with the family. Why would he have? They might well have been virtual neighbors, but they inhabited different universes. In the provinces, class divisions were stark and unequivocal. There wasn't a single occasion in which they would have crossed paths. He had once glimpsed them, however, at least partially. It was a distant, blistering summer day. Quim and his brothers were bound for the river to fish, and as they passed the entrance to Quinta Amelia, the great iron gates swung open and a Hispano-Suiza, gleaming and majestic, a uniformed chauffeur behind the wheel, rolled slowly out of the drive and onto the road. The windows of the car were rolled down on account of the heat and Quim saw the mother sitting in the rear, staring straight ahead of her, as still and enigmatic as a sphinx. Around her he could just make out the tops of her children's heads, nothing more. The car sped away, kicking up dust, and a gatekeeper hurriedly closed and barred the gate. The man stared blankly at Quim and his brothers before gesturing wordlessly with a jerk of his head for the boys to be on their way. And that was as much as Quim had ever seen of the Grau-Vidals.

Years later, the same gatekeeper, slower, slightly stooped, opened the gate for the staff car in which Quim and the coronel were traveling to pay a visit to Doña Eugenia Grau at Quinta Amelia. As they proceeded up the drive and the house came into view, the coronel scoffed at the turrets and multi-colored tiles, the twisted-iron balconies and crenelated parapets. In Madrid, he insisted dryly, they weren't taken by such fancy. They had called ahead, but at the front door they were kept waiting. It was a silent, yet unmistakable slight. Quim had the distinct sense that they were being watched, scrutinized from some upstairs window. A housekeeper finally let them in and left them standing in the entrance hall. The walls were bare, Quim noticed, but he could make out unblemished spaces where paintings had once hung. Their hasty removal, he imagined, was a precaution against pillage. What would they do with the twins? he wondered. Somewhere upstairs doors were being opened and closed and there was the sound of heels, a woman's step, progressing down a corridor, growing nearer and suddenly halting. It was then that Quim looked up and saw her. She stood hesitating at the top of the stairs, wearing a slim white dress made of some diaphanous material. She might have been an apparition. As she descended the stairs with slow, measured steps, she came gradually into focus. Quim felt like an explorer gazing at an exotic species for the very first time. She was young, not yet twenty, he estimated. Her face was still half-formed, tender, the skin radiant. Honey-colored hair, parted on the side, spilled in gleaming waves to her shoulders. Her hips were shapely, her waist small, and with each footfall her breasts moved gently beneath the material of her dress. Quim felt himself grow weak. Both he and the coronel were watching in silent awe. And then she was before them, pale hazel eyes, a mole on her left cheek.

"I am Lucía Vidal. I'm sorry if you have been kept waiting. I'm afraid that my mother is indisposed" she said, extending a languid hand to Quim.

"I am Lieutenant Soler," said Quim, taking her hand, but gently correcting her "and this is *Coronel* Zuloaga."

"Ah, forgive me, gentlemen. I am not at all versed in the subtleties of rank." And she smiled, revealing a slight gap between two front teeth.

Perfect, Quim thought, she was beautiful, but not flawless, or rather he found her beautiful precisely because she bore a flaw. Finally, it was that innocuous gap that made her irresistible.

So began their affair. He still found it hard to credit. All that Quim had thought of when the coronel queried him about houses in which to billet troops was comfort, his and that of his men. What he had in mind was a fine place to lay their heads. He had not been counting on love.

* * *

Quim stayed on with Puri for nearly five weeks, resting and trying to regain his strength. Never had time passed with such excruciating indolence. It struck him that no one knew where he was, not even fate. His world had shrunk to the size of Puri's diminutive cottage in the delta. He felt like a man confined to a ship during an interminable voyage, bobbing on a placid sea, praying for wind to fill the sails, scanning the horizon for the sight of land. His recovery was slow and sometimes he lapsed into bouts of debilitating fever and delirium. Suddenly, he would not know where he was; he would shrink from Puri, call out for his mother, or shout commands to imaginary men as if in battle. And then the fever would pass and his mind would grow calm again, but he would be exhausted and frail. Through it all, Puri was unwaveringly good to him, redressing his wound, feeding him, making sure that he was comfortable in the confines of her cozy refuge amidst the rice paddies. Yet they spoke little; she was not interested in conversation and he did not press her. One evening after dinner, however, as they sat in the tenuous candlelight with ominous shadows dancing across the whitewashed walls like ancestral ghosts, Quim asked her what she knew of the progress of the war. He was astonished at her reply and her detachment.

"I hear the great guns echoing and see the war planes overhead, but I know nothing of these things," she offered, her tone dismissive. "Men will always kill one another. I will try to heal the wounded if they come to me. For the dead I would pray if I thought it would do any good, but it doesn't, so I don't."

"Some of us have been fighting for a better world, for justice," Quim insisted, but somehow his words had a hollow ring; his voice did not seem his own.

"Yes," replied Puri wearily "it is always the same."

* * *

For weeks the weather had been foul with lashing rains, sleet, and unsettling winds, and then in the third week of December, just days before Christmas, the skies cleared and the temperature rose and the world seemed a different place. On that first bright morning Quim sat on a bench outside, leaning his back against the house and basking in the sun with his eyes closed and his mind unperturbed. At that moment he imagined that he could very well stay on there in the delta, detached from the world and the war that seemed to have momentarily passed him by. But he knew at once that the idea was pure folly and knew too that his prolonged convalescence had come to an end. It was time to report back to his superiors wherever they might be. He felt a mixture of anxiousness and foreboding, but of what precisely, he wasn't sure. Suddenly, a shadow fell across him and the warmth of the sun vanished. "What is it Puri?" he asked, his eyes still closed.

There was a loud guffaw, and Quim leapt to his feet to find himself face to face with a toothless old man, barefoot and clad in rags. His face was creased like something reptilian, the skin burnished a deep copper. Despite his apparent age, his chest and arms looked powerful.

"*Cago en l'hòstia!*" the stranger exclaimed. "That is the first time that anyone has taken me for Puri!"

"Who are you?" Quim demanded.

"I am Ximo."

"The fisherman?"

"The same."

Quim relaxed and extended his hand. "Well, in that case, it is a great pleasure to meet you."

Ximo looked at Quim's hand warily, but finally grasped it briefly. They sat down together on the bench.

"Thank you for rescuing me from the riverbank."

"It was nothing."

"All the same, you saved my life."

The fisherman didn't respond, but simply jerked his head in acknowledgement. Quim was accustomed to country people and their often laconic ways, but this fisherman seemed to mistrust words, to flee from them. Quim couldn't think of what more to say to the man who had so casually delivered him from death. He asked about the fishing.

"All the warring is scaring the fish."

He asked about the fighting.

"They say it is the beginning of the end."

And then they fell into a prolonged silence. Quim wondered whether the man might want some sort of recompense for having saved his life, something more than chitchat, but when Quim broached the subject, Ximo said only: "Don't insult me." How could it be, Quim reflected, that he and his comrades in arms were fighting for a more equitable world, a more selfless society, and that here in the delta, a place that he had always understood to be dangerous and backward, life seemed to be decent by nature? Why were there not more Puris and Ximos in the world?

It was time to leave the refuge of the delta and return to the war-torn world. Ximo agreed to ferry Quim upriver to Tortosa in the evening under the cover of darkness, but first he went off to find out what he could about troop movements in the vicinity. Puri had boiled Quim's uniform in a cauldron of river water and managed to get rid of both the blood stains and the lice. She also mended the hole in his tunic where the bullet had entered and pierced his side. Best of all, she produced a pair of battered hobnailed boots, relics that her father had worn as a soldier in Cuba during the Spanish-American War, and into which Quim just managed to squeeze his feet. When Quim shed his convalescent clothes and put on his uniform for the first time in more than a month, he felt like a soldier again, but also strangely alien in a place so removed from the conflict. When Ximo returned at dusk, Quim bade farewell to Puri in front of the house as the sun was sinking below the mountains to the west and clouds, dark and forbidding, were massing behind the horizon. The innocent seeming days were over. Puri gave Quim a bundle of provisions wrapped in a woolen blanket, and they embraced awkwardly. "Thank you for your kindness," said Quim, aware of the inadequacy of his words.

"With all your warring, don't forget about Lucía," was all she replied before turning quickly and disappearing into the house.

Ximo ferried Quim out of the marshes as night descended, poling the skiff through the stagnant fetid waters, and all the while bringing him up to date on the fighting. Quim was amused to see how the fisherman's role as a scout had transformed him, for he was now positively garrulous. The Republicans were in retreat, Ximo announced, but they were hoping to halt Franco's Nationalist forces at the Ebro. It was, as everyone seemed to know, a last and largely futile stand. The Nazis and the Italian Fascists were supplying Franco with troops and ample materiel, particularly artillery and fighter planes, and the Republican army and air force were hopelessly outgunned. Morale was dismal and deserters were being publicly shot, or so he had been told. In Tortosa, a good many residents—and here he paused to spit voluably—were waiting to welcome Franco as a liberator. Quim knew all this already, but he hadn't the heart to cut Ximo off. The fisherman finally ended with a bit of his own advice: "Do what you have to do," he urged Quim "but if I were you, I would either return with me to the delta or make for the French frontier as fast as you can."

When they reached the Ebro, Quim had to bury himself beneath a heap of reeking fishing nets and remain silent for the rest of the journey upriver to Tortosa. Along this fluid front one might come across friend or foe alike. The heavy rains of the previous fortnight had swelled the river and made the progress against the current excruciatingly slow. Apart from some scattered gunfire, the moonless night was calm and dismayingly quiet. Quim dozed off, but sometime in the dead of night the bow of the skiff ground and settled on a sandy bank. Ximo lifted the nets and Quim climbed out of the boat with his bundle of provisions.

The two men shook hands silently, maintaining the grip longer than was customary. Then Quim slipped through the reeds and climbed the riverbank as the fisherman poled back into the current and drifted downstream without a backward glance. Before setting off, Quim crouched above the shore, waiting and listening and getting his bearings in the funereal darkness. In the middle distance a dog barked and then grew silent. Further off truck engines shifted and groaned. Finally, he realized that he was just downstream from Tortosa. Not a single light shone in the landscape, but he could just make out the silhouette of La Suda, the massive Moorish fortification that rose above the town and gave the place a vague air of the Levant. Quim rose and moved off cautiously. He didn't make for Brigade Headquarters in Tortosa, however, or seek out any Republican force dug in along the left bank of the river, or attempt to reunite with his own unit, whose members, no doubt, took him for dead, swept off by the Ebro in their retreat and washed out to sea. Instead, he hurried cross country, avoiding all roads and lanes and paths. He planned to cross the railroad tracks, pick up the ancient Via Augusta to Coll de l'Alba, and come into Tortosa from the east, a route that led directly to the gates of Quinta Amelia. If he maintained a good pace and didn't encounter any unforeseen obstacles, he could arrive by dawn. It would be the 25th of December; he would surprise Lucía for Christmas.

Desire was what had led Quim to shirk his duty and instead make for Quinta Amelia in an attempt to reunite with Lucía. Desire and love. It was not his nature to act on impulse. He had always been a man of his word, or so he liked to think. *Do the right thing*. That is what his father had always told Quim and his brothers, and that did not mean what one's heart desired, but what one knew to be right, what duty obliged one to do. In the present circumstances, he was obliged to report to his superiors after weeks of having gone missing in action and presumed dead. *Lieutenant Quim Soler reporting for duty;* that is what he should have heard himself saying instead of slipping behind his own lines to get to the one he loved. Never would he have imagined himself doing such a thing, but then again, he had never met anyone like Lucía

Vidal; he had never been in love. It had only been a matter of weeks since they had last seen one another, but it seemed an eternity, so much had transpired: a battle lost; his near death on the river; fever, delirium, and idleness. And so he pushed on through the darkness, indifferent to duty, propelled by the memory of their last encounter.

* * *

The autumn rain had been pouring down in great sluicing sheets, and Quim's men prayed that, like some biblical deluge, it might never cease, but carry on forever, washing away the death and destruction. For weeks they had been incessantly bombarded by enemy aircraft until they could no longer think or sleep or hear their own panic-filled voices. Now the foul weather was all that kept the bombers grounded and provided Quim and his men a brief respite. The roads were thick with mud and few vehicles were moving. There was a lull in the fighting. Killing, Quim had learned, was best carried out under clear skies.

They were holed up on an abandoned farm in the shadows of the Sierra de Pandols, south of Gandesa, short of men, food, ammunition, hope, everything, it seemed, save exhaustion. Quim stood leaning in the doorway, watching a crepuscular light descend. All the landscape, observed through veils of rain, looked liquefied, as if it were fathoms down beneath the sea. He heard the horses before he saw them, a far-off whinnying came through the din of the downpour and Quim looked out across the fields to see a pair of mounted riders picking their way slowly up the muddy track. He raised the field glasses that hung around his neck, but it was difficult to see clearly. The rain distorted everything. All he could make out were two horses and their riders, neither of whom appeared to be bearing arms, at least he saw no rifles, nor were their long coats military issue. Still, Quim alerted two of his men who were dosing before the stove in the kitchen behind him to take up positions in the windows with sights over the idle, weed-choked fields and the track. He told them not to shoot unless someone drew a weapon and in that case to aim above their heads. As the figures drew closer he could see that the horse flesh was magnificent. Quim ordered his men to by no means harm the animals. They waited. As the strangers approached, Quim could hear their voices, one of them, that of a woman; it was a fine voice, an unmistakable voice, even as it came to him half-drowned by the torrent. It belonged to Lucía. Quim told his men to lower their weapons and walked out into the rain to greet her. He was elated. They hadn't seen one another since his summer leave in Barcelona.

"We are looking for the bravest men in the Republican army," Lucía called out as she approached.

"In that case you have found them," Quim answered.

"We come bearing gifts."

"You are gift enough. How on earth did you find us?"

"You underestimate this woman's determination," came a voice from the hooded second rider.

"This is Ryszard, a Polish journalist," said Lucía, gesturing to the second rider, who drew back his hood to reveal white-blond hair and a boyish face.

"Welcome," Quim offered.

The two dismounted, Lucía with the easy practiced grace of a horse woman. She and Quim embraced, but they did not kiss, not in front of the men. He shook hands with the Pole. Some of Quim's men unstrapped the saddlebags and others led the horses, a chestnut Andalusian stallion and a dappled mare from the stables at Quinta Amelia, to a nearby barn.

Inside the house, the visitors shed a layer of sodden clothes and huddled around the stove. All the men had gathered around now; they had a desperate look, sunken cheeked, eyes vacant, lips cracked. They were close to starving. Lucía told them to open the saddlebags. They tugged eagerly at the straps of the bags and gasped as they withdrew a leg of cured ham and links of chorizo, rounds of cheese, fresh bread, dried figs, dates, and bacalao, apples and pears, potatoes and rice, bars of chocolate, skins of wine and bottles of brandy. It was more food than the men had seen in months, more than some of them had ever seen. A sergeant named Porras, one of the veterans of the column, stepped forward to impose order. A table was cleared, some chairs and makeshift benches found, and bread, cheese, and ham rationed out along with wine. Hardly a word was uttered. One of the men, a former cook at one of the great beach hotels in Tarragona, set to preparing a stew of potatoes and chorizo. Quim stood back, making sure that he was the last to be served. At meal's end, one of the soldiers, a young law student and poet, an intellectual from Barcelona, quiet and withdrawn, stood and raised his battered tin cup of wine and offered a toast to Lucía. They had been starving, he explained, and through the storm an angel had come to deliver them from death. All the men stood and raised their cups and intoned in unison: "To Lucía Vidal, *viva!*" Quim looked around the table at a group of men hardened by battle and loss and want, and saw hardly a dry eye among them. Later, the brandy came out and the men began to sing mild, plaintive songs of love and longing, the moon and the sea, home. Ryszard interviewed some of the men about the Ebro front. The will had not been beaten out of them, but the bravado of the early days of the war was gone. There was no boasting now, no talk of victory or stamping out fascism, just a kind of weary soft-spoken resignation. Quim and Lucía sat in the shadows on the room's periphery, touching furtively, whispering, and waiting for the moment to discreetly retire. The rain beat down steadily and sleep overcame some of the men. Sergeant Porras assigned the night watch. Quim took Lucía's hand in his, rose and withdrew from the room without a word.

They climbed the stairs tentatively, Quim leading the way with a candle, the flame flickering wildly with the drafts. They emerged into a single spacious room beneath the eaves, where an iron bed with a sagging straw mattress, the sole piece of furniture, stood askew and forlorn in the corner. They didn't so much climb as fall into bed, and covered themselves with a thick woolen blanket that Lucía had thought to bring. Quim was astonished at her readiness. They had never slept together, only kissed and groped in stolen moments at Quinta Amelia where they had been constrained by propriety. There had always been soldiers about, siblings, servants, a fearsome mother. Here at the front, however, there were few conventions to be observed, no reticence, only a willingness to succumb to desire when one knew that life might be extinguished at any moment. They left the candle burning in a recess in the wall. Beneath the blanket they helped to strip one another of their clothes. After months at war, Quim was delirious with the smell of expensive soap that rose from Lucía, captivated by the softness of the skin of her breasts and thighs, in awe of the silken texture of the hair between her legs. Rough, calloused and dirty, he felt as if he were somehow violating her. He told her so, but she dismissed his reservations by climbing atop him silently and taking him inside her with a gasp and rocking steadily, rhythmically to the end. The world had changed forever, Quim thought rightly. They scarcely slept, but talked long into the night, long after the candle had burned down and extinguished, leaving them in perfect darkness and their hushed voices strangely disembodied. Love made their every utterance seem urgent and full of meaning; even the pauses, the silences were highly charged. They spoke of their childhoods; the windswept landscape that they shared; the social milieu that they did not; their siblings; their mothers; their fathers—one who had run off and died alone, the other who had been led off and murdered. Their conversation shuttled wildly from topic to topic, as if they were trying frantically to make up for lost time, to know each other through and through. They were laying face to face, their arms and legs intricately intertwined.

"How odd life is," said Quim after a lull.

"Yes," Lucía replied.

"We are in the midst of a war; the battle of all battles is fast approaching. I have lost men and the ones who have survived, the men downstairs, have lost all hope. We are doomed, convinced of it. And yet, never in my life have I been so happy. How is that?"

"I suppose that you are hopelessly in love, as I am," said Lucía.

"Your family will oppose us," Quim cautioned. "They will forbid us a life together."

"Is that a proposal of marriage?"

"I cannot imagine a life without you at my side, but we will have another war to wage."

"They have already lost," said Lucía, but even as she uttered the words they seemed somehow specious. In the radiant light of the Republic anything seemed possible, even a love and a future life that defied the constraints of class and family. What would become of them in defeat? she wondered. Would her passion for Quim Soler wane like the diminishing moon? Would they even survive? She thought of Quim's rank as an officer and her own contribution to the Republican cause as *Lucía the Red*. They were damned, she realized with a shudder.

In the early morning before light, they made love again. Quim lay behind her. It was even better than the night before; everything was dreamily soft and warm. When it was over and they were spent, the sound of the men stirring rose from the floor below like distant echoes from another world. Suddenly, Quim bolted upright.

"What is it?" Lucía asked, alarmed.

"The rain," Quim replied, "it has stopped."

"Thank goodness."

"No," he said, bounding from the bed. "The war will now resume."

An hour later, at first light, Lucía and Ryszard were mounting the horses. All the men had gathered outside to bid farewell. Quim gave Ryszard instructions to head south before crossing the river at Amposta. He then moved to the side of Lucía's horse. She leaned down from the saddle, tears streaming down her cheeks, and the two kissed, no longer caring about the eyes of the men upon them. Before rising to turn and go, Lucía whispered in Quim's ear: "You know where I will be waiting."

* * *

Recalling these episodes of love fulfilled were what enabled Quim to push on. He was somewhere due east of Tortosa in a dry river bed that, on account of the recent rains, was anything but dry. In fact, he was up to his ankles in mud, and what would have been a moderate march had become a slog. There was no moonlight or stars to guide him. The temperature had plummeted. He could feel his fever returning and his wound ached. After more than a month of lying infirm in the delta, pampered by Puri, he felt weak and winded. What's more, Puri's father's boots were pinching his feet irremediably. No, he was decidedly not doing the right thing and he cursed himself for his impetuousness and his vanity and his self-indulgence. But then he thought of Lucía and all his self-recriminations dissolved. *You know where I will be waiting.* And so he groped forward in the unmitigated darkness. How precisely he managed to finally get to Quinta Amelia he could not say. In his feverish state he recalled next to nothing of the journey. The last thing that he did remember was collapsing against the cold iron of the entrance gate at first light on Christmas morning and finding his way barred.

* * *

Quim must have cried out because Estela was standing at his side, tugging on his sleeve and making a sort of low gurgling sound of panic. Quim opened his eyes, blinking in the sunlight. His brow was beaded with sweat. It took a moment for him to regain his bearings, to transpose himself from the hard, frozen ground of the past to the heat of the present spring day. "*Tranquila,*" he assured Estela, taking her hand in his "it was just a bad dream." He was astonished at how vivid a memory could be, how full of minute details and subtleties after so many years. He was also left mildly uneasy by the possibility that these mental reenactments fraught with too telling precision might not constitute a kind of madness, a fanciful replacement for the paucity of the present. He was tired of the past, loathed it. And yet he never seemed to be able to escape it. Why did the past shadow him so? Why could he not be so fortunate as to forget? There were times when he thought he would actually welcome senility and the curtain that it would lower on everything. But then he thought the better of it. Death, he suspected, would be preferable to imbecility.

Judging by the height of the sun in the southern sky, as well as the sheer quantity of helichrysum that filled their basket, Quim realized that he must have been daydreaming for quite some time, hours it seemed. In his slumber Estela had gone on gathering flowers until they were spilling over the edge of the basket. She was obsessive like that; she could not stop herself once she set upon a task. Quim wondered what the future had in store for this child. If he went on living and resisted the urge to do himself in, as he sometimes thought he might when things looked especially bleak, it was because of Estela. She was his lifeline.

"Now, there was something that I had wanted to do, but for the life of me I cannot remember what it was," said Quim to Estela. He knew what it was all right, but he liked to watch her being coy and feigning ignorance. "Was it your shoes that needed mending?" he asked, looking down at her bare feet. She shook her head no. "Did your nails need cutting?" Again, she indicated no. "Ah, it must be your ears that need cleaning!" Now she was stomping her feet and shaking her head and emitting a kind of high-pitched giggle. Finally, she began to chew a lock of her hair, looking at him with wide eyes. "That's it! It's your teeth that need brushing! Come along, we'll do all those things and wash your hair too." And they descended the hillside hand in hand, their basket spilling wild flowers, their ears abuze with the droning of bees, and the sun beating down on them.

He sent her home clean and contented at midday, watching her walk and skip down the track, her tiny figure growing ever smaller in the landscape until she disappeared around a bend and was swallowed up by the valley. Just as he lost sight of Estela, however, Quim saw someone peddling slowly up the track on a bicycle. He could see a skirt billowing and knew it was a woman, but he couldn't imagine who; he received so few callers to Cal Soler and less in the heat of the day. It wasn't until the visitor had gotten off the bicycle to walk up the final steep approach to the house that Quim recognized Rosa from Quinta Amelia. He had seen her on occasion in the village during a feast day celebration or on market day, when they would nod at one another in greeting, but they hadn't exchanged a word since she had tended to him during his convalescence at Quinta Amelia at the end of the war. What could possibly have brought her here now? he wondered.

He was sitting on a wall in the shade of a fig tree in front of the house when she turned into the entrance, pushing the bicycle beside her. Quim stood as she drew near. She was flush and out of breath.

She wore a pale grey cotton dress and white canvas shoes. Although she had grown plump and her hair had gone grey, Rosa had clearly aged well. She must have been approaching seventy, Quim calculated. He had always thought her attractive with her dark Levantine eyes and sturdy legs, and wondered why she had remained a spinster and carried on working for the Graus. He could never fathom the unwavering devotion that some servants displayed toward their masters. Before he had even uttered good day, or gestured for her to take a seat on the wall, or offered her cool water from a clay jug, or asked first after her wellbeing and only thereafter what had brought her to Cal Soler, Rosa fixed him with an urgent, penetrating gaze, and with no preamble or note or warning, said simply: "She is back."

CHAPTER SIX

WHEN LUCÍA VIDAL STARED OUT THE WINDOW of the train bound for Tortosa and saw once again that ancient azure sea and the golden shore of diminutive coves and sheltering pines, jagged rock and gleaming white-washed houses, she realized all at once how dearly she had missed the landscape of her youth. New York, she knew deep down, did not suit her, not really. She loved the city in spite of herself, for it had been generous and unquestioning, welcoming her as an exile and allowing her to fashion a new life. Still, there was something callous about the place. Perhaps it was the inability to revel in the simple things that she had never grown accustomed to; that, and the city's relentless pace, which obliged everyone to scramble and charge about without a moment's pause. Never mind, she thought, as she sat back, determined to focus instead on the view, voluptuous and timeless. If only for that she was glad she had come.

Alas, it was not the mere view that had drawn her back.

When she had boarded the train in Barcelona, following closely behind a porter bearing her bags, she had actually stopped abruptly in the aisle of the train car, looked out the sooty window at the station platform, and considered descending in a rush and bolting, leaving her belongings and her longings behind. She could have made straight for the airport, she had calculated frantically, and caught the next flight back to New York and the comforts of life on Park Avenue and the love of her son Paco and her husband Adam. Or could she? Perhaps it was too late for that, she had realized with a sinking sensation. Her Spanish family would be expecting her, although what sort of reception she would receive she could scarcely imagine. It didn't matter. Her mother was stricken. Lucía had lived removed from it all for far too long. The time of reckoning was upon her and there was no turning back now. And so she had taken her seat on the train, resigned and uneasy. Then a whistle had sounded, there was an abrupt lurch and a screech of steel, and the train entered the darkened tunnel, homeward bound.

Lucía was relieved, at least, to find the train car sparsely occupied. A few solitary men, sad types with harried looks, sat bent over paperwork. There was an elderly couple traveling with their granddaughter; Lucía could hear the child address them as *àvia* and *avi,* the Catalan terms for grandparents, words she had not heard for years. Just across the aisle sat a family of British tourists, starring out the window seemingly in awe of the sun-soaked beaches and towns fronting the sea, and speaking only sporadically in the hushed, reserved tones of unpracticed travelers in a foreign land. The milky pallor of the whole family, mother and father, a son of perhaps eight or nine, and a strikingly beautiful teenage daughter with a fine golden mane that reached her waist and the long bare legs of a colt, was offset by their rather garish dress which boasted all manner of brightly colored flowers and stripes and nautical motifs, a British department store's idea of "holiday" attire, Lucía surmised. Otherwise, the car was empty, or so she thought at first. Only when she returned from the vile loo, where water sloshed in the toilet with every jolt and pitch of the train, and she found no paper, did she realize that behind her seat were two young soldiers. They must have been on leave from their military service. They were dozing, their legs splayed, their raw shaven heads lolling, their mouths agape, and so very still that they might have been dead, thought Lucía with a shiver. She sat down and tried to gaze out the window impassively, but the image of the soldiers at her back summoned memories from long ago, haunting memories that she could not dispel. Why did she dwell so on the past when all it stirred was a kind of nameless foreboding? She could not say, nor could she quite resist the urge to venture there.

* * *

It was December of 1938. Lucía had accompanied a group of foreign journalists, Adam Fates among them, back to Barcelona in the general retreat. The city had the air of a place under siege. The aerial bombing had reduced countless buildings to rubble; there were craters about, filled with black stagnant water. Handbills exhorting the populace to resist Franco and his Nationalist forces, who were closing in unchecked in a relentless advance, were scattered around the city, blowing down desolate streets, trodden by the haunted, the panic stricken. The roads to the north and the French frontier were still open and every day great multitudes could be seen bearing bundles and pushing carts and bicycles laden with possessions most of which would prove useless and unwieldy in flight: bedsteads and armoires, dining room chairs and dressing tables, picture frames and electric lamps. How they ever imagined reaching France weighed down with such detritus, Lucía did not know. She stood by and watched Adam photographing these desperate new refugees and wondered with distress how long it would be before she would have to join the exodus. But she could not leave, not yet, not without Quim.

For weeks Lucía and Adam tried to track down Quim, to find out something, anything about his fate or whereabouts. They made inquiries day after day at Army Headquarters in Las Arenas bullring, where the military personnel were either maddeningly indifferent or offered scant hope. They scoured the city's military barracks and garrisons from San Andrés to the castle on Montjuich; they visited the hospitals, hoping to find him alive among the wounded; they scanned the cafés and canteens. Adam even inquired discreetly in the brothels. Nothing. With each passing day Lucía grew more frantic and her speculations more outlandish. Quim might have gotten cut off in the retreat, she would suddenly insist to Adam, or stuck in the general crush somewhere on the road leading to Barcelona, or wounded and recovering in some field hospital or private house, or taken prisoner, or...anything, it seemed, than consider, even briefly, that he may have perished. That she would not do. Then one evening as they were sitting exhausted, hungry, and despondent, drinking rancid brandy in lieu of food in the trade union canteen that had been set up, of all places, in the Ritz hotel, Lucía recalled the last words that she had whispered in Quim's ear as she was leaving that farm at the front only weeks ago: *You know where I will be waiting.* Of course, she suddenly explained to Adam in a frenzy, that was it, that was where Quim was, hiding out in Tortosa or El Perelló, laying low, biding his time, waiting for her. She had to return immediately to Quinta Amelia, she insisted. She rose to her feet and demanded that Adam come with her, but he only stared at her with a look of weary incredulity.

"What?" asked Lucía agitated, "don't you believe me?"

"I'm not quite sure what to believe," Adam responded calmly. "I suppose it's possible."

"Are you going to just sit there?" She was shouting now and heads began to turn in the canteen. Lucía didn't care.

"Yes, at the moment I think I will. What do you propose we do, set off into the night, directly into the advancing Nationalist army and slip through their lines and stroll down to Tortosa?"

"Get up!"

"I suggest rather that you sit."

"Coward!" A hush fell over the whole canteen. All eyes were focused on the scene.

Now Adam did get up, rising slowly, never taking his eyes off of Lucía. Then he grabbed her by the shoulders and sat her down forcibly, and when she tried to shrug him off and stand up again, Adam drew a hand back and proceeded to slap her hard across the face, the sound reverberating throughout the silent room like a thunderclap. Lucía sunk into her chair and buried her face in her hands and began to weep inconsolably, whereupon heads turned back to their business, conversations resumed, and Adam ordered two more brandies.

The following morning they went on with their agonizing search. Neither Lucía nor Adam mentioned the scene of the night before; they didn't have to. There was nothing peculiar about frayed nerves and near hysteria in times of war; certainly there was no need for an apology. They plodded along Barcelona's streets and squares, walking miles upon miles, just like the refugees, thought Lucía, but never really making any progress. All the while, Adam never stopped taking pictures of the last doomed days of the Republic—the dust-chocked aftermath of the air raids; the victims of sectarian violence within the Republican ranks, whose corpses would appear in the morning strewn in gutters or hanging from lampposts, startling one at first light; the bread lines; the aimlessly wandering widows; the quick-witted orphans. Lucía often wondered how he could endure it, training his eye, pointing, and focusing his camera, capturing all that misery. But she admired him too, oh how she admired him. He didn't have to be there, didn't have to risk his life, didn't have to give the world a taste of what the century had in store. Nor did he have to accompany her on her quest to find the man she loved. Perhaps that was what puzzled her most. Why was he forever at her side? she wondered. What compelled him precisely? If he felt something more for her than mere friendship, he never let on, never made a pass at her, never insinuated anything amorous. And yet there were moments when he would stare at her in a way that seemed somehow heated and utter something like, *I wish there was a woman who would search for me so tirelessly.* Other times, when they were pursuing Quim, it almost seemed that Adam hoped that they wouldn't find him. It wasn't anything that he said specifically, just a certain weariness in his voice and manner. Lucía never admonished him for this; it was enough that he didn't abandon her to the search. Neither of them mentioned the fact, but the quest for Quim was becoming increasingly hopeless. Lucía could not help but sense that Quim was lost to her. Perhaps Adam knew as much.

And then one bitterly cold day, the 6th of December, Lucía would never forget it, she and Adam were walking down Las Ramblas on their way to the barracks at Atarazanas to ask yet again after Quim, and they came across a group of soldiers in the process of looting a small grocery store. It wasn't the looting that was altogether surprising, the city was becoming increasingly lawless with each passing day, but to see regular army soldiers plundering was further sign, if any was needed, that the end was drawing near. Lucía stood by watching despondently as Adam photographed the scene. They were on the central promenade of Las Ramblas, looking across the adjacent street just in front of the shop, and as the soldiers began to emerge, their arms laden with foodstuffs, their wide eyes in an almost feral cast, Lucía caught sight of one of Quim's men. At first she wasn't sure, everything was happening so fast, but then it was the soldier who paused, looking directly at Lucía, and she knew. It was the young poet, the soft spoken intellectual type from Barcelona who had toasted Lucía at the farm at the front. She could hear his words…*and through the storm an angel had come to deliver us from death.* Yes, it was him. He turned quickly, making off up the sidewalk at a trot, but Lucía followed him, chased him down, and implored him to stop. He finally came to a halt, but wouldn't look Lucía in the eye. She could see that he was ashamed.

"Never in my life have I stolen, but they have given us no food at the barracks in days," he offered by way of explanation. "And now to see you, you who fed us all so selflessly, forgive me."

Lucía didn't care about the food, or the looting, or the apology, she had only one thing on her mind. "Where is Quim?" she asked excitedly, thinking, at last, that he must be near.

The soldier looked up and into Lucía's eyes for the first time. "Quim?" he murmured softly.

"Yes Quim! Where is he?"

"Haven't you heard?"

"Heard what?" Lucía demanded, her voice shrill. "Tell me for God's sake."

"He was lost in the retreat, it appears he drowned while attempting to cross the Ebro."

"What do you mean 'appears'?"

"They never found his body. He was swept out to sea. I'm sorry."

The soldier went on talking, but Lucía did not hear another word. Adam came up then, he must have seen her stunned expression, her face leeched of all color, her bottom lip trembling, for without a word he opened his arms to her. Lucía fell into his embrace, buried her face in his chest and, almost imperceptibly, began to whimper.

They were staying in a small flat that Adam had managed to rent above a *lecheria* in the barrio of Gràcia. The owners, an elderly, childless couple, sold milk from a storefront on the ground floor, behind which was a courtyard occupied by two Holsteins. Not surprisingly, the flat had the fecal air of a barn, but, in fact, it was spotless and well lit. Lucía slept in the bedroom and Adam on the sofa in the living room. They had hardly spent any time there, what with all the incessant searching for Quim, but now Lucía scarcely left the place. She locked herself in the bedroom and only emerged to use the loo or to eat something meager when Adam was out or asleep. She didn't speak. She could hear Adam occasionally approach her room and put his ear to the door, but mostly he just let her be. What else could he do? Meanwhile, the bombing was growing more frequent and sustained, and Lucía could hear neighbors on the street below abuzz with rumors of Franco's advance. And then one morning a bombing raid struck so close that all of the windows in the flat were blown out. Adam was unscathed, but Lucía emerged from the bedroom bleeding from cuts caused by shards of glass that had lodged in her forehead and arms. Astonishingly, the wounds were superficial. She sat on the edge of the bathtub, silent and docile, as Adam treated her.

"That was rather too close for comfort," said Adam.

Lucía looked at him, but said nothing.

"We have to get out of Barcelona," he said.

"What about Quim?" she asked.

Adam paused from treating her wounds and looked away.

"What is it?"

"I went around to Army Headquarters today," he said. He looked at her now, placed his hands over hers, and slowly shook his head. "It's about Quim...his death...it's official."

"No, no, no" Lucía insisted. "He is presumed dead. He may have been swept downstream by the river, but not drowned. He knows that river. He's alive. I know it."

"I'm afraid not," said Adam, wearily. He reached into his breast pocket and withdrew and unfolded a sheet of paper and handed it to her silently. The letterhead was that of the *Ejército de la República;* it was duly stamped. Lucía handed it back to Adam.

"Read it," she said.

"Are you quite sure?"

"Read it."

Adam cleared his throat. "Lieutenant Quim Soler Masoliver, V Corps, Army of the Ebro, fallen in battle in defense of the Republic…"

She snatched the paper out of Adam's hands and began reading silently, mouthing the words as her watery eyes scanned the page, her mind attempting to grasp the sense of the official language that bore the news of death. It took her a moment to make the connections, *Lieutenant Soler…Ebro…fallen…Republic.* She handed the letter back listlessly to Adam. She did not weep or wail or lash out. Why was that? she wondered. All she felt was an unspeakable emptiness, that, and a degree of cold that she had never experienced before, as if her very heart had frozen and ceased to beat. Adam was saying something. She could see his lips moving, forming words, but she heard nothing. She thought for a moment that perhaps all this was a kind of trauma, a delirium induced by the bombs, that none of this was real, but it was no use. Quim was gone. It was done. She felt something like…what? Relief was it? No, not relief, more like a manner of supreme resignation. Yes, that was it. She didn't care what happened now. Let the bombs fall, she thought. Let the roof come crashing down, the fire consume her. It didn't matter, nothing mattered.

"So, as I said, I've been doing a lot of thinking…"

"What?" Lucía asked, bewildered.

"Lucía, listen to me. I know how much you loved Quim, but Quim is gone, and you must think of the future. You are young. You have a life to live and, at the moment, that life cannot be lived here in Spain. You cannot stay here. Do you understand what I am saying Lucía?"

She did understand him, but she was too weary to form the words into a coherent reply. She looked at him dolefully and nodded her head.

"Good, now listen to me carefully, please," he said, and proceeded to drop to one knee in front of her.

Lucía wanted to tell him to be careful not to cut his knee on the glass strewn floor, but he kept on talking, looking at her very intently.

"Lucía, I want you to marry me and to come back with me to New York."

It took her a moment to grasp what he had said. She was not so much surprised as shocked, and she teetered on the edge of the bathtub, wondering if the bomb blast had not caused some momentary sleight of mind. She tried to imagine herself, bleeding and half-mad with loss, a physical and emotional wreck, and she could not credit how any man, but especially this man, could want her. She blinked and looked back at Adam, focusing on his eyes and trying her best to read his thoughts. "Why?" she asked at last.

"I've got to get you out of here," Adam pleaded. "We can be married and you'll be issued a U.S. passport in a matter of days."

Lucía continued looking at him, taking this in. Of course, she realized, it all made perfect sense, although she would never have conceived of using marriage to such ends. She felt her eyes grow wide in astonishment, then she let her head drop onto Adam's shoulder and in an almost inaudible whisper uttered simply "yes."

They were married the following week in the town hall in Gràcia. Martha Gellhorn and Robert Capa were their witnesses. It certainly was not the sort of wedding that Lucía had always envisioned for herself. It was hardly a wedding at all, in fact, more like a bit of bureaucratic paperwork, like signing a lease or opening a bank account. Afterward, they went to lunch at that place on Paseo de Gracia, La Pasarela or La Pubilla, was it? No, La Puñalada, that was the place. What a name for a restaurant, *The Stabbing*. Martha Gellhorn had some story about why it was named thus, but Lucía couldn't recall what it was. To be honest, it wasn't much of a celebration, although Adam appeared genuinely elated. Lucía put on the best face she could muster. It was only later, much later, when she was installed in New York and far from the war and its brutal aftermath of reprisals and imprisonment and deprivation that she fully realized what good fortune had befallen her. Adam Fates had saved her life.

The day after the wedding they walked up to the U.S. Consulate on Avenida Tibidabo to apply for a passport for Lucía. It was in one of Barcelona's poshest neighborhoods, perched high above the rest of the city, high above the misery, the suffering, and, it seemed, the war itself. The weather was clear as crystal, everything appeared finely-etched in the sharp winter light. They walked past imposing villas with gardens sequestered behind high walls, and chauffeurs shining great gleaming automobiles parked in the entrances. No one seemed to be in the street but for the occasional nanny pushing a pram. In the summer, many of the city's best families moved their households up here where it was cooler, the air more salubrious. Lucía remembered this part of Barcelona from her childhood, before the fall of the Vidals, before the unraveling. She and Inés used to visit an aunt who lived nearby, but then that world closed to them. Scandal can shut doors tight, never to be opened again. What had become of auntie? Lucía wondered. Dead, most likely.

There was a long line of people waiting to get into the Consulate offices, but as it happened, Adam had a personal letter of introduction to the Consul General from someone he knew in New York. He had been saving it, like a card up his sleeve, for just such an eventuality, he told her. It was the way things worked; social connections could move mountains, or evidently, make a waiting crowd all but disappear. Adam strode to the front of the line and gave his calling card and the letter to the secretary in the lobby, whereupon they were promptly ushered in to a library and offered tea. It didn't take long for the Consul himself to appear.

He was exceedingly tall, taller even than Adam, and dressed in an impeccable pin-stripe suit, every inch the diplomat. His gaunt, mournful features reminded Lucía of a figure from El Greco. He had a haggard look with dark half-moons suspended beneath his red-rimmed eyes and a jaundiced tone to his complexion. His name was Clement Strauss. He wasn't much older than Adam, and he too was from New York. They soon established a sequence of shared references—schools, clubs, summer retreats, common acquaintances –that constituted a kind of gentlemanly shorthand and concluded with the Consul asking affably: "How may

I serve you." Lucía was astounded at the breezy efficacy of it all. She had never seen Adam behave in this patrician manner, but she had no intention of protesting. Adam explained their situation—Lucía's Republican sympathies and collaboration, even her radio work—and their need to flee the country in advance of the inevitable Nationalist victory. "I see," said the Consul gravely, looking at Lucía, or so she imagined, with an expression of forbearance. He then rose from his chair and excused himself. "I'll just be a moment." Adam and Lucía remained on the sofa. She reached for her tea, but it had gone cold. Her hands were shaking.

"Everything is going to be all right," said Adam in such a way that she believed him.

This is what she wanted now, what she needed, someone like a guardian to watch over her. She could not have borne this burden alone. Adam took her hands in his and stroked them tenderly, reassuringly. It was the first husbandly liberty that he had taken with her, she suddenly realized. The night before, their feigned wedding night, Adam had slept on the sofa and Lucía in the bedroom as before. She wondered how long that could go on?

When the Consul returned, he strode briskly into the room and spoke with what seemed a new urgency. "I have just had a word with my French colleague and the situation at the frontier is not good; in fact, it is rather desperate. I'm afraid you really have no time to lose." He gave Lucía some documents to fill out, and when she had done so, he told them to return in the morning at dawn. "Bring just one bag each and nothing that would betray you as refugees or Republicans on the run. Dress in the best clothes that you have. You are just a Yank and his Spanish bride caught in the crossfire on their honeymoon."

"I take it you've done this before," said Adam.

"Too many times," he replied wearily "and I'm afraid the worst is yet to come." He fell silent, looking down at the intricate patterns of the fine oriental carpet, lost in thought. Then all at once he came to again, focused and attentive. "Your wife's passport will be ready in the morning. The coast road is out of the question; it is collapsed, and Nationalist aircraft are strafing refugees. And the scene at the border, from what I've been told, is worse. The French are not very keen to accept Republican combatants, many of whom are being forced into camps at gun point. It's shameful."

"So what's the alternative?" asked Lucía, who had been mostly silent.

"My driver will take you on an interior route to Puigcerdà, and you can cross the frontier from there."

"Your driver?" Adam repeated, surprised.

"Yes, he's a local chap and a fervent Republican, don't worry. And the car has diplomatic plates, which is always a help. I would accompany you as well, but I'm afraid I can't get away. You saw the line outside." And then he rose to his feet and so too did Adam and Lucía. The Consul saw them to the door, where he shook Adam's hand and bent to kiss Lucía's. "It's not every day that I get to assist a radio star. *Lucía the Red,* I always looked so forward to your broadcasts."

"We are indebted to you," said Lucía.

"It is the very least we can do. I am sorry that my country did not come to the Republic's defense. He then turned back to Adam. "Dawn," he insisted. "Don't be late."

When they emerged from the Consulate the cold winter light was blinding. Adam lifted his arm to hail a taxi, but Lucía stopped him, asking if he wouldn't mind if they walked. "Who knows when I'll be back, perhaps never?" They descended Calle Balmes in silence, walking slowly, Lucía's arm linked in Adam's. Despite the glaring light, Lucía somehow perceived the world cast in shadow. She felt at once relieved at the prospect of her imminent departure, but also oddly craven. Here she was strolling with a man—her husband!—and readying her flight when Quim was somewhere at the bottom of the sea, only recently drowned, and seemingly forgotten. But he wasn't forgotten, not by her. Lucía decided then and there to never forget him, to always reserve a place for him in her thoughts and in her heart. She would do so silently but faithfully. He deserved more, yet to cherish him secretly was all that she could do for him now. No one would ever need to know.

They stopped for a vermouth at a bar in Putxet. It was a well-to-do barrio, and they found the atmosphere in the street and inside the bar strangely animated. They sat by the window with the December light falling over the table, and when Adam lit a cigarette they were suddenly enveloped in a billowing blue radiance. A white-jacketed waiter took their order. He had a pink face, a shiny bald pate, and a pronounced stoop. He addressed them with the formal *ustedes*.

"Well, I haven't heard that for a while," said Lucía when the man had moved off to fetch their vermouth. "For years it's been nothing but comrade this and comrade that."

"Waiters are always the first ones to sense which way the wind is blowing," Adam declared.

Lucía looked around the bar, which was filling up for the midday *aperitivo*. There were rituals not even war could obliterate. Suits and ties were back, she noticed; there was little sign of the once rife proletariat garb, no boiler suits or red scarves knotted around soiled necks, at least not in this part of town. Two young women in elegant dresses were seated at a nearby table, alternately whispering and eying Adam. "They will line the streets in welcome when Franco marches into town."

"Who?" asked Adam.

"All of these people, they never believed in the Republic. They're already jockeying for position in the future regime."

"That sounds a bit harsh."

"Does it?"

"Yes, who knows what they're thinking?"

"I know."

"Well, you're not going to be a part of it, thank goodness," said Adam, rather too glibly, thought Lucía.

"I will always be a part of it," she shot back.

The waiter returned with their vermouth. Adam paid him and included a modest tip, something that would have been frowned upon only a few months before. The waiter made to return the change, but Adam said merely, "new times," and the man bowed his head slightly.

"Any chance of getting something to eat?"

The waiter looked toward the kitchen for an instant and then back at Adam. "A bowl of lentils, perhaps some stale bread."

"That sounds splendid," said Adam. "We'll have two of those."

The waiter slouched off.

"Must you do that?" asked Lucía, miffed "the tipping, I mean."

"Darling, the revolution is over."

For a long time they did not speak. Adam stared out the window at the passersby and occasionally raised his Leica to take a photograph. Lucía closed her eyes, let the sunlight warm her face, and tried as best she could to think of nothing, but it was useless. Her mind was racing. Everything was in flux. Quim was dead; the Republic was falling; and she was poised to cross the frontier and go into exile. Awaiting her was a new life in a vast, teeming city in an unknown land. Even her identity would change. Henceforth, she would be Mrs. Adam Fates. She slowly repeated the name to herself with different accents, different inflections. She wasn't sure she liked the ring of it. How could American women abandon their very names so readily? she wondered. No, it would not do, not for her. She was Lucía Vidal i Grau, that was the name she was born with and it was the name with which she would be buried.

"Adam," she said, breaking the silence.

"Yes, darling?"

"I want to keep my name."

"What do you mean?"

"I mean I want to be known as Lucía Vidal, not as Lucía Fates, or Mrs. Adam Fates. Do you have any objection to that?"

"No, of course not, I've always loved your name. Lucía: she who was born with the first light of day," he uttered melodiously. "And Vidal: one who is full of life. How could I ever ask you to renounce such names? It would be like dismissing poetry."

Perhaps she could come to love this man, Lucía realized at that moment. All she needed was time.

They walked all the way to Plaza Cataluña. But for the sky of robin's-egg blue, the center of town had a dystopian air. Hardly anyone was about. Occasionally, a military vehicle or an official government automobile would scream past, their horns blaring at nothing. There was no other traffic. The streetcars were idle. Sporadic gunfire came from the rooftops, but Adam said he couldn't imagine who was being shot at; the enemy was still hundreds of miles away. "The Republic has been lost through military incompetence," he declared, exasperated. Lucía did not care to speak. There was nothing to add at this juncture. They made their way to the heavily barricaded Central Telephone Exchange, where they were only allowed to pass after Adam had relinquished sufficient tobacco to a pair of frightened young soldiers. A certain arbitrariness was settling over everything. The familiar rules no longer applied. Inside, a single clerk stood behind a counter in the cavernous hall. He had a pistol tucked into the front of his trousers. Adam sent a telegram to his editor at the *New York Herald Tribune* informing him that he was returning home…with a Spanish wife.

"They will not be pleased that I am missing the entrance of the Nationalists into Barcelona," he told Lucía "but it is not a spectacle that I care to see. I've seen quite enough."

When they turned to leave, Lucía hesitated before turning back to the clerk and asking for another telegram form.

"What is it?" Adam asked.

"My family."

"Oh, yes, quite, sorry for not having thought of that."

For a moment Lucía stood motionless, gazing down blankly at the form, pen in hand, unsure of what to write or, indeed, to whom. Finally, it was to Inés, her twin, that she addressed the note. Her hand trembled slightly as she wrote:

```
INÉS VIDAL I GRAU

QUINTA AMELIA

CARRETERA LA SIMPÁTICA S/N

TORTOSA

HAVE MARRIED ADAM FATES STOP

NOW ON ROUTE TO FRANCE WILL SAIL FOR NEW YORK STOP

LOVE TO ALL WILL WRITE STOP


FORGIVE ME
```

Lucía handed the form to the clerk, who glanced down at the message, and then raised his eyes to Lucía's. "New York," he muttered "lucky you."

The following day they were back at the Consulate before sunrise. They had had to walk from Gràcia through the ebony darkness, stumbling along like some hapless figures from a fairy tale lost in a deep, dark wood. The owner of their flat had given them each a bowl of fresh warm milk before they set off, but otherwise they had eaten little in days. When they reached the Consulate they were already weak and famished. Adam rang a bell at the front gate and presently a man emerged from the darkness dressed in a silver-buttoned tunic, breeches, and knee-high boots. Without a word he opened the gate and let them in. Lucía spoke to him in Catalan, telling him who they were. Yes, he said, he had been told to expect them. His Catalan was measured and formal, not what Lucía was accustomed to hearing in Tortosa. He was probably from the interior, she surmised, from Vic or Olot or one of those recesses of Catalonia untainted by Castilian culture and language. The man led them to the shadowy bulk of an automobile parked in the darkness before the front door of the Consulate. Only when the light from the sconces that flanked the entrance suddenly flickered on and the Consul came out of the front door did Lucía and Adam get a look at the machine, a great sweeping black thing with whitewall tires and an abundance of polished chrome. Adam whistled in admiration.

"Good morning," said the Consul, as he approached. He and Adam shook hands, and he bowed toward Lucía. The chauffeur took their bags and stowed them in the trunk.

"Well," said Adam, turning to face the automobile, "from the look of it we are to flee in style."

"Yes, isn't she beautiful," said the Consul, rubbing his hands together and cocking an eyebrow.

They might have been leering at a strumpet the way they sounded, thought Lucía.

"It's a '36 Fleetwood," the man continued. "Had it shipped over myself at great expense, but I consider it a rolling testament to

American ingenuity. Ildefons here treats it as one would a spoiled and cherished child," he said, looking to the driver. "You have met Ildefons I assume?"

"Yes," said Lucía. Adam nodded vaguely and continued to ogle the automobile.

"You will be in very able hands." He then handed an envelope to Adam. "Permit me to give you your wife's passport, transit visas for France, and a letter of safe passage. The letter is, from a legal standpoint, utterly useless, but the official seal of the Consulate General of the United States of America tends to impress. You never know when it might come in handy with some local policeman or frontier guard."

"We cannot tell you how grateful we are for all your assistance, and now this to boot," said Adam, turning back to the beloved Fleetwood.

"Think nothing of it. I am only doing my duty."

"No!" said Lucía, perhaps a bit too emphatically. Both men started and looked at her slightly bewildered. "Forgive me," she said "but all this is not mere duty. It is so much more. How can I ever repay you?"

"Put in a good word with Mr. Roosevelt," he said, winking.

"Look us up when next you are in New York," Adam insisted, as he shook the Consul's hand, sounding, or so thought Lucía, like he was addressing an old school chum.

The man then took Lucía's hand as if to kiss it, but she drew him toward her and kissed his cheek.

"Well, well, it's not every day that I get kissed by so beautiful a woman," he stammered. "But now I must insist that you be off! The best of luck to you both, and send me a telegram when you have safely crossed the frontier. I do worry so."

Ildefons opened the rear door of the Fleetwood and the two slid in. Adam rolled down the window and the Consul bent down to offer some final words: "You shouldn't have any trouble on the backroads. You will cross the frontier after Puigcerdà, from there you're on your own. Then he stepped back and straightened and raised his right fist and proclaimed: "Viva La República!"

Ildefons started the automobile and revved the engine grandly before they slowly rolled out the drive just as the first rays of golden light touched the crowns of the palms lining the avenue.

They raced north for the frontier, hurtling through somnolent villages and sullied factory towns where the houses were still shuttered and little stirred. When they did pass people, villagers huddled in a square or refugees slouched on the side of the road, the silent figures stared with mouths agape as the great machine sped past. Ildefons had clearly made this trip before; he seemed to know all the turns and curves and forks in the road, knew where he could open up the aptly named Fleetwood on long, level stretches. He steered the automobile with a kind of relaxed mastery, like a jockey who knows how to manage his thoroughbred mount. Adam and Lucía sat in quiet awe, not quite believing their good fortune. For months they had been cold and cramped and uncomfortable and mostly uncomplaining. Now they sprawled across the rear seat, the leather caressing them, the voluptuous suspension cushioning them from the imperfections of the road, the heat blasting through the vents, the chill of the morning, the very world, it seemed, at bay. It was what heaven must be like, thought Lucía. "God bless America," Adam had murmured only half in jest, and she wondered if that were possible, for God to bless one country above all others. She moved Adam's hat from where it sat on the seat between them and eased herself against him in a languorous movement, resting her head just beneath his shoulder. Adam drew an arm around her and together they gazed out the window as the subdued morning light grew to a sharp winter brilliance.

It suddenly struck Lucía that there were things that she might well be seeing for the last time. She looked at the bent, long-suffering widows clad in black and silently said goodbye. She bade farewell too to the Romanesque campaniles, rising above the tile rooftops, to the cypress all huddled around the village cemeteries, to the neat ranks of olive trees, to the well-tended vegetable patches with their rows of winter cabbages, to the donkeys and asses tethered to trees, to women in headscarves and men sporting *boinas*, to chestnuts roasting in braziers in town squares. To all these things she said goodbye. The past and her place in it were receding as fast as the world rushing by outside the window. The moment had arrived to embrace the future, but what exactly lay in store for her, for them, she hadn't a clue.

As Lucía lay limply in Adam's embrace, listening to the murmur of his heart, she realized, not for the first time, that she hardly knew this man. Who had she married so hastily? she asked herself. He was not a complete mystery, of course. She knew he was intelligent, not an intellectual perhaps, but curious and well-spoken, and engaging. He was clearly well-bred; his impeccable manners gave him away. Lucía recalled that even Quim had said as much. "He's polite to everyone," he had said one evening at Quinta Amelia as they both sat observing Adam making small talk with Rosa, the maid, but at the same time treating her with the utmost respect, as if she were the lady of the house. Quim had liked that; so had she. Lucía suspected too that Adam loved her, otherwise, why would he have married her? Why would he be doing all of this, if not for love? In time, she supposed that she would come to know him and love him too, or at least to respect him deeply, like one of those arranged marriages of old. Didn't old ladies say that those were the ones that endured?

"I was just thinking," she said finally, breaking a silence that had gone on for miles, "I know so little about you and nothing at all about your family."

"What would you like to know?"

"Everything."

Adam laughed. "That's too broad; I don't even know everything about me. You'll have to narrow it down, I'm afraid, one question at a time."

"Very well, what does your father do?"

"My father?" Adam pondered this for a moment before responding. "Mostly what he likes."

"What does that mean?"

"Nothing. Let me see, well, he owns things, many things, property mostly and stores, great big department stores, lots of them, where you can buy anything and everything."

"Where?"

"Oh, all around the country. 'Fates Department Stores: Where America is Destined to Shop.' That's our slogan, a bit trite, I know, but everyone knows it."

Lucía brightened. She hated to admit it, but it was true all the same, wealth mattered to her. Perhaps it was the result of coming from a family that had had everything and then lost it all, or rather a father who had lost it all. What on earth had she been thinking when she fell for Quim? She didn't know.

"Your father, does he gamble?" she asked.

"No, he and my mother play bridge, but never for money. My father always says that gambling is the easiest way to lose your shirt."

"And a great deal more," Lucía added.

By midday they had passed Ripoll and began to climb toward the snow-capped peaks of the Pyrenees, floating in the dazzling alpine light like icebergs at sea. The road grew narrow and serpentine, and Ildefons proceeded slowly for fear of ice or encountering oncoming vehicles. Their progress became painstaking. And then, ascending a switchback, they came around a curve and found two soldiers and a young woman blocking the road. Ildefons cursed and braked and brought the automobile to a halt about fifty feet short of the group.

"What do you want me to do?" he asked over his shoulder.

"What do you mean?" Adam asked.

"I could ignore them and speed ahead. They'll get out of the way in time."

"No!" Lucía insisted "they haven't even drawn their weapons for God's sake."

One of the soldiers began to approach, limping slightly, while the others remained behind, watching. Adam reached into his coat pocket and withdrew the envelope with the American Consul's letter of safe passage. Ildefons rolled down his window, but just a crack, enough to hear and speak. Stooping to the gap in the window, the soldier wearily offered a greeting: *"Buenos días."* He was unshaven and burnished by the sun, his eyes lost in a squint, his head wrapped in rags.

Ildefons nodded, but remained silent. Lucía rolled her window down and Adam began to brandish the letter, but she turned to him and told him firmly to put it away. She then leaned her head toward the open window. "What is it that we can do for you?" The soldier peered inside the automobile and blinked at Lucía and Adam as if he hadn't understood the question.

"My name is Alejandro," he finally responded, barely audible. "I am with my sister Isabel and her husband Ramón. We are trying to reach the border. We have been walking for many days, but I fear that my sister cannot go on. She is," he said, turning to look at the woman before continuing, almost apologetically "expecting a child."

"Expecting a child!" repeated Lucía. "For the love of God, tell her to get in. All of you get in!"

The soldier waved for the other two to approach.

"Now wait just a minute *señora,*" said Ildedons, looking nervously at Lucía in the rearview mirror. "I have been instructed by the Consul to drive the two of..."

"Ildefons!" Lucía interrupted, "this is no time to quibble. This woman is pregnant. Are you proposing that we leave her, leave them, behind?"

"She's right," said Adam meekly.

The strangers, who were now huddled together alongside the automobile, said nothing; they didn't have to, the expressions on their faces looked like a triptych depicting hunger, exhaustion, and despair. The chauffeur sighed, muttered under his breath, and climbed out from behind the wheel. "There will be no fire arms inside the Cadillac," he announced, as he strode to the rear of the automobile and opened the trunk.

The soldiers complied readily. "You needn't worry," said the second soldier, speaking for the first time, as he relinquished his rifle, "we have no ammunition, haven't had any in weeks. Like that one cannot win a war. That is why we are fleeing."

The three were careful to clean the mud from their boots before climbing into the back seat with Lucía, while Adam moved up front with Ildefons. Before continuing on, Lucía leaned forward and addressed the chauffeur: "Forgive me, Iledfons, this is your automobile. It wasn't my decision to make."

"Sometimes, *señora,* we need others to encourage us to do the right thing."

"Yes," she agreed, leaning back. *Do the right thing;* she recalled wistfully, that is what Quim always said.

They were from Barbastro in Aragon, they explained. For weeks they had been trying to cross the frontier over several passes but had been thwarted by foul weather and French border guards. Now they were going to attempt to cross at Puigcerdà; if unsuccessful, they didn't know what they would do. They were spent.

Isabel and Ramón were an unlikely couple only because they appeared little more than children. His innocent, boyish face brought to mind nothing so much as a cherub. It was hard to believe that he was in uniform and not at play in short trousers. He was clean shaven if, indeed, he shaved at all. Only above his upper lip was there a trace of a downy shadow. Lucía had seen women with moustaches more prominent. As for his wife, she was slender and not unattractive, with hair as black and glossy as a raven's wing, and pale alabaster eyes. Her high forehead and graceful movements were not those of a peasant girl, nor were her fine hands. Lucía suspected that she was from a well-to-do family. Perhaps they were running away from more than the war. Only when the girl opened her coat inside the automobile did Lucía notice the slight swell of her belly.

"Four months," she said when she saw Lucía looking. "We want the child to be born in France, to be born free."

"Yes, of course," replied Lucía, forcing a smile. What more could she say? She hardly envied her predicament.

Isabel's brother Alejandro was older. He had been studying at the university in Zaragoza when the war broke out. For nearly two years he had been living and fighting in the trenches on the Aragon front. His spirits rose when he discovered that Adam was an American. He had fought alongside many soldiers from the Lincoln Brigade, he said. "You could always count on *los Yanquis.*"

Adam didn't acknowledge this bit of praise. In fact, he hardly appeared to be listening. Lucía wondered if he wasn't miffed at having to take on these desperate passengers. She couldn't say if it was unlike him, for she didn't know exactly what that was. He kept up a hushed conversation with Ildefons. What were they talking about so intently? she wondered.

On the outskirts of Puigcerdà Ildefons pulled the Cadillac off the road and onto a dirt track and came to a stop in a small clearing surrounded by towering pines sighing in the mountain air. Patches of dirty snow endured in the shadows. The day had suddenly grown overcast and raw. Adam turned around in the front seat and addressed the two soldiers.

"I presume that you know very well that if there are any Republican military units in town and they catch sight of you, you will be taken as deserters and most likely shot."

The soldiers nodded sullenly. Isabel bent her head and began to weep copiously into her hands. Lucía gave Adam a look of reproach before turning to console the young woman.

"However," Adam declared, pausing and lifting an index finger like an actor on the stage, as all eyes looked to him in anticipation, "I have a plan."

Alejandro and Ramón stayed behind, hidden in the underbrush, while Ildefons drove Adam, Lucía, and Isabel into Puigcerdà. They parked in the Plaza de Santa Maria in the shadows of the campanile. It was a Saturday, market day, and the square was full of shoppers and vendors bearing baskets and pushing carts laden with produce. The air smelled of wood smoke and roasted chestnuts. After the penury of Barcelona, the war seemed decidedly far off. A group of men and boys soon gathered, and in that guileless way that provincials have, stared baldly, silently at the Cadillac. Ildefons remained with the automobile, while Adam and the women set off to do some shopping.

On the Calle Mayor they found a dress shop, where the saleswoman, wearing a dress of moss-green silk and altogether too much rouge, looked the three of them up and down, lingering on Isabel's soiled coat and boots, and offered a perfunctory greeting: "How exactly can I help you?" she asked haughtily.

"By showing us some smart dresses naturally," Lucía replied, refusing to allow the woman's smugness to go unchecked.

"Very well," said the woman, sighing "if you ladies will follow me."

Before being led to the changing area, Lucía leaned into Adam and whispered: "What can we buy?"

"The works," he said.

"What is the works?"

"It's an American expression; it means everything."

"I like the works," she said, smiling up at him.

Adam slipped her a wad of bills and went off in search of a haberdasher. They agreed to meet back in the square.

It didn't take long for Lucía to set about choosing a complete outfit for Isabel: a navy blue crepe dress with a high belted waist, puff sleeves, and a bow collar; square-heeled pumps; silk stockings; a slouch hat; leather gloves, and a pale grey woolen coat with a fur collar and cuffs. By the time Lucía paid for this extravagant make over, the sales woman had become positively obsequious, insisting on dabbing their pulse points with complimentary perfume.

"We *do* hope to see you again soon," said the woman, beaming and bowing, as she opened the door for Lucía and Isabel as they left.

"I'm sure," said Lucía, smiling at her icily, and stepping into the street.

When the women returned to the square, Ildefons did not recognize Isabel.

"Well?" Lucía said to him, what do you think?"

"Of what? Madame."

Lucía laughed. "Of Isabel, of course."

He appeared dumbfounded. "Goodness me," he finally stammered, stepping back and looking at Isabel. "You look like one of those elegant young ladies on Avenida Tibidabo."

Isabel was too stunned to speak. Then Lucía caught sight of Adam's head above the multitudes as he approached from across the square; the crowd seemed to part before him, like the sea before the prow of a ship.

In his wake bobbed a tower of boxes balanced by a young shop boy. When he reached them, Adam looked at Isabel approvingly and said to Lucía: "Well, you have certainly done your part. She looks marvelous."

"I feel like someone else," said Isabel in disbelief.

"You *look* like someone else," said Adam. "That's the point."

Ildefons packed the boxes in the trunk, but before they set off, he insisted on buying some provisions in the square. "I don't know what you people survive on, but I am famished." Adam tried to press some money in his hand, but Ildefons refused it. "This is something that I would like to pay for."

When they returned to the clearing outside of town, Ildefons tooted the horn and Alejandro and Ramón emerged from the woods looking relieved, as if they hadn't been entirely sure that they would come back for them. Then Isabel stepped from the automobile and Ramón looked at his young wife and seemed to visibly swoon. She bowed her head slightly, trying to hide her smile. Her brother gasped.

"Now it's your turn," said Adam to the men, as he opened the trunk and brought out the stack of boxes. "Off with the uniforms, I'm afraid."

The men began to unbutton their tunics, but stopped suddenly, glancing shyly at Lucía.

"Oh, forgive me," she said. "I'll just wait in the automobile with Isabel."

A short time later, Adam tapped on the rear window of the Fleetwood and gestured for the women to come out. As they stepped from the automobile it was their turn to gasp. Alejandro and Ramón stood before them clad in tweed suits, fine white cotton shirts, silk ties, and highly polished oxfords. They each had a charcoal grey overcoat slung over an arm and a fedora worn at a rakish angle on their heads.

"You look every bit the dandies," said Isabel.

"Everything fits them perfectly," said Lucía, astonished. "How ever did you know what to buy?"

"As a young man, my father insisted that I spend a good portion of my summer holiday working in the men's department at the Fates department store in Manhattan. I can size a man up in a glance."

"Remarkable," said Ildefons.

Suddenly, however, Alejandro grew solemn. "We can never pay for all of this," he said, looking down at his attire and shaking his head.

"He's right," said Ramón. "We cannot accept this; it is all too much."

"Don't be silly," Adam said dismissively. "Consider it my contribution to the war effort."

"But we are running *away* from the war," said Alejandro.

"You have been given no choice," said Ildefons. "There is no dishonor in what you are doing. And now, for the love of God, for I don't believe I will endure another minute, let's eat!"

They built a small fire in the clearing and spread out their old coats and sat down to a meal of white and black sausage, goat cheese, roasted chestnuts and sweet potatoes, bread and wine. Lucía recalled the provisions which she had brought to Quim and his men at the front and the makings of the feast which she had come to regard in her recollections as the Last Supper. How famished they all had been; how famished they all were now. More than anything else, that was what the war meant for so many people, hunger, forever gnawing at one's thoughts. It was worse in the cities. In Barcelona, people foraged in the parks and outskirts for weeds, scavenged in the trash, netted songbirds, trapped cats. There was nothing that one wouldn't eat. In the mountains and throughout the countryside far from the front and the bombing it was different. There was always something to be had, however meager. The country folk, always disdainful of the city, had their moment. They knew that the only thing worth possessing was land, where one could always cultivate something, raise something.

After the meal, Adam took pictures of the group; everyone looked happy and satiated and impeccably turned out. They might have been on holiday. And then the sun sunk below a mountain peak, the light quickly faded, the temperature dropped, and it began to snow. They sought shelter in the Cadillac and waited for night to descend. An hour later darkness was pressing in at the windows and Ildefons eased the automobile out to the snow-blanketed road and turned for the frontier.

"The cold and the snow are a blessing," said Ildefons. "The frontier guards will be less likely to linger over details and procedure. Remember, I am to do the talking. If you must speak, try to do so in English, it tends to throw the French off. You are an important American journalist," he went on, looking at Adam in the rearview mirror. "And these are your rich Spanish friends. All you are looking for is a fine meal in France."

The road skirted Puigcerdà and swung north toward the lights of Bourg-Madame, France in the near distance. No one said a word, but Lucía could almost hear the collective pounding of their hearts, their nervous, uneven breathing. And then the automobile rumbled over a wooden bridge and the din of the Rahur River, and on the far side the silhouette of a helmeted figure in a long coat bearing a lantern emerged from a sentry box and raised a hand, gesturing for them to halt. Lucía glanced at Isabel and saw that she was clutching a rosary, her lips moving silently in prayer.

"*Tranquilos,*" said Ildefons, as he slowed to a stop and rolled down his window. "*Bonsoir Monsieur le douanier.*"

"*Bon soir,*" said the guard flatly. He lifted his lantern to the window and peered in, looking at them all arranged there, as still as corpses. For a long time he did nothing but stare; he seemed to be waiting for something to give way. There was a knowingness to his expression, thought Lucía, something wily that suggested that he was on to their ruse, that he had seen it all before, but still he said nothing. And then Adam broke the unnerving spell, speaking in an exaggerated twang that Lucía had never heard before: "Say, can you tell us where to get a decent meal hereabouts?"

The guard looked at Adam and shook his head. "*Les américains, qui les comprend?*" he muttered. He leaned back toward Ildefons. "*Qu'est-ce qu'il dit?*"

Ildefons cleared his throat. "*Il veut de la cusine française raffinée. Voilà des jours qu'il se plaint de la nourriture espagnole. Je n'en peux plus de l'entendre, alors j'ai pensé l'emmener avec ses amis à l'hôtel de Lac, sur la route de Foix. C'est là que mon patrón va quand it veut bien manger.*"

"*Et c'est qui votre patrón?*"

"Le cónsul des États-Unis *d'Amérique. C'est son filleul derrière, le grand."*

"What on earth are they going on about?" Adam whispered to Lucía.

"The guard didn't understand a word you said, and he's asked Ildefons to explain. It seems that you have been complaining bitterly about the Spanish food. Ildefons can't listen to it anymore so he's taking us to a fancy restaurant near Foix. He says it's where his boss goes when he wants to eat well. 'And who is your boss?' the guard wanted to know. Why the Consul of the United States of America, and evidently you are his godchild."

"Really, well, that's nice to know."

The guard pursed his lips and nodded, clearly impressed. Then he walked to the rear of the vehicle to inspect the number plate, circled the automobile slowly, and came back to Ildefons' window.

"C'est un voiture magnifique. C'est quelle marque?"

"Une Cadillac Fleetwood."

"Elle a combien de cylindres?"

"Huit. Elle file à toute allure."

"Now what?" whispered Adam.

"He likes the automobile; wants to know the make and model; how many cylinders it has. Ildefons says it goes like the wind."

"Formidable." said the guard, admiringly. *"Bon…c'est dommage parce que vous allez devoir rouler doucement. Les rues sont glissantes avec la neige."*

Lucía smiled. He says it's a pity because Ildefons will have to drive slowly. The roads are treacherous with this snow."

The guard glanced back at them one last time and smiled slyly. *"Bon dîner,"* he said. Then he stepped back and waved them on. *"Allez-y."*

They were free and clear.

In the end, they did actually drive to the Hotel de Lac for dinner. Adam insisted. It would be a celebration. The dining room, hung with still lifes of harvest plenty and game, and paintings of kitchen scenes and banquets, was nearly full but very hushed, not like Spain at all, more like church. The waiter did not know what to make of a uniformed Ildefons in the formal dining room. He bent discreetly, whispering to Lucía: "Shall we make a place for your chauffeur in the kitchen, Madame?"

"No," said Lucía firmly, "*merci.*"

The food was exquisite. Ildefons said that it was often so in the stead-fast restaurants in the provinces; it was the true French cuisine. They got very drunk, except for Isabel, who sipped a single glass of wine through-out the night. They toasted the three republics: Spain, France, and the United States of America. Of course, there were tears too. They wept for Spain, for those who had been lost or had not been able to flee. Naturally, Lucía thought about Quim, but already less so. He was no longer among the living. He now occupied that exclusive and shifting terrain that was memory. They all vowed to return. "But when?" someone asked. None of them knew.

Adam had taken rooms for them all. Well after midnight they stag-gered up the hotel stairs, propping each other up, mumbling. Only Isabel could walk straight. They slept in enormous brass beds, beneath feather comforters as light as air. For the first time Lucía and Adam lay together, but they dropped off to sleep immediately, overcome with exhaustion, made drowsy by the wine.

In the morning it was different. What woke Lucía was not the warm, dazzling light as it streamed through the irregular window panes, or the muffled voices of other guests that drifted in from the hallway, no; what roused her from the deepest of sleeps of the sort that she hadn't man-aged in months was the weight of him. Lucía opened her eyes to find Adam straddling her, looking down with an expression at once bleary-eyed and vaguely lecherous. She was too startled to scream.

"Good morning, wife of mine," he said in a proprietary voice.

Lucía didn't answer, didn't know what to say. He kissed her lightly on the lips, just for an instant, as if to say, I'll be back. Then he kissed her everywhere, all over. He ran his hands along the contours of her body, grazing his fingers around her breasts, up and down her thighs, behind her knees. He was taking possession of her, Lucía realized, inspecting the goods, and she felt not so much powerless as unqualified to stop it. He rolled her over and continued over her buttocks, along her spine, reck-oning every inch of her. It hadn't been like this with Quim. She thought back to their lovemaking at the front in that big bed with its sullied mattress and rough woolen blanket. There she had surrendered herself willingly, wholeheartedly, and it was like nothing she had ever experienced before. Nothing of the shabby surroundings had taken away from the sublimity of that night. There was nothing sublime in this now; it felt more dutiful. Quim was dead and Adam was her husband. And so, she went slack and parted her legs. It didn't matter that the linens were crisp and the room spotless. She felt sullied somehow, like a courtesan. When he entered her, he stopped suddenly and looked at her, taken aback. *Ah, so you've done this before,* she imagined him thinking. And then he seemed to shrug and resume his efforts. Soon enough he was hurtling along and came soon after, whimpering through clenched teeth and rolling his eyes into his head. They lay spent, tangled in damp sheets. Lucía wanted to cry, but did everything she could to hold back the tears. She rose from the bed and walked to the window naked. The day was luminous. Snow blanketed the frozen lake. She had to shield her eyes from the glare. From far off across the lake the sound of gunfire echoed, but it wasn't the sound of war, just some hunters after game on a Sunday morning.

They bid farewell to Ildefons and the others in the hotel lobby. It was hard to believe that all of them had met only the day before; they seemed like old friends, relatives even. The ordeal had established something between them, something intangible but true. Adam slipped an envelope stuffed with franc notes to Ramón, "for the christening," he said, although Lucía knew that the money was meant for the three of them. Ildefons was returning to Barcelona. Adam attempted to press a tip into his palm, but the man refused. Finally, Adam gave them all his, or rather their, address and telephone in New York. "Look us up," he said gleefully.

He was always saying that, Lucía realized, *look us up*. He had said it to Gellhorn and Capa, to the Consul in Barcelona, and now to this strangely incongruous band. What's more, he seemed genuinely to mean it. She began to envision a steady stream of miscellaneous visitors knocking on their door. "Remember us?" they would ask. Remember? How could she possibly forget?

* * *

They took the sleeper train from Toulouse to Paris, arriving in the Gare d'Orleans on the morning of the 24th of December, just in time for Christmas. A sharp winter wind was blowing off the Seine; the surface glimmered like quicksilver in the morning light. Along the avenues the trees were naked and still. Lucía had never been to Paris. France was the place her father had run off to; no one in the family ever mentioned it. Still, she had always known that Paris must be like life itself. Now she pressed her face to the window of the taxi and tried to take it all in as they sped past monumental palaces and hallowed churches, imposing ministries and immaculate gardens, luxurious shops—oh, the shops! Suddenly, Barcelona seemed like a village. Adam sat back very composed. Lucía could feel his eyes on her. They crossed the river, turned onto the Avenue Montaigne, and pulled up to the Hotel Plaza Athénée. *"Voilà"* said the driver.

"What is this?" Lucía asked.

"Our hotel. This is where the honeymoon begins."

"We're staying here?"

"I've booked a suite."

At the reception desk the concierge seemed to recognize Adam. "Anymore bags Monsieur?" he asked, looking down questionably at Adam's Gladstone and Lucía's single valise.

"No," said Adam "but more are on the way."

Really, wondered Lucía, *from where?*

Everyone in the lobby was smartly turned out. Women were coming through the front door wrapped in furs, the men with coats draped over their shoulders like princes. Lucía had never felt like a provincial, but she did now. She and Adam looked precisely like what they were, two people who had just come from a war. Adam must have sensed her unease. He leaned over and whispered to her: "Presently we will see to our wardrobes. We can't go around Paris looking like a couple of refugees."

Refugees, well, that's what she was, wasn't it, thought Lucía. She knew that he had meant the comment to be lighthearted, but it stung.

A wiry bellboy in a snappy crimson uniform with brass buttons rode with them up the elevator and led them down a carpeted, dimly-lit corridor. Muffled voices, strains of music, came from different rooms as they passed. It was almost comical the way the boy strode ahead of them, carrying their two insubstantial bags. He opened the door with a practiced flourish and stepped aside for them to pass. Lucía gasped when she crossed the threshold. She had never seen such luxury. Not even the distant memory of her family's Barcelona townhouse could compare. The gilded mirrors, the Empire furniture, the fine carpets and paintings, the velvet curtains, everything was manifestly grand. Through French doors that gave on to a balcony, the Eiffel Tower was perfectly framed.

"Oh Adam…" she said, hesitating, not quite sure what to say, "it's… divine!" Then she went to the bathroom and squealed when she saw the size of the tub. Immediately Lucía ran the bath and began to undress, throwing her clothes out the bathroom door and onto the bedroom floor. The water was steaming. She stepped in, slid down, and closed her eyes. Yesterday she had been in a war zone and now she was soaking in the bath of an elegant hotel in Paris. She could hardly credit it. Adam came in carrying a gilt armchair from the suite's salon, placed it at the foot of the bathtub, and sat down, eying her covetously.

"Don't you look lovely," he said.

"Tell me I haven't married a voyeur."

"When the object of scrutiny is one's wife it is not considered voyeurism, but the act of a dedicated husband."

Lucía laughed. "I had no idea that you were capable of all this," she said.

"Of what exactly?"

"Everything. Buying all those clothes in Puigcerdà; putting everyone up at the hotel in Foix; passing money to Ramón, Alejandro, and Isabel; booking the first-class train compartment from Toulouse; and now this," she indicated, raising her hands from the water palms up.

"Well, I don't like to talk about money; I was brought up to believe it vulgar."

"So say those who have it."

"You're not going to admonish me for my discretion I hope."

"No, no, I'm sorry, that's not it at all. I think that's wonderful. I think it's wonderful the way you helped those people, the way you are helping me. What I mean to say is…" What *did* she mean to say? She wasn't sure. "Well, it's just that I want you to know that I didn't marry you for your money. I didn't even know you had any."

"I'm glad."

Then there was a sudden silence, somehow freighted. Lucía was certain that they were both thinking the same thing. It wasn't for money that she had married Adam, but for an ulterior motive all the same, and that was to flee. They both knew it; they had discussed it openly. Finally it was Adam who spoke.

"So much has happened in recent days. It's hard to believe that little more than a fortnight ago we learned that Quim was dead…"

Quim was dead. Lucía winced when she heard the phrase. Somehow she still half believed that she might receive a letter or a telegram, a phone call even, and there would be Quim's words, Quim's voice. *It had all been a misunderstanding, he would explain, part of the chaos and confusion of war. Miraculously, he had survived; he could scarcely believe it himself, but now they could pick up where they had left off.* Or could they? Did she, the now betrothed Mrs. Fates, really want that? Lucía could no longer say for sure. She went on listening to Adam.

"…I know very well how much you loved him, and I know that you are suffering still. All I can do is, in time, hope to make you happy."

Lucía didn't know what to say, or rather she had an inkling of what she might say, but couldn't quite find the words. All the customary phrases seemed inadequate, if not banal. *Be patient with me.* Would that do? Perhaps, *give me time to heal,* or something of that nature. She couldn't say. Adam remained there quietly watching her, unhurried, poised, like a man who knows that his wager has paid off. He has won. He need not say more. Finally, Lucía rose to her feet in the tub and stood glistening before him, her arms limp at her side, her whole body laid bare like some sort of primitive offering.

For the moment, it was everything she could muster; it would have to be enough.

* * *

It was Christmas. Paris was like paradise, otherworldly. The very air seemed joyous, to promise fulfillment. The dazzling storefronts and window displays beckoned. The streets were crowded with shoppers bearing bags and packages wrapped in decorative paper and tied with colored ribbons. Everyone seemed to greet one another with glee. *Joyeux Noël!* they exclaimed.

For her Christmas present, Adam took Lucía to Coco Chanel's boutique on the Rue Cambon, to the "Schiap Shop", Elsa Schiaparelli's salon in the Place Vendôme, to Le Bon Marché, and Printemps. Sheathed in a Schiaparelli knit dress and splashed with Chanel Nº5, Lucía felt as if she had had a change of skin. She accompanied Adam to Charvet, to Cifonelli, to Moynat for luggage. He had impeccable taste, she discovered. In fine clothes he looked like a duke. They had their purchases sent to the hotel and wandered the streets of Paris like plutocrats, which, Lucía was coming to realize, they were. It all felt like a dream. She would not have been altogether surprised to wake up suddenly in that cold flat in Barcelona that smelled like a barnyard, wearing an ordinary dress, hungry, the sound of gunfire not far off. But no.

They had Christmas Eve dinner at Le Select in Montparnasse. The dining room was only half full. People were home with family in their glowing Parisian flats or away in the beloved towns and sleepy villages of the provinces. The waiters tried to be cheerful, but somehow it only compounded the melancholy. Adam was undeterred and ordered Krug. She had never tasted anything like it; it was like sipping gold. The bubbles made Lucía think of Christmas at Quinta Amelia, not that they ever drank champagne, just *cava* from the Penedés, but still. She tried to envision the gathering at home. The occasion could hardly be full of good cheer. The family had grown progressively smaller, consumed by life's myriad tragedies. Her father, of course, was long dead and buried;

Carlitos had been murdered less than a year before; Borja was off fighting with the Nationalists; and now she was on her way to exile. She thought of her telegram to Inés, and imagined it opened and discarded on a side table or a bookshelf, or worse, tossed in the fireplace, the message—"…have married…on route to France…will sail for New York stop"—up in smoke. Her mother would insist on attending midnight Mass in the Tortosa cathedral. Lucía could see her walking up the aisle of the central nave with Inés on her arm and Francisco trailing behind, the tap, tap of his crutches sounding on the cold stone floor. It would be just the three of them now, and the other parishioners would wonder and whisper about the family's diminished ranks, and watch them slide into their habitual pew near the altar and see that they no longer filled it, and the yawning gap would plainly indicate to anyone who had failed to notice just how reduced the family had become. Lucía saw her mother kneeling, her face veiled, her fingers playing over the worn beads of her rosary, and she couldn't help but wonder what exactly she would be praying for, her family reunited? No chance of that plea being answered.

"Where on earth are you?" Adam asked, interrupting her reverie.

"What?"

"You're a million miles away."

"Oh, I'm sorry," said Lucía, smiling, but knowing full well that her expression must have looked contrived. "I was thinking of Christmas at Quinta Amelia."

"You looked decidedly glum."

"Yes, well, it's sad to think what Christmas must be like for my mother, for Inés, for Francisco."

"I should think they'd be raising their glasses to Franco."

Basta! exclaimed Lucía, surprising Adam, even herself with her reaction. But like a lightening flash it didn't last. She reached across the table and took Adam's hand. "I'm sorry," she said, "but forget about politics for a moment. God, I'm so sick of it all, the war, the factions, the country divided, families divided. I don't want to think about any of that, at least not tonight."

"Quite right," said Adam "forgive me. I have no right to judge them."

"The sad truth of the matter is that they are probably doing precisely what you imagined, toasting Franco," said Lucía, smiling wanly, resignedly.

"Well, that's not for us," said Adam, filling their glasses with champagne. "Here's to our first Christmas together. May it be the first of many, a lifetime's worth."

"Yes," said Lucía, raising her glass to his, "*salud.*"

A lifetime's worth, she hadn't really thought of that. It sounded so definitive, so irrevocable. She wasn't accustomed to thinking so far into the future. To her relief, the waiter suddenly appeared with their first courses.

"*Et voici...pour Madame, les artichauts et pour Monsieur, les huitres*" said the waiter, placing her artichokes and Adam's oysters before them with a certain exaggerated panache and a click of the tongue.

"Ah..." said Adam, closing his eyes and dipping his head to the milky grey and gleaming oysters as he inhaled, "the smell of the sea."

Lucía watched him squeeze lemon over the oysters, and one by one, lift the shells to his lips, and slide and slurp them and their juice into his mouth. He was a sensualist, Lucía was quickly discovering. She liked that he enjoyed things.

"Would you care for one darling?" he asked. They were disappearing quickly.

"No thank you, I'm enjoying myself too much just watching you."

Perhaps it was the smell of the sea as Adam had mentioned or the image of the oysters lying lucent in their shells, but suddenly Lucía recalled a day walking with her father on the beach, she couldn't remember where precisely. She must have been very young, probably eight or nine, because her father was still on the scene. They stopped and spoke to a fisherman, who gave them fresh oysters. Lucía had never eaten them before. She could remember it still, the oyster's silky gelatinous texture, the unfamiliar, but not unpleasant taste of brine, the look of approval on her father's face. It was one of the only memories that she could conjure up of her father. Why did her mind choose to preserve that scene above so many others? Perhaps it was the look of approval from her father. Is that what she needed so desperately, approval?

"I think I *will* have one of those," said Lucía to Adam.

"But darling, they're long gone."

"Oh," she said, suddenly noticing the empty shells on his plate, "I see, never mind."

"Are you sure? I can order another plate."

"No, no, that's all right," but immediately she regretted it. "On second thought, yes, please do. I haven't tasted an oyster in years."

And sure enough, Adam seemed immensely pleased somehow. He signaled to the waiter and ordered another plate. *"Outre plat, s'il vous plait,"* he pronounced haltingly.

"So tell me," said Lucía, trying to consciously rest her thoughts from herself, her family, her past, and feeling that perhaps she had been neglecting Adam, "what is a Fates Christmas like?"

He didn't answer at once. He was looking off vacantly, imagining something, another place, times past. Lucía could see him trying to conjure it all up. It had been an innocent question, but who could say, perhaps behind his blithe façade Adam too was burdened by the past.

"I hope I haven't stirred up any dark memories."

"Oh, not at all," said Adam. "It's just that Christmas was always a rather solitary time for me. I've told you that I was an only child. My parents would always throw an annual Christmas Eve party; it was a tradition. They would fill up the apartment with friends, some of my father's business associates, the odd relative. Everyone would drink too much, sing, become rather maudlin. And there I was in the midst of it, feeling oddly detached from it all."

"That doesn't sound all that bad." said Lucía.

Adam continued, as if he hadn't heard her.

"When I was a boy, I would get up early and run to the Christmas tree in the drawing room looking for my presents and invariably find the maids cleaning up from the night before—emptying ashtrays, cleaning up spilled drinks, dropped hors d'oeuvres. My parents wouldn't emerge from their bedroom until quite late in the morning, usually hungover. I would have already opened my presents hours before, wonderful presents, splendid things. I was immensely grateful, but they seemed somehow incapable of participating in my world, a child's world of wonder, even for a moment. They inhabited a resolutely adult sphere.

"Poor Adam," said Lucía in a not insincere voice.

"Nothing of the sort," said Adam, shaking his head and smiling. "That's the thing, I couldn't have been happier. I showed my gifts to the maids and Ruby the cook, and James the butler, and Sammy who operated the elevator. I never resented my parents for their air of indifference. That was just the way they were."

"I think that it's wonderful that you are so without rancor."

"Rancor? Good heavens, I had the most privileged upbringing. All I can say is that I will be a very different sort of father. I intend to be involved in the lives of my children, all of them."

All of them. What did he mean by that precisely? Lucía looked down at her hands, her fingers laced tight. There was a lull.

"What? You do want children, don't you?" asked Adam in a mildly puzzled tone.

"Yes, I suppose," she replied unconvincingly. "I hadn't really thought about it too much. I'm only twenty. I think I'd like to live a bit without children."

"Of course, no rush," said Adam, clearly relieved "but just imagine how beautiful they'll be...and bilingual! You can speak to them in Spanish and teach them that lispy thing that you all do."

The waiter approached with the second plate of oysters and tried to place them before Adam.

"*Non, non,* Adam indicated, holding up a hand in front of his place, *pour Madame.*"

Suddenly, Lucía felt ravenous. Was it the talk of children? she wondered. They devoured the oysters noisily, followed by a succession of dishes: *côte de veau,* a *frisée* salad, assorted cheeses, and finally a heavenly *bûche de Noël.* In addition to the Krug, they drank two bottles of velvety Burgundy, and several glasses of cognac.

Two waiters were required to usher them unsteadily out the door and into a waiting taxi. Adam rolled down the window and leaned his head out. "Merry Christmas," he told them, jollily.

"Joyeux Noël, Monsieur, Madame," they replied, amused.

"Feliz Navidad," Lucía called out, but it was too late, the waiters had turned and the taxi was already pulling away.

* * *

Two days later they departed St. Lazare station on a special train bound for Le Havre, where they were to board the S.S. Normandie. Adam was ecstatic. "By the end of the week we'll be in New York."

"So soon?" asked Lucía.

"Yes indeed, it's the fastest ship on the high seas and the most luxurious. I've managed to book us a cabin in first class. I wouldn't want my wife to have anything less on her honeymoon."

Lucía didn't quite know what to say. "Yes…wonderful," she managed, determined not to appear or sound ungrateful. In truth, she was beginning to find the unbridled largesse slightly overwhelming.

When they rolled out of Paris, Lucía and Adam had had the train compartment to themselves, but just as they were getting comfortable and the bleak suburbs were giving way to open country, a porter knocked and slid open the door and showed an older couple to the seats facing them. Adam offered a clear, if perfunctory greeting, but the man and the woman either did not hear or chose to ignore him. Adam looked at Lucía, arched his brow and frowned. Lucía watched them. They were smartly dressed, she in a mink coat, which she didn't remove despite the stuffy air of the compartment, he in grey tweed, but the cut of their clothes was a bit passé. Lucía guessed that they were French, perhaps Swiss, although it was hard to say as they hadn't uttered a word to one another. No sooner had they sat then the man buried himself behind the pages of *Le Figaro,* while his wife looked blankly out the window, as if hoping to find solace in the landscape, even though there was precious little to see. A cold rain was falling and the countryside lay obscured in a winter mist. They might have been utter strangers.

"I hope that is not what becomes of us," said Lucía. She spoke in Spanish, telling Adam that the French would never understand Spanish. "They look down their noses at all things Spanish."

"I would never ignore you in such a manner; if ever I do, you may knock me off."

"What is 'knock me off'?" she asked.

"To kill me. It's a gangster expression."

"Oh, that's nice to know, although I hope it won't ever come to that."

"It won't."

Lucía was about to say something else when she suddenly caught sight of the image. There on the front page of the newspaper, which the man was holding up spread open in front of him, appeared a photograph showing a multitude of Spanish refugees amassed at the French frontier; they were being held back by a formation of French soldiers and border guards. They looked like what they were, the vanquished cast out of their land. Shattered, homeless, and hungry, they formed the very picture of misery. All at once Lucía felt like one of those people who have come through some devastating natural disaster—a hurricane, say, or an earthquake—miraculously unscathed. How tenuous was the line between survival and doom, Lucía realized. She might well have been among that horde, desperate and beseeching. Had it all been mere happenstance, or had she been somehow touched by the hand of Providence? Why had she been spared and others not?

And then the man folded over the front page of the newspaper as he continued reading, and the image disappeared from view. Adam hadn't seen it, or if he had, he didn't let on. What would he or she gain by calling attention to it? What good would it do to torment herself with the guilt of the survivor? She had been lucky, plain and simple; she had been delivered.

* * *

They stood on the quay in Le Havre, craning their necks and gazing up in awe at the S.S. Normandie. The ship's navy-blue hull, white trim, and towering scarlet and black funnels stood out against the swirling dove-grey sky. Lucía had never seen anything like it, nothing so colossal. It was hard to grasp that the thing was man-made and not some majestic wonder of the natural world.

"Just look at her," said Adam with a boyish sense of wonder.

"I'm trying, but it makes me slightly dizzy."

"It's like a floating city; it lacks for nothing." He began to read from the ship's brochure: "'The first-class dining room, illuminated with glass columns and sconces crafted by Lalique, seats 750...' We shall ignore where the lower classes feed," he added with a mock-haughty air. "There is also a grill room, an indoor pool, a theater, a winter garden, a library, a smoking room, several bars—thank goodness, and for the spiritually inclined, a chapel. One can stroll along several miles of decks, and also play croquet, shuffle board, and deck tennis." He trailed off, but continued reading silently.

Alas, Lucía would see little of it. No sooner had she crossed the gangway and boarded the ship then she began to feel ill, before, in fact, they had even set sail. She was mildly embarrassed at her weak constitution, saddened that she was disappointing Adam, but like so much else he took it magnanimously. They had the steward bring their meals to their cabin, although Lucía kept down little of the ship's excellent food. When she was feeling slightly less queasy, she and Adam bundled up against the cold and strolled the upper decks. The ocean was the color of slate, and rough, at least the look of it. In truth, the ship was so imposing, even in those boundless surroundings, that one only perceived a kind of measured listing and rolling, nothing too alarming, but disquieting enough. They stood at the rail and looked out at the perfectly-etched rim of the world.

"It makes one feel rather insignificant," said Adam, stating the obvious, thought Lucía, or was she just irritable on account of her malaise?

"I'm afraid that the only thing I feel is nausea."

"I think you just need to get your sea legs," he insisted. "In a day or so you'll feel fine."

But she did not.

On the third day of the crossing, Adam returned from a solitary lunch in the Grill Room with the ship's doctor in tow. He was a tall, older man with fine blond-white hair and eyes of the palest blue. Lucía thought that he was Nordic, but it turned out that he was a Russian, a White Russian. Dr. Perov was his name.

He stood in the middle of the cabin, a white smock open over his black suit, a black leather bag in his hand. "Your husband tells me that you are not well."

Lucía was sitting up in bed. "No, not since we boarded," she said. "I'm afraid I'm not much of a sailor."

The doctor smiled and waited. Finally, he looked at Adam and cleared his throat. "Perhaps..." he said.

"Oh, of course, forgive me doctor," said Adam. And then to Lucía: "I'll just go and have a coffee in the lounge. Then he bent to kiss her cheek and quietly slipped out of the cabin.

The doctor drew a chair alongside the bed and proceeded to examine her. Lucía liked his manner, calm and deferent. Perhaps he had once treated Romanovs, she thought. He took her blood pressure, listened to her heart, peered down her throat, gently felt her glands and breasts, and for a long time examined her eyes. All the while he spoke to her softly, asking questions not only about her health and history of assorted childhood ailments, but about her origins, her plans for the future. He knew at once, he said, that she was Spanish, but couldn't determine from where precisely. He spoke of his admiration for Goya, for Machado and Cervantes, especially Cervantes. He said that *Quijote* was a work that Russians understood as if it were by one of their own. And he lamented how her country was being torn in two. Regrettably, he too had lived through such things, he said wearily. They spoke about the sadness of exile. "One can always make a life in a new place, among new people, in a new language, but you will always carry Spain with you here," he indicated, placing a hand over his heart, "as I carry Russia with me." Then he was quiet, looking off blankly, losing focus. Lucía imagined him in some frozen landscape, clad in furs, a dacha in the background. When he turned back to look at her he was smiling.

"Madame, in my opinion, it is not the rhythm of the North Atlantic that ails you," he said. "Notwithstanding a blood test, which I strongly suggest that you have upon arrival in New York, I would say that you are with child."

You are with child. It took a moment for the slightly antiquated expression to register, but when it did Lucía felt the blood drain from her face. She would have burst into tears if she hadn't been so overcome with panic.

"Are you absolutely certain?" she asked, almost in a whisper.

"No, for that you will need a blood test, but I should add that I have never been mistaken in cases such as this. You have all the signs."

The signs, of course, how could she have been so unaware? She *had* missed her period, but she sometimes did. She had attributed it to the chaos and anguish of the last weeks. And then there was her slightly bloated belly, the result, she had naively imagined, of the rich French food and wine. Fool!

"I sense that you are less than enthused at the news."

"What?" asked Lucía absently.

"You seem displeased."

"Well, it's a shock, to say the least."

"You have been blessed."

"Have I really?" She almost laughed, but stopped herself. She would have cried if she hadn't been before a stranger. "Tell me, doctor, how far along do you think I am?"

"Several months I should say; it's impossible to be precise. There is something else, however," he added, his tone becoming suddenly somber "it's your heart. You have a slightly irregular beat, be sure to mention it to your doctor…"

Lucía closed her eyes. She stopped listening. She didn't give a damn about her heart beat. Her mind began to race with calculations, but she could have spared herself the effort. The child could hardly be Adam's;

she was too far along for that. No, it was Quim's child she was carrying, a child of the deceased and dearly departed. Death had seemed so near, so certain that night at the farm on the Ebro front, she recalled, that caution or precautions seemed somehow superfluous. But one night of lovemaking was all it had taken. The whole episode seemed so distant now, as if it had all been part of another life, which was not too far from the truth. Yet just when one imagined that the past had been abandoned, left behind, and half forgotten, back it came in a fresh guise, born anew, appearing unbidden like an awkward, unwanted guest.

When she opened her eyes the doctor was gone. She must have dozed off. Through the cabin's porthole she saw that the early winter darkness had descended. Lucía did not turn on the light, but remained lying there in the sullen shadows, contemplating her fate. There were women who might have made straight for the deck and hurled themselves in the icy depths and put an end to it all. Who knows, perhaps she would even be reunited with Quim in some watery netherworld where the drowned floated for all eternity. But she hadn't the courage to do such a thing, or rather the foolishness. No, no, Lucía thought, she hadn't given up so much to say goodbye to it all. She had a life to live and what's more, a life to give. This child which she would bear would be her everlasting link to Quim, not something misbegotten, but something blessed, just as the doctor had said.

Hours passed before Adam returned, stumbling through the cabin door, groping in the dark, cursing. Lucía knew at once that he was drunk. She could smell the liquor wafting from him in the closed quarters of their cabin, hear his fitful breathing. She feigned sleep. Adam did not attempt to rouse her or speak to her, he merely approached the bed and stood over her in silence. She could almost feel him swaying there uncertainly. The hovering unnerved her, but she could not face him, not now, not in his state or hers. Eventually, he stepped back, stumbled, and fell into a chair, muttered incoherently for a time, and finally began to snore. And that is how the interminable night progressed. She tossed and turned and called up scenes that did little to settle her mind. She imagined Adam encountering Dr. Perov in some passageway or perhaps on deck, the oceanic swells providing an unforgettable backdrop for the delivery of the portentous news.

Congratulations, Monsieur Fates!

But what on earth for?

Lucía could envision the doctor clasping Adam's hand and shaking it vigorously.

Why, you are to be a father!

What would Adam's reaction be? Lucía wondered. Would they make for the first-class bar to have a congratulatory drink, buy a round for all those in attendance, and raise their glasses to the father-to-be? Or would Adam's face sink and go pallid. Perhaps he would utter some false pleasantry and turn away sullen and confused and make for the lowly bar in steerage, where he would drown his bad luck and bemoan under his increasingly whisky-laced breath the tarnished woman that he had made his wife. Would he still want her? Would she suddenly be used goods? And what of the child? Oh, how could she possibly guess these things, Lucía thought with frustration, she was only coming to know the man.

* * *

Lucía woke to the sound of Adam whistling in the cabin bathroom as he shaved. She sat up in bed, tried to compose herself, tried to steel herself for whatever confrontation awaited her. A dull, Atlantic light pressed weakly through the porthole. The ship seemed to pitch to and fro ever so slightly, or was that just her feeling adrift in her unmoored state? When Adam emerged from the bathroom, drying his face with a towel, he hesitated ever so slightly when he saw that she was awake.

"Good morning, I hope I didn't wake you," he said, coolly, and came and kissed her on the forehead.

"No, no...not at all," said Lucía, surprised. She hadn't expected the dispassion.

Adam sat facing her on the edge of the bed and took her hands in his. "And what did the good doctor have to say?" he asked, looking at her with eyebrows raised and an unwavering stare.

Lucía looked into his eyes and tried to read his thoughts, to gauge his temper, but she could not, he gave little away. She froze, for how long she wasn't sure. All through the night she had been bracing herself for unbridled hostility. She hadn't anticipated this prosaic scene.

"Darling?" said Adam.

"Yes."

"The doctor, what did he say?" he asked again.

"Oh, nothing serious," Lucía replied, trying her best to sound poised "just your average, run-of-the-mill seasickness."

Adam looked at her without speaking, expressionless, as if he were now trying to decipher her thoughts. "Well, thank goodness for that," he said, finally. "Before you know it we'll be in New York and back on terra firma."

Lucía tried to smile as she considered this, but even she could feel the deceit quivering in her expression. She changed the subject.

"And where were you last night, if you don't mind me asking?"

"Me?" said Adam, hesitating. "Oh, I bumped into an old school chum. What an impossibly small world, eh. We talked old times in the bar. I had no idea it was so late. When I got back here you were sound asleep and I didn't want to wake you. What a terrible husband I've been. Will you forgive me?"

Forgiveness. Now there's something she hadn't been expecting to provide.

"But of course, darling."

* * *

It was a tugging and a tapping that finally roused her. Lucía opened her eyes, blinking, to find the train conductor staring down at her and tugging at her sleeve. "*Señora,* we have arrived in Tortosa, last stop." She looked around bewildered and saw that the train car had emptied. The tapping, however, persisted; in fact, it grew more insistent. She turned to look out the window and was startled to see a peculiar reflection of herself. It was her countenance all right, but the image staring back at her seemed somehow worn, more seasoned, as if she were seeing herself a decade hence. And then she heard the muffled voice come dimly from outside the window: "Lucía, it's me, Inés!"

CHAPTER SEVEN

T HEY STOOD ON THE STATION PLATFORM at the mercy of the mid-day sun, locked in an awkward embrace, as sisterly tears rolled down their near-identical cheeks. The porter stood off at a respectful remove, waiting with Lucía's bags, smoking a cigarette, dully gazing at the women. The reunion was even more emotive than Lucía had antici-pated. She and Inés had not seen one another for thirty-seven years, half a lifetime, so much had transpired. It was hard to know precisely what to say, where to begin. When they unlocked their embrace, and held each other at arm's length, Inés said: "Welcome home, sister." The tone was ironic, not entirely sincere, but it was enough.

The two of them walked arm in arm out to the street in front of the station, the porter following behind. Stark buildings of cinder block and shabby brick had sprouted up everywhere, Lucía observed; the town seemed denser. She was astonished at the traffic. The last time she had been in Tortosa one still saw horse-drawn carriages, mules and donkeys bearing loads. Suddenly she felt old.

"How is *mamá*?" Lucía asked as they walked away from the station.

"Stable."

"What does that mean exactly?"

"She is not improving, but she's not growing worse either. She can-not speak; she tries to put words together, but they all come out a jum-ble. Otherwise, she is aware, or mostly."

Lucía tried to imagine the one-sided conversation that they would have, but she could not.

"Here we are," said Inés when they came to a squat car the color of flesh. She opened the trunk and the porter deposited the bags inside. Lucía tipped the man and he touched the brim of his cap and said, "Welcome back", before walking off.

Did she know him, or was he just being polite? Lucía wondered. She stood looking at the car, smirking; it was similar to the taxi that she had taken from the airport into Barcelona. Inés must have read her expression.

"What were you expecting, the Hispano-Suiza?" she asked, sardonically.

Lucía didn't answer. They climbed in and Lucía watched her sister silently as she started the engine, adjusted the rearview mirror, and reached for the gear shift.

"What?" Inés asked, stopping suddenly and looking at Lucía.

"Nothing, it's just that I've never seen you behind the wheel of a car."

"There are a good many things you've never seen me do," said Inés, pulling onto the street and setting off.

"Whatever did happen to the Hispano-Suiza?" Lucía asked.

"It's gathering dust in the old stable."

"Is there a new stable?"

"No, we just call it the 'old' stable because there are no longer horses. Much has changed, Lucía, don't be too shocked."

She was right, of course; Lucía had an image in her mind of Quinta Amelia and all the family that resembled a sepia photograph circa 1938. She would have to brace herself. It was already a shock to see Inés so, well, heedless of her appearance. She had grown slightly thick, her makeup carelessly applied, her hair not entirely clean.

"So what became of the chauffeur? What was his name?" asked Lucía.

"Sebastián."

"Yes, that's right, Sebastián. He only came on when we were older, but I always thought that he was wildly handsome in that smart grey uniform and those polished boots."

"What he is, is wildly rich. He owns car dealerships all over the province. In fact, he wanted to buy the Hispano-Suiza. He appeared one day unannounced and at the front door no less. Wanted to pay in cash, he had a big wad of it in his fist. Borja refused, of course, out of principle."

"What principle is that?"

Inés gave Lucía a look of exasperation. "You've been in America too long. You've forgotten what life is like here."

"Thank goodness," Lucía replied dryly.

"Yes, well, for some of us it's the only life there is."

Sitting there in that tinny, insubstantial car alongside her tainted twin, Lucía pondered her own sheer good fortune. In truth, none of it had been any of her doing, not really. She felt vaguely undeserving.

They drove on, climbing one of the steep streets that led away from the river and the city center. So much looked unfamiliar or transformed beyond recognition. It was the same sensation that she had had in Barcelona, and again she wondered with a sense of misgiving if she should have come. As they approached the lofty brick edifice of the Convento del Sagrado Corazón, where she and Inés had gone to school, Lucía felt a sudden pang of relief at finding something familiar and abiding. She asked her sister to stop the car, and Inés parked beneath the high wall that surrounded the convent compound. Everything was quiet. It was Sunday; school wasn't in session, inside, a few lonely boarders, the nuns fulfilling their devotions. Lucía opened her bag and took out her cigarettes.

"Now there's something I've never seen you do," said Inés.

"I only smoke when I'm nervous."

"You're nervous?"

Lucía did not answer. She lit a cigarette and rolled down the window. "Who will be at the house?" she asked.

"Everyone...Borja and Paulina, Francisco, Javier, Victor is down from Barcelona for the weekend and so too are the twins with their families, and, of course, *mamá* and her nurse. It's a full house."

"She has a nurse?"

"Naturally, she can't do anything for herself; she needs constant attention."

"Oh, I didn't realize it was that bad."

"It is that bad."

They sat in silence, the only sound an occasional door slamming shut somewhere inside the convent, footsteps along a marble corridor.

"I've never met them," said Lucía.

"Who?"

"Your daughters, their spouses and children, Victor...I feel like some sort of phantom figure appearing out of thin air."

"Well, you certainly vanished like one."

"Yes, I suppose I did. I didn't have much choice."

Inés snickered, unnecessarily, Lucía thought, but she let it go.

"Do they know anything about me? I mean, did any of you ever talk about me, mention me in passing?"

"No, I'm afraid not. At first you were a whisper, then a silence. It was as if you were dead, worse than dead really, people talk about the dead with a certain tact."

Lucía shuddered despite the heat. This would be the general tenor of her homecoming, she knew, a succession of slights and barbs meant as retribution for her perceived betrayal. She would have to steel herself, she wasn't accustomed to such wickedness.

"I was quite happy here," said Lucía, leaning her head back and gazing up at the convent. "All those brides of Christ trying to make good submissive ladies of us, do you remember?"

"They didn't seem to make much of an impression on you."

"That's not true, in the beginning I believed it all," she insisted, staring off, recollecting. It was the Republic that changed everything. How sheltered we were. I don't know what would have become of me had it not been for the war. It was like a great awakening. All at once the Church calendar, the meaning of sin and redemption, the Creed, the lives of the saints, all of it, seemed slightly ludicrous."

Inés said nothing. Lucía wondered if she hadn't offended her inadvertently; as if to say without the war perhaps she would have ended up like her sister. She didn't know quite how to go on, everything seemed so loaded, so inclined to misinterpretation. They sat in disconcerting silence.

Finally, Inés started the engine and put the car in gear. "We better be off, lunch is waiting."

To Lucía's surprise, the entrance gate to Quinta Amelia was flung wide open, the keeper absent, and the gatehouse shuttered, but she held her tongue for fear of appearing too critical of the home that she had left behind. As they advanced up the drive past the orchards and olive groves she saw that the grass had grown too high and the trees were in need of pruning. The property wasn't ruinous exactly, just unkempt, something it had never been, or was her memory, fragmented and selective, playing tricks on her again, imagining everything from childhood to have been pristine and orderly? She wasn't sure. Then the house rose up in the near distance and Lucía knew at once that the impression of neglect was no illusion. There were tiles missing from the roof, shutters askew, cracked panes of glass in the windows, and weeds sprouting from the gutters. Scaffolding obscured part of the south wing, but no works appeared to be underway. The gardens were scarcely recognizable, the parterres ill-defined and overgrown, the flowerbeds a tangle. Lucía sighed.

"I told you much has changed," said Inés dryly.

"Yes, but I wasn't quite prepared for this."

"It gets worse. This is merely what one can see."

"Surely not everything is…" Lucía began to say, but her train of thought was suddenly cut off by the sight of Rosa standing, waiting at the foot of the stone steps that descended from the front door. Despite the years, Lucía recognized her immediately. Unlike the house, she had aged gracefully.

Inés parked in front of the house and tooted the horn to announce their arrival. Lucía hurried from the car and made straight for Rosa. The two women fell into a fond embrace, hugging one another like the long-lost friends that they were, all the while swaying gently from side to side.

"*Mi niña,*" Rosa kept repeating.

"*Amiga mía,*" said Lucía.

Inés leaned against the car, watching silently. No one from the family emerged from the house to greet them.

"Go to your mother," said Rosa, separating herself from Lucía. "We can talk later. I will ask Victor to bring your bags to your room, which is not your old room, I'm afraid, but the small extra room on the third floor."

Lucía shrugged and smiled. "That will be perfect," she said.

As she ascended the steps to the front door, Lucía looked up at the façade of Quinta Amelia. Something had happened to the place, she couldn't help feeling, something more profound than mere creeping decay. The fantastical architecture of mosaic tiles and stained glass, twisted iron and undulating lines, once a source of delight, especially for a child, now appeared strangely threatening, like the distortions of a carnival fun house. When she reached the front door, Lucía stopped suddenly, unsure whether to knock or to saunter right in, as one would to one's own house. And there was her quandary perfectly framed, she realized. Was she a proper member of the family or an intruder? Was this place really home? Inés must have sensed her predicament, for she reached past her and opened the door. *"Adelante,"* she said, allowing Lucía to enter first.

It was the smell of the place that struck her first. Despite the passage of time there clung to the interior a scent of candle wax and wild herbs, must and olives, and, faintly, the sea. In all the years of her absence, Lucía had been unable to conjure up that precise smell; the recollection of it had always eluded her. As for the look of things, she had tried to carry in her mind's eye the composition of the rooms at Quinta Amelia, all of them, every nook and corner and closet and secret space beneath the stairs. Retaining the details of this intimate domestic geography helped her to hold onto the past and her place in it. But as she gazed now at the entrance hall with its dark, heavy furniture long out of fashion, it's faded crimson velvet curtains, sweeping staircase, and hanging lanterns of colored glass, she saw that her cherished recollections were not so much erroneous, as subtly altered and out of proportion. Lucía stood for a moment taking it all in, allowing her mind to register the reality anew and dispel the faulty stuff of memory. She wondered how many more of these mental adjustments and corrections of perception awaited her.

And then Lucía felt eyes upon her, and she turned her head and saw Borja standing in the doorway to the drawing room, observing her with a smile, or was it a grimace, she wasn't sure. He hadn't aged well; Lucía could see that at once. He had never been a handsome man, but now he resembled a comically fat figure from a nursery rhyme, Humpty Dumpty, say, with his trousers hoisted high above a prominent belly, and spindly legs and diminutive feet that looked as if they couldn't possibly support his weight. A few wisps of hair were combed, to little avail, across the gleaming dome of his skull. He had a receding chin.

"Well, well, if it isn't the prodigal daughter come home at last."

"Hello Borja," said Lucía coolly.

He moved toward her, waddling slightly, and grasped her shoulders and kissed her cheeks. "America has treated you well I see. You are as beautiful as ever."

"Thank you, you too…" but he didn't let her finish. All the better, she wasn't sure exactly what she was going to say.

"No, please, don't try to return the compliment. I have grown fat, bald, and gouty, but I have other qualities."

What those were he didn't say.

"Come in, everyone is waiting for you."

When they entered the drawing room, an awkward silence fell over the room as all heads turned and eyes lifted to stare at Lucía. Arranged before her was the whole family, assembled as if in a scene from a play, waiting for the cue of the long-lost daughter's entrance on stage for the drama to be set in motion. "Hello," said Lucía, almost in a whisper, as she stood surveying the faces both familiar and unknown, before setting her gaze on her mother, who sat wheelchair-bound in front of the French doors, bathed in a sun-slashed light, looking absent and unaware. Around the room others murmured greetings and rose to their feet, but Lucía made straight for her mother, dropped to her knees at her side, grasped a hand, the skin as fragile as paper, and bent to kiss it. "Mamá, soy yo, Lucía," she said, looking into her mother's eyes and feeling her own well up. The face that starred back at her, of course, was not that of the mother who she had left behind. It wasn't the transformation that the

years had wrought—the spotted, wrinkled skin, or the thin white hair—
that shocked her, no; these were the inescapable effects of age. What filled
Lucía with a combination of heart-wrenching grief and something that
she would be loath to admit, even to herself, repugnance, was the dev-
astation that the stroke had left etched on her mother's face. Her mouth
was twisted into a kind of wretched scowl with her lower, spittle-covered
lip hanging limp and lifeless. Her head too was off kilter, drooping piti-
ably to one side, as if it hadn't been screwed on straight. Only her eyes
remained alive and unfazed, and they peered at Lucía now with a kind
of ferocity before abruptly looking away. She began to mumble something, but the garbled sounds which escaped her throat were incomprehensible, at least to Lucía. Then a hand appeared suddenly with a cloth
and discreetly wiped the drool from her mother's chin. Lucía turned to
see a woman who she assumed to be the nurse. "Thank you," said Lucía.
Although the woman wore neither a habit nor a headpiece, there was the
look of a nun about her—the hair cropped short, the absence of makeup,
the crucifix around her neck, the hushed, meek manner.

"She says that every day she has prayed for your return," said the
nurse.

Lucía heard someone behind her scoff, perhaps understandably. How
the woman could possibly decipher this heartening message from such
a register of guttural grunts Lucía did not know. What she had always
dreaded about her homecoming more than anything else was the possibility of her mother's rejection. Now Lucía watched her mother's eyes
flutter and close, and her breathing become fitful, and in an instant, she
was asleep. For a horrifying moment Lucía thought that her mother may
have expired, but the nurse spoke up: "Your mother tires easily," she said
"we must let her rest a moment before lunch."

"Yes…yes, of course," said Lucía, relieved, as she rose to her feet and
turned to find the whole family standing, watching her. "Oh, forgive
me; I didn't intend to keep you all waiting."

"We've been waiting for thirty-seven years, what's a few more min-
utes," said her brother Francisco, who was swaying between two canes
and looked as if he would topple over at any moment.

Lucía approached him and hugged his limp body to her. He smelled as if he had been dipped in gin. How little some things change, she thought.

"Forgive me," said Francisco under his breath, before sliding back into a chair.

The rest of the family, which had grown considerably larger, now lined up, dutifully offering cheeks to kiss, and gaping at her all the while, as if she were some sort of exotic species come from afar. She couldn't quite keep track of the names of the new members of the family, the children and grandchildren and various spouses, as they paraded before her...Elena, was it, Elizabeth...Manuel, Miguel, Marta, Jesús...it all became a jumble. It took her a moment too to adjust to the way the years had transformed the old ones; some had grown thick, others grey, still others slightly stooped. But it was Francisco's state which shocked her most. Of course, he had always been burdened by his lameness, but what impeded him now was clearly drink. Over the years she had read his sodden, incoherent letters, and listened too to Paco recount episodes of his uncle's binges during that distant summer, but now she saw with her own eyes just what a wasted, broken figure he had become.

Lucía took a seat on the sofa and slowly everyone settled into their places, although they did not stop scrutinizing her, looking her up and down, gawking. Countless times Lucía had tried to imagine what the initial scene of her homecoming would be like, but she had never imagined this. She felt as if she were being introduced to someone else's family.

"What about a drink then?" asked Francisco, finally.

"Yes, thank you," said Lucía with a combination of nervousness and relief. "I'd love a gin and tonic, please."

"Victor, fix your aunt a drink and refresh mine while you're at it," said Francisco, rattling his glass.

"Another?" said Borja.

"Yes, another, what of it? This is cause for celebration."

There didn't seem to be much of a celebratory spirit, thought Lucía, but she hadn't really been expecting one either.

Victor rose, took Francisco's glass, and went to a corner table where there was a makeshift bar. "Lemon, aunt Lucía?" he asked over his shoulder.

Aunt Lucía, well, no one had ever called her that before. Still, it was an acknowledgement of some sort, she supposed. "Yes, Victor, thank you, and not too much gin."

Everyone seemed to be waiting for something to flare up, something long pent up and fettered, but there was no such outburst, just a quiet, persistent lack of ease. No one seemed sure of what to say. Had all these kin really nothing to ask her? She looked around the room distractedly, trying to appear content to be back home.

"You must find all of this positively provincial after New York," said Paulina at last.

"Oh, no, not at all" said Lucía, lying. "There seems to have been great progress."

"Spain has progressed because we had the *Caudillo* to lead the way," said Borja, using the title with which the supporters of the regime fondly referred to Franco.

Victor approached Lucía and handed her her drink. "Now that he's finally dead and gone maybe we'll see some true progress," he said to Lucía, but loud enough for the others to hear.

"You and your leftist friends will only bring chaos, just like the last time," said his father.

"Please, let's not talk politics, not now," said Lucía, whereupon the silence resumed.

"I've always wanted to go to New York," Paulina said, at last "but Borja has always forbidden it, too many Jews, he says."

Lucía bristled at the comment; she had forgotten how some people spoke in Spain. "Well, you're welcome anytime. Perhaps you should leave Borja home."

"A woman alone in New York, imagine it," said Borja, incredulous.

"She wouldn't be alone, that's the point," said Lucía, smiling tight-lipped at her brother.

"What about the Jews?" asked one of the young girls; Lucía couldn't recall her name.

"What about them?"

"Don't they, well, corrupt everything?"

"No, where did you get that idea?"

"At that miserable convent school, no doubt," said Victor.

"Victor, please!" said his mother, Paulina.

Conversation was going to be fraught, Lucía realized; she would have to tread carefully. "The wonderful thing about New York is the tremendous variety, the mix of people, of cultures, of languages." She had not imagined herself defending New York, but it seemed the right thing to do. "No one ever held it against me that I was Spanish, on the contrary."

"I wouldn't think it so wonderful to mix with the blacks," said Borja.

"I have no problem with that," said Lucía, although she knew very well that she would be hard pressed to think of any blacks with whom she had any sort of true contact.

"Well, thank goodness we don't have to worry about that here," said Inés.

Lucía was trying to think of a suitable retort when Rosa appeared in the doorway. "Lunch is served," she said, smiling at Lucía.

"You've made paella! It smells heavenly. Oh, Rosa, thank you."

"Now, there's something I'm sure you can't get in New York," said Borja.

"Don't be silly. There is wonderful paella to be had in New York," said Lucía, defensively.

"Who would know how to make it properly?" asked Paulina.

"Why, Republican exiles like me, of course," said Lucía. She couldn't resist.

They filed out of the drawing room, her mother in the wheelchair silently leading the way.

It was too hot to have lunch on the terrace, where the sun was beating down on the flagstones and the air was dead still. They sat down at the long table in the dining room. Everyone had their prescribed place except for Lucía, who was given the seat at her mother's right for the occasion. The nurse occupied a stool on her mother's left, ready to feed her with a spoon and offer wine from a straw. No one paid her mother much mind save the nurse, Lucía noticed. It was as if she wasn't present, or already half dead.

"Where is Javier?" Lucía asked Inés, seeing the empty chair at her sister's side.

"Who knows?" said Inés indifferently, looking away.

"Papa called and told us not to wait," said one of the twins, Antonia or Alejandra; Lucía would have to learn to distinguish them.

"When have we ever?" said Inés.

"At least he has the courtesy to call," said the other twin.

Inés shrugged.

There was a rapid murmuring of grace. Lucía noticed that both Inés and the nurse watched her to see what she would do. She merely sat passively, waiting for the others to finish.

They passed around several platters containing mushrooms, ham, salad, and *pan con tomate*. The talk was of local politics, some trouble with new neighbors, the rising prices of things. Lucía stopped listening and let her eyes wonder about the room. Nothing had changed: the furniture, the china and crystal, the portrait of her grandfather, Jofre Grau, hanging above the sideboard. The painting was by Sorolla; her mother always said it was the most valuable object in the house. As a child, Lucía had never understood how it was that he looked directly at her no matter where she was in the room. It spooked her then; it did so still. As she listened now to the clatter of knives and forks determinately at work on plates around the table, Lucía recalled a long-forgotten scene. It was an early morning during the war. She was standing in her room, looking out the window at the garden below, where her mother was standing over one of the gardeners as he dug a hole in a flower bed. She watched for a time, wondering what they were up to at that hour. Then the gardener stopped his digging and reached for a sack at her mother's feet. There was a rattle of metal, as the man lowered the sack into the ground, and Lucía realized suddenly that her mother was burying the family silver. The Republican officers—Quim and some pompous coronel—had been around to the house the day before arranging for troops to be billeted at Quinta Amelia, and her mother feared, no doubt, that they would pillage the place. They didn't take a single thing, as it turned out, although they had defiled the chapel somewhat with some hastily scrawled graffiti beneath a statue of the Virgin.

Rosa appeared with the paella dish in hand and displayed it to the table as was the custom. There was a smattering of praise. Victor served wine to all but the youngest children.

"Thank you again for making paella," said Lucía to Rosa.

"We have it every Sunday," said Borja.

"Not like this one," said Rosa, glancing at Lucía.

Conversation waned as the loud and disorderly mechanics of properly eating paella commenced. Shrimp were peeled and sucked, clams and mussels slurped and consumed, their shells tossed aside, and rice was scraped across plates. Lucía had forgotten how ritualized meals could be in Spain. They ate strawberries for dessert. Afterward, when her mother had been wheeled away for her siesta, and the young people and children excused, it was just the siblings and Paulina left at the table. Coffee was served, then brandy. Everyone smoked. The talk became more serious. They discussed their mother.

"It's a shock to see *mamá* so deteriorated," said Lucía.

"Not when one has had to live with the slow, prolonged decline," said Inés. "You have been spared all the lesser afflictions."

It was true, but still. Lucía resented being made to feel guilty for her absence. She wanted to defend herself, but she didn't want a row, at least not so soon after her arrival.

"We must begin to make plans for the future...for eventualities," said Borja.

It appeared as if he were looking and talking only to her; Lucía sensed that the rest of them had already had this conversation of "eventualities."

"*Mamá's* not dead yet," she said.

"No," said Francisco, almost in a whisper "just eighty-seven."

He hadn't said anything for almost the entire lunch. Lucía was surprised that he had actually been following the conversation.

"She could live to be a hundred," said Lucía.

"It's not a question of years, but of her mind," said Inés. "She has become increasingly…muddled."

"I didn't notice that, I mean despite her speech," Lucía said.

"You saw her for all of an hour," said her sister, dismissively.

"I've had letters from her in her own hand that were perfectly coherent."

"Yes, well, when they begin to go, they go fast," said Borja.

"You speak of her as if she were a dog."

"No need to get nasty, dear sister," he said, archly.

"You make it rather easy."

"I think I'll leave you siblings to talk while I have a bit of a siesta," said Paulina, rising.

"Perhaps we should leave this for another moment. You must be exhausted from all your traveling," said Borja, as he pushed his chair from the table and made to get up.

"I'm not the least bit tired. What is it that you're all cooking up? I have the feeling that you are all in agreement about something."

Borja sighed and looked at the others with eyebrows raised.

"The moment of truth," said Francisco, reaching for the bottle of brandy.

"Very well," said Borja, settling back into his seat. "We think that the time has come to declare mother, how shall we say… unfit."

Lucía gasped.

"It's a legal issue, nothing more," said Inés, trying to placate her.

"Really?"

"There are decisions that need to be made, crucial decisions that mother is incapable of making," said Borja.

"Because she is, as you claim, 'unfit' or because she doesn't agree with the decision?"

No one answered. All eyes were downcast.

"What decisions are we talking about?" Lucía asked.

"Decisions involving resources," said Borja.

"You mean money."

Borja only nodded.

"Oh, I see."

"I don't think you do," said Borja. "You've been gone a long time."

"Some things, like avarice, resist the passage of time."

"Oh, listen to you," said Inés. "It's very easy to talk like that when you live on Park Avenue."

"I never conspired to attain anything."

"No, of course not," said Inés "fortune just fell into your lap, so to speak," she added, cackling, but she laughed alone.

Well, thought Lucía, that didn't take long.

"What is it about sisters at odds that seems so…beastly?" asked Francisco, his eyes closed now, as if he were deliberately shutting out the unpleasantness.

Was he in favor of whatever it was Borja and Inés were proposing? Lucía wondered. She didn't hold out much hope: a drunk is too easily manipulated, too erratic.

"I think we're getting off track," said Borja.

"Yes, it appears so," she said.

"Perhaps what I should explain is the general state of things," said Borja, adopting a pedantic tone that Lucía found insufferable; it was as if he were speaking to a child. "You see, agriculture is not what it once was, alas. The estate is struggling. You've noticed, no doubt, that the house is in desperate need of repair. At the same time, the family is growing." His voice trailed off, and he stared at the wall.

"In other words, as they say in New York, you're strapped for cash."

"I am not familiar with American argot," said Borja haughtily.

"You need money."

"Let's say that there are better ways to employ the family assets."

"Such as?"

"We have certain plans for the land."

"Do you really?"

"Yes, of course, you don't think we've been idle?" said Inés.

"From the look of it, all too idle, or you wouldn't be in such dire straits."

Inés made a sort of scoffing sound, shook her head, and looked away.

"So, tell me about these so-called plans of yours," said Lucía to Borja.

"We have large tracts of land in El Perelló and L'Ampolla, some of it along the coast. We could develop the land—hotels, holiday apartments, restaurants and bars, a club perhaps."

Lucía's mind flashed back to that turkey farm on Long Island where she and Adam stopped every Thanksgiving. What was the name of it? Sunrise Farms or Sunshine Farms, something like that. She recalled the hideous development that was going up in its place. Implacable progress, it was always the same.

"Tourism, that's the new industry. The northern Europeans are flocking here for sand and sun," said Borja, growing animated, sounding like a promoter.

The role didn't suit him; Lucía wasn't sure why. Perhaps because he didn't look like he benefited from sand and sun. She tried to imagine him in a bathing suit, but quickly abandoned the thought.

"Yes, I saw some of them on the train coming down," said Lucía. "I'm not sure where they got off."

"Probably in Salou or Cambrils, anyway, there you go. That's our clientele."

"And let me guess, *mamá* finds the idea abhorrent."

"She has certain old-fashioned notions."

"That land should be cultivated, for example?" Lucía asked.

"She cannot see the future."

"Perhaps she can see it all too clearly. It's a gamble after all, this scheme of yours, and she's already seen one fortune gambled away."

"Well, if you're going to look at it like that."

"Like what?"

"Like mother."

"So what you'd like to do is eliminate *mamá* from the picture, is that right?"

"You make it sound positively criminal."

"I don't think I could have said it more clearly."

They sat in silence, everyone looking off at nothing, avoiding eye contact. The sound of shouts and laughter came from the garden where the children were playing. Inés was fuming; Lucía could feel her rancor. Borja was harder to read, but he appeared calm. He was accustomed to getting what he wanted. He likely saw this as the first skirmish in a long, protracted war. Francisco still had his eyes closed. Was he sleeping? she wondered.

"And now I think that I will lie down for a siesta. This has all been rather a lot to digest," said Lucía. As she rose from the table, she looked at the portrait of her grandfather. "What would old Jofre Grau have said of such a scheme?" she asked, speaking to no one in particular.

"Times change, Lucía," said Borja, still avoiding her gaze.

"Yes, don't they, but some things are worth preserving," she said, before turning to go.

Just as she was leaving the dining room, Francisco called out from behind her, his voice loose, but spirited: "Lovely to have you back Lucía!"

They put her in a diminutive room on the third floor, neither the splendid part of the house, nor the servant's quarters. Never mind, thought Lucía, it was a relief not to be surrounded by the others, not to have to hear their every murmur and footfall. This was where Carlitos had liked to come and play, away from the general mayhem. It was also where Paco had slept all those summers ago. She recalled him describing the room to her in a letter and how she had felt vaguely insulted when she realized where the family had relegated him. But it had been a blessing she now saw. The room was spare, but clean, with the essential furniture and a single window overlooking the olive groves and providing a view of the peaks of Els Ports in the far distance. It suited her just fine.

Lucía undressed and lay down naked on the bed. The heat was unforgiving; the air was motionless, the birds silent. All that could be heard was the dull whir of cicadas. Lucía rolled over to find a faded photograph of herself and Carlitos propped against the lamp on the bedside table. They were posed in the garden beneath the jacaranda. It was spring, the tree in bloom. She was shocked to see this tender version of herself and her brother. She had never had any old family photographs to contemplate, she had left in too much of a hurry. It was one of the things that she had always longed for in exile. And now there she was, a young, innocent Lucía and a lost brother, staring back at her from a lost world.

* * *

All through that pivotal spring of '38, with Quinta Amelia teeming with Republican troops, Lucía had watched Carlitos grow from a mere boy to...what? Not yet a man, he was still only 14, more like a fledgling, yes, that was it, one of those small birds that suddenly learns to fly. She and Carlitos had always been close, but during that season their relationship deepened. Her brother idolized her, Lucía knew, but she found herself coming to admire him. Unlike her other siblings—Borja, with his fascist sympathies, Ines, who blindly assumed her mother's conservatism, or Francisco, whose only loyalties lay with liqueur— Carlitos seemed to embrace the Republican cause naturally. At first, Lucía thought it was mere boyish enthusiasm, but soon she became convinced that her youngest brother understood, as many adults of their class did not, the underlying justice of the Republic. Perhaps he was freer than the rest of his siblings, Lucía thought, less damaged by their father's abandonment and the loss of the Vidal fortune, which he was too young to remember. He had no recollections of Barcelona. His was a country life, rooted in the land and the rhythms of the seasons and the habits of the locals and the farm hands. He was gregarious and unaffected and passionate in ways that escaped the others in the family. And so, when the soldiers billeted at Quinta Amelia formed in the mornings to drill in the olive groves, squatting and jumping and doing pushups and the like, Carlitos was at their side and in their ranks, obeying the commands of the Sergeant just like the rest of the troops. He became their mascot, following them everywhere. They called him

Camarada Carlitos and he grew before their eyes. They talked to him about the cause of freedom, taught him all the revolutionary slogans and how to raise his clenched fist high and shout: *Viva la República!* or *La razón es la muerte del fascismo!* And Lucía encouraged it all, taught him not to be afraid to voice his convictions, to resist the urge to remain silent and complacent.

Carlitos' awakening hardly went unnoticed at Quinta Amelia. Lucía recalled one fine spring evening when the family was gathering on the broad terrace at the rear of the house that overlooked the gardens. It was one of the few spaces off-limits to the soldiers. Lucía's mother had insisted on it. The almond trees that extended in near-perfect rows beyond the far edge of the garden were in flower, and their white and pink blossoms filled the air with an almost oppressive perfume which never failed to evoke in Lucía a slight queasiness. Carlitos was the last to appear, and as he came through the French doors from the library onto the terrace, he promptly spouted some newly acquired dictum, something like, *I'd rather die on my feet than live on my knees!* Lucía couldn't quite remember the precise phrase. Whereupon their mother called him to her side and slapped him hard across the face, something that she had never done to any of them. There was a moment of shocked silence, before Carlitos fled in tears and their mother made a wordless exit, leaving Lucía, Inés, and Francisco alone and oddly disconcerted, as dusk descended and a dying light lingered on in the west. It was a long time before one of them spoke up.

"I don't think that was quite called for," said Lucía, finally.

"Really?" Inés asked. "Perhaps you're right. It would have made more sense if she'd slapped you."

Lucía stared at her sister in disbelief. How was it that they had been so inseparable as children? she wondered. Now, she could hardly fathom the fact that they were twins.

"Don't look at me as if you were surprised," her sister went on in a voice brimming with reproach. "It's you, after all, who's been corrupting Carlitos, turning him into a perfect little radical."

"Better than a fascist like Borja," she replied.

"Borja is a grown man. He can take responsibility for his political beliefs. Carlitos cannot, he is too young."

"He's old enough to know right from wrong."

"Oh, yes, just as you made so clear in your now notorious 'I have a brother' broadcast. You should be more careful," Inés warned "there are plenty of people about only too willing to silence such opinions."

It was true. Lucía knew it. Nearly every day, victims of death squads were found hanging from trees, floating in the river, face down in some gutter. It was the more intimate violence of the war, conducted far from the front, under the cover of darkness, between neighbors, and all the more chilling for its quiet, anonymous nature.

"People have lived in silence too long." It was all Lucía could manage to reply.

"My God!" said Inés, with a jeer. "That's just what Carlitos said when I confronted him, those very words. How thorough you've been."

"What of it? And what right do you have to confront Carlitos, anyway?"

"Evidently, he's been very vocal in town of late. You have emboldened him. It's dangerous."

"You know how he always wishes to please you," said Francisco, absently.

Why was it that her brother always interjected something just when he seemed so far off and uninterested in the conversation? She had thought that he wasn't paying the least attention.

"Well, he needs someone to look up to, doesn't he?" she said, but immediately regretted it.

"Hmmm…I suppose we can't all be role models, now can we?" he said.

As spring gave way to summer, Lucía found herself spending scarcely any time at all with the family. Her work translating for foreign journalists, the weekly radio broadcasts, which were becoming the talk, not merely of the town, but of the province, the entire Republic even, and the occasional excursion that she so looked forward to with Quim and

Adam, and sometimes Carlitos too, kept her far from the tensions and scrutiny of the family. Her mother did not approve of her behavior, but she could do little to stop it. Lucía didn't care what the family thought of her. Never had she felt so alive, so engaged, and so utterly in love. Quim became the center of her life.

The sun climbed to its zenith, the sky grew white. Nothing stirred, not a breath of air. When one inhaled, the torrid atmosphere scorched one's lungs. The heat sapped the life from everything and everyone, even the olive trees drooped and grew slack. Quim complained of the lethargy of the troops.

"Who would think of attacking in this heat?" asked Adam.

The three of them went to L'Ampolla and spent hours floating in the sea. When they came out of the water and lay in the scorching sand, Lucía and Quim stretched out together, Adam at a slight remove. Later, they strolled into the village and found a bar in the port where they ate inky black rice and drank two bottles of wine chilled in the sea.

"I wish we could give the troops such food, they would fight to the death," said Quim.

"Your concern for your men is admirable, honestly," said Adam.

"Apart from my mother, they are all I have."

"That's not true!" said Lucía, a little taken aback by the force of her outburst.

There was a sudden silence. She could feel herself blushing. Quim put his hand over hers on the table. It was the first sign of physical affection, trivial, but unmistakable. When Adam excuse himself and went to the men's room, Quim leaned across the table and kissed her.

"How I have longed for you to do just that," she said.

"Me too."

When Adam returned he sensed at once a subtle shift. "It seems I've missed something," he said, smiling.

They drove back to Quinta Amelia in the early evening, the sun still high in the sky. When they turned into the entrance, Lucía saw Hilario, one of the caretakers, leading a pack-laden mule up the drive ahead of them. She wondered what the mule could be hauling. It was too early for almonds, too early for carob. When the man heard the car approach, he led the animal to the side of the drive and stopped to let them pass. And then Lucía saw it, a human hand dangling down beneath an oil cloth at the mule's flank. Quim saw it too and told Adam to stop the car at once and for Lucía to stay where she was. He got out and spoke with Hilario, who didn't stop shaking his head and gesturing toward the mule and its burden. Finally, Quim lifted the oil cloth just enough to reveal a lifeless torso and a bruised and ashen face in profile.

"Good God," said Adam "it's Carlitos!"

He was interred in the Grau family crypt in the cemetery above Tortosa. Apart from the family, scarcely anyone from the wide circle of prominent friends and acquaintances attended. It was like a final indignity. Had Carlitos succumb to fever, say, or perished in an unfortunate accident, the funeral would have drawn a crowd. As it was, he had died declaiming "Bolshie" propaganda, and the social silence surrounding his death was meant to infer that he had had it coming to him. Adam and Quim attended, but they stood alone at the rear, not wishing to impose on the family's privacy. Of the ceremony Lucía recalled little, except that her family all seemed to turn their backs to her slightly, to shun her. In their eyes, she was to blame for Carlitos' murder, not the gang of anonymous fascist thugs who had set upon her brother as he made his way home from town on a summer evening, and marched him to a secluded spot among the olives and there slowly, but relentlessly stoned the boy to death. No, it was Lucía who had killed Carlitos. At the conclusion of the funeral, as soon as the family was outside the sacred ground of the *camposanto*, Lucía's mother turned to her, and in a voice that she had never heard before, a kind of vitriolic whisper, a hiss, uttered the last words that she directed to her daughter.

"I should have put a stop to your wayward Republican sympathies, your radical ideas, your disgraceful radio talk, and, worst of all, your evil power over Carlitos. You have betrayed all that you are. Henceforth, you are dead to me."

When she got back to Quinta Amelia, Lucía moved to the servants' quarters. Rosa took her into her room. They shared a bed, sleeping head to toe.

* * *

When Lucía woke from her siesta, the room was cooler and the light dim. She was relieved to be awake and once again in the present, although the almost feverish, hyper-real recollections of Carlitos' death had left her with a sensation of deep disquiet. So many years had passed, so many occurrences large and small, and yet Carlitos' murder seemed so recent, not like a distant memory at all. Perhaps this is what it meant to be haunted by traumatic events. Lucía reached for the photograph of her brother and placed it face down on the bedside table. She rose and went to the window. The sun had descended beneath the mountain peaks and the sky was a garish pink. A flutter of sparrows was soaring and swooping above the garden and groves. Behind her she heard a steady thumping of canes and a dragging of feet, as Francisco approached down the hall. Lucía quickly slipped into her dress and switched on the light. She had hardly exchanged a word with her brother over lunch and she longed to speak with him in private. She hoped that he was sober. Lucía opened the door before Francisco had a chance to knock.

"I suppose it's no mystery why I never seem to be able to sneak up on anyone," he said.

"No sneaking necessary," said Lucía, smiling "come in."

Francisco made his way through the threshold and took a seat in the only chair, exhaling loudly. "Do switch off that horrid light, would you?"

He was sweating, Lucía noticed; it must have been a strain to climb the stairs to the third floor.

"This must take some getting used to after the comforts of Park Avenue," he said, looking around as if seeing the room for the first time.

"Actually, I rather like it up here; I'm not lacking for anything," she said, taking a seat on the bed.

"This is where Paco stayed."

"Yes, I know."

"When they put someone up here in the rafters, it's to make them feel banished."

"I know all about banishment."

Neither of them said anything for a time. Outside, the evening birdsong had commenced.

"Why did you say 'forgive me', when we first greeted one another in the drawing room? Lucía asked finally.

"Did I?" said Francisco, looking away.

"Yes, you did."

"I couldn't say, really. Habit, I suppose. There's always something to apologize for."

He began to tap an index finger on his chin, as if trying to think of something, anything for which he could apologize. Suddenly, he lifted the finger in the air, indicating that he had found what he was looking for. "Ah yes, you know I can't do much to prevent all this development business, this grandiose scheme of Borja and company."

"That may well be true, but that wasn't why you apologized when I arrived."

"Wasn't it really? Well, it will have to do."

Lucía wasn't accustomed to conversation of this nature. It was as if she were speaking with a petulant child. She wondered what kind of relationship they would have had if she had never left Spain. Chances are they would have fallen out long ago.

"Why is it that you can't oppose Borja's scheme?"

"It's rather simple," he said, sighing wearily. "I depend on them for everything, you see."

"They can't hurt you."

"Oh, can't they just."

"*Mamá* would never stand for it."

"My dear Lucía, mamá will likely never *stand* again. I'm afraid Borja and Inés are right about that. Soon they will be in charge and if I don't play my prescribed part, they will not hesitate to cast me out."

"*I* would never allow it."

Francisco snickered. "Your reach from New York might not be entirely effective. I'm afraid this is not a question of principle, but of survival, mine."

He was right. For all his boozing, he had a better grasp of the circumstances than she. What did she know? She hadn't been back in more than thirty-five years. It was as if she were traveling in a foreign land and only spoke the language haltingly. She felt nothing so much as impotence.

"I don't suppose you have anything to drink up here," he asked, changing the subject.

"No, I'm afraid not."

"That's a pity. I have bottles stashed about the house, but not up here, too much of a climb and then the treacherous descent."

"I could go fetch something."

Francisco merely raised a hand, indicating for her not to bother. "You know if I weren't so impaired, I would actually go off and do something on my own," he said, looking up at the ceiling as if searching for what that "something" might be.

"Your lameness shouldn't stand in the way of that. You could look for some sort of office job."

Francisco began to laugh hysterically, slapping his lifeless legs. Lucía looked on in alarm. When he finally stopped and caught his breath, he said: "I wasn't referring to my legs. I'm a drunk, Lucía, have been nearly all my life; that is my true disability, not these useless limbs. Oh, I go off to the convent of the good Sisters of Mercy across the river to dry out now and again, but those spells of sobriety, which are worse than any torture that you could imagine, are just interludes from my habitual dissolution." He began to laugh again, but it was more restrained. "Your lameness shouldn't stand in the way...Ah, that's a good one, sister."

Lucía felt a fool. How could she be so clueless? She sat with her head bowed, looking at her hands.

Her brother took his canes and hoisted himself out of the chair with a grunt. "And with that I think I will leave you. It's cocktail hour.

Do come down and join me when you're ready, but give me a bit of a head start; I'm painfully slow on the stairs."

She let Francisco out and closed the door behind him. Lucía listened as he clattered away, and then she heard him mockingly repeat in a high-pitched voice: "Your lameness shouldn't stand in the way…" followed by a burst of derisive laughter.

* * *

Lucía did not appear for cocktails, but went instead to her mother's bedroom, where she knocked gently on the door and was let in by the nurse. Her name was Concepción, she told Lucía, but insisted that she call her Conchi. She was just giving her mother her medication, she explained, and then she would leave them alone.

"Look who's come to pay you a visit," said Conchi in that buoyant sing-song voice that nurses seem to favor.

Her mother was sitting in her wheelchair, slumped and slack, although Lucía thought she saw her eyes brighten when she appeared at her side. Conchi placed a succession of pills in her mother's mouth and managed to get her to swallow them with sips of water from a straw. Lucía looked on warily.

"Don't be alarmed," said the nurse. "The medication is mostly to allow her a good night's sleep. Rest is crucial. The key is to keep her engaged during the day. Speak to her and oblige her to speak, move her limbs, insist that she eat to keep up her strength, and to walk, even if it's only a few steps. Above all, don't lose hope. I have seen some miraculous recoveries in my time."

"Yes, of course," said Lucía, astonished. She hadn't contemplated the possibility of recovery; she had imagined her mother's condition irreversible. "Thank you, thank you for everything," she added, more animated now. "I will do precisely as you say."

"I know you will," said Conchi, nodding her head and giving her a measured look, before turning to leave and then stopping short and turning back. "Allow me to clarify something, something that I fear your siblings don't seem to understand, or don't wish to understand," she said in a tone that was halting, almost apologetic, as if she wasn't sure if she was exceeding her duties. "Your mother has suffered a stroke and she faces a long and difficult recovery, but it is principally her motor skills that have been diminished, not her mind. What I mean to say is that there are no signs of senility. In fact, apart from the stroke, your mother's health is remarkably sound for her age."

"Then she might live for years yet?"

"God willing."

"Yes," said Lucía, softly repeating a phrase she hadn't uttered in years, "God willing."

She would be just outside the door, the nurse explained to Lucía. When the two had finished their visit, she would come back in to put her mother to bed.

Lucía wheeled her mother onto the balcony where it was cooler. The sky had turned to mauve. In the fading light she massaged her mother's legs and feet, brushed her hair, rubbed cream into her hands, and all the while, spoke with her. It wasn't much of a conversation, of course, more of a monologue really, but Lucía was determined to recount and reveal so much of what had gone unsaid for decades, and she sensed that her mother was listening; she could see the flickering recognition in her eyes. At first, Lucía didn't quite know where to begin; it was like narrating an entire adult life. She decided to focus on chapters, as it were: the birth of Paco, life with Adam, discovering New York, weekends in the country, assorted friends and family, her teaching position, and, naturally, the predicament of exile. Sometimes she had the feeling that her mother grasped her every word, but at others Lucía thought that perhaps she didn't understand a thing. She wondered whether or not she was talking more for her own benefit than for her mother's. Finally, as night enveloped them, and her mother's eyes began to grow heavy with sleep, Lucía asked for something which she had always steadfastly denied she ever needed, namely, forgiveness.

She hadn't expected a reply, but suddenly her mother looked at her with an expression of pained supplication, and her misshapen mouth emitted a series of bleats, which she repeated again and again. For the life of her Lucía could not understand what she was saying. She contemplated bringing Conchi back in to interpret, but she didn't want to interrupt the intimacy of the moment. And then the labored syllables: *que...da...te,* repeated like a mantra, suddenly made sense.

"*Quedate!*" Lucía exclaimed. Stay, of course, that's what her mother wanted; she wanted Lucía to stay! Her mother nodded her lopsided head, closed her eyes, and drifted off to sleep. Lucía sat watching her, but the contentment quickly gave way to doubt. What, after all, had she meant by stay? Lucía now asked herself. To stay in the room with her at that moment? To stay on at Quinta Amelia for a time? To remain in Spain and not return to New York? What had her mother wished to express precisely? It pained her not to know.

* * *

She rose at first light and made her way quietly out of her room and down the stairs. The house was still, not a sound could be heard, the halls near-dark with only a weak glow of dawn caressing the windows. She was astonished that after so many years she still knew every odd step and turn, the boundaries of walls and bannisters. She could have proceeded with her eyes closed. On the second-floor landing she stopped suddenly and froze. There was someone in the shadows in the corner, standing dead still and silent. She felt something akin to terror.

"Who's there?" she asked, her heart pounding. She had meant to sound threatening, but her words came out choked and tentative.

A tall figure stepped forward into the half-dark. "For a moment I thought I was dreaming and seeing Inés as she might have been," he said.

It was Inés' husband Javier; she recognized him from photographs, even in the low light. She hadn't expected to meet him like this. What was he doing lurking in the shadows?

"Christ! You scared me half to death."

"I'm sorry, I didn't mean to."

She couldn't quite see his eyes, but she sensed that they were looking her over. She crossed her arms in front of her.

"It's a pity Inés doesn't take after her twin and take better care of herself."

"Perhaps you should give her a reason to."

"Touché."

He was standing in her way, blocking the next flight of stairs. Was he coming or going? she wondered. "If you don't mind, I'm going down to breakfast."

He stepped aside. "And I to bed, see you around," he said, as she brushed past him.

So he was coming, she realized.

Lucía found Rosa sitting alone at the breakfast table in the kitchen, her hands folded in front of her. She looked to be waiting serenely, with infinite patience, like a saint. There was bread baking, a *tortilla de patatas* on the counter, coffee brewing. The smells of morning in Spain.

"You're up early," said Rosa.

"I knew I'd find you here."

"And I knew that you would come. There is no one to disturb us now…or almost no one."

"Yes, I met Javier on the stairs. Are those his habitual hours?"

Rosa did not comment, but raised her brow and frowned. She got up, took two cups from a cupboard, and served them coffee.

"Still two sugars?" she asked Lucía.

"Yes," she said, smiling. "The things one remembers."

They sat at the table and spoke in turn of her mother's condition, the good fortune to have found Conchi, the growing family, the lamentable state of the house, and Rosa's health, which was robust. Lucía told her that she was more beautiful now than when she was young.

"You look like Georgia O'Keefe."

"And who would that be?"

"A very famous painter."

Rosa scoffed.

They were mentioning every subject but the one that was most on their minds. After a moment of silence, Lucía finally relented.

"It was quite a shock."

Rosa said nothing.

"Discovering that Quim was alive, I mean."

"I know what you meant."

"Have you known for long?"

"Yes, of course."

"But you chose not to tell me."

"To what end? You have a life and a family in another country. You couldn't travel here previously, even if you had wanted to. Why would I have submitted you to that torment?"

For a long time neither of them spoke. They drank their coffee and looked straight ahead, avoiding each other's gaze.

"Quim came here looking for you on Christmas Day," said Rosa, breaking the spell.

"What Christmas Day? When?"

"Christmas Day, 1938. Borja found him unconscious at the front gate. Your brother carried him into the house, put him to bed in the room you are in now, in fact, and called Dr. Romeu. He was here for weeks recovering."

Lucía could feel the blood draining from her head. She felt weak, as if she might collapse, black out. She closed her eyes and began to breath deliberately. Rosa asked if she was alright, but Lucía only raised a hand as if to silence her. Her first reaction was incredulity, surprise, but the more she thought about it, the more it made perfect sense. Of course he turned up at Quinta Amelia. It was she who had picked up and fled to Barcelona with that pack of correspondents, Adam among them. She began to make calculations in her head. The 25th of December, that was just two days after she and Adam crossed the frontier into France and left Spain behind, just ten days after they had been married. How could fate be so fickle as to allow her entire future, her life, to hinge on a mere handful of days? She had wanted to get back to Quinta Amelia, that much she could remember, but Adam had dissuaded her. Had he done so a bit too readily, she now wondered? Still, what difference did it make? She had seen the official death notice from the army, hadn't she? What was the use of all this speculation in hindsight? She couldn't keep up with it all, what was said, that is, and when precisely. So much time had passed. She opened her eyes again and looked at Rosa blankly. She did not ask her again why she hadn't chosen to tell her what she knew of Quim. *To what end?* Rosa was right.

"Have you seen Quim lately?" Lucía finally continued.

"I visited him the day before yesterday to tell him that you were coming, to give him a bit of warning."

"Is he married?"

"No, he lives alone at Cal Soler, some neighbors help him out."

"Help him?"

"Lucía...he has suffered greatly; it's a miracle he's alive."

"Yes," Lucía mumbled "a miracle."

* * *

Lucía could not remember the last time she had ridden a bicycle, and as she pedaled unsteadily now, wobbling down the gravel drive of Quinta Amelia, she wondered why she had agreed to take Rosa's on an excursion to El Perelló in search of Quim Soler. The answer, of course, was that she did not have a car, and did not wish anyone in the family to drive her and discover her destination, not yet anyway.

It was a brilliant morning, the sun still low and the air fresh, and as she rode through the Coll de l'Alba valley, she grew more confident on the bicycle. When she came to a gentle downhill stretch, she let herself glide, lifting her feet from the pedals, splaying her legs, and allowing her skirt to billow up around her. It had been a long time since she felt so... what? Not happiness, exactly, but rather giddiness. That was the word and the feeling; she felt giddy, like a girl off to see a beau. But immediately she checked herself. It wasn't a beau that she, a married woman, was going to see, but an old love who was now racked by age and loneliness.

She rode on through miles upon miles of olive groves. The trees stretched all around her, planted in immaculate rows as far as the horizon, as far as the sea. In truth, the soil thereabouts, baked by the sun until it was parched and hard as stone, was suitable for little else. Only occasionally did Lucía pass some almond or carob trees, a lone fig. Where the terrain wasn't flat, generations of field hands had built stone terraces, which rose up the steep hillsides and clung there improbably as if mocking the laws of gravity and inertia. It was remarkable how little had changed in the countryside since her youth. She still saw more mules working the land than tractors; and when she passed whole families, including small children, toiling at some task, they would stop and straighten up, and raise a hand in greeting, and watch her pedal past until she was out of sight.

Halfway to El Perelló, she stopped and sat in the shade beneath a fig tree on the side of the road and drank water from a *bota* that Rosa had given her. Without it she might have suffered sun stroke. It was only midmorning, but already the heat had grown oppressive, the landscape shimmered with it. She looked over the groves and saw a small farm house nearby; it belonged to her family, she knew, and looked much like others in the vicinity—white-washed, with a tile roof, wooden shutters in the windows instead of panes of glass, and a few palms, cypress, and fruit trees growing around the periphery. She suddenly recalled that she had been to the house once with her mother when she was a young girl of eight or nine. She remembered her mother telling her that the house was called Cal Foraster, The House of the Stranger, because it was occupied in the autumn and winter months by a family who came down every year from the Pyrenees to work the olive harvest. Her mother was in the habit of making the rounds of various of their properties unannounced and at first light, the better, she would say, for the workers to see that their patrons were not whiling away the day in bed. She always insisted that one or another of her children accompany her to understand the responsibility of being a landowner. On this occasion, it was late autumn, the harvest was on, and the wind was howling so that one had to shout to be heard above the gale. They were in a small horse-drawn trap, which her mother maneuvered with unyielding determination, not sparing the switch if she thought the horse needed coaxing. When they pulled up to the house, the family, which had been gathering olives nearby, stopped their work. The man approached the carriage, removing his hat, and proceeded to answer the questions that her mother put to him, looking at the ground, or the horse, or the sky, anywhere, Lucía recalled noticing, save her mother's eyes. The wife stood silently behind the husband, ready to step forward if addressed. A clutch of children huddled farther back still, looking curious, ragged, and of oddly indeterminate ages. When her mother had finished questioning the man on the prospects for the harvest, the appearance of blights, or the price of a mule, and was satisfied with her show of social and economic prerogative, she turned to Lucía and instructed her to hand over a basket of eggs, a bag of rice, or a side of bacon—some token of munificence from the *patrona*, Lucía couldn't recall what exactly. It was the moment that the wife stepped forward, for the man could not be seen to be accepting charity from a child. *Gracias Doña Eugenia,* the woman shouted above the wind, bowing. Her mother nodded curtly, promptly took up the switch, and off they went to the next visit.

Cal Foraster, The House of the Stranger, Lucía said to herself. She liked the ring of it.

She mounted the bicycle and rode on in to the noon heat. There was no time to dawdle.

* * *

He was waiting for her, or so it seemed from a distance. As Lucía rode up the track that led to Cal Soler, she saw Quim seated at a small table under a tree in front of the house. Only when she turned from the track into the entrance to the property did she see that it was someone else, a small, hunched man in ill-fitting clothes. Lucía suspected that he was a neighbor and she approached intent on inquiring after Quim's whereabouts. Suddenly his head jerked up. He must have been dozing, Lucía thought, and she began to apologize: "Forgive the intrusion, I was looking for…"

And then she saw it, the strong jaw gone jowly, the thick hair turned grey, and as she drew closer, the hazel eyes. The features were unmistakable. It was Quim. He rose shakily to his feet, trying to stand as tall and as unflinching as possible. She wasn't sure if she didn't let out some audible gasp or whimper. How could she not? Never had she seen a man so diminished, so much a shadow of his former self. It was as if he had been ground down somehow.

"Yes, I'm sorry to say, it's me," he said, as Lucía stood staring, speechless.

"Forgive me, I…"

"Don't apologize; sometimes I don't even recognize myself."

Lucía stepped toward Quim hesitantly and leaned in to offer her cheeks to be kissed.

"You, on the other hand, look marvelous," said Quim, as he brushed her cheeks with his lips "just as I remember you."

Lucía smiled nervously. She found it an effort to look at him without betraying a certain aversion.

"Please, sit" he said, gesturing to another chair at the table.

For days, no weeks, she had been rehearsing in her mind what she would say when they finally met—the words love and longing kept cropping up—but now that they were face to face she could not find the words. They sat in anxious silence. Finally, it was Quim who spoke.

"How is your mother? I understand that she is unwell," he asked politely.

Lucía made as if she hadn't heard. She bowed her head and looked down at her wringing hands. She tried to order the words in her mind.

"I thought you were dead," she said at last, almost in a whisper.

"People are forever telling me that. It makes me feel like a specter."

"I was *told* you were dead," she went on, louder now. "You must believe me!" she pleaded, her eyes welling up.

"But of course I believe you," Quim assured her. "Why would I not believe you?"

He reached for a book on the table—something by Delibes, she couldn't read the title, tears were blurring her vision—and from its pages Quim withdrew a telegram, faded and brittle looking, like a treasured piece of memorabilia. He unfolded it carefully and handed it to Lucía. She brushed tears from her eyes with a hand and read:

```
DATE: DECEMBER 21, 1938

TO: TRINIDAD MASOLIVER
    CAL SOLER
    EL PERELLO, TORTOSA

MOST SINCERE CONDOLENCES ON PASSING OF YOUR SON QUIM STOP
JUST DISCOVERED THE NEWS STOP
QUIM IN OUR HEARTS ALWAYS


LUCÍA VIDAL
```

Lucía hand dropped to her side, still holding the telegram between two fingers. "We searched for you for weeks," she said, looking off into the distance, as if reliving the far-off events she was describing. "in barracks and bars, canteens and hospitals, even a brothel or two."

"Who?"

"Adam and I."

"Ah, Adam…yes, I can imagine."

What did he imagine? Lucía wondered, but she didn't press the point.

Quim rose from his chair carefully and excused himself as he shuffled into the house. Lucía sat looking out over the olive trees and the lay of the land at Cal Soler. She glanced at the house—not crumbling exactly, but much in need of repair—the overgrown vegetable patch, the former hen house where nothing stirred, and the abandoned pig sty, all of it. Had things turned out differently all of this could have been hers. She almost wanted to laugh. Would she have been happy at Quim's side? She didn't wish to dwell too much on the question.

Quim returned carrying a tray with a bottle of wine, two glasses, and a dish of olives. Lucía rose and made to help him, but he shook his head. "I'm not dead yet," he said.

He meant the comment to be humorous, but it had the opposite effect. The truth was he wasn't far off. He placed the tray on the table and poured the wine with an unsteady hand, spilling a bit. Lucía looked away, pretending not to have noticed.

"To old times," said Quim, raising his glass to hers.

"Suddenly, it feels like yesterday," she said, trying to sound light-hearted.

They sipped the wine, eying each other over their glasses.

"Yes, seeing you brings it all back."

They settled back into their chairs, both reflecting, or so Lucía imagined, on events long passed, but hardly forgotten. She recalled drinking wine with Quim and Adam in the garden at Quinta Amelia, but she didn't bring it up.

"That young law student from Barcelona, the one who made me that lovely toast after dinner at the farm house on the front, what was his name?"

"Carlos Prim."

"I don't think I ever knew his name, but I recognized him immediately. We bumped into him by chance as he was looting a shop on Las Ramblas."

"Carlos Prim… looting? I can't believe it. He was obsessed with rules and regulations."

"Everyone was starving in Barcelona. He said that they hadn't been fed at the barracks

in days. He was desperate. We all were."

Quim said nothing.

"He was the one," Lucía went on.

"He was the one, what?"

"The one who told us you had been swept away by the river."

Quim waved his hand. "Stop it, don't go on," he insisted, clearly exasperated. "I don't want to hear it."

But Lucía went on, as if she hadn't heard him. "The 6th of December," she said absently.

"What about it?"

"That was the day."

"You remember the actual date?"

Lucía looked at him slightly stunned. She found the question insulting. "It is not a day I would likely forget."

A prolonged silence followed. The sun was at its peak. Even in the shade there was little relief from the heat. Lucía would have to be careful with the wine; she had a long ride back to Quinta Amelia. Still, the wine was helping to loosen her tongue and Quim's too presumably. He gazed at her for a moment in stillness.

"You did know that I was there at Quinta Amelia, no?"

"I thought that you didn't want to hear any of it."

"Answer me."

"I only discovered as much this morning."

"My, my, you certainly are discovering things late in life. It must be quite a shock," he said, his tone almost mocking.

"As a matter of fact, it is," she said, annoyed.

"I'm sorry, there's no reason why you should have known about any of this."

"I certainly would not have imagined that it would be Borja who took you in, Borja of all people."

"Yes," said Quim, nodding "Borja is full of surprises."

"Why *did* you go back there, to Quinta Amelia, I mean?" She regretted the question as soon as she posed it. Now it was Quim who gave her a look of reproach.

"That was our plan, wasn't it?"

It was.

* * *

Quim came to on that remote Christmas day enfolded in crisp laundered sheets the likes of which he had never known. He felt euphoric, but relaxed, so, so relaxed, as if he were floating on air. The pain in his side was gone. And there was a man looking down at him, a pleasant looking sort with grey pomaded hair, a well-kept goatee, and dark, slightly blood-shot eyes peering from behind wire-framed glasses balanced atop a sharp, rather prominent nose. His breath reeked of brandy. Someone coughed, a delicate feminine cough, and Quim realized that there was someone else in the room. He turned his head to look over the bed to a far corner where a woman stood silently in the shadows. She looked vaguely famil-iar to Quim, but he couldn't quite place her—an old friend, a distant relative—he was not sure. He looked back at the man. "Who are you?" Quim asked weakly, his voice little more than a whisper.

"I am Dr. Romeu."

"Where am I?"

"You are at Quinta Amelia, the home of Doña Eugenia Grau and the Vidal family."

Quim smiled. "And where then is Lucía Vidal?"

A gasp came from the corner and the doctor closed his eyes and frowned in irritation. "That is enough questioning for the moment," he insisted gently. "I have removed a bullet from your side; that is what was causing such high fever. Now you must rest. I have given you morphine to ease the pain."

Quim wanted to speak, to ask again after Lucía, but he could not, his mouth would not form the words. His eyes were drawing closed, the lids as heavy as lead, and he could do nothing to prevent it.

The days that followed were long and indistinguishable as he lay languishing in a narcotic daze, falling in and out of consciousness. Morpheus filled his dreams with a confusion of figures distorted and out of context, so that his mother appeared not to recognize him, his brothers to taunt him, and a beloved childhood teacher to examine him wordlessly. He saw Lucía as a child and the soldiers from his col-umn as stooped and wizened old men. Again, and again, he would find himself on a mountaintop where his dead father was waiting for him with something urgent to tell him, but when he opened his mouth there appeared a deep black void from which rose the roar of a fierce wind. These indecipherable dreams tormented Quim, but when the morphine wore off, the torment in his side was worse still, until he was given another dose and the madding cycle resumed. And then one day the pain had mostly ceased, but Quim demanded the morphine regardless, beseeched Dr. Romeu to give him a dose, but the man said no and turned away and left the room, locking the door behind him, and a new sort of torment began that left him at turns raving and docile. All the while he called out for Lucía, pleaded with the doctor to let him see her, asked the servant girl Rosa to relay a message to her that he was a prisoner at Quinta Amelia, a captive in her very own house. But she never came. Who did appear sporadically and always hopelessly drunk was her crippled brother Francisco. He would hobble in, unsteady on his crutches, and talk nonsense and bluster and curse Quim and the country and the war and his slack, lifeless legs. When Quim tried to question him about Lucía, he would cry and utter something incomprehensible and childish as if he were still with her in the nursery, before staggering out.

At last a day dawned and Quim found that he was calm and lucid again, although strangely broken, like a wild horse that finally submits to the saddle. In the afternoon, there was a knock at the door and in walked not Rosa or Francisco or Dr. Romeu, the only people he had seen in days, but a Nationalist officer, a captain of the cavalry, wearing breeches and lustrous riding boots and three gold stars on his sleeve. Quim froze. Never had he felt so helpless, so exposed. He could not breathe for panic. For days he had heard distant artillery and planes flying over the house, rattling the panes of glass in his bedroom window, but he never imagined that the rebels would have advanced quite so quickly. The retreat must have been headlong and desperate. The Republican cause, he knew at once, was lost. The officer stood at the foot of Quim's bed and looked at him directly, his face expressionless. He was short, the kind of lack of stature that doesn't go unnoticed, so that if Quim too had been standing, he would have loomed over him as with a child. What, Quim wondered, had this diminutive man done precisely to rise to the rank of captain of the cavalry? His wavy sand-colored hair was brushed back from his forehead. There was something ill-defined about his face, perhaps it was the weak jaw or an excess of pudge. Above red, rather sensuous lips, rosebud lips, there was an attempt, not altogether convincing, at a moustache. His eyes were narrow, as if he was perpetually squinting, and Quim could not make out their color. Although his uniform was impeccable, somehow, he did not fit it adequately. His shoulders sloped and his chest was slightly sunken. He reached into a side pocket of his tunic and removed a silver and gold cigarette case and a lighter. He opened the case, removed a cigarette, and then moved to the side of the bed and held the case open to Quim. It had been weeks since Quim had smoked and he longed for a cigarette. After hesitating briefly, he accepted. When the officer bent to offer the flame from his lighter, Quim observed beautiful, manicured hands that might have belonged to a surgeon. The two men smoked, eying each other silently.

"How are you feeling?" the officer asked at last.

"I would have thought that you would rather see me dead than ask after my health."

"I make it a point of being considerate to anyone who is a guest in my house."

My house. Christ, thought Quim, this was Lucía's brother, the one who had run off to join up with Franco and his lot. Lucía had spoken of him with shame. "I see," he said, looking at him for traces of Lucía but finding none. "So, you must be Borja."

"That is correct."

For a moment neither man spoke. This was the closest Quim had ever been to the enemy, he realized, closer even than that unfortunate young soldier who he'd had to shoot along the riverbank. He wondered if he would be able to kill this man, the brother of the woman he loved. He doubted it. "Would it be too much to ask why Lucía has not come to see me?" he finally asked.

Borja Vidal pulled up a chair alongside the bed and sat down unhurriedly. Quim watched him tug at his cuffs each in turn, smooth the front of his tunic with one of those fine hands, and pick a piece of lint from a leg of his breeches. Only then did he begin, looking not at Quim, but out the window at the leafless branches of a poplar. "From what I gather Lucía has managed to make her way to New York, to Park Avenue no less. In the manner of the Americans I believe that she is now known as Mrs. Fates."

Quim's heart seized and seemed to weigh him down, to push him into the bed. He felt himself gasping for air. He tried to speak, but he could not. He wanted to lash out at Borja, to point out the absurdity of what he was saying, to accuse him of fabricating the tale so as to thwart his and Lucía's love. He began to sweat, a cold panic-stricken sweat the likes of which he had only felt during the interminable instant before a battle, when time hung suspended and immeasurable. He closed his eyes in an attempt to think more clearly. It couldn't be true, he thought, not with a woman like Lucía, not after the love that they had professed and sworn in the face of every conceivable obstacle. No, no, no, what this man was saying was a deliberate ploy. Hadn't Lucía always said that her brother Borja was a damaged soul, cynical and sinister, that he enjoyed torment? Well, here was yet more proof, confirmation of what Lucía had claimed. At the time, Quim had found her judgement shocking, surely, she was exaggerating, he remembered thinking. For his own brothers he had felt only the deepest love and camaraderie. Now he could see what Lucía was referring to. Like an evil figure in a fairy tale, Borja was wicked. And yet he could not help but contemplate what he had heard. His mind raced, attempting to refute the news, or to fathom it. *Adam Fates,* he repeated the name to himself again and again, conjured up the man's face in his mind's eye, recalled how they had met, and remembered fragments of conversation that they had had. And suddenly, nothing of what Borja said seemed quite so fanciful.

* * *

Quim recalled the spring day that Adam Fates first turned up at Quinta Amelia where he and his men were billeted. Some overly eager commissar from regimental headquarters dropped him off along with a few other journalists, Yanks and Brits mostly, with the aim to show them how the Republican troops were living side by side in harmony with the local population. This, of course, was a fiction, at least regarding the Grau-Vidal clan, most of whom treated the troops with undisguised disdain, but the commissar, a young officer, younger even than Quim, delivered those very words—*living side by side in harmony*—without a hint of irony. Quim remembered being annoyed, at least initially; he didn't have time for propaganda, what with trying to get his men to learn to shoot straight, to become familiar with the terrain, and to submit to a measure of discipline. But his reluctance soon faded when he got to know these foreigners who had come from so far, risking their lives to tell the world what was at stake in Spain. They were so open and earnest, Quim discovered immediately, so forthright, not like most Spaniards at all, who were forever hiding something, or saying one thing yet doing another, or conspiring against whatever authority reigned at the moment. He especially remembered Dos Passos and Capa, and Martha Gellhorn, the bravest woman he had ever met, and, of course, Adam Fates. He was the one Quim liked the most. There was something about the man, it wasn't just his physical presence, his towering height, which he never used to lord over one, but rather a quiet intensity that came from within. He was always calm and unruffled, but at the same time determined. And there was something else, perhaps it was an American trait, certainly it was astonishing to a Spaniard; he treated everyone equally. He was just as polite to Lucía's mother as he was to Rosa the maid. Quim felt drawn to him instantly. The only problem was Adam's Spanish, which was rudimentary at best, and on account of it, their conversations were halting and tedious. It was then that Quim asked Lucía Vidal, whom he had heard chatting in English with Gellhorn, if she would consider serving as an interpreter, and he was surprised and delighted when she readily agreed. For weeks thereafter, Quim, Adam Fates and Lucía Vidal became inseparable; they worked well together, setting off to visit regular army units and columns of the International Brigade, comprised of volunteers from France and the U.S., Britain and Germany, Belgium and Ireland, Yugoslavia and the Netherlands, Cuba and Mexico, all of them still jaunty, full of idealistic fervor, and confident of victory. Those were heady spring days. When they weren't working, the three of them took excursions in the vicinity, to Miravet Castle, to the Cistercian monasteries of Poblet and Santes Creus, or to the sea, where they swam in the still frigid waters and lay afterwards in the warm sand and almost managed to forget about the war. All the while, Quim watched as Lucía blossomed before his eyes. He could see that she felt engaged, useful, and had been won over to the Republican cause, something uncommon for a young woman of her class and social standing. At first, she confined herself to merely translating Quim's statements for Adam, but soon she began to offer her own insights and perspectives, and Quim found himself learning from her, admiring her intelligence and the workings of her mind. Then came the radio broadcasts. He had been against the idea, but he couldn't help but admire her commitment, her willingness to renounce so much for what she thought was right. How could he *not* fall in love with such a woman? Quim admitted as much to Adam. He recalled the moment perfectly. They were sitting in the garden at Quinta Amelia, drinking wine as the soft evening light set the world aglow. Lucía rose to fetch another bottle and both men watched her silently as she lithely climbed the stone steps to the house. Even in fatigues, Quim remembered thinking, she somehow looked alluring. He did not speak easily of his emotions, but there was an openness about Adam that invited confidence, that, combined with the intoxicating effects of the wine and the light, prompted him to abandon his inhibitions.

"I am falling in love with that woman," Quim offered.

"Yes, I can see that," replied Adam, turning to Quim and nodding knowingly. "All I can say is that you would be a fool not to. I have never met a woman quite like her."

"You make it sound as if you were the one in love," Quim shot back, a bit too defensively, he realized at once.

"If it weren't so obvious that she is crazy for you, I would have tried to steal her away weeks ago."

"You think she feels something for me?"

"Good God, man, are you blind?"

Quim smiled. "Yes, I suppose I am. Isn't that how the song goes?" And then a shadow seemed to descend over him. "Still, I worry," he added nervously.

"What about?" Adam asked.

"So many people have seen us together," said Quim. "They have watched Lucía collaborating enthusiastically with the Republican effort. They have surely tuned into her radio broadcasts. *Lucía the Red* is famous and they know just where to find her. What do you think would become of her if the Republic were to fall and the Fascists were victorious?"

"Yes," Adam acknowledged "I see what you mean."

"Do you?"

"Yes, of course, there would be reprisals."

"Reprisals?" repeated Quim incredulously. "She would be shot."

The two men fell silent. The evening was full of birdsong. It was hard to believe that there was a war on. Finally, Quim spoke. "We are friends, are we not Adam?" His tone was vaguely imploring.

"Yes, of course we are," Adam replied.

"Then promise that if I am unable to be at her side, to protect her, you will do whatever it takes to get Lucía out of harm's way."

Adam was contemplating this when Lucía appeared in the distance, descending the stairs, a bottle of wine in each hand. Both men were watching her approach, but she was still out of earshot.

"Promise me," Quim repeated, his voice low, almost a whisper.

"Yes," said Adam, without taking his eyes off Lucía, "I promise."

"And do make sure to let me know where you've taken her. You will do that, won't you?"

"Yes," Adam repeated, absent-mindedly "yes, of course."

"Now what have you two been talking about?" asked Lucía as she reached them. "You both look positively spooked."

"Love," the two men answered in unison.

Oh, how could life be so tangled and tortuous? he now thought as he lay helpless in a bed in the house of the woman he loved, a woman now far away and married to his...friend was it? He could not even fully grasp the convoluted plot of it all, and yet it appeared to be true.

He felt like the hapless character in some picaresque novel—something by Quevedo or Cervantes, say—whose destiny is ruled by a cruel and inscrutable twist of fate. *Promise to get Lucía out of harm's way.* Well, well, Adam Fates had done that admirably, hadn't he? What a fool he had been, Quim realized, what a complete and utter fool.

In all his agitation, Quim had almost forgotten that Borja Vidal, the enemy, was sitting at his bedside. He stared at Lucía's brother, trying to guess what this man had in store for him, but his expression was indicative of nothing so much as tedium. He did not look like a man who was plotting another's execution, or so Quim hoped. "What do you intend to do with me?" he asked finally.

"Now, you see, I have been thinking long and hard on that very subject, what to do with you," said Borja with an air of mock solemnity.

He was pretending to pick lint from his impeccable uniform again, Quim noticed. Nothing he did or said seemed genuine.

"I do not wish to sully my hands with the blood of the man who my sister loved, however unseemly that love affair may have been." He laughed suddenly, a laugh full of ridicule. "Really," he added contemptuously "did you think that she was going to live her life with an olive farmer, scraping by in the backwater that is El Perelló?" He did not expect or wait for a response. "I am astonished by some people's capacity for self-delusion."

Quim chose not to respond to this barb. "I don't suppose you would allow me to return to my unit."

"Your unit?" Borja repeated in disbelief. "I'm afraid that you have missed a good deal while bedridden with us. There is no unit, or column, or company, or battalion, or brigade, or army. The Republic is finished. I don't wish to sound overly dramatic, but we are on the brink of a new dawn, ushering in a New State," he proclaimed with false fervor before his tone grew cynical again "which, of course, is the Old Spain, but without most of your red comrades."

Quim looked away, not wanting to give this man the satisfaction of seeing the profound disillusion that must have been etched on his face. "I take it that I am to be spared."

"Does that surprise you?"

"Lately, I am beyond surprises," said Quim glumly.

"Yes, I can well imagine. But you see, even I am not thoroughly rotten; I too am capable of a measure of compassion…on occasion."

"I suppose I should thank you."

"I suppose you should, but don't get your hopes up. You may leave this house freely, but I will do nothing to protect you once you are outside the gates."

There came a muffled clatter from outside the door, both Quim and Borja heard it.

"That would be Francisco, I suspect, always hobbling about and eavesdropping," said Borja. "Best watch out for him." And with that he rose and looked down on Quim with an expression close to pity. "Good luck to you, you'll need it." He then strode to the door, the metal taps on the heels of his boots clicking smartly, opened it, and stood still, silently looking at something or someone that Quim could not see. Then Borja stepped out without a word, leaving the door wide open. Suddenly Francisco appeared in the threshold, slouching unsteadily against the door frame. He was drunk, Quim could see at once, but then realized that he had never seen him in any other state.

"Good afternoon," Quim offered sullenly.

"Truly? Tell me, what's so good about it?" Francisco slurred.

"Well, it seems that I am to live, at least for the moment."

"Is that so? I for one think you should die," he said matter-of-factly. "Would you like to know why?"

"No, I don't think I would."

"Still, I will tell you." He was silent for a moment, his head lolling and his eyes closed, and then he took a deep breath and continued. "Because you drove her away. If it hadn't been for you, Lucía would still be here. My only consolation is that if we are not to have her, neither shall you." And then he gathered his crutches and teetered off, mumbling incoherently as he went.

At nightfall, Quim climbed out of bed, dressed in his uniform, and quietly made his way down the back stairs and out the kitchen door.

The night was bitterly cold and the wind was blasting fiercely through the olive groves, causing the branches of the trees to lurch and pitch wildly. With the war on, no one had seen to harvesting the fruit, and there were dark shadows under the trees where the olives lay unpicked. The air was ripe with the mildly rancid smell of them. Quim stayed off the gravel track and kept to the inky shadows under the trees as he headed away from the house. He did not turn to take a last glimpse of Quinta Amelia. With Lucía gone, he thought, the place was dead to him. When he reached the entrance, he was surprised to find the gate slightly ajar; he slipped through, closing the latch behind him with a creak. Quim turned north toward El Perelló, bound for home, intending to make for Cal Soler where he hoped to find his mother and refuge. There he could hide out before deciding where to go and what to do. During the last year, his plans had always included Lucía, but now that she was out of reach and out of his life, he felt lost and unsure, or worse, indifferent as to what lay in store. He hadn't taken more than a dozen steps before a dark figure appeared before him in the road. "Halt!" came a dim voice that seemed to have been swallowed up by the wind. And then there were other shadowy figures closing in on him, and he knew that he was doomed. Despite the chill of the night, Quim could feel the sweat at his temples. He was afraid; it wasn't the fear that overtakes one before battle, but something closer, more intimate, like a childhood fear of the dark. His mind jumped to Borja Vidal. What was it that he had said? Quim tried to recall. Ah yes. *I will do nothing to protect you outside the gates.* When the blow came, it did not take him by surprise; he was expecting it, almost desiring it. There was a dull thud and a paralyzing pain at the back of his head. He dropped to his knees and fell face first into the frozen ground.

* * *

"You're sweating profusely, perhaps we should go inside," said Lucía.

"What?" said Quim, dazed from his reverie.

"The heat," she said "we should move into the house. We're going to get sun stroke."

"Yes, of course," he said, rising carefully to his feet. "We shall carry on inside."

Quim insisted that Lucía sit at the kitchen table while he prepared a light lunch of salad, cheese, and plums. She watched him move about the space sluggishly, but with a certain practiced assurance. It was, after all, the house he had been born in. There was something about the way he focused on the tasks at hand, a simplicity and economy of movement that was so quintessentially Old World, Mediterranean even. One did not usually find such scenes in America. She couldn't say why really, couldn't put her finger on it, but she found herself suddenly overwhelmed with a sense of nostalgia and contentment. Lucía was happy to be back, happy to be with Quim.

The talk grew less pointed, not so consumed with the traumatic events of the past. Quim inquired about the States, and Lucía spoke of the peculiarities of American customs and politics, the dynamism of New York, her work, and Adam's travels. She found herself touching upon everything, in fact, except her son, Paco. Finally, it was Quim who broached the subject.

"Any children?" he asked, matter-of-factly.

"What?" said Lucía, her voice cracking.

Quim looked at her with a puzzled expression. "Children, do you have any?"

"Oh, yes, of course," she said, trying to sound composed. "I have a son, Paco."

"How old is he?"

"How old?" Lucía repeated unnecessarily. It was the most innocent of questions and there didn't seem to be anything calculating in Quim's voice or manner, but she felt herself grow flush. She should have anticipated this conversation, Lucía thought, practiced it, in fact, before the mirror. She quickly decided to shave a year from Paco's age, just to be safe. "Ah, let's see, in August he'll be thirty-eight."

"Just the one?" Quim asked.

"Yes, just Paco."

She watched Quim carefully. He couldn't possibly suspect anything, Lucía thought. Still, she was determined to steer the conversation elsewhere. "So what of your life?" she asked. The question was borne of equal parts panic and courtesy, but even to her ears it sounded ludicrous under the circumstances.

"My life?" Quim responded, confounded. He began to laugh before succumbing to a violent fit of coughing and wheezing. Lucía didn't know quite what to do. She tried to offer him water, but he waved her away. When at last he recovered his composure, he said: "Lucía, my love, I don't believe that my life, at least since I saw you last, is really the stuff of polite conversation."

She could hardly blame him, of course, but Lucía pressed him all the same. She wanted to know the truth, wanted to face the grim reality— or the recounting of it anyway—of all that she had escaped. And so Quim relented and began to narrate a tale of unremitting woe, describing in lucid detail the appalling conditions of prison life and forced labor, the relentless hunger, the numbing cold, the disease and despair. He did not raise his voice, did not speak in a tone of mordant indignation, but rather chronicled everything in a measured, dispassionate manner that struck Lucía for its utter lack of rancor.

"You don't seem particularly angry or bitter," she said, perplexed.

"I am beyond anger and bitterness. I am simply trying to cling to whatever meager life is left in me."

"Have you seen a doctor?"

"There is little that modern medicine can do for me, I'm afraid. It's silicosis that I'm suffering from, the result of excavating in that godforsaken mountain. We all contracted it to a greater or lesser extent. I've been lucky, believe it or not, many others died from it. They dug their own graves." He stopped speaking for a time, as if he were silently recalling those lost companions who never made it off the mountain. "The hardest thing to bear was the near perpetual darkness," he went on. "We led sombrous lives, so that after a time we became like certain nocturnal animals: bats, owls, lemurs... To never feel the warmth of the sun, to never see the play of natural light on the simplest objects, to never look up and find the sun suspended in the sky, that is my notion of hell."

Lucía pressed him no further. She shuddered to think of the hell that she had been spared.

They ate lunch at the kitchen table, but Lucía found it hard to savor anything. They scarcely spoke. When they had finished eating, Quim got up to make coffee.

"How exactly do you get around?" she asked.

"Get around?"

"Yes, to do your shopping, to visit the doctor or the local bar."

"I don't. This is my world now. My neighbors, the Curtos, lend me a hand from time to time, especially their daughter Estela, who brings me my groceries, but otherwise I don't really see anyone or go anywhere," he said without a trace of self-pity.

"Does she drive?"

"Who?"

"This Estela woman."

"She's eight years old."

"Oh, I see."

"It's funny, when I think about it," said Quim "but I don't believe I ever got around so much as when you, Adam, and I went off on those excursions to the sea, or to visit a monastery, or some village. I rather miss that."

In the late afternoon the heat subsided. Lucía said that she would have to get back to Quinta Amelia. She had been gone all day: they would be worried. Quim walked out of the house with her to see her off. They were strolling slowly toward the track, Lucía pushing the bicycle beside her, when Quim stopped suddenly.

"Adam..." said Quim, hesitating for a moment, as if pondering the question even as he was asking it, "has he been a good husband to you?"

She wanted to be truthful. "A woman couldn't ask for more."

"I'm glad," he said, then added, "that's why I made him promise me to look after you."

She had been listening half-heartedly, the wine had dulled her senses and it took a moment for the statement to sink in.

"What does that mean?" Lucía asked, a note of agitation in her voice.

"Oh, just that. We had a pact, so to speak."

There was a look of contentment on Quim's face, as if he were enjoying this late revelation.

"If anything was to happen to me. Adam was to take care of you, get you out of Spain. I must say, he certainly kept his promise."

Lucía did not say anything more, she was too astonished. She mounted the bicycle and rode off silently.

"Come back and see me again," Quim called after her. "I'm always at home."

As she rode back to Quinta Amelia, Lucía could not stop thinking of Quim and Adam's so-called pact. Why had Adam never told her as much? The whole notion seemed to call into question Adam's love for her. Was it genuine, she suddenly wondered? Yes, of course it was, she told herself. Perhaps Quim was inventing the lot. What difference did it make, really? She had been spared, that was the important thing. It only made her think all the more of the tragic waste that was Quim Soler's life. How doomed he had been to have gotten entangled in the web of the war and its dreaded aftermath. How blessed she had been to escape it. She tried to imagine what would have become of her had she too been sent to prison or a camp to toil at some soul-grinding task that would have left her as unrecognizable as Quim, so that upon encountering someone she had known from her former life, she too would have to say: *Yes, I'm sorry to say, it's me.* All at once Lucía grasped the cause that would shape her immediate future. How long she had lived without one! She resolved to devote herself to Quim's final days, Quim's and her mother's. She would live for them, providing succor and at least a measure of the love that had long been denied them. That would be her sole purpose. *Stay,* isn't that what her mother had implored with those strained, misshapen syllables? Well, so it would be. She certainly had the time, a whole long, hot summer stretched before her with no real commitments. The new academic year would not begin until mid-September. Yes, that is what she would do, she convinced herself as she pedaled faster. She would stay.

CHAPTER EIGHT

A FITFUL NIGHT'S SLEEP, full of incessant tossing and turning, did nothing to dampen Lucía's enthusiasm for her new…what was she to call it, this new-found sense of purpose that had overcome her? Activity? No, that sounded too much as if she were bent on taking up gardening or needlepoint. Vocation was too detached, pastime too trivial. No, what had gripped Lucía was more like a calling; that was it. To care for Quim and her mother above all else would be her new calling.

By seven o'clock, Lucía was bathed, dressed, and sitting in the breakfast room waiting for her sister. Inés appeared at last just after nine, still in her robe, a cigarette dangling from her lower lip, her hair a tangle.

"Good morning, Inés."

Her sister ignored her.

"Do you have any plans this morning?"

"At the moment, the only plan I have is to drink a strong cup of coffee." She served herself a cup from the coffee maker on the counter, sat down opposite Lucía at the table, rubbed her eyes, and looked at her sister wearily through blue-grey ribbons of smoke. "My, aren't we chipper this morning."

"Yes, well, I need your help."

"Do you really? It's been a long time since you have; wouldn't you say?"

"Oh, don't start," Lucía said, her tone pleading.

"Start what?"

How easy it was to get off track when she spoke with her sister, Lucía thought. "Didn't you say that Sebastián…"

Inés cut her off. "Sebastián who?"

"Our former chauffeur."

"Him again?"

"No, or rather yes. Didn't you say that he had a car dealership?"

"Did I? I suppose I did. He does."

"Good, will you drive me there?"

"What for?" her sister asked.

"To buy a car, of course."

"Why of course...when did you decide on that?"

"Yesterday."

"You Americans, so impulsive," she said with a smirk. She looked pleased with herself for the comment.

"Will you?"

"What on earth do you need a car for?" Inés asked. "You're only going to be here for ten days."

"Actually, I've decided to stay on a bit."

Inés tilted her head to one side, squinted, and pursed her lips. Lucía had seen this very same exhibition innumerable times in childhood. How little people change, she thought.

"What do you mean stay on? For how long?"

"I'm not sure, not permanently, to be sure, but at least through the summer."

"Did you decide that yesterday too?"

"Yes, in fact, I did."

"While on your mysterious excursion, I suppose."

Lucía did not answer. She didn't like her sister's insinuating banter. "Will you take me or not?" she asked dryly.

"Yes," said Inés, as she stubbed out her cigarette slovenly in her saucer, "after my bath."

It was nearly noon and steamy by the time the sisters walked into S. Amat Autos, but the showroom, despite its floor to ceiling windows, was crisp and cool. Somewhere an air conditioner was humming softly. The place smelled of gasoline, fresh paint, rubber, and something else that Lucía couldn't quite identify. Success was it? Parked at various angles around the showroom was a bevy of shiny cars, looking at once captivating and slightly stagey for being parked incongruously indoors. It was as if they wanted out.

A young receptionist with blue-black hair and a pinched face sat behind a desk filing her nails with the utmost concentration; she did not get up to greet them, or indeed, acknowledge them in any way. Lucía approached the desk: *"Buenos dias,"* she said. The woman raised her eyes to Lucía's and repeated the greeting listlessly before returning her attention to her nails. Inés strolled aimlessly amongst the automobiles.

"I would like to see Sebastián, if you don't mind," said Lucía.

The woman looked up at Lucía. "You mean Señor Amat?"

Lucía had never known his surname. "Yes, I believe so."

"What is it in regard to?"

"Buying a car, of course," she said coolly. "You do sell cars, do you not?"

The young woman sat up suddenly. "Yes, naturally, one moment please." She picked up the telephone receiver and dialed awkwardly with a perilously-long lacquered nail. "Sr. Amat, there is a woman here to see you." She covered the mouthpiece with her hand and asked Lucía: "Your name please?"

"Lucía Vidal."

Inés approached Lucía and whispered in her ear: "Don't be surprised, this is Spain, women do not walk into showrooms and buy cars."

"It appears not," said Lucía.

An older man soon appeared from a rear office, buttoning his suit jacket and smoothing his hair with a hand. Although he had gone grey and put on some heft, Lucía recognized him immediately. He looked rather distinguished in a cream-colored linen suit and a robin's egg-blue shirt with an open collar.

"I thought it might be a mere coincidence in the name," the man said, as he approached, smiling broadly "but I see it *is* you, welcome *señorita!"* He bowed his head slightly as they shook hands.

"Señora," Lucía corrected him.

"Of course, forgive me, just an old habit."

"How nice to see you again, Sebastián. May I still call you Sebastián?"

"Please do. You are here visiting?"

"Yes, an extended visit," she said.

"Wonderful." He then looked at Inés and seemed at a loss as to what to do.

"You remember my sister Inés."

"Of course," he said, smiling nervously in her direction.

Inés nodded, almost imperceptibly.

"Tell me," he said, focusing his attention back on Lucía. "How may I be of service to you?"

"I would like to buy a car."

"Ah, splendid, did you have a particular model in mind?"

Lucía hadn't really thought about it. Adam had taught her to appreciate fine cars, the sound of their engines, the smell and details of their interiors, their distinctive lines. Every so often he even allowed her to drive the Bentley. She knew for certain that she didn't want one of those diminutive Spanish models—a Seat was it?—of the type that Inés drove, although, of course, she would hardly say as much. She hesitated.

"What, if you don't mind me inquiring, do you drive in…America is it?"

"Yes, America…" she was about to say *a Bentley,* but she thought that it sounded a bit too pompous. "A Mercedes," she decided, elegant, but not too rarefied.

"An excellent automobile," he said, his eyes growing wide. It just so happened that he had recently acquired a very special Mercedes-Benz, he explained, pronouncing the name with a flourish. The car had belonged to a German tourist who was on holiday in Ampolla and, alas, had drowned while taking a midnight swim in the sea. It was in all the papers, he said, in case they didn't believe him. A tragedy, of course, but what can one do, he asked rhetorically. He then led them to the far side of the showroom where the imported cars were on display. The royal blue, two-seat convertible with tan leather interior caught Lucía's eye immediately. She walked directly toward it, opened the driver's door, and slid into the seat.

"It's a 280 SL, 1971, the last year they were made. It has an automatic transmission, multi-port fuel injection, power steering, sheet steel unibody construction, and a top speed of 200 kilometers per hour. I hope that I'm not boring you with unnecessary details." And then, as if one detail might trump all the others, he added in a hushed tone: "Sophia Loren drives one, but I doubt that she looks as good as you do in it."

Inés made a chuckling sound of disbelief.

Lucía hadn't really been listening to either of them. She had already decided that she wanted the car. "I'll take it," she said.

"But I haven't yet mentioned the price," he said, astonished.

"Oh, I'm sure you won't cheat me Sebastián, after all, we're practically family," Lucía said, staring at him and grinning knowingly. "Work out the price in dollars and I'll have my bank wire the funds."

"I do believe that is the fastest sale I've ever made."

"Please have another look under the hood to make sure everything is in order," said Lucía, remembering just such a comment that Adam had made to a salesman when Paco was buying his first car. "Also, see to the insurance, full coverage." She was enjoying herself, adopting this resolute tone, playing out the impulsiveness of it all. "And one last thing," she said, speaking to Sebastián, but looking all the while at her sister, "please register the car in Inés' name."

"As you wish, *señora*. The paperwork should take two or three days. I could deliver the car to Quinta Amelia personally."

"That would be splendid."

Sebastián chattered away and bowed low repeatedly as he saw them to the door. When they reached the threshold, he kissed Lucía's hand. "*Servidor de usted*" he said. There was an awkward moment when he hesitated, not knowing quite how to bid farewell to Inés. Her sister ignored it and walked straight past him and out the door.

Outside, as they walked to the car, Inés said to Lucía: "Well, sister, you certainly are full of surprises. They'll be talking about that performance for years to come." Then she grasped Lucía by the arm and they stopped for a moment, facing each other in the parking lot. "No one has ever given me so extravagant a gift; I don't know what to say. Thank you," said Inés, for once sounding sincere.

"Think of all those birthdays of yours I've missed," said Lucía.

* * *

Three days later Lucía drove up the track toward Cal Soler, blaring the Mercedes' distinctive low-pitched horn as she went. Coming around a bend she nearly hit a young girl walking in the same direction. Lucía stopped the car, shaken and intent on scolding the child, but when she got a good look at the waif with her bare feet, tattered shift, and dirt-smudged face, she decided against it. The child stood staring at her expressionless.

"Can I give you a lift?"

The child looked at the car and back at Lucía and nodded her head vigorously.

"Hop in."

The child did not open the door, but rather climbed over it and fell into the seat.

"There's an easier way to do that," said Lucía.

The girl did not reply.

"Cat got your tongue?" she said, before setting off again.

When Lucía started to beep the horn again, the child reached over and did the same, squealing with delight. As they pulled into the entrance to Cal Soler, Quim was standing out front looking alarmed, but when he saw that it was her, his face brightened. Lucía parked and turned off the engine, but remained behind the wheel.

"Well, what do you think?" she said, beaming.

"I think that it suits you perfectly."

"I just bought it; isn't it marvelous?"

"Yes," said Quim "it certainly is." He looked at the girl. "I see the two of you have met."

"Actually, we haven't. She hasn't uttered a word. Do you know her?"

"That's Estela, the neighbor's daughter that I mentioned. You will not hear her utter a word; she's mute."

"Oh. Good God, why didn't you tell me?"

"I didn't think to. I never really conceive of her as mute, just exceedingly quiet," said Quim, before walking around to the passenger door and opening it for Estela.

Lucía let herself out and stood admiring the car, but it looked palpably out of place in front of the half ruin that was Cal Soler; it needed a striking background to do it justice. The house in Southampton would have done admirably. All at once she realized how ostentatious she and her shiny new car must have appeared, and wondered if she shouldn't have bought one of those Seats after all.

"I thought I'd take you to lunch, someplace on the coast perhaps. We could drive down to Cap Groc."

"You mean lunch in a restaurant?" asked Quim, blinking.

"Why, yes," said Lucía. Although he *did* look rather shabby, she noticed. She had anticipated as much and deliberately dressed down in beige linen pants, a blue polo shirt, and espadrilles, but still. If only Adam were here, he would size up Quim in a glance and dress him head to toe, just like those two young soldiers they shepherded across the frontier all those years ago. But Adam wasn't here. "Perhaps you could put on a clean shirt, different shoes," she said as delicately as she could.

Quim looked down at himself and seemed to consider this. "I'll do my best," he said, turning and padding into the house, grumbling.

Lucía sat on the wall under the fig tree and watched Estela skip about the place aimlessly. Mute, she thought, how on earth would she get on in the world? A shudder ran through her just thinking of it. Life was hard enough with a tongue. But there was also something unmistakably beautiful about the child, Lucía couldn't help but notice, she looked like some mythological nymph whose domain was the grove. Perhaps she was the tainted one with her flashy car and urbane ways. How was she getting on in the world? Lucía thought. She preferred not to think about it.

Before long Quim emerged from the house wearing a clean white shirt, a blue suit jacket and blue trousers, although the blues did not match. The clothes were enormous on him, so it appeared as if they might swallow him up. He had shaved and pomaded his hair.

"Just so you know, I am aware that I look ridiculous, but it is what it is," said Quim.

"You look very handsome," said Lucía.

Estela had stopped playing and was gawking at Quim, grinning.

"And what are you grinning at, if I may ask," he admonished her playfully.

The girl chortled and resumed her play.

"What are we to do with her?" Lucía asked, under her breath.

"Nothing," said Quim "we cannot take her along. She is not permitted to leave the valley. It is the only condition that her mother insists upon. The woman is terrified that someone will steal her, gypsies perhaps, who knows?"

Lucía watched as Quim approached Estela and whispered something in her ear. The child then turned and skipped off down the track.

"What a curious creature," said Lucía, as they climbed into the car.

"I love her more than anyone in this world," he said with the utmost conviction.

After all he'd been through, she was astonished that he still had the capacity for it, love that is. "What did you tell her just now?" she asked.

"That I would bring her a shell from the sea," he said, then "a sea she has never seen save from the tops of these hills."

* * *

Lucia had been longing to go to the sea. From the train she had gazed out the window at the azure water and sequestered coves, the beaches that stretched for miles with little more than an occasional fisherman's hut, but the images had flashed past like visions in a dream, beyond reach and subtly distorted. She wanted to listen to the sea's tireless repetition, feel the sand and the water, even swim if it wasn't too cold. The day was achingly beautiful. The sky, ash-blue and bright, contained great cumulus clouds hovering on the northern horizon, their snow-white slopes and peaks towering above each other and forming distant sierras. They drove with the top down, of course, and Lucía let her hair flow with the wind. Quim's pomaded hair did not stir. She enjoyed driving the Mercedes; it was so responsive, so swift and smooth. She loved the feel and smell of the leather. She looked over at Quim and saw him leaning forward slightly in his seat like an excited child.

"Enjoying yourself?" she asked, raising her voice over the sound of the rushing wind in the open car.

Quim turned to her smiling broadly. "I have never traveled so fast!" he shouted.

She was scarcely speeding.

They followed a sinuous road along the coast, olive groves on one side, the sea on the other. There was little traffic, just a few cars, young people on bicycles and mopeds, a horse or two, an occasional mule.

"I remember those beautiful horses you rode to the front, you and that Pole."

"There are no more horses at Quinta Amelia, Borja got rid of them, too expensive."

They drove on in silence. Quim was sitting back in his seat now, his hollow face raised up to the sun, his eyes closed. She could see his transformation, and all on account of a mere drive. How little it took. She decided to pull over and stop for a moment on the side of the road where there was a view looking south along the coast. They were high up, with cliffs below them that dropped to groves of pines and a small cove with a rocky beach. All was silent but for the wind in the creaking pines, the tempo of the tide, and the odd ticking of the car's engine as it cooled. Lucía had visited the same cove with Quim and Adam in the late spring of '38. They had brought a picnic, and drank wine, and swam in the sea. She didn't mention it, but she wondered if Quim remembered the place, the day.

"They want to develop this stretch of coast," Lucía said, breaking the long silence.

"Who?"

"Borja, Inés and her husband Javier, Francisco, they have a whole scheme worked out." She went on to explain their plans for hotels and apartments and clubs, her mother's opposition, their desire to declare her mother unfit, the whole unseemly business. Quim remained silent.

"Don't you have anything to say?" she asked.

"I know nothing of these things," he replied, shrugging.

"Would you like to see this landscape sullied with tower hotels, restaurants, and bars?"

"No, I suppose not."

"Well, there you go, you *do* know something of these things," she said, slightly annoyed, but immediately she regretted it. "Are you hungry?"

"Yes, in fact, for the first time in ages I have an appetite."

"Rosa told me of a small restaurant belonging to a fisherman's family at Cap Groc. Shall we?" She reached for the key to start the engine, but Quim stopped her, placing a hand on her arm.

"Wait," he said. "Do you remember that you, Adam, and I came here and picnicked in this cove, and swam, and later lay drying off on the rocks in the sunshine?" he asked.

"Yes, I do. I remember feeling that the war seemed so far off, unreal almost."

"How often I thought of that day, those days, while in captivity. Everything that came after was like a nightmare. Apart from childhood and certain moments with my brothers, it was the only time that I had the sensation that I was actually living life." He paused a moment before going on. "I just wanted to know whether or not you remembered it that way as well, or if perhaps it had become romanticized in my mind. Memory is so unreliable in that way."

Wasn't that the truth, thought Lucía, but she didn't say that. "It was just as you describe it. For me too it was a time of happiness."

"I'm glad to know that," said Quim, gazing at her raptly.

That's when Lucía saw it again, something in Quim's eyes, a glint.

The restaurant had no name; in fact, it wasn't really a restaurant at all, just the house of a fisherman where one could get a meal. They sat under a pergola on the terrace with a view of the sea. At another table nearby were the only other customers, a middle-aged German couple and a local man. The Germans seemed to be looking for a house to buy, but it was hard to tell. The three had no language in common, and after some strained attempts at conversation and translations gone awry, they fell into silence. There was a heady smell of salt air and grilled fish. From the kitchen came the sound of clanging pots and pans and a woman's voice, clear and melodious, singing *coplas*. An older man with the rough, cracked hands of a fisherman came and told them what was available: razor clams, fried sea nettles, sardines, salad, and white wine.

"We'll have all of that," said Lucía.

They made small talk about the goings on at Quinta Amelia, the slow decline of Tortosa, and the expectations aroused by Juan Carlos, the new king. And then, in a lull, Quim suddenly asked:

"Tell me more about Paco… I hope that he has something of Adam's nature, his generosity."

"Well, thank you very much."

"Oh, I didn't mean it like that. I'm sure that he takes after you in many ways, but you know I always admired Adam's way with people, all sorts of people."

Was this just polite lunch conversation? Lucía wondered. There was nothing pointed about the tone of his voice, but who could tell?

"He does have that quality of Adam's, that same openness. He also looks very much like him." She added this as a means to dispel any suspicion, but, oddly enough, it was true somehow.

Lucía was relieved when their food arrived. They ate the sardines and clams with their hands, periodically licking their fingers. The food was simple, but delicious. Lucía couldn't remember the last time she had had such fresh seafood. She thought suddenly of the time that she and Inés and their father ate oysters on the beach. She could still taste them, their brininess. It might even have been nearby, but she couldn't be sure.

"How Spanish is he?" Quim asked.

"Who?"

"Paco, of course, he said. "I mean his manner, his speech, his attitudes."

"Well, let's see. His Spanish is fluent, although he does make an occasional error—verb tenses and articles, mostly. Like so many Americans he is an optimist, but he also has a streak of Spanish fatalism. And, of course, he's a Republican, in the Spanish sense, that is. He's really a mix of the two of us," she said, "Adam and me, I mean to say."

Quim looked at her, puzzled. "Yes, naturally," he said.

How could she have said such a thing? Lucía scolded herself. She changed the subject.

"Tell me, what became of your mother?" she asked. "Forgive me for not having inquired sooner."

"Oh, that's quite all right, thank you for asking. She died while I was incarcerated, of old age, I suppose, that, and loneliness. I wasn't allowed to attend the funeral."

"I'm sorry."

After a long pause, Quim said: "Borja paid for it," as if it were an afterthought.

"Paid for what?"

"The funeral, he paid for it all: the coffin, the flowers, the priest, the niche in the cemetery."

"I can't believe it," said Lucía, shaking her head, her eyes wide.

"Nor could I when I learned of it upon my return," he said, shaking his head too. "Soon after, I made my way to Tortosa one Sunday and waited for him to emerge from the cathedral after Mass to thank him."

"What did he say?"

"'I'm sorry for your loss' or something of that nature, something conventional, correct."

"Did you ask him why he had betrayed you?"

"No, it didn't seem quite the time or the place. I'm not even entirely sure that he did betray me. It certainly seemed that way, but oftentimes things are not as they seem. I had enough time to think about it. I can't imagine who else it could have been. It doesn't really matter anymore."

For a long time neither of them spoke. Lucía was trying to fathom Borja's actions. Perhaps she didn't know him as thoroughly as she imagined.

The old man came to clear away their plates and then returned with bowls of wild strawberries and blackberries. "On the house," he said. They finished with coffee as black as tar.

When I learned of my mother's death, I thought that I would never come back here," said Quim. "In fact, I was free to go, free to leave the Valley of the Fallen in 1960, but I stayed on, working for a wage."

"What compelled you to do that?" Lucía asked in disbelief.

"What else was I to do? I had lost my brothers, my father, and finally, my mother. I was alone in the world." He was quiet for a moment, looking out to sea. "The strange thing was," he went on "it wasn't death that I feared. Death had become so familiar; we lived in its shadow; it visited us almost every day, descending upon the weak, the infirm. We were all half-dead already. What I had come to fear most, believe it or not, was life." He laughed, but it was a joyless laugh. "Eventually, of course, I did come back, but only when I could no longer manage to put in a day's labor and was no longer of any use to the authorities or anyone else."

Lucía didn't say as much, of course, but she found it exhausting listening to this litany of misfortune. During a pause she asked for the check. The old man shuffled off and returned with a scrap of paper on which the sum had been scrawled in a childlike hand: 500 *pesetas*. It was next to nothing. She left twice the amount. Quim raised his eyebrows. They got up from the table and walked down to the deserted beach, where they took off their shoes and strolled along the water's edge. The sea was colder than Lucía had expected. She doubted that she would swim. They sought out some wavering shade beneath the pines above the beach and sat for a time looking out to sea, before laying back and, lulled by the steady rhythm of the surf, drifting off to sleep.

When they woke from their siesta, Lucía knew at once that she had slept too long, or drank too much wine, or both. She felt dazed and torpid, her head ached slightly, and her mouth was parched. The light had grown diffuse; even the sea looked a dull grey. Lucía squinted at her watch; it was almost six o'clock. She would have to hurry if she intended to get back in time to sit with her mother in the garden. She had two charges, she reminded herself. They roused themselves and walked back to the car arm in arm.

"What a wonderful afternoon," said Quim.

"It's just the first of many," Lucía said.

"Is that so?"

"It is," she said "too much solitude is good for no one."

Quim nodded and after a pause added: "At last, I feel as if I have returned amongst the living."

They were halfway back to Cal Soler when Quim suddenly groaned and slapped his knee.

"What is it?" Lucía asked.

"I forgot the shell."

Lucía turned the car around immediately and went back for it. Quim said that it wasn't necessary. "To Estela, it will be like priceless treasure," she insisted.

* * *

As the days passed lazily by Lucía's life took on a certain routine. She devoted the mornings to her mother, who she would wheel out to a patch of dappled shade in the garden and remain there for hours, engaging her mother in physical therapy, exercise, and conversation. She obliged her to speak, and walk, and write, and recollect, and as the days advanced, Lucía detected a growing clarity of her mother's speech, an increased assurance in her steps, an improvement in her powers of concentration. Her mother's head no longer lolled so markedly; her mouth had lost much, if not all, of its twisted grimace. Conchi was astonished at Lucía's mother's recovery; so too was Dr. Romeu, who, as it happened, was the son of the doctor who had treated Quim during his convalescence at Quinta Amelia. How odd it was, and at the same time how gratifying, Lucía reflected, to find such unexpected continuity in life.

The afternoons Lucía reserved and devoted to Quim. Sometimes they remained at Cal Soler, talking, reading, and passing the time with Estela; but more often than not, they drove off into the countryside or along the coast. They visited the Roman ruins in Tarragona, the medieval monasteries of Poblet and Santes Creus, and the wineries of the Priorat. They returned frequently to Cap Groc, where Lucía swam regularly in the sea. She liked not having to brave the pounding surf as she did in Southampton. Here, she could swim along at a leisurely pace and sometimes stop and float on her back and look up at the sheltering sky and think of nothing. No amount of coaxing, however, could get Quim into the water. He was no longer cut out for such things, he claimed; besides, he had no wish to bare his wasted physique before such a beautiful woman. He had his dignity, he insisted, drolly. But like Lucía's mother, Quim too was improving. He had put on weight; his deathly pallor had disappeared; his spirits had risen. Lucía no longer saw Quim as a man with a wasted frame who deserved her pity. She began to understand anew how it was that she had loved him above all things.

For the first time in years, perhaps since Paco was a boy, Lucía felt that her life had taken on a certain significance that it had previously lacked. She had only been vaguely aware of this void, but her dedication to both her mother and Quim had woken something in her, something ill-defined but powerful. Lucía had written as much to Adam in a letter that she had sent imploring him to come and join her, although, of course, she had made no mention of Quim. He would discover that Quim was alive, if not well, when he arrived. He would see the good that she was doing and realize at once how important a moment this was not only in her life, but in Quim's. She was sure of it. And so, every day Lucía eagerly sorted through the mail that arrived at Quinta Amelia, hoping to find a letter postmarked Brazil, but none arrived.

Driving back to Quinta Amelia one evening after an outing, Lucía stopped on the side of the road to look down again at Cal Foraster, as she had done that first morning when she set off on Rosa's bicycle to find Quim. There was something about the house that she found appealing;

perhaps it was the lines of the local vernacular architecture, so spare and pure and humble in a way that exuberant Quinta Amelia was not. She began to imagine herself installed there, not just her, but Adam too. She did not wish to submit him to the strained family dynamic at Quinta Amelia. They would have no privacy there; they certainly couldn't occupy that diminutive third-floor room for long. Here they could live out the summer season in a kind of rustic idyll.

The following morning Lucía went out in search of Hilario, the gardener and caretaker, and found him in the kitchen garden behind the old stables. She had always thought of him as somehow elderly, even when she was a child, but now he appeared positively ancient. Rosa had told her that her mother kept him on, even when she had let so many others of the staff go, because he had no family and no other place in the world. Quinta Amelia was his home. He was a fixture. It was Hilario, she recalled with a shudder, who had found Carlitos and hoisted his battered lifeless body atop his mule and brought him home. Lucía watched him silently for a time as he weeded and hoed between the impeccable rows of vegetables with a slow, dogged determination. She wished she had something of that constancy. Lucía walked down one of the garden paths until she stood beside Hilario's stooped figure. He must have seen her shoes, for he suddenly ceased his hoeing and stood up straight and wiped his brow and greeted her as if he hadn't noticed that she had been absent for nearly forty years.

Buenos dias, señorita Lucía, he said, squinting at her against the sunshine.

She did not correct him, in fact, she was beginning to like being called *señorita.* "Hello Hilario, wonderful to see you again."

He looked at her blankly, waiting for her to reveal why she had come and interrupted his gardening, or so she imagined.

"I was wondering if you could tell me whether anyone is living at Cal Foraster at the moment," she asked.

"Cal Foraster? No, *señorita,* not until October," he said.

"Would you have a key to the house? I would like to take a look at the place."

"I do, indeed, *señorita,* but I will have to accompany you. The door is a bit tricky to open."

"I'm sorry; I hate to take you away from your garden." But, of course, she already had.

"No matter," he said, laconically.

They drove out to the house in the Mercedes. Hilario looked excruciatingly uncomfortable, as if he were afraid to touch anything for fear of soiling it. He sat rigidly with his hands in his lap, his shoulders not quite touching the seat back. Lucía tried to engage him in some small talk, but it was useless. He answered in monosyllables. They drove on in silence. When they turned off the road and proceeded down the track toward the house, a rabbit dashed across the path in front of the car. Hilario lifted his arms as if he had a gun and was training the animal in his sights.

"Bang," he murmured.

They parked in front of the house. From the outside, at least, the place looked to be in good shape, better, thought Lucía, than Cal Soler. Hilario produced the key from his trousers' pocket. It was an ancient-looking piece of iron, and enormous, probably a foot long. He fit the key into the lock on the front door and strained to turn it. When the door swung open, Lucía started, as geckos scurried across the walls.

"Pay them no mind," said Hilario "they eat the flies and mosquitos. Don't kill them, it is bad luck."

He went about opening the inside shutters and as he did so the light streamed in to reveal an interior that was stark, but spacious, with a minimum of furniture—a few odd chairs, a trunk, a chest of drawers, a long rough-hewn table—and a gossamer-thin layer of dust settled over everything. Despite the heat outdoors, the air inside the house was cool on account of the thick stone and mortar walls and tile floor. The ground floor consisted of a large common room and a contiguous kitchen with a blackened open hearth, a stone sink, a butane stove, and a larder and cold storage. There was no electricity and so no refrigerator or artificial light. A few kerosene lamps hung from the lower ceiling beams. A door in a corner of the kitchen led to a primitive bathroom with a small sink, a toilet, and an ancient zinc tub. From the common room a narrow stairway led upstairs to a single large bedroom with an imposing four-poster mahogany bed and a few canvas-covered folding cots pushed against one wall. The bed looked singularly out of place, like a gleaming item of silver amidst a collection of pewter. Lucía wondered how it had gotten there. The whole place, but the upstairs room especially, reminded her of the farm house on the front that Quim and his men had occupied. She gazed at the bed and an image flashed in her mind of Quim and her making love beneath the rough woolen blankets, the sounds of his snoring men rising up from below. The prospect of lying here with Adam, she suddenly thought, seemed strangely disloyal, although she wasn't sure to whom.

"Why are you interested in this old place?" Hilario asked.

"I'm going to live here for the summer."

"Just yourself, *señorita?*"

"No, with my husband," she said, hopefully.

"Your husband? Ah, forgive me, *señora*. Allow me to offer my congratulations."

"Thank you, Hilario," she said, trying her best not to laugh. What would it be like, she wondered, to live perpetually in the present?

When they got back to Quinta Amelia, Lucía dropped off the ancient retainer by the old stables so that he could get back to his gardening. He was turning to go, when suddenly he stopped and spoke: "How I miss Carlitos," he said, quietly. "Such a lovely boy he was."

He made it sound as if her brother had only just left this world. Sometimes, Lucía felt the same. "Yes," she said "a lovely boy."

Around the lunch table at Quinta Amelia conversation had waned as the family members busied themselves consuming *bacalao a la llauna,* another of Rosa's specialties. Lucía thought it the perfect moment to announce her imminent change of address.

"I have decided to move into Cal Foraster for the remainder of my stay," she said, scanning the table and registering the subtle reactions—eyebrows rising, jaws halting, lips pursing—in the faces of her family.

No one spoke, not at first; they seemed to be contemplating just what to say. Her mother, whose reaction was the only one that truly mattered to Lucía, remained still, her eyes downcast. She watched Borja, as he placed his knife and fork open on his plate, wiped his mouth with his linen napkin, took a leisurely sip of wine, and cleared his throat. He would have made a fine actor, thought Lucía, not a leading man, to be sure, but a memorable character actor.

"I wouldn't have guessed that you went in for such rustic surroundings," he finally said.

"On the contrary, I love the countryside and I've always loved that house. I'll be out before the tenants arrive in October for the olive harvest."

"But it seems like you've only just arrived," said Francisco "and already you're…" He trailed off.

"Fleeing," said Inés. "I think that's the word you're looking for."

"I am not 'fleeing'. I am moving down the road because I think that I'll be a bit more comfortable. The room on the third floor is lovely, but since I'm planning to stay on for a while, I'd like a bit more space."

"Aren't you afraid to be there alone?" asked Paulina.

"Oh, I suspect she won't be entirely alone," said Inés, as she smiled her wicked smile.

"No, you're quite right; I won't be alone," said Lucía, calmly holding her sister's gaze. There was a weighty silence. Lucía could sense that everyone gathered at the table was speculating as to who might be joining her. She left them hanging for a moment before adding: "Adam will be joining me." She hoped it was true.

"*Señor* Fa-tes…is w-w-wel-come…in my house always," her mother managed to pronounce, giving Lucía a sly, knowing smile.

Her mother had given her blessing. It was the final word, nothing else mattered.

"Oh, by the way," said Inés "there's a letter for you on the hall table with a lurid stamp from some exotic locale."

"Why didn't you tell me?" said Lucía, jumping up from the table.

"I just did."

She did not tear open the envelope there in the hall, but took it to her room instead and sat on the bed and looked at it for a moment, admiring Adam's elegant script, the stamp depicting a brightly-colored toucan, and the alluring tropical return address:

AV. VIEIRA SOUTO, 76

IPANEMA

RIO DE JANEIRO, 22420

BRASIL

She opened the envelope with care, unfolded the fine airmail paper, and read:

Dearest Lucía:

*Please forgive me for the long silence and my failure to answer your letters. I have been working night and day on a photo project in the Rio slums (*favelas*) which are at once unspeakably grim and curiously cheerful. I can't really explain it. I hope the photos manage to capture the paradox. I feel more inspired than I have in many years. Frankly, I think that this separation has been good for me. I hope that you realize that the reason I was so upset with you for wanting to return to Spain alone was on account of the ill treatment and hostility that your family has always submitted you to, at least since the tragic loss of Carlitos. Don't forget that I was with you when they found your brother. I saw how your family blamed you so unfairly. I know what they are capable of, and I wanted to protect you from the beasts.*

How relieved I am to learn that your mother has received you well. As for the rather rocky relations with your siblings (I loved the portrait that you painted of rotund Borja! That of Francisco, of course, is more distressing) well, what of it? Do they really matter at this stage in your life? I realize that this is all coming from me, an only child, but just think how lucky we've been not to have been exposed to all of them over the years. Now I understand Paco's bitter memories of that summer spent among the Vidals. Poor chap!

Naturally, I was saddened to learn of your mother's stroke, but the progress that she is making thanks to your dedication is perhaps a sort of silver lining, no? It is wonderful that you are able to be there for her and I thoroughly understand your wish to stay on.

So, I will not be making the trip to Spain, not any time soon anyway. I think that what I am working on is truly important. I hope you understand.

All best,

Adam

P.S. Very sad to hear of that development scheme of Borja and Co. I remember that stretch of coast. Do you recall that you, Quim, and I used to swim there? How curious that we managed to find moments of happiness in the midst of war.

P.P.S. Please send my best to Rosa and to your family as you see fit.

The letter was everything that Lucía had silently feared. She was glad for Adam's work, of course, but the overall message seemed plain enough—he was doing just fine without her, thriving even. And what was she to make of him signing off "All best"? What did that imply? A dull panic rose up in her. Lucía sat down at once and wrote back imploring Adam to hurry with his work and come to her. She would wait.

* * *

As spring gave way to summer, the days grew long and sultry. The air hung motionless and the heat took one's breath away. Everything one looked at seemed to quiver as in a mirage. The evening of the 23rd of June, Lucía and Quim went to the main square in El Perelló to join in the celebrations of the Feast of San Juan. They sat on the terrace of a café and drank *cava* and ate *coca*, while an orchestra played *pasodobles* and *boleros*, and farmers in starched white shirts danced stiffly with their stout wives. Lucía wanted to dance, but Quim said that he wasn't up to it, and besides, he didn't want the locals to get the wrong idea.

"And what idea might that be?" Lucía asked, although she knew very well what he was referring to.

"That Quim Soler has taken up with a married woman."

"They don't know me or anything about me."

Quim gave her a look of disbelief. "They know precisely who you are and more about you than you could possibly imagine."

It was probably true, Lucía knew. She was aware of the power and profusion of local gossip, especially in these tiny villages, but all the same, she was annoyed at Quim's provincial constraint. After all, what did she care? But then she remembered that before too long she would be gone and Quim would remain. Perhaps he would become the butt of jokes. She resolved to be more respectful of his predicament.

"I'm sorry," she said. "I suppose you have a reputation to uphold."

"It's not my reputation that I'm concerned about," he said, shaking his head.

When darkness descended, a bonfire was lit in the middle of the square, and locals stepped forward in the flickering light to toss broken furniture and unwanted objects—the detritus of the preceding year—into the growing flames. Quim contributed a bundle of old clothes, and Lucía a battered stool that she had fetched from Cal Foraster. The fire was said to purify and renew those who fed and contemplated it. They rose and joined hands with a circle of villagers and danced around the fire like pagans until Quim began to wheeze and they returned to their table. Later, when the flames had died down somewhat, local boys took turns leaping over the fire, competing in bravura, as girls watched and shrieked and egged them on.

"I'm going to live at Cal Foraster for the summer; have I told you?" Lucía knew very well that she hadn't. She wanted the statement to sound somehow spontaneous, but it had the opposite effect.

"No, you haven't" said Quim, not looking at her. "Now the villagers will really have something to talk about."

"Oh. Why is that?"

"Beautiful rich married women don't tend to move into houses re-served for seasonal laborers, alone no less."

There was something about the way that Quim summed up the sit-uation that suddenly made her feel a fool. He sounded like her siblings. What was it about them all that made them so resistant to anything that veered from the norm? Why couldn't a grown woman go and live in a house for God's sake? What harm was there in it? She began to see her exile in America as a kind of blessing. How would she have lived amidst these stifling social norms?

At midnight, the sky filled with fireworks, but the explosions, too similar to ordnance perhaps, made Quim and many of the older locals in the crowd nervous, Lucía noticed. She and Quim left the square and as they walked down a dimly-lit street toward the car, a group of rau-cous boys passed and one of them shouted at Quim's back: "Filthy Red!" Lucía turned quickly, incensed, and was about to respond, but Quim pulled her back. "They're just silly boys," he said. "It doesn't matter."

* * *

For several days after the Feast of San Juan, Lucía did not see Quim, not out of spite for anything he did or did not say that night in the square, but because, apart from the morning visits with her mother, she poured all of her time and energies into putting Cal Foraster in order. She swept, mopped, and scrubbed; changed the mesh screens in the windows; white-washed the interior walls; oiled the front door lock; scoured the bathtub, sink, and toilet; and beat the mattress until her hands were blistered. She washed all the plates, glasses, cutlery, and pots and pans, as well as the sheets and towels. Never in her life had she toiled so and more than once she had to sit and rest, overcome with fatigue and at times spells of dizziness. It didn't mat-ter; she pushed on, rarely had she felt so content. It was curious, she thought, but somehow reconnecting with Quim and putting their old love to rest, as it were, had made her love for Adam that much more pronounced. She longed to see him, yet she also began to question the wisdom of reuniting the two men. Of course they *had* been friends, but that was before, well, everything really—Quim's supposed demise, her marriage to Adam, Paco's birth. Good God, the two men had every reason to loath one another, she suddenly realized. What had she been thinking?

One afternoon as Lucía was on her knees scrubbing grime from the earthenware floor tiles, she looked up, startled, to find Inés standing in the doorway.

"I'm not at all sure that the cleaning lady look suits you," said her sister.

"Christ, don't you knock or anything; you scared the hell out of me."

"Sorry, I did beep the horn to alert you as I came down the track, but you must have been lost in the task at hand. May I?" she asked, stepping inside.

Lucía got to her feet and watched Inés as she looked around, examining the place, nodding her head approvingly. "Well, well, so this is your little love nest. I'm impressed, it's so…charming," said Inés. "Are you quite sure it will do for Mr. Fates of Park Avenue and Southampton?"

Lucía didn't answer. "Couldn't you dispense with the barbed tone on occasion?"

"Is that what my tone is, barbed? I don't even notice anymore, but not to worry, that's what I've come to talk about, in part."

"What exactly?"

"Oh. Let's not rush things, shall we. I've brought along some *merienda*: *croquetas*, compliments of Rosa, and cold beer, compliments of me," she said, holding up a shopping bag.

They sat at the kitchen table which Lucía had covered with a pale blue linen tablecloth. A vase of wild flowers stood in the middle.

"I must say, I never took you for much of a homemaker, but I see that I've been wrong. This place really does look lovely," said Inés, her tone unusually sincere.

"Thank you," said Lucía. "I've been working like a mad woman. Adam could arrive at any time."

Inés opened two bottles of beer and unwrapped the *croquetas* from some wax paper. They drank from the bottles, ate with their hands. The moment seemed to call for it.

"*Madre mía*" said Lucía, affectionately "what does Rosa put in these *croquetas*; they are divine."

"Love, I suspect," said Inés. "She made them for you."

Lucía smiled weakly. She looked down at herself and exhaled loudly. "Goodness, just look at me, what I sight." She was wearing an old flowered cotton smock that Rosa had given her to do the cleaning; a scarf was tied around her head; she had cheap canvas sneakers on her feet. Her skin was glistening with sweat.

Inés looked her sister up and down, took a sip of her beer, and said: "The truth is you even look good dressed as a charwoman."

"Well, I don't feel it," said Lucía, trying to be self-effacing. She suddenly regretted having brought up the subject of appearances at all, for now the focus shifted inevitably—as it always did with twins—to her sister, who was not cleaning house but still looked badly turned out in too-tight jeans from which unflattering curves were spilling, and a faded sleeveless yellow top. Inés must have sensed the sudden, subtle scrutiny. She looked away as she spoke:

"You know, we were once equally beautiful; do you remember? My figure was just as good as yours, my features just as fine. My hair too was lustrous."

Lucía was silent. She didn't know quite what to say. What her twin sister was saying was true.

"And yet," Inés continued "both Quim and Adam were crazy for you. Everyone at Quinta Amelia could see it. Why was that? I couldn't stop wondering. I hated you for it. I mean I really, truly hated you. I was so pleased when you left. Isn't that awful."

Lucía felt a chill run through her. Inés must have noticed it.

"It's taken me the better part of a lifetime to come around, a lifetime to realize that your looks, our looks, had nothing to do with it. It was your manner that drew them to you; the way you have with people, and not just men, but everyone. Look at Rosa, for God's sake, didn't you see how she welcomed you back, how she missed you? She's never displayed any special sort of caring toward me, but that's because I never gave her anything to care about. I always treated her more or less as a servant, while you always treated her as a companion, a friend, a… person." Her voice trailed off, almost to a whisper. "I see all that now." She bowed her head. "Forgive me," she managed, before the tears began to fall.

Lucía leaned forward in her chair and put her arms around her sister and drew her toward her. "Of course I forgive you," she whispered in Inés' ear. "How could I not? You are like a part of me." They remained there locked in an embrace for some time, Lucía rubbing her sister's back, consoling her as she would a fragile child, Inés sobbing and trembling with years of pent-up bitterness. Finally, Lucía rose and fetched Inés a handkerchief. Her sister slumped back in her chair, exhausted, and wiped her eyes and blew her nose.

"How could it have taken me so long for Christ's sake," said Inés. "In the meantime, life has passed me by."

"Well, it's not too late," said Lucía, doing her best to sound positive.

Inés looked at her and smiled wanly. "Isn't it? If I'd come to that realization earlier, my life might have been different. Perhaps I would have run off with you and Adam. You were right to have left. I see that now too. I thought that I was being loyal and true to the family, to mother, to our class and country. What nonsense! I have stayed on here all my life and slowly but surely I have become invisible. The family takes me for granted; my daughters don't respect me; my husband is unfaithful to me. What a fool I've been. You say that it's not too late, but it is really. You are the woman that you are because you have devoted a lifetime to the task of living."

Lucía wanted to tell Inés to leave Javier, to stand up for herself and show some resolve before the family, especially her daughters. But she held back. "Why don't you come back to New York with me, with us," she said instead, her voice rising expectantly. "God knows we have room enough. We could catch up, I mean, really catch up, without all this," she raised her arms and gestured vaguely "Spain, Quinta Amelia, Javier, Borja, all of it."

"And what would I do precisely?" Inés asked skeptically.

"Whatever you like…anything…nothing at all."

"America, the land of opportunity," said Inés, mockingly.

They sat without speaking for a time. Lucía could see Inés gazing off, considering a different future—*anything… nothing at all*—and wondering if perhaps it wasn't too late after all.

"Who knows? I might do," her sister said finally. "I have been such a coward all my life. It won't be easy to change my ways."

"It's an open invitation," said Lucía. What's more, she meant it.

"Christ, you do make it hard for one to hate you."

* * *

Lucía moved into Cal Foraster in early July. The house, she had to admit, looked wonderfully inviting, and everyone, like Inés, who came to see the place—her mother, Rosa, Paulina and Borja, Francisco, even Hilario—said as much. Only Quim, who came reluctantly one afternoon and gave everything a cursory glance, seemed indifferent, if not vaguely hostile. He declined to sit down and hovered close to the front door, as if ready to beat a quick retreat.

"What is it?" she asked him.

"What is what?"

"Don't you like what I've done to the place?"

"Yes, I suppose, but…"

"But what?"

"Well…to be honest, the house seems a bit tarted up, that's all."

"Tarted up? Really?" she asked. The expression made her feel cheap. "How so? You mean the curtains in the windows perhaps, or the few comfortable chairs…"

"I guess, I'm not sure. These houses never really look like this, so homey, that is."

Of course, it had nothing to do with her decorating abilities, Lucía realized later. No one had ever made a home for Quim except his deceased mother. He never visited the house again, never so much as mentioned it.

Lucía continued to frequent Cal Soler to see Quim on his terrain, to prepare an occasional meal, to pass long afternoons engaged in simple activities with Estela—improving her reading and writing skills, drawing, sewing—while Quim looked on, but in the evenings she returned to Cal Foraster alone. She took advantage of summer's protracted light to sit in front of the house and write letters to Adam and Paco and Katia, and postcards to Margaret and the Candees, a few colleagues from her school, and friends like Lorenzo de Marco. She missed them all, missed New York life, she was surprised to realize. And yet she also felt uncommonly able and useful, not just to her mother and to Quim, but beyond all expectation, to herself. There were long stretches of the day and the sometimes sweltering, sleepless nights when Lucía was free to think and reflect and come to know herself as she never really had. Being alone, she realized, had given her a certain degree of empowerment. She thought back with a tinge of embarrassment to her first hours in Barcelona, when she was reluctant to even leave her hotel room on Las Ramblas. What had she been so afraid of exactly? She wasn't sure she could say, perhaps just ordinary run-of-the-mill failure. For years Lucía had sensed that in her life she had somehow fallen short. She viewed her existence in America as comfortable, if serenely inconsequential. There was her life on Park Avenue into which she had slipped with a kind of tailored ease; the not-terribly-demanding teaching stint at the Lindley School; the caring for a husband and a son with the aid of devoted domestic help; and her remove from her own family, which had freed her of certain obligations that would have been expected of a dutiful daughter had she remained in Spain. Why, she wondered, did all of this good fortune leave her with a sense of ill-ease? And then she thought of Inés' life of dull despair, or worse, of Quim's, and she cursed herself for even daring to question her blessings when all she should have done was given thanks and praise.

August drew to a close. The heat began to subside ever so slightly, the light to diminish. Almonds were ripe for the picking, so too figs, their thin skins splitting and oozing nectar and attracting the bees. The very air was sweet with the end of summer. Lucía had again readied everything at Cal Foraster for Adam's arrival and was expecting him any day, when Rosa appeared one morning on her bicycle with a letter from Brazil. Lucía did not regard the colorful stamp, or dwell on the exotic return address, or admire Adam's fine handwriting, but tore open the envelope and unfolded the letter and began to read. She felt her face drop, heard herself let out a sort of bleat, and bit her lower lip; Lucía noticed Rosa stepping back and away, the better to allow her a measure of intimacy.

It took all of her concentration to read the letter through. He wasn't coming, not now, not ever. What leapt from the page were certain phrases, loaded words, that she could scarcely credit. "Not a good idea… something really changed on that Thanksgiving Day…this is for the best…have always wanted your love and happiness…finally my needs must come first…divorce…hope you understand…" A self-portrait was enclosed. The photograph showed him standing on a ruinous street, towering above a circle of ragged children. He looked perilously thin, Lucía thought. On the reverse side he had written: *Para Lucía, luz de mi vida.*

"Not bad news, I hope."

"What?" Lucía asked. She had almost forgotten that Rosa was there with her. "Oh, no…or rather yes. Adam's had to postpone his arrival." She couldn't think of what else to say, couldn't bear to offer up the truth, couldn't even register it.

"There is more than enough to occupy you here," said Rosa. "As for *Señor* Fates, don't worry about him, he adores you."

How could she say such a thing with such conviction? Lucía wondered. Rosa, who hadn't seen the man in forty years. But it was true, she told herself, he did adore her, would always adore her. It was Lucía who had realized too late that she adored him.

* * *

And so, she attended to her mother and Quim, and watched the days grow shorter. She had already written to her school, asking for a leave of absence for the semester on account of family matters, and they had readily complied. As summer gave way to autumn and the date neared for the family of seasonal workers to occupy Cal Foraster, Lucía managed to find them another house nearby. They arrived at the end of October. Lucía woke early one morning to the sounds of unfamiliar voices, distinct accents, and a persistent sound of thrashing outside the house. When she stepped outside, she found the family harvesting the olive trees around Cal Foraster. Lucía greeted them, but they went on working, eying her askance. *So there she is, the strange woman who had tossed them from the House of the Stranger,* Lucía imagined them thinking. She didn't care.

The mornings now dawned cold, and in the garden at Quinta Amelia a fine blanket of hoarfrost gave everything a ghostly cast. Lucía and her mother could no longer pass the mornings outside, but sat instead in front of the French doors in the library, warmed by the autumnal rays of light slanting through the glass. Her mother's powers of speech had improved markedly, so that slowly the two of them could begin to carry on a semblance of proper conversation. Initially, Lucía had tried to confine their talks to more or less innocuous subjects—comments on the youngest members of the family, the changes that had occurred in Tortosa, some innocent reminiscence from childhood—so as not to unsettle her mother. Both women, however, eventually grew weary of this small talk.

"Because I am o-o-ld does not mean that you have to talk to me as if I were f-f-eeble," her mother said one morning.

It appeared as if the stroke and the long months of recovery during which she had been moot or struggled to form the most rudimentary phrases had left her with an aversion to idle chitchat. Her mother wanted to get to the heart of it. Perhaps she sensed that her time was short. They discussed Inés' unhappiness, Francisco's doleful drinking, Borja's ambitions, and, of course, Lucía, her marriage, Paco, and her sudden return. All of it, Lucía was relieved to find, without vengefulness; on the contrary, her mother seemed to have acquired a trait which Lucía had never known her to possess, namely, a sense of humor.

"Ironic how you f-f-ell in with the Reds and ended up a r-r-ich woman," she said with a crooked grin. She had yet to completely recover from the partial paralysis in her face. "Of course," she went on "you almost ended up with that local Soler character. Not a bad man, I'm sure, but I never saw you on a f-f-arm, needless to say."

"Yes," said Lucía, smiling "it's funny how things turn out in life."

"Funny and sometimes unspeakably cr-r-uel, I started out r-r-ich, very r-r-ich indeed, but from one day to the n-n-ext it was all gone."

"Yes, but we never lacked for anything," said Lucía, in an attempt to assuage her mother.

"Just a f-f-ather."

There was a long pause. Lucía closed her eyes and tilted her head back to the meager light, seeking warmth. "And a brother," Lucía added, almost in a whisper. They had broached every subject, it seemed, but one.

"Is that why you re-returned, seeking f-forgiveness f-for your original s-sin?"

Was that why she had returned? Lucía wondered. She wasn't at all sure. "I'm sorry, I..."

"Sorry means nothing," her mother interrupted, her face darkening. The measured tone was gone. "I cannot f-forgive you. Do not ask that of m-me. It is too m-much. Carlitos' death is on your conscience, s-something between you and God. If, that is, you still b-believe in one."

"I'm not sure I do."

"That is your a-affair."

Lucía looked out across the barren garden bathed in bleak autumnal light. The jacaranda tree beneath which she and Carlitos had posed for that photograph so many years ago was bare of leaf and flower. She turned back to her mother.

"You cannot forgive me?" she asked, incredulous, her voice rising. "Perhaps it is I who cannot forgive you! Have you ever considered that? You have submitted me to a lifetime of ostracism and bitterness. You cannot forgive me, indeed! I was not responsible for Carlitos' death, but you didn't hesitate to blame me. How easy it must have been for you. How did you feel putting the onus for such a tragedy on your very own daughter? How does that sit on *your* conscience? What killed Carlitos was envy and ignorance and your stultifying class pride. He embodied all that was positive and noble in life. No wonder he sympathized with the Republic. Carlitos was the purest thing that ever came out of this family precisely because he lived the farthest from your idiotic social norms. It is not in your power to forgive me? No? Ah, but it is in your power to continue to persecute me. I am not seeking your forgiveness! *You* should seek forgiveness before your God, forgiveness for your sins of spite and pettiness, bitterness and narrow-mindedness. Beg Him for forgiveness, go on, implore Him for it before it is too late!"

When she was finished, when she had said all that had gone unsaid for the better part of a lifetime, Lucía felt a certain lightheadedness, a euphoria, even, as if some impossibly weighty burden had been lifted from her. Perhaps that is why she had really come, not to ask forgiveness, but to unburden herself of the guilt that her family had attributed to her. Neither of them spoke, neither of them seemed even to move. Her mother's face had taken on the twisted scowl anew, and Lucía wondered if her outburst hadn't induced another stroke. Perhaps she had been too vehement, or not vehement enough, she wasn't sure.

Finally, her mother spoke up, breaking the freighted silence, but something in her voice had changed, grown feeble, almost childlike. "I too have done many things wr-rong. I adm-mit it. Perhaps what you say is t-true, but as you say, that is b-between me and my G-god. I have b-been so alone. F-forgive me for shutting you out."

Was it going to be that easy? All those years of suffering atoned with a mere *forgive me?* Perhaps so, thought Lucía. Still, she resisted.

"No one loved Carlitos as I did," said Lucía.

Her mother shook her head in disbelief. "How c-can you s-say s-such a thing to a mother?"

"I wanted to defend him, to be at his side."

"H-he was a boy, h-he didn't n-need your defending."

"I tried to arm him, arm him with principles."

"M-my G-God, how p-presumptuous of you," her mother said, with a violent, trembling jeer.

Lucía was silent.

"D-don't you seeeee? It wasn't C-Carlitos they were after. They didn't c-care about a m-mere boy. It was *you* they wanted to silence, *Lucía the R-Red!*"

Lucía closed her eyes and from the darkness tried to grasp what her mother was saying, the significance of it, the long-obscured truth of it. How could it be that she had not realized it sooner? She had been so thoroughly consumed in herself—her loss and brother, her love and pain…her life. She could see that all of a sudden with the utmost clarity, like some sort of epiphany. Good God, what had she done? She opened her eyes. The library was cast in shadow. Only a weak light touched the glass.

"What do I do now?" she whispered.

"Do?" her mother answered. "You l-live."

"That won't be so easy, I'm afraid."

"It n-never is."

Lucía wanted to flee, to be someplace alone with her thoughts, but her mother insisted on remaining there. Time was running short, she said, and there was still something that she needed to explain. Lucía wasn't sure what time her mother was referring to, the immediate time, the time that remained to live. What did she mean?

"C-come c-close, now," her mother said, in a hushed, secretive tone. "I n-need you."

Lucía was taken aback. How seldom her mother had ever needed her. She couldn't imagine what this was about.

"It's those two men," she said, referring to Borja and Javier and shaking her head, "I know very w-w-ell what they are p-p-lanning. They think I'm senile, oblivious. I'm g-g-lad that you are h-h-ere with me. I'm not at all sure that I would be able to op-p-ose them alone."

"I don't really see that there is much I can do to alter their plans in the long run."

"Ah, but t-t-here is."

"How is that exactly?"

"The land t-t-hat t-t-hey are aiming to develop…it is your land, or w-w-ill be. But, of course, t-t-hey don't know t-t-hat, not yet."

Lucía shook her head slowly, she wasn't sure that she understood what she was hearing. Her mother understood her surprise. She had drawn up her will and testament years ago, she went on to explain. There was nothing especially unusual about it. As was customary in Cataluña, the eldest son, that is to say, Borja, was slated to inherit the best agricultural lands in the hopes that he would continue to manage the estate. She had set aside certain holdings for Inés and money for Francisco so that they would have an independent income and not be dependent on anyone. As for Lucía, she was due to inherit lands along the coast, which traditionally were little valued because they were scarcely arable. She hadn't done it out of spite, her mother insisted, but because Lucía had married into money and her position was secure. All of this was done before the speculative fever for tourist development had set in, but now it seemed oddly prescient.

Her mother was grinning that crooked grin again. Lucía was speechless.

"If I h-h-aven't t-t-old them yet, it is because I don't want to witness my children quarreling over t-t-heir inheritance. So, I b-b-eg you, not a word to anyone. You w-w-ill all h-h-ave to w-w-ork it out when I am g-g-one."

"Of course," said Lucía, still shocked, "not a word." She made to get up, but stopped short. "*Mamá,* how is it that you care so much about that strip of land and what's done with it?"

"It is l-land that s-saved this family, l-land that r-redeemed us after your f-father's f-foolishness, G-God have m-mercy on him." Then, after a pause: "L-land…it's the only t-thing worth p-possessing."

* * *

Lucía decided to stay on for lunch. Rosa had prepared *carn d'olla.* The mood around the table was characteristically muted, only more so. Inés and Javier were quarreling wordlessly, Lucía could tell. Perhaps her sister had given her husband a piece of her mind at last. Francisco appeared to be suffering from his habitual hangover. Paulina looked to be elsewhere,

Borja preoccupied. Lucía tried to engage her mother in conversation, but she seemed spent from their earlier talk. The food, thank goodness, was delicious.

Lucía looked around the table and wondered if any of her siblings knew of the details of their mother's will. Is that why they had tried to interest her in their scheme that first day she was back? The topic had barely come up since then. Why would they have bothered to try to persuade her of their plans if it weren't because they knew that she held all the cards, as it were? Lucía hoped that her mother had years yet to live and none of these issues of inheritance and lands and development projects would come to the fore anytime soon. Perhaps time would temper all these ambitions; more likely, it would exacerbate them.

The monotony was broken, at last, when Borja rose suddenly and announced that he was going to see how the harvest was progressing.

"Would you mind if I joined you?" Lucía asked.

"Not at all…taking an interest in the crops, are we? Every day you are becoming more and more of a country girl." His tone was mocking, but without rancor.

In the entrance hall, Borja put on a Barbour and a tweed flat cap and took up a walking stick. The perfect guise for the *patrón,* thought Lucía. Her brother certainly knew how to play the part. Again she imagined him on the stage. Lucía wrapped herself in a thick woolen shawl and tied a scarf over her head. The season of the fierce *mistral* winds had begun, and as they walked out of the front door and up the track behind the house they leaned into the gale. When Lucía linked her arm into Borja's, she felt him grow tense. He was not a man accustomed to displays of intimacy, she knew, but she wanted him to feel that she loved him despite everything. Or perhaps love was too strong a word. They were siblings; never close, it was true, but brother and sister nonetheless. What other word could she use? She wasn't sure that she respected him exactly. In reality, she scarcely knew him, as recent revelations only seemed to confirm. That was why she had wanted to join him on the walk. At first they did not speak, as they climbed the gradual slope that lead away from the house and up to the high terrain where the best olive groves lay. Lucía had never seen the trees so abundant with variegated fruit; the bowed branches hung low with the weight of it. They reached a group of workers harvesting a series of enormous, centuries-old trees on a plateau at the top of the property. It was the same family that had been working the trees around Cal Foraster, Lucía saw, but they did not ignore Borja as they had her. They all stood up straight as Borja, the *patrón* approached, and the father came forward and touched the rim of his cap, but did not shake hands with her brother. The two men stood talking, while Lucía waited behind. She could not hear what the men were saying on account of the wind, but she knew what their exchange entailed: blights and yields and weather and the price of the fruit. Lucía had heard her mother discuss as much; she almost wanted to step forward and hand over a basket of eggs or a sack of sugar or some such show of largesse from the ruling class, but those days were past. Times were changing, she had heard from Rosa and others, now the workers wanted a fair wage, a percentage of the crop. Thank goodness, Lucía thought. Borja shook the man's hand before turning to go, and he and Lucía set off again.

"Every year they want more," said Borja exasperated. "Do you know what the man told me? He needs the extra money to pay for his son's university, his son's university!" he repeated, as if she hadn't heard. "I didn't go to bloody university!"

Lucía did not comment. It wasn't necessary. She hadn't come to discuss the harvest or the estate or social mobility in the new Spain, but rather to acknowledge a debt long overdue.

"I believe that I owe you a measure of thanks," she said, after her brother had calmed down somewhat.

Borja stopped and turned to her. He looked shocked, as if no one ever thanked him for anything. "Is that so, on account of what?"

"On account of saving Quim's life," she said.

"Oh, that, good Lord, why are you dredging up that bit of the past now?"

"Because I only learned about it upon my return," Lucía said. "I've been meaning to mention it, but the occasion never arose."

"Well, if I recall correctly, I didn't want my sister's lover's blood on my hands, nothing more."

They continued walking.

"Then why did you betray him? Lucía asked. Her tone was less accusatory than one of bewilderment.

"Betray him, how so?"

"By setting your men on him as soon as he was outside the gates."

"I did nothing of the sort."

Lucía took his arm and obliged him to stop. She wanted to look him directly in eyes. "Is that the truth?"

"Of course it's the truth, although I would have been perfectly justified to do so. He was the enemy."

"Quim is convinced that it was you who betrayed him. Evidently you told him that he was safe under your roof at Quinta Amelia, but that you would not protect him once he was outside the gates."

"I do recall having said something to that effect. Still, I must insist, it wasn't me or my men who captured him. I'm afraid that you and Quim will have to look for a more suitable culprit. I shouldn't think that you would have to look too far."

"What does that mean, exactly?"

"Lucía, there were people very close to you who wanted you to remain just that, close. They felt, we felt, that Quim was drawing you away from everything that was dear: family, class, and country."

"Who was it?" she asked, pleading.

"I don't know, to be honest. I haven't thought about these things in years."

They walked on in silence. Lucía tried to imagine who would have betrayed Quim, but immediately she had misgivings. In truth, she wasn't sure she wanted to expose someone close for some long-forgotten deception. Perhaps she should take after Quim more; what was it that he always said when confronted with some wretchedness from the past? Ah, yes: *It doesn't matter.*

When they arrived back at the house, Borja saw Lucía to her car.

"It seems that you're the talk of the town," Borja told her.

"Is that so?"

"Oh, yes, very much so," he said, grinning. "The story of your car purchase still resonates."

"Oh that," said Lucía, smiling back at him. "Well, not to worry, I don't do that sort of thing often."

"The newer episode, your installation at Cal Foraster, that has them a bit more perplexed."

"Let them speculate all they want," said Lucía, as she opened the car door. She was about to slide into the seat, but stopped short. "That was a beautiful gesture of yours for Quim's mother. The funeral expenses, I mean."

"My dear Lucía, your brother is not a monster," he said, before turning toward the house.

"Borja! One more thing," she called after him. He stopped and turned back to look at her. "I'm going to fight you and the others every step of the way on this development scheme. You know that."

He only shook his head and waddled off, his walking stick tapping the gravel drive.

Lucía drove toward Cal Foraster, but when she arrived to the entrance to her track, she continued on instead. It was mere impulse; she didn't wish to be cooped up in the house with the wind gusting outside and darkness descending early. The days were short enough now; she wanted to take advantage of what light was left in the day. She made for the coast. At Cap Groc, she parked at the same spot where she had stopped with Quim on their first outing months before. She did not get out of the car, but sat looking south where the cliffs dropped steeply to the water's edge. The day was cloudless and bright with a hard wind roaring in from the sea. Whitecaps, thick and churning, broke against the rocky shoreline. No one was about. The fishermen's houses clustered in the cove were shuttered and quiet. At a slight remove from the beach, the pine groves rose up, thick and dark. My land, Lucía thought. She couldn't quite believe it. She had never understood the desire to possess land that consumed some people, but now she had an inkling of it. What would she do with this land of hers? she wondered. She certainly had no ambitions to develop it, to see the trees cleared, and the roads go in, and the buildings rise up, and the people arrive in droves. No, that is not what she wanted for her land. Let the solitary walkers come instead, and the small groups of picnickers and bathers, and let them stretch out on the rocks to dry as she, Quim, and Adam had done. Wasn't that a good enough use of the land. Her siblings, she knew, would loathe her for it, but Lucía hoped that it would be a short-lived kind of loathing, like the brief fury of a squall, and later calm would settle over everything. Or was that just a chimera, the longing for calm? Lucía suspected as much. No, on second thought, she knew it to be true.

Lucía arrived back at Cal Foraster just as the sun was dropping beneath the peaks of Els Ports. The wind was still howling and as she opened the front door, a small cloud of dust rose up in the entryway. She would have to sweep in the morning, she reminded herself. She had felt slightly dizzy on the drive back from the coast; perhaps she had sat too long contemplating the sea and the distant horizon and her precious land. Lucía slowly climbed the stairs to the bedroom and lay down to rest for a moment, hoping to regain her equilibrium. From the bed she had a view of the sky, and she looked out to see a few stars dimly glowing above the first flush of pink. Suddenly she felt terribly cold and decided to get up to light a fire in the wood-burning stove downstairs. She managed to sit upright, but immediately grew light-headed and found herself unable to stand. There was a dull pain spreading through her chest and she lay back down in a panic. Her breathing became fitful. Suddenly her mind flashed back to that White Russian doctor on the S.S. Normandie. In all the years since she had scarcely thought of the man, but now she saw him perfectly: his blond-white hair and pale arctic-blue eyes. She recalled his love of Machado and Cervantes. That old ship's doctor had seen something that other doctors had failed to see. He had detected her pregnancy by merely examining her eyes, she recalled. How strange that had been. And he had been right too about the more profound implications regarding the child, regarding Paco. "You have been blessed," he said. She could still hear his voice with that peculiar Russian inflection. She hadn't wanted to believe it, but it was true. Paco had been a blessing. To think that she had actually contemplated hurling herself over the rail and into the depths of the Atlantic and a watery grave. She thought now of all the precious gifts that would have been denied her: Paco, first and foremost, but also innumerable friends and acquaintances and students, and the likes of Margaret and the Candees and the doormen on Park Avenue, and, of course, Adam Fates, the finest man she had ever known—yes, she knew that now. Perhaps the gods had been conspiring all along, twisting fate to put Adam in her path and keeping him there against all the odds. Alas, it was a love that she had squandered. That was her greatest regret, to have allowed such a love to go unrequited.

Her heart. Must it fail her now? She shuddered to think of it, shuddered from the cold. A blanket lay neatly folded at the foot of the bed, but she could not reach it; could not make her arm do what her mind demanded of it. She felt like a beached whale, lying helpless, out of its element. There was no one about, nothing to do, no sense in crying out above the bellowing wind. She turned her head again toward the window. The sky was darker now, more stars dotted the firmament. She began to have visions, so that she saw her father wearing evening clothes and dancing with Lucía and Inés, while Borja, Francisco, and Carlitos sat silently on a staircase, watching them whirl across a floor of checkered tiles. And then the scene changed abruptly and it was her mother who appeared, sitting before her dressing table, brushing her long hair and singing a kind of lullaby. Perhaps it was sleep that was beckoning her, thought Lucía, hearing that melody from the nursery. But at once she feared that it might be a sleep from which she would never wake. No, she must resist sleep, she told herself. There was still too much yet to see. She then had a vision of Paco as a boy, swimming toward her in the ocean as the surf crashed around them. And she saw Quim and Adam in fatigues, staring out wordlessly, a castle towering up in the background. Miravet was it? She couldn't tell. Save for the fleeting faces, which were almost preternaturally distinct, everything else in this illusionary parade of loved ones from the past was ill-defined or misshapen. What did that mean? she wondered. Try as she might, she could not conjure up images of her loved ones as they were now. Why was the past always looming up to cast a shadow over her present? Why did it have to determine everything? Maybe that's why she had always felt slightly out of sorts in America, where the past counted for so little. Perhaps it was only fitting that she should expire here in these ancestral lands. Is this what she had come home for in the end, to die the finest death of all?

She no longer felt cold. The pain in her chest had receded. In fact, she felt nothing at all, just a kind of weightlessness and the feeling, as her eyelids fluttered and closed, that her heart had missed a beat.

CHAPTER NINE

ADAM FATES STOOD LEANING against the balustrade above the left bank of the Ebro River in Tortosa, smoking and thinking and killing time. Storm clouds, bruised and low, roiled overhead, threatening to swallow him up like the ocean waves that herald a tempest. It smelled like rain, but not a drop fell. With the last of a cigarette Adam bent his head, cupped his hands, and lit another, exhaling smoke into the raw December air. In a half-empty lot nearby, some boys were playing football. A group of men stood looking on from the sidelines, rising on their toes suddenly when a player took a shot on goal, shaking their heads when the shot went wide, calling out commands that Adam could not quite make out above the blustering wind.

The funeral Mass was scheduled for noon, more than an hour yet. It was to be in the cathedral, presided over by the bishop no less. They had come down on the train from Barcelona, he and Paco, all riled up and ready to reject the notion of a church funeral for Lucía, the anticleric, the Republican, the free-thinker. And then they had learned that the mother too had passed, not two days after her daughter, and suddenly it didn't seem right to protest. Eugenia Grau had died at the age of eight-seven from old age, as they say, but also—and they said this with more conviction—from the grief of having a daughter precede her. They were to be buried side by side. Both Adam and Paco had to admit that there was something fitting about that, something indisputable that they didn't have the heart to question; and if the bishop was to perform the rite, what difference did it really make? Lucía had come home to die, even if she hadn't known it.

Paco had gone off earlier with his cousin Victor to attend to certain details: the eulogy, seating, flowers and the like, the customary details of disposing of the dead. Adam didn't think that he was up to such details, nor did he wish to arrive early to the cathedral and feel obliged to engage in small talk with assorted Vidals. What would they all say exactly? He thought he knew.

Such a tragedy.

It was all so sudden.

She had seemed in the best of health.

He thought too of what would go unsaid, but what would be on so many of their minds.

She had been expecting you for months. Why had you kept her waiting so?

Why indeed.

He could so easily have come. It wasn't as if Rio's *favelas* couldn't have waited; they weren't going anywhere, God knows. Suddenly, his professional ambitions, his artistic achievements seemed so paltry, irrelevant even. He recalled his last letter to Lucía in which he had broached the subject of a divorce. Now, the content of that missive filled him with shame. How it must have hurt her, Adam knew. What he would now do for a last few months with her, a last few weeks, a last few hours. The idea of the lost opportunity, the finality of it, tormented him like retribution.

Adam walked away from the river toward the Old Quarter, allowing the cathedral towers to guide him. He still had time to spare and ducked reflexively into the first bar he saw. As he came through the door he was met by the distinctly Spanish stench of frying oil, rancid liquor, and stale cigarette smoke, that, and a din of male voices. But as the patrons leaning against the bar and seated at the marble-topped tables raised their eyes to see who had come through the door, all conversation came to an abrupt halt, as if on some unspoken cue. The silence was so immediate, so pronounced that Adam almost laughed. He felt like the stranger coming through the swinging doors of a saloon in some hackneyed Western. He approached the bar, waiting coolly as the bartender sidled over eying him suspiciously. Everyone seemed poised to hear what words the intruder would utter.

"*Un café solo y un g*üisqui sin hielo," said Adam, flawlessly.

And throughout the room the chatter slowly resumed.

The coffee was bitter and the whiskey, some coarse local label, wretched, although not so much as to prevent him from ordering another. He propped an elbow on the bar, half turned, and surveyed the scene. No women about, the television blaring, men shouting one above the other, dominoes slapping down on tabletops, clack, clack, clack. A portrait of Franco hung on a far wall above a team photograph of the local football club. The New Spain, where was that precisely? Adam wondered. Not here in Tortosa, evidently. He wasn't surprised. He had never liked the place, not during the war, not since he and Paco had arrived the day before; he wasn't sure why. There was a fine medieval quarter, some pleasant residential districts; the mountains of Els Ports provided a dramatic backdrop; the river fed the orchards and gardens to luxuriance; and the sound of flowing water bestowed a certain calm over the place. It was the people rather. Adam had always found them haughty as only true provincials can be. How was it that Lucía had emerged from such a place? he asked himself. He lit a cigarette and looked at his watch. A quarter of an hour, time enough for one last whiskey. He signaled to the barman to fill his glass. Adam picked up the drink, swirled it in a slow motion, raised the glass and drank. The stuff no longer tasted so wretched. He paid the bill but left no tip and ground his cigarette butt on the sawdust strewn floor.

Outside, it had begun to rain and the cobblestones were slick and treacherous. Adam nearly slipped and fell and realized belatedly that he had drunk too much too quickly and eaten too little. His temples were throbbing. Suddenly he was overcome with shame as he stumbled to his wife's funeral. He prayed that he was heading in the right direction. In the midst of the narrow streets he could no longer make out the cathedral towers to guide him. He tried to ask the way from a woman he came upon, but she took one panicked look at him and scurried away wordlessly. Only when the cathedral bells chimed at noon did Adam realize that he was hard by the church. He came around a corner and found Paco waiting for him on the cathedral steps looking vexed. Adam knew at once that his son could see that he had been drinking. How could he not?

"You're late…and tight."

"Neither terribly late nor remotely tight," Adam said, lying.

Paco merely shook his head before they both turned, and father and son climbed the grey rain-streaked steps and passed beneath the Baroque portal. Adam stopped just inside the entrance, removed his overcoat, passed the flat of his hand over his hair, and buttoned the jacket of his charcoal-grey suit. Then he took a deep breath, steadied himself, and proceeded down the center aisle with Paco at his side. The tentative light pressing through the stained-glass, and the dim, draft-flickered candles did little to dispel the dense shadows of the interior. The church smelled of incense and lilies and wet wool. Despite the dankness in the atmosphere, the cold, Adam was sweating; his upper lip was moist, his forehead beading. Whiskey had left his tongue and throat raw and burning. From somewhere deep in the church came the baleful notes of a requiem, a few coughs, a baby crying, scattered whispering. What were they saying these whisperers? Adam wondered. *There goes the widower, the American, the one who took Lucía away; the one who kept her waiting in vain; the one who wasn't at her side when she passed.* The walk up the aisle seemed interminable. He did not look at the other mourners, but trained his eyes forward and concentrated on walking a straight course. In the distance, growing ever closer, lay the two closed caskets, their brass fittings and polished wood gleaming in the half light. Only when he reached the first pew and turned to step in did he see that seated in the row behind him were a collection of familiar faces: Katia, Lorenzo de Marco and Gabriela, Paul Weems, Jeremy Branch, Margaret, Archie and Dorothy Candee, a few of Lucía's colleagues from the Lindley School, some Park Avenue neighbors, assorted friends. Adam had not been expecting this showing of friends and colleagues and servants, and for a moment he felt a pang of melancholy descend over him. He wanted to weep, but he did not. He sat and swiveled around in the pew and grasped Lorenzo's hand and Paul Weems' and nodded at the others with a weak, uncertain smile. Then he whispered to Margaret and Katia to join him and Paco in the front row. They were as close to immediate family as one could be. Just before turning back around, Adam caught sight of a hunched figure seated a few rows behind and couldn't help but think that there was something familiar about the man. He was not a New York friend or acquaintance, of that Adam was sure. In truth, the elderly stranger looked slightly down at the heel in a shabby overcoat that seemed to consume his meager frame. He reminded Adam of a Bowery bum. Perhaps he'd just come in out of the rain to seek shelter and found himself at a funeral and hoped to go unnoticed in the crowd. Lucía would have liked that, he thought. Adam was about to turn back in his seat when the man, perhaps sensing Adam's scrutiny, raised his head and looked directly into his eyes and held his gaze as if trying to convey some wordless message or appeal. And in a sudden flash of recognition Adam knew at once who the man was, although he could not quite credit it. He blinked and wondered if drink or grief weren't wreaking havoc on his senses, or the dim sepulchral light distorting his vision, but no. A shudder ran through the whole length of him. He turned back around and felt the blood draining from his face, his breathing growing erratic and labored. For a moment he thought he might blackout. Paco leaned toward him, looking alarmed, and whispered in his ear: "Papa, what is it? You look as if you'd just seen a ghost."

"I'm not sure I haven't," Adam mumbled, and stared off, transposed to another world, another time.

* * *

He had left Lucía holed up in a state of near-certain mourning in that diminutive flat in Gracia with the irremediable stench of the barnyard. He made his way to the Barrio Chino in the hopes of procuring foodstuffs on the black market and was astonished to find the illicit trade going on quite openly. Business, in fact, was booming. He waited in line behind hollow-cheeked locals bearing paintings in gilded frames, assorted silver, fine crystal. In wartime, these prized possessions, these treasured heirlooms were mere trifles and readily exchanged for a tin or two of sardines, a packet of rice, a kilo of sugar. With such treasures one could feed a family for a week, procure a woman, buy a car, even alter official records. Everything had a price; nothing was off limits. For a few meager dollars—less than the price of a cocktail at the Knickerbocker, Adam reckoned—he walked out of the Barrio Chino with his satchel brimming, bound for Las Arenas.

That the Republican Army Headquarters should be housed in the bullring struck Adam as darkly comic. Two enterprises devoted to slaughter sharing a venue. Surely there was some notion of economy in such a coupling. He found the place a picture of mayhem, yet another sign that the Republic was doomed. Adam made his way quite unimpeded to the records department, where he had been innumerable times with Lucía to inquire after Quim's fate. He immediately recognized a haughty clerk who had treated Lucía on more than one occasion with undisguised indifference. Now, however, things would be different, Adam knew. He managed to get the corporal's attention with a mere jingle of his satchel and promptly allowed him a quick peek inside. He saw the soldier's face grow flush and the man actually lick his lips.

"I need a bit of information," Adam said, nonchalantly.

"How may I assist you?"

Ah, that's better, Adam thought. "I need to know the status of one of your comrades in arms, one Lieutenant Quim Soler Masoliver, V Corps."

It didn't take long. In the end, even Adam was surprised how quick and cheap it proved to be. For a few links of chorizo, a loaf of stale bread, a tin of tuna, and a jar of peaches—this last luxury thrown in as a sort of gratuity—Adam bribed the clerk to alter Quim's status from "missing in action" to "fallen in battle" in the service of the glorious Republic. He did not see it as treachery, not really. He was doing it for Lucía, or so he told himself. All that hopeless searching and inquiring was taking its toll on both of them. They had to get out of Barcelona, out of Spain, before it was too late, at least for Lucía. Anyway, the chances that Quim had survived were...what? Minimal, less than minimal, miraculous would be more like it. Adam was simply providing a means of closure, a suitable conclusion to a tragic loss. Still, he did feel the pangs of a rotten conscience, however briefly. How glib it was to do away with a life, at least on paper.

* * *

The first notes of Mozart's *Ave Verum Corpus* rang out in the chill cathedral air and roused Adam from his distant memories. The mitered bishop, clad in princely purple, entered from the sacristy surrounded by a retinue of priests and altar boys bearing candles and unlit censers. The entire congregation rose, and as Adam stood, he glimpsed furtively over his shoulder just to confirm that it was indeed Quim Soler sitting off behind him and that his mind hadn't been playing tricks on him. He would have preferred the latter, but, alas, Quim was there still; he even nodded gently toward Adam, as if to say: *Yes, it is me, alive, if only just.* But how? Adam wondered. His mind was reeling. Over the next hour he could scarcely concentrate on the long ritualistic proceedings of his own wife's funeral. There were successive readings from Job, the Romans, and the Gospel according to Mark, but all the words of succor and hope, mercy and compassion were tangled and confused and lost to him. The Eucharist, the priests circling the caskets swinging censers billowing clouds of incense, the hymns...all it of conspired to make Adam feel slightly bewildered. It wasn't the whiskey that was impairing his ability to focus, for he had sobered up fast enough, but the past, a past that was supposed to have been surmounted, put to rest, duly forgotten. Instead, the past in the guise of his deceased wife's first love, his former friend, the true father of the son who was sitting at his side, was hunched a few pews back, waiting. For what, precisely? Adam could not be sure. He looked down and saw that he had a white-knuckled grip on Paco's hand. His son regarded him with that forgiving, indulgent look that grown sons adopt when their fathers become feeble.

"What?" Adam asked in panic, a bit too loudly.

"Papa," Paco whispered patiently "you've got to let go of my hand."

"Where are you going?"

"To deliver the eulogy."

Adam grasped little of it; something about the lessons that his mother had taught him, principles of liberty, fraternity, and solidarity, Republican principles all. He spoke of a woman who had carried her country and her culture in her heart always, and how he, her only son, had been enriched by her foreign ways, her peculiar take on things, even her inability to fully adapt to life in America. And of course, he spoke of his mother finally coming home, something that had not been possible for decades on account of a murderous regime. Adam looked around and saw that much of the congregation, including Katia and Margaret and the Vidal clan across the aisle, were weeping. The bishop and priests, on the other hand, looked piqued. Adam felt something rend within him and all at once he too was weeping. They were the first tears that he had shed over the loss of Lucía, the first tears, in fact, that he had shed since he was a boy. At his parents' funeral he had been stoic and dry eyed. It's not that he considered himself a callous person, just not exceedingly emotional. But this, of course, was different. He didn't bury his face in his hands, but just allowed the hot tears to stream down. He couldn't even summon up the wherewithal to wipe them away. Through the liquid veil Adam stared at the casket and realized he wasn't even sure which one held Lucía, but he was glad that they were closed. He couldn't deny that he had an urge, powerful and decidedly morbid, to kiss his wife's lips one last time, to stroke the skin of cheeks as smooth and cold as marble. But who knows, perhaps she wasn't there at all, he suddenly realized. Perhaps she hadn't died. Everyone is so convinced that death is final, but just take a look at old Quim Soler huddled back there. Hadn't he been swallowed up by the river and washed out to sea. If he had cheated death, why couldn't Lucía?

Adam wasn't sure how long he had sat there lost in his reverie, but suddenly Paco was grasping his arm and helping him to his feet. The tears on his cheeks were dry and crusty. Up at the altar, the bishop muttered some concluding rite. Bells sounded and soon Mendelssohn's *Prelude* accompanied them down the cathedral nave and out of the gloom.

The rain had stopped, but it was just a respite; slate-colored clouds rushed overhead, reflected in the shimmering puddles of the square. Far off one could hear thunder rolling down from Els Ports. Waiting at the foot of the steps in front of the cathedral was an antique glass-paneled hearse drawn by a pair of black-plumed horses, the driver turned out in a top hat and an Inverness cloak of black satin. The whole arrangement struck Adam as vaguely ludicrous; he turned to Paco, smirking and cocking an eyebrow, but said nothing. His son went off in search of the New York crowd. The congregation gathered on the church steps and spilled into the square, talking, smoking, peering up at the ominous sky, marveling at the hearse and the horseflesh. It was that brief interim moment—there was no word for it, at least none that Adam knew— between the funeral Mass and the actual burial. The mourners had submitted grave-faced and decorous to the solemnity of the church proceedings and now they were back in the open air and relieved, although they would be loath to admit it, that it was someone else, and not them, who had expired. Giddily grateful to be alive, that's the way they looked, thought Adam. He bent to light a cigarette and when he straightened up he suddenly found himself face to face with Inés Vidal. He let out an audible gasp, actually more like a whimper. Dressed in rigorous black and veiled, she looked like a macabre and slightly spent version of Lucía.

"I didn't mean to startle you," she said, as she lifted the veil from her face.

"Forgive me," said Adam, taking her hand and leaning down to kiss her salty, tear-streaked cheeks, "the likeness was always so striking."

"Not so much in later years, unfortunately," said Inés, frowning.

"It's good to see you again," he said politely. In fact, he had been dreading this moment.

"We're so glad that you could come…finally."

Adam felt himself wince. To his relief, Inés turned away to watch the caskets borne out of the cathedral and down the steps and placed into the hearse. The pallbearers were hired hands from the funeral home.

Adam scanned the crowd, looking for Quim. It shouldn't be too hard to make out his ravaged frame amidst the crowd of well-to-do mourners, he thought, but Quim was nowhere to be seen. Where had he disappeared to? Adam caught sight of the New York contingent huddled together in a corner of the square, looking at a loss as to where to go or what to do. He was about to excuse himself and go to them when a bloated little man approached with Francisco hobbling up behind.

"At last," said the stranger, extending a hand to Adam to shake. He realized suddenly that it was Borja Vidal and took the hand with certain reluctance.

"The two of you have never met?" Inés asked, surprised.

"No," said Adam, shaking Borja's hand, but looking at Inés "your brother was not at Quinta Amelia when I was there." Then, turning to Borja, he said: "You had run off to join the Fascists, if my memory doesn't fail me."

"I prefer the term Nationalist," said Borja coolly.

"In this case they are synonymous," said Francisco from somewhere behind Borja, before clattering forward. "Hello, Adam."

"Hello, Francisco. You haven't changed a bit."

Francisco beamed. There was a long silence, as if no one knew quite what to say, perhaps because there was too much to say. *I wish we were meeting under other circumstances.* Or, *the bishop did a fine job with the ceremony,* seemed to Adam too stale, so he said nothing. The ill-ease was relieved by the sudden pealing of the cathedral bells.

"Not a moment too soon," said Francisco, grinning witlessly.

Adam could see that Francisco too had been drinking. He appeared slightly addled, as if he wasn't sure why they were all standing there. Borja gave his brother a long-suffering look before leaning toward Adam's ear to be heard above the clamor of bells.

"Please tell your American guests that there will be a reception at Quinta Amelia. The burial, however, is a more intimate affair. I'm sure they will understand."

"Yes, of course," replied Adam, "thank…" but Borja had already turned away.

The caravan of automobiles, headlights lit, crept slowly through the streets of Tortosa, following the horse-drawn hearse and the sound of clicking hooves on cobblestone. Adam rode in a car with Paco, Katia, and Margaret; Victor drove. People crowded the sidewalks and the balconies and removed their hats and crossed themselves and stared as the funeral cortege passed. The flag on the façade of the Town Hall flew at half-mast, Adam noticed. The official gesture was not for Lucía, of course, but for Eugenia Grau, one of the last of the Old Guard gone. He felt a grudging respect for the lady. As they passed through a narrow lane of the Old Quarter, Adam suddenly saw Quim standing aside, his back pressed to an ancient, pock-marked wall, watching the procession pass. He could have reached out and touched him, they were so close. Adam pressed his face to the window and for an instant the two men caught each other's eye, before the car rolled on.

"What are you staring at?" Paco asked him.

"Nothing," said Adam "I thought I saw someone I knew."

"Ghosts again?"

"No, flesh and bone, or what's left of it," he said, his voice trailing off.

The walled cemetery, perched on the hillside above the city and guarded by an enclosure of towering cypress trees, was called San Lázaro, of course. How different the place was from the cemeteries of America. Adam thought of the lush green acres of graves and tidy rows of headstones that he always saw from the expressway on the drive to Southampton. Here, the niches were stacked one atop the other, the dead as cramped and crowded as captives on a slave ship. Unless, of course, like the Graus, one had the means to be interred far from the rabble in a roomy family crypt. Adam and the other mourners—family, intimates, a few faithful retainers—filed solemnly along an immaculate gravel path to a well-kept corner of the precinct where the private crypts were located. Even here, the Grau crypt—or was it a mausoleum, Adam wasn't sure—stood slightly apart from the others. It was an impressive, if rather ponderous neo-Gothic pile with an abundance of pointed arches, slender spires, elaborate tracery, and wholly unnecessary flying buttresses. Above the portal, the name Grau was wrought in stone in a kind of Germanic Blackletter script. At once Adam regretted that Lucía would be forever confined in such an aesthetic aberration and that it was here that he would have to make his way each year to lay flowers at his beloved's tomb. But what was he to do? If Lucía had died in New York, he would have found a lovely spot, perhaps in the Southampton cemetery beside his parents, or had her cremated and her ashes dispersed in the rose garden or in the crashing surf at the beach. Was that even legal? he wondered. It didn't matter now. Nothing mattered. He hadn't the strength to impose his will. In fact, he felt as if he had no will at all. He felt nothing so much as relief that others were making the crucial decisions.

The caskets lay side by side on a dais at the entrance to the crypt. The bishop stood on the front step, while the mourners gathered around the dead roughly in a semi-circle. It was a quick affair. The bishop droned on for a spell, but Adam could barely make out his rapid Spanish. The gist couldn't have varied too much from the English conventions… ashes to ashes… and all the rest. There were a few hymns, tentatively sung. Margaret and Rosa and Inés sobbed quietly. Paco put his arm around Katia, the two hung their heads, and they too began to sob. Adam maintained just enough composure to read, first in Spanish, then in English, Lucía's favorite verse by Lorca, *Tengo miedo a perder la maravilla* or *Sonnet of the Sweet Complaint*.

Tengo miedo a perder la maravilla
de tus ojos de estatua, y el acento
que de noche me pone en la mejilla
la solitaria rosa de tu aliento.

Tengo pena de ser en esta orilla
tronco sin ramas; y lo que más siento
es no tener la flor, pulpa o arcilla,
para el gusano de mi sufrimiento.

Si tú eres el tesoro oculto mío,
si eres mi cruz y mi dolor mojado,
si soy el perro de tu señorío,

no me dejes perder lo que he ganado
y decora las aguas de tu río
con hojas de mi otoño enajenado.

* * *

Never let me lose the marvel
of your statue-like eyes, or the accent
the solitary rose of your breath
places on my cheek at night.

I am afraid of being, on this shore,
a branchless trunk, and what I most regret
is having no flower, pulp, or clay
for the worm of my despair.

If you are my hidden treasure,
if you are my cross, my dampened pain,
if I am a dog, and you alone my master,

never let me lose what I have gained,
and adorn the branches of your river
with leaves of my estranged Autumn.

Finally, the pallbearers carried the caskets into the crypt and placed mother and daughter in adjacent vaults amidst an assemblage of silent Graus. Two laborers waited outside at a discreet distance, smoking and quietly preparing a batch of mortar. The mourners, led by the bishop, filed out of the cemetery, but Adam lingered behind and watched the workmen brick up the opening of the vault. He wanted to make sure that they did a proper job of it, that they didn't leave any gaps or chinks where cold air or vermin or light might enter to disturb Lucía's eternal sleep. When the men finished their task, Adam thanked them, and they nodded and looked away and said that they were sorry for his loss, before gathering up their tools and departing. Adam was left alone and he sat on the steps of the crypt in the pale, diminishing light and lowered his face into his hands. He stayed on at the cemetery until darkness had fallen and his teeth chattered from the cold. Then he said his last goodbye to Lucía and turned his back on the dead and walked down the hillside with little more than the distant lights of the town to guide him. He made his way to the train station and found a taxi to take him to Quinta Amelia.

"A sad day for the Graus," said the driver, after Adam had told him where he wanted to go. "And that daughter, so beautiful and full of life and come home at last."

Adam watched from behind as the man alternately shook his head and spied him in the mirror.

"A mother and daughter should never be buried together," the driver added "Isn't natural."

No, it wasn't natural, Adam agreed, but he didn't speak. What could he say? They drove on in silence, climbing up the winding road past stately villas ensconced behind high stone walls and iron gates. When they turned into the drive at Quinta Amelia the driver made a clicking sound with his tongue.

"Now here's a place that's seen better days," he said.

The house was lit up inside and out, making its outlandish architectural details, which Adam had never liked—until now he had forgotten just how much—look all the more like figments of some fevered imagination. Adam felt a sudden chill and a sinking of his heart. He would have turned and fled if it weren't for Paco and the slew of New York mourners. He paid the driver and told him to come back in an hour.

"Oh, no need for that," the man said. "I'll just park off to the side there and listen to the game on the radio. I'll be here whenever you're ready."

"Thank you," said Adam.

It was Rosa who answered the front door. They had seen one another at the burial and greeted each other decorously, but they were constrained by the occasion and had scarcely spoken. Now Adam opened his arms and embraced her warmly. Then he held her at arm's length and gazed at her, shaking his head.

"*Querida* Rosa," he said. "How we missed you."

"It was we who missed you," Rosa said, looking up at him, her eyes welling up.

Which *we* was she referring to, Adam wondered, which *you*.

"I have so many questions," he told her, his voice graver.

"The guests will be leaving soon," said Rosa. "We can speak later in the kitchen."

"I just have to make an appearance. I'll come as soon as I can get away."

"Don't be in such a rush, there are many people in that room who loved Lucía," she said with a hint of reproach.

"You see how I missed you," he said, smiling gently.

Rosa took Adam's overcoat and he walked toward the low collective murmur of conversation that was coming from the drawing room. From the threshold, he looked over a somber sea of black and grey suits and frocks. Standing around in clusters, chatting, drinking, balancing plates of tapas, clinging to their age-old provincial privileges was the elite of Tortosa, such as it was. Landowners, politicians, lawyers and their wives, a few military officers, and, of course, the clergy, plenty of clergy, they were all there, gathered to pay tribute to the Graus. These were the war's victors, Adam saw at once, those who were suspicious of progress and social justice and foreign ideas. They would remain forever faithful to Spain's inveterate traditions; the less that changed, the better. Suddenly, Adam was overwhelmed with a sense of contentment for having enabled Lucía to escape this stifling world. What would have become of her had she remained, he wondered. Seeing Inés, standing off in a corner, looking stolid and slightly plump, gave him more than an inkling. He made his way to a bar set up on a table in the corner and helped himself to a generous glass of whiskey. There was a tap on his shoulder. Adam turned and found Paco looking rather spent, his eyes swimming in and out of focus.

"We've been waiting for you; where on earth have you been?" his son asked.

"With your mother," he replied.

"Oh," said Paco, seeming to teeter.

"Are you quite alright?" Adam asked, although he could see that his son was not.

"No, in fact, far from it," said Paco emphatically. "I am bereft. I have made a mess with Katia. And I am positively exhausted from translating condolences from English to Spanish and Spanish to English."

Paco poured himself a whiskey. How alike they were, Adam realized, not for the first time.

"Best to take things one trouble at a time," said Adam. "Where are our New York friends?"

"In the corner," said Paco, jerking his head in the general direction "talking to the bishop, of all people."

"Oh, good God, we better get over there."

"No, no, no, I've just come from that gathering. It's your turn," said Paco, before moving off unsteadily.

Adam worked his way across the room, catching bits of conversation, small doses of laughter, glances. Occasionally he was pulled into a group, introduced to various Vidals, distant Grau relations, strangers. They expressed their condolences, looked at him compassionately, touched his arm. He began to understand his role as a widower, the finality of it. He had lost his parents; now he had lost his wife. Only Paco remained and he suddenly realized with dread that he might well lose him too. By the time he reached the corner of the room his glass of whiskey was empty and he was feeling light-headed. He found the Americans huddled together in a corner looking surprisingly animated. Adam made his way among them, shaking hands, embracing, taking in their whispered words of comfort.

"How on earth did you all get here?" Adam asked, incredulous.

"By taxi, "said Margaret.

"No, I mean to Spain," said Adam.

"Jeremy chartered a plane for all of us," said Paul Weems.

"What?" Adam exclaimed, turning to Branch, looking dumbfounded.

"Yes, it's true," said Jeremy Branch. "Best money I ever spent."

"We wouldn't have missed it for the world," said Dorothy Candee. "Lucía meant so much to all of us."

"I don't know quite what to say except that I am touched beyond words. I can't tell you what it means to Paco and me that you came all this way."

"Well, I must say that the Spaniards, or should I say the Catalans—they seem to be rather touchy about that around here, by the way—certainly know how to put on a funeral reception," said Paul Weems.

"Yes, excellent wine," said Branch.

"And the ham!" said Margaret.

"The only problem is that no one speaks any English, or comprehensible English anyway, not the hotel manager, or the taxi driver, not even the bishop," said Branch.

"Yes, well, we're not in England, after all," said Adam. "Paco and I will translate anything you'd like to say."

Just then Adam heard Lorenzo's voice, insistent, agitated. "Tell him that if Jesus of Nazareth were alive today he would be a Marxist, perhaps an anarcho-syndicalist, at the *very least* a Socialist!"

Adam turned to see his friend and Gabriela backing the bishop into the corner. The Most Reverend looked out of his reckoning.

"Go on," Lorenzo prodded Gabriela, "tell him."

Ordinarily he wouldn't have minded watching this clash, this affront, for Adam had more than a few misgivings regarding the ways of the Church, especially in Spain, but on the day of his late wife's burial, in her childhood home, he did not wish to witness a fracas. Adam swooped in on the trio just before Gabriela had a chance to engage the bishop.

"Excellency!" said Adam, interrupting. Was that the proper title or was it Eminence? he couldn't remember. He didn't really care. "There you are. I've been searching for you. I wanted to thank you for such a distinguished ceremony."

The bishop instinctively extended his ringed hand for Adam to kiss. Adam hesitated, taken aback momentarily, and then simply grasped the man's hand and shook it vigorously. The bishop looked bewildered.

"Now, if you'll forgive me, I must care for my New York friends who have come such a long way and are understandably exhausted. Excuse us, please."

Whereupon Adam grabbed Lorenzo and Gabriela by their arms and whisked them away.

"I was just making a very salient point," Lorenzo insisted.

"They shot people during the war for saying as much."

"That doesn't make it any less true."

"Yes, of course, but not here, not today, if you don't mind."

"Very well," said Lorenzo, appearing resigned "but it's not every day that I get a bishop on the ropes."

"We must get food," said Gabriela, glaring at Lorenzo. "You talk so much, we have nothing to eat."

"Can we get you something?" Lorenzo asked Adam.

"Yes, whiskey."

"Nothing more?" said Gabriela. "You must eat something."

"No appetite today, I'm afraid," said Adam, sighing.

Lorenzo and Gabriela drifted into the crowd, leaving Adam to scan the room. He was hoping to catch a glimpse of Quim, although what exactly he would say to the man if they came face to face he didn't know. *Well, well, look who's alive...Ah, fancy meeting you here...Son of a bitch, we thought you were dead!* Suddenly he remembered having been in this very room with Quim during the war. Adam had been surprised by the young officer's deference toward Quinta Amelia and his hosts. He had wanted to sit in the drawing room with Quim and take some portraits of the Republican officer juxtaposed in the rarefied interior. Quim had refused. It's not a question of me sitting here and putting my boots up on the table, he had said. The family has opened their home to us— although both men knew very well that Eugenia Grau had not been in a position to refuse—we are billeted here, not the new lords of the manor.

How struck Adam had been by that attitude, that sense of a man doing the right thing. It was then that they had become friends.

"You won't find him here," said a voice.

Adam looked down to find Borja Vidal. What a little man he was, Adam noticed again. It was hard to believe that he had been an officer in the war, that he had led men.

"Who do you mean?" asked Adam.

"Oh, come now," said Borja, raising his eyebrows, a trace of a smile on his lips "Quim Soler, of course."

Adam did not deny it. "And how can you be so sure that he won't appear?"

"The power of pride, I suppose. Quim is a wasted man, a broken man. I can't imagine him wanting to turn up here in his state."

"The one that got away, was he?"

"On the contrary," said Borja. "I even managed to have him spared the firing squad," he added boastfully, rising on his toes.

Neither man said anything for a time. They both looked out over the room and the guests. The crowd was thinning; people looked weary from drink and hours of forced solemnity.

"I suppose that Quim should thank you," Adam said finally, his tone derisive.

"Oh, he already has, in fact, on more than one occasion, and I accepted his thanks. All the same, it must have been a shock to you to discover that he was alive; it certainly was to Lucía."

Adam felt at a distinct disadvantage. It was hard to spar when he was so in the dark as to the facts. But who was he to question Borja, anyway, he who had orchestrated Quim's removal from the rolls of the living? He felt like a fraud. At last Lorenzo appeared bearing his whiskey. He did not introduce the two men.

"Permit me to express my condolences at the loss of your mother," Adam said, hoping to strike a closing note to the conversation.

"Ah, there we are; I knew that there must be some graciousness in you, otherwise Lucía would never have married you...except perhaps to flee. Thank you for your sentiments." Then Borja bowed his head slightly and actually clicked his heels, before turning neatly and striding off.

"Who on earth was that?" Lorenzo asked.

"Borja, Lucía's eldest brother."

"Well, he must be a bastard. He certainly bears no resemblance to Lucía."

"No," Adam agreed, "not at all."

When the last of the guests had departed, only the family remained, lingering slack on the sofas and gathered in small groups around the room—Paco and Katia with Victor and Inés' twin daughters; Borja and Paulina with some or another Grau; Francisco with Inés and Javier. Adam made his way around and listened to them discuss the events of the day, the guests, family lore. Eventually, he slouched over to the bar, served himself a last whiskey, and stole off to the kitchen in search of Rosa. He was surprised to discover that even in the half dark he still knew the way after all these years. He found her helping a young scullery maid with the washing up. Rosa did not see Adam at first, her back was to him, and he stood watching the two of them for a time. He was astonished at how well Rosa had kept herself—her figure, her legs, her whole bearing. Why on earth had she never married? he wondered. Or had she decided long ago to simply wed the Graus? His mind was skipping about, thinking disjointed, drunken thoughts. He looked down at the glass of whiskey in his hand, but he did not raise it to his lips. He had already drunk too much, again. His empty stomach felt queasy. He lurched suddenly, but caught himself. Rosa turned and looked at him, shaking her head and giving him a look of reprove. She went to him, drying her hands on a kitchen towel, and took his glass of whiskey.

"Go sit," she said, motioning with her head toward a breakfast table in the corner.

She made him strong coffee and a plate of eggs with *pan con tomate* and white sausage. Adam felt like a schoolboy, needy and vaguely remiss.

"One day you will make a man very happy," said Adam, mockingly.

"Shush," said Rosa.

He had always liked this woman, could have married her and been perfectly happy, he thought. "I envy you the time you had with Lucía these last months," Adam said, serious now.

"And I the years you had with her."

"I almost wish I could trade them," said Adam in a whisper, staring unfocused at the window. All he could see was his and Rosa's ghostly reflection in the dark glass.

"It wouldn't be much of a bargain," said Rosa, frowning. "You didn't miss much here. Lucía filled her days with her mother. Think of how sad it would have been had Lucía died without returning and reconciling with her mother."

"So, they did reconcile, at last."

"Yes, I think they did, on a certain level, at least."

Adam was silent for a time, thinking about the truth of what Rosa had said. But he thought too of what, or rather whom, she had failed to mention. "Apart from her mother, who else did she fill her days with?" he asked.

Rosa looked away toward the young maid who was finishing her chores, ignoring what Adam had said. He could see her face grow tense, her jaw tighten.

"What is it?" Adam asked. "You seem ill at ease." He could hear his own voice growing hard.

Rosa turned back toward the table, but she did not look at Adam. "What is it that you want to know?" she asked, her eyes downcast.

"How long have you known that Quim Soler was alive?"

"For years, of course."

"Of course," said Adam sarcastically. "So is that how Lucía filled her days, entertaining Quim Soler?"

"You are insulting your wife's memory."

"Am I? I don't quite see it that way. I'm just trying to discover a bit of the truth."

"The truth? The truth is that Lucía cared for her mother and reconnected with her family and with Quim Soler too, yes."

"No wonder Lucía was so keen on coming back alone."

"For goodness sake, don't be a fool," said Rosa in an unexpectedly harsh tone, eying him narrowly. "You saw Quim at the cathedral, or I assume you did. The man's life was ruined, he is alone and on his last legs, and you're insinuating some sort of romantic reunion." She made to get up from her chair, but Adam reached for her arm and stopped her.

"No, please, don't go," said Adam. "I'm sorry, but I feel like I'm the only one who is unaware of what has been going on. I feel like I've been made a fool of."

"The only thing that has been 'going on', as you call it, was Lucía caring for people who she loved, that and pining for you, waiting for your letters, and wishing desperately for you to come and join her."

For a long time Adam was silent. He felt slightly ashamed. "Perhaps you could take me to her room," he said finally. "I think that I'd like to sit there for a moment before gathering her things."

Rose nodded slowly and turned her head to look off toward the kitchen, but the young maid had gone. She sighed deeply.

"What?" Adam asked.

She turned to him and shrugged. He could see her gathering her words, deciding what to say. He was growing impatient.

"Lucía hadn't lived here for months. She moved out in the summer."

"Where on earth did she go?" Adam asked, feeling more and more the fool. Why did he have to ask these questions, discover these revelations, about his own wife?"

"She was living at Cal Foraster, a small house not far from here that belongs to the family."

"I see," said Adam wearily. "She didn't mention it in her letters."

"It was to be a surprise."

"Is that where she died?" he asked.

"Yes."

"Alone?"

"Yes."

What an irony, he thought. She'd come all this way to be surrounded by family again and ended up dying alone. If he had been there he might have saved her. He suddenly realized that he now had a burden that he would never shed. "Will you take me there?" he asked. "In the morning, I mean."

"Yes, naturally."

He stood up slowly to leave. He felt better for the coffee and eggs. "Thank you for taking the time to explain all this to me," he said, looking down at her. Again he noticed how attractive this woman was. What a pity she hadn't managed to get away from Quinta Amelia, he thought. "May I ask you something, something intimate?" Adam asked. She merely looked up at him and waited for his question.

"Why have you never married?"

Rosa closed her eyes and lowered her head.

"Forgive me," said Adam. "It's not my business."

"No," she said, shaking her head. She opened her eyes and looked up at Adam, smiling weakly. "Love…you know, not everyone finds it. How lucky you and Quim were to have found Lucía."

He had almost forgotten about the taxi. Adam found the driver slumped behind the wheel, his cap pulled down over his eyes, snoring gently. The football match was long over; boleros were playing on the radio. The man started when Adam opened the back door of the car; he looked around, blinking, and for an instant seemed to have forgotten where he was.

"Sorry to have kept you waiting so long," Adam said.

The driver shrugged and started the engine. "Where to?" he asked.

"The Parador," said Adam.

"You're not from here are you?" the driver asked.

"No."

"You a distant member of the family, maybe?"

"Husband of the deceased," said Adam for the first time. He didn't like the sound of it.

The driver pulled abruptly to the side of the road, stopped the car, and swung around in his seat. "I had no idea, sir, please accept my condolences."

"Thank you," said Adam, somewhat taken aback by the exuberance of the gesture.

They started off again, the driver shifting his gaze from the road to the rearview mirror. "I drove your late missus once," he said proudly "a beautiful woman, a true lady."

"Yes," Adam agreed "the best any man could hope for."

* * *

He woke with a shriek, entangled in sheets, trying to break free of—of what? Something had been restraining him or pursuing him, he wasn't sure which. He tried to grasp it, but the thread of the dream vanished; perhaps it would return in a flash later in the day when he least expected it. Adam sat up and looked around the room with its ghastly trappings: the dark, heavy furniture and wrought-iron fixtures, the light sconces in the form of torches, the crenelated chandelier suspended from black chains. No wonder he'd had a nightmare, Adam thought. He rose from the bed and went to the window and peered out. It was past seven o'clock, but only the dimmest light glowed in the winter sky. The rain and the clouds had moved off, so too the wind.

All of the New York guests were staying at the Parador, a sprawling Moorish fortress-turned-hotel rising on a hilltop above the city. Most of them intended to stay on for a few days and take advantage of the journey to soak up a bit of Spanish culture, as one of them had confessed the night before. Adam would have time enough to attend to friends, but they could wait. He wanted to see where Lucía had been living these last months, where she had met her end. What had Rosa called the place? Some Catalan name, Cal...something...Cal Foraster, that was it, The House of the Stranger. He almost laughed.

He showered and dressed, stole past the night clerk dosing behind the reception desk, and set off into the morning, walking fast to keep the cold at bay. By nine o'clock he was at the kitchen door at Quinta Amelia. Rosa was waiting for him, car keys in hand. They walked around to the side of the house where the car was parked. It was a very splendid machine, and Adam felt a certain degree of pride—silly, he knew, but nonetheless—on account of his wife having chosen so well. Still, there was something ghostly about the car that made him shudder. When he first opened the door and ducked his head inside, he got an unmistakable whiff of her, and almost collapsed from grief. Then he contorted his lanky frame to squeeze himself into the driver's seat and froze suddenly, not wanting to adjust the seat or the side and rearview mirrors to suit him for fear of losing something of Lucía's measure in the world. In the end, he relented, but only reluctantly; he had no choice. They rolled out of the gravel drive and headed north, Rosa indicating the way through the endless olive groves.

He hadn't known quite what to expect, not really, so when they turned off the road and proceeded down the dirt track and the house came into view, Adam smiled and made a pleasant kind of humming sound. He parked the car and got out and stood in front of the house, silently training his eyes over the place, studying it.

"Lucía loved it," said Rosa, who was standing behind him at a respectful remove. "She thought you would too."

He did. He liked the white-washed brilliance of it; the spare lines and weathered tiles of the ridge roof; the enormous rough-hewn wooden door. He liked the lay of the land with olive trees stretching in every direction. He liked the view of the mountains to the south and the sea to the east. He could see Lucía here, even more so the two of them together. The mere thought of how happy they might have been filled him with unspeakable sorrow. Suddenly, he wasn't sure if he wanted to go inside. Perhaps he shouldn't have come at all, he thought; but then he remembered Rosa telling him how hard Lucía had worked fixing up the place and he felt he owed her the effort of admiring what she had accomplished. And so he approached the door, inserted the almost comically large iron key into the lock, opened the door, and crossed the threshold. The first thing that struck him was a waft of dead cold air, that, and the sight of geckos clinging to the walls. Rosa followed him inside and proceeded to open the shutters, and the interior filled with a sharp winter light that illuminated every object and surface. Adam was stunned by the beauty of the place—its proportions, its economy, the perfect restraint of the furniture. Here, he thought, was the absolute essence of a house. It looked as if it might have survived from antiquity. To add anything would have been excessive; to take anything away would have disturbed its delicate equilibrium. He thought of the Park Avenue apartment and the cavernous Southampton house and all the thoroughly unnecessary things that filled those spaces. Adam proceeded to wander about the house, upstairs and down, gazing from every window, peering into every corner, sitting in every chair. He even lay on Lucía's death bed and looked out the window to behold the piece of sky that Lucía had last contemplated. He was searching for her, he realized, trying to capture something of her presence still lingering in the place. On the bedside table he found his letters to her kept neatly in their original envelopes with their exotic Brazilian stamps. And when he carefully unfolded the brittle airmail stationary and read his own words, he was at once full of remorse for the excuses that he had proffered to stay on working in Rio, and something verging on disgrace at the suggestion that they should perhaps consider a divorce. He folded the letter and carefully put it back in the envelope and slipped it into his jacket pocket.

Before setting off, Adam stood in the middle of the living room intent on bidding the house and Lucía's association with it farewell. But when he looked around the room, Adam realized that what the space needed was life. "Rosa," Adam shouted.

Rosa rushed into the house from the garden where she had been waiting for him. "What is it?" she asked, looking alarmed.

"We are going to organize a memorial lunch for Lucía, here, with all her New York friends, the people she loved and who loved her in return. We can set up a long table, give them proper paella, teach them to drink wine from a *porrón*."

Rosa's face dropped.

"What's the matter?" asked Adam.

"I think it's a wonderful idea, truly, except for the *porrón;* they'll just make a mess of themselves."

"Most likely, but they'll love it."

"How many people are you imagining?"

"I'm not sure, a dozen perhaps. Can you make paella for that many?"

"I could make paella for a hundred."

"Really?"

"Naturally."

"We can all help," said Adam eagerly.

"No, no, no," said Rosa, shaking her head. "You take care of the guests, the wine, some extra chairs, but leave the paella to me."

"Do you think it's a crazy idea?" Adam asked, suddenly unsure. "I mean celebrating at a time like this."

"Not at all, I think Lucía will love it."

Adam locked up the house and they got into the Mercedes and drove back up the track. When they reached the road, Adam stopped and turned to Rosa. "There's just one more stop," he said flatly. He didn't have to explain where.

Rosa nodded. "Take a right," she said.

* * *

He was sitting in front of the house, wrapped in a greatcoat, his back against the façade, his eyes closed, warming himself in the sun. Only when Adam got out of the car and approached him—was standing right over him, in fact—did Quim finally raise a hand to shield his eyes from the glare and look up at Adam.

"You're late," said Quim, matter-of-factly.

"By nearly forty years from what I understand."

"Yes, but I'm afraid I wouldn't have been here to greet you."

"We were told that you had died, swept away by the Ebro."

"Yes, I know, but the river spat me back and here I am."

"Alive."

"Just barely."

Rosa, who had been hovering behind Adam, waiting for an opening, stepped timidly forward. "Hello, Quim," she said, sounding relieved.

"Welcome, Rosa, you are looking well, as always."

She blushed like a school girl. "Have you got a basket? I think I'll go gather some mushrooms and leave the two of you to catch up."

"On the kitchen table, help yourself."

The two men watched Rosa enter the house and emerge soon after with a wicker basket hooked on an arm. She disappeared around the side of the house.

"Have a seat," said Quim, gesturing to another chair at his side.

Adam sat, and for a long time neither man spoke. It was not an awkward silence. The men had secrets between them. Everything in time, Adam thought.

"So," said Adam finally "the woman we loved is gone."

"It doesn't seem right. I'm the one who should be dead," said Quim "although I don't imagine I'll have to wait much longer."

"I'm sorry," said Adam in a low voice, looking down.

"What about?"

"I'm not really sure. The way things turned out for you, I suppose." In fact, he was altogether sure. He was sorry for having manipulated the records and killing off the man, as it were. Still, he lacked the courage to come clean. He would have to learn to live with that particular stain on his conscience.

"You have nothing to apologize for, I asked you to promise to get Lucía out of harm's way."

"That wasn't hard. I loved her."

"I know, but all the same, you gave her the sort of life that I would never have been able to provide."

Adam sighed, shaking his head.

"What?" Quim asked.

"I don't think it made much difference to her, the material comforts, I mean."

"Is that so? What about the car?" said Quim, looking over at the Mercedes gleaming in the late morning light.

Adam smiled. "Yes, well, you've got a point there. Still, I've just come from Cal Foraster and the way that Lucía prepared the house, the simplicity of it, really struck me. I think that house is more a reflection of her character than our New York apartment or our grand house at the beach. Have you seen it, by the way, Cal Foraster?"

"Yes, once."

"Just once?" Adam asked, surprised.

"Once was quite enough," said Quim sharply.

"Why do you say it like that?"

Quim gave an empty laugh. "Because I was jealous, blindly so. Lucía labored to get that house into shape and she did it for you. Before she moved into Cal Foraster, she had had lots of free time to devote to me, but once she set her mind on fashioning a place for the two of you, I saw her less and less. It was as if I was losing her to you yet again. It sounds silly now."

It didn't sound silly to Adam. He couldn't help but feel a slight sense of satisfaction, although he knew that it was unbecoming. "Jealous?" he said. "It seems as if I spent my whole marriage being jealous of you, jealous of a dead man, if you'll forgive me. You were her first love. I never seemed to be able to get over that."

Both men began to laugh, but soon Quim was overcome by a fit of wheezing, gasping for breath and clutching Adam's arm. Adam looked on, alarmed, before rushing into the house and fetching a glass of water from the kitchen. When he came back out, Quim had recovered somewhat.

"Forgive me," said Quim, taking the glass from Adam and drinking.

"Have you seen a doctor about that?"

"Of course," said Quim wearily "but there's nothing to be done. It's silicosis from excavating Franco's blasted tomb."

"I'm sorry," said Adam for the second time. He didn't know what else to say. Perhaps Quim would rather have been swept away by the river. They both closed their eyes and let the sun's rays warm them. Gunfire punctuated the silence from time to time; Sunday hunters were out for rabbit and partridge.

"I hope Rosa's careful," said Adam. Quim made no comment. Perhaps country people didn't comment on such things, he thought. It was assumed that they knew what they were doing. Adam took out his silver case and offered a cigarette to Quim, but immediately felt foolish for plying tobacco to an invalid suffering from a lung disease, and for brandishing the exquisite case. Quim merely raised a hand silently to decline. Adam smoked and looked out over the olive trees, their branches bending nearly to the ground with the weight of ripe fruit.

"Handsome man that son of yours," said Quim suddenly.

"Thank you," said Adam, at once feeling somewhat fraudulent. Had Lucía and Quim discussed Paco? he wondered. Adam didn't think so, but he couldn't be sure.

"He bears an uncanny resemblance to my brother Pere," said Quim. Then, keeping his eyes closed all the while, and in a seemingly practiced motion, he reached into the breast pocket of his coat, withdrew a photograph, and held it out to Adam. "Have a look," he said, calmly.

Adam reached for the old sepia-tinted image and saw that his hand was trembling. When he first glimpsed the photograph he heard himself gasp. The photograph must have been taken in a studio or perhaps at a fair. It showed the three brothers astride a mock zeppelin each with a hat in an upraised hand. They were dressed in modest suits, their hair pomaded, their expressions oddly grave given the levity of the montage. And there in the middle sat Pere Soler. His resemblance to Paco wasn't merely uncanny; Adam felt as if he were indeed gazing at an image of his son. He stared at the photograph for a long time. The proof was indisputable, but rather than feeling crushed by the revelation, he suddenly felt strangely buoyant, as if a burden had been lifted and a secret so long and scrupulously guarded had at last been revealed. What was the sense of perpetuating the ruse any longer?

"It must be the Soler genes," said Adam, nodding.

Quim lowered his head and opened his eyes and fixed them on Adam. "Is it true?"

"Yes," said Adam with a sigh of relief.

"I knew it the moment I set eyes on him."

They were silent for a time. Quim had closed his eyes again and was smiling broadly. As well he should, thought Adam; it's not every day that a man discovers he's a father. But what of Paco? Adam wondered. How would he take the news? Something told him that his erstwhile son would not be smiling so broadly.

"I will need time to speak to Paco about all this," said Adam, anxiously.

Quim opened his eyes again and stared at Adam. "What good could possibly come of that?"

"He should know the truth," said Adam without conviction.

"The truth? Quim repeated. "The truth is overrated; it can be a curse. Some things are best left unsaid. *You* are Paco's father; you have been all his life and he's a lucky man for it. *Joder,* the young man just lost his mother and now you want him to discover that this old bag of bones is his father. No, it's too late to change all that now. Promise to me that you won't tell him."

"You're always demanding oaths of me" said Adam, trying to sound slightly annoyed, but failing.

"You haven't done too badly by them," said Quim pointedly.

"No, I suppose not," Adam admitted. After all, Quim had given him the two things he cherished most in life, his wife and his son. "Very well, I swear."

"However…" said Quim, pausing. "I would like to see him, to meet him, even briefly."

"Yes, of course," said Adam. He was not a religious man, but suddenly he felt somehow blessed.

Quim leaned back in his chair, closed his eyes, and tilted his head up to the sun. "Now," he said in a contented tone "tell me a bit about the young man."

* * *

They came down the track, walking in pairs and small groups, stepping gingerly in their heels and city shoes, laughing, stopping to admire the landscape or marvel at the gnarled, centuries-old olive trees. Adam and Paco stood in front of Cal Foraster, watching their approach, talking softly.

"New Yorkers always look so misplaced in the countryside, but never so much as in the Spanish countryside," said Paco.

"They are like fine wines that don't travel well, but I love them still," Adam said.

Father and son laughed together, and Adam realized how long it had been since they had last done so. Behind them, he could hear Rosa moving about in the kitchen, preparing the paella, singing quietly. An aroma of the sea hung in the air. In a great tub of ice wine was chilling. Inside, they had set up a long table with mismatched chairs and a few makeshift benches. There would be room enough for everyone, if not, they would squeeze.

"The taxi driver refused to drive his car down the track," said Jeremy Branch, as he approached "or so I gather, I couldn't make out a word he said."

"A bit of a stroll never hurt anyone," said Margaret, half-scolding.

"What a striking house," said Paul Weems "it looks like Miró's place in Montroig, but smaller."

"Oh, I can just see Lucía here," said Katia.

More guests came drifting down. "Welcome to Cal Foraster everyone," cried Adam, above the chatter.

The day was sunny, but brisk. They gathered outside around an open fire. Paco served vermouth as an *aperitivo* and offered plates of *jamón* and dishes of olives and fried almonds.

"I think I could get used to this," said Lorenzo "now that Franco is dead and gone."

"I bet you can buy a house here for a song," Branch said.

"And make your own olive oil," said Gabriela.

"And live off the fat of the land," said Paco, in a mock twang.

They all liked it here, Adam could see. He began to better understand why Lucía had made a temporary home here. He wondered what would happen to the place. Adam looked around, surveying the property, and suddenly saw Quim coming slowly down the track with the help of a walking stick. He called Paco over. "Would you be good enough to go and help that guest coming down the track?"

"Who is it?" Paco asked.

"A very dear friend of your mother's and mine, an old comrade," said Adam.

"The man in the photograph with you and *mamá*, the one on the mantle in the library in New York?" Paco asked.

"Yes, how on earth did you know that?"

"Every time I asked *mamá* who the other man in the photograph was, she always said 'just an old comrade.' Tell me, does this old comrade have a name?"

"Yes, Quim Soler, now go to him."

Lorenzo approached and began to describe an excursion that he and Gabriela had taken the day before, something about the river, a castle, and two members of the Civil Guard, but Adam scarcely listened. His eyes continually shifted to the track, watching Quim and Paco's progress, wondering what they could be talking about, gauging their chemistry. Quim had an arm hooked in Paco's; they stopped from time to time to allow Quim to catch his breath or make a point. Adam could see Paco stooping to listen, laughing, looking surprised.

Rosa called them inside to the table. It was a tight fit, but everyone was in fine spirits. Adam seated Quim between Paco and Gabriela so that he could speak Spanish. They had just settled into their places when there was a gentle knock at the door and Victor appeared, followed by Inés and Francisco. A lull fell over the table. Adam jumped up to receive them.

"I am aware that we are uninvited, but I hope that we are not unwelcome," said Inés.

"We wanted to be a part of any memorial to Lucía," Francisco said.

"But of course," Adam insisted.

Everyone made room at the table, conversation resumed, and soon Rosa appeared with assorted salads, dishes of artichokes and wild mushrooms, and platters of oysters and fried fish. They drank wine from *porrónes* with mixed success, and mercifully, glasses were procured.

Before the paella appeared, before he consumed too much wine to speak lucidly, Adam rose from his chair at the head of the table, called Rosa in to join them, and addressed the band of friends and family.

"I am delighted to see that this is a joyous celebration and not a somber gathering. Lucía, or to use the full name of which she was so proud, Lucía Vidal i Grau, would approve. Her spirit is at this table and in this lovely house. I must confess that at first I was sorry that Lucía had passed away here in Spain and not in America, but I now see that I was mistaken. She died and is buried in her native soil and in a country that she never wished to flee and to which she forever longed to return. It is fitting that here she has been laid to rest. To the ancients, Lucía was the goddess of childbirth, the one who brought forth light. She certainly illuminated my life and Paco's and all of yours. That is why we are here. So please raise your glasses and join me in toasting Lucía, the giver of light."

Everyone at the table got to their feet—Quim helped up by Paco, Francisco by Victor—raised their glasses, and chimed: "To Lucía, the giver of light!"

Rosa and Inés retreated to the kitchen and returned carrying the enormous paella between them. The Americans had never seen such a thing and gasped. The plates were served and passed around. Rosa took a seat at Adam's side.

"*Bon profit,* which is to say, enjoy your meal," said Francisco, before everyone took up their forks and dug in.

Victor demonstrated the proper manner to peel a shrimp, Quim to eat with the half shell of a mussel, Inés to scrape the bottom of the paella pan in search of the golden, crusty rice that the Catalans call *socarrat.*

"This is a veritable education," said Paul Weems.

"We are thinking of retiring here," Archie Candee announced.

They all told stories about Lucía: Inés from their childhood, Paco from his, Margaret from Lucía's early days in New York, Adam from their travels. Finally, Quim recounted, and Paco translated, the time during the war when Lucía rode across the river bringing food and drink to his half-starved men in a farm house at the front. "She risked her life," he told them, just managing to hold back the tears. "She was not only beautiful and intelligent, capable and loving, but brave, so very brave. I have never known a woman like her."

As the plates were cleared away, and the afternoon wore on, and the guests lingered, drinking coffee and brandy, and drifting into smaller groups and more intimate conversations, Adam surveyed the table and felt a peculiar happiness. He saw Paco and Katia together again, Quim with his arm around Francisco's shoulder as Lucía's brother confessed something quietly, Gabriela and Lorenzo urging Victor to come to live in New York.

"Just look at all the lives she touched," said Rosa to Adam, as if she had been reading his thoughts.

"How fortunate we are to have been a part of it," he said.

Inés approached. "I have some rather important news for you," she told Adam. Rosa began to get up from her chair, but Inés stopped her. "No," she said "stay, this is a family matter. Perhaps Paco should hear it too."

Adam gestured to his son and Katia across the table for them to join him. When they were all seated together, Inés asked for more wine for everyone. Ah, thought Adam, another toast, but no.

"This morning my siblings and I met with the family lawyer for the reading of our mother's will and testament," she explained. "I will see that you receive a copy. There is much that will not concern you, but a good deal that will. In her great wisdom my mother saw fit to leave this house and property to Lucía."

Adam looked at Inés and then at Paco with an expression of astonishment, but he said nothing.

"And not just this house and property," Inés continued "but perhaps more importantly, a considerable strip of land on the coast around and including Cap Groc."

"Where Borja and Javier have plans for a development?" Adam asked.

"We were all part of that scheme," Inés admitted, shaking her head, "everyone except Lucía and our mother."

"And now?" Adam asked.

"And now it is in your hands," she told him.

"Actually, it will be Paco's concern," Adam said. He turned to his son with a faint, quizzical smile. "In your mother's will, you are the sole beneficiary."

Paco paused, his eyes wide, and exhaled audibly. "Goodness," he said "suddenly I'm a landowner."

"I cannot imagine a better ending to all of this," said Inés.

Paco looked at Katia, smiling warmly, and then at the others. "Actually," he said "it may well be a beginning."

And they all raised their glasses and drank to that.

EPILOGUE

PACO ARRIVED AT THE TRAIN STATION just as the 11:07 rolled in from Barcelona. He rushed to the middle of the platform, craning his neck, looking up and down the track, watching for the first glimpse of her. Students, home for the weekend, brushed past, so too assorted day trippers, elderly couples, some army conscripts hauling duffel bags and looking haggard, a solitary priest…but no Katia. She may have missed her flight from London or the train from Barcelona, Paco told himself; or perhaps she wasn't coming at all, he thought anxiously. He felt a tightening in his chest, a low, dull beating of his heart, an emptiness.

A day after that fateful memorial lunch for his mother nearly six months before, when he discovered that he had inherited a house and property and a new dimension to his life, Paco had asked Katia to marry him at last. No, she had said, brusquely, surprising him; she did not want him making such a decision in the wake of Lucía's death. She intended to return to London and her role in *The Cherry Orchard*, but she promised to come back to Spain in May when the Chekhov run ended. They would talk about the future then. He was not crushed; he understood her. Paco installed himself at Cal Foraster, hoping to absorb something of his mother's world, to write, to care for Quim Soler, "the Old Comrade", to wait.

Now he waited until he was the last one on the station platform. He watched a conductor emerge from the rear of the train bearing a weighty bag, which he placed on the platform. And then before Paco caught sight of her, he heard her. "Much obliged to you," said Katia in that delicious Texas cadence, and at last Paco saw her alight from the train car. As he walked toward her he felt a moment of immeasurable happiness. He knew at once that he was saved.

Magical days followed, the hours of light growing ever longer, the sun radiant but not yet blinding. Paco felt like he was living life for the first time; everything that had come before seemed now like a simulacrum. Cal Foraster became their haven; for days at a time they scarcely left the property. In the mornings Paco rose early and wrote at the big table in the living room, light streaming in through the windows and the open front door, everything quiet save for birdsong or the whirring of a tractor far-off. The Gaudi book had been laid to rest, a distant memory; he wanted to write something about his mother's life, something about war and exile, love and memory, life. Slowly he made progress. When he heard Katia begin to stir upstairs, he brought her coffee and they made love in the bed in which his mother had died. Funny that, he thought, it didn't bother him; on the contrary, he felt a certain sense of continuity on account of it.

Paco had bought a car from Sebastián Abad. The man recognized him immediately despite the passage of time; he offered his condolences, spoke fondly of his mother. Then his eyes grew wide and he ushered Paco to a corner of the showroom where the luxury cars were on display.

"No," said Paco. "I think I'd like something…*más humilde.*" He eyed a black and maroon *Deux Chevaux.* "That one," he told Sebastián.

"You are as decisive as your mother," Sebastián told him.

Before Paco drove off, Sebastián leaned down to the driver's window. "You know, even when she was a child I knew she was different."

"How so?" Paco asked.

"Hard to say, it was something she radiated."

Every few days Paco and Katia drove to Tortosa to do their marketing. Katia carried a large wicker basket on her arm and made lists of everything she wanted in Spanish and Catalan: *berenjenas, champiñones, huevos...pebrots, julivert, formatge...* She had an actor's natural ear for language. The merchants loved her, even the women; they gave her things—flowers, special pieces of fruit—adding them to her basket with a wink. When they got back to Cal Foraster, they cooked together, then set up a table beneath an olive tree and ate like peasants, propping their elbows on the table, talking with their mouth's full, drinking wine from the *porrón,*

"Never in my life have I been so happy," said Paco one day as they lingered at the table after lunch, cast in golden light, heady with wine.

"Yo tampoco," said Katia.

"Now will you marry me?" he asked, pleading.

"Sí!"

Two days later they invited Rosa and Quim to lunch at the fisherman's restaurant on Cap Groc. It was mid-June. The day was searing, not a cloud in the sky. A sea breeze relieved some of the heat.

"They are going to rename this stretch of the coast Cap Paco on account of the new owner," said Quim, straight-faced.

"Is that true?" Katia asked, excitedly.

"No it is not," said Rosa, slapping Quim's hand.

They all laughed, but Quim contained himself so as not to set off a wheezing attack. The four of them had not been together since Lucía's memorial lunch, but there was an easiness between them, as if they'd all known one another for years. What they had in common, of course, was Lucía; even with her gone it was enough to bind them. Paco had seen Quim a good deal over the past six months. He had visited him often at Cal Soler, run errands for him, took him out. Mostly they just talked, sometimes about the war and the friendship between Quim and his parents. Paco wanted to know everything. He said it was for his new book, but he knew it was more than that; he suspected Quim did as well.

The owner came out to take their order. When he asked after Lucía, everyone at the table grew silent and looked away.

"I'm afraid she is no longer with us," said Quim finally.

The man pulled up a chair and sat down, visibly shaken. *"Me cago en Deu,"* he whispered. It was the sort of blasphemy that one reserved for the most extreme circumstances.

"This is her son Paco," said Rosa.

"I am sorry for your loss," the man said. "Your mother was like a ray of light. The world is a darker place without her."

What a lovely thing to say, thought Paco. "Thank you."

Eventually the man rose and walked slowly toward the kitchen. He never did take their order. He simply emerged over the next two hours with a series of dishes. "These were the things that Lucía liked," he said by way of explanation. They ate mussels and urchins, razor clams and spiny lobster, black rice and sea-bass. With every dish their spirits rose.

"Gracious, I thought we ate copiously in the South," said Katia.

They passed on dessert. The owner brought out glasses of brandy instead. They all drank to Lucía. Paco said to refill the glasses.

"I have another toast, and I know that my mother would have been very pleased to hear it," he said. "Katia has agreed to marry me."

Everyone cheered and drained their glasses.

"Furthermore," said Katia "we would like you, Rosa and Quim, to be our witnesses at the ceremony."

Both Rosa and Quim began to cry. Paco tried to soothe them, but Quim shook his head. "You don't understand," he said, "these are tears of joy."

"Yes," Rosa agreed, reaching out and taking hold of Katia's and Paco's hands.

After lunch they moved to a spot of shade beneath the pines above the beach for a siesta.

"I hope the owners of this property don't mind if we sprawl out here," Quim said in mock earnest.

"Oh, no," said Paco, smiling "that's what they want people to do with this land."

Soon Rosa and Quim dozed off, the two of them snoring lightly. Katia lay with her head on Paco's chest. Neither of them could sleep; they were too excited.

"I'm so glad that we asked them to be our witnesses," Katia whispered. "Did you see how happy it made them, especially Quim?"

"Yes."

"It's the sort of honor that a son would ask of his father," she added.

"Yes," said Paco "that's it exactly."

The End

OTHER WORKS BY NICHOLAS SHRADY

Sacred Roads: Adventures from the Pilgrimage Trail

Tilt: A Skewed History of the Tower of Pisa

*The Last Day: Wrath, Ruin, and Reason in the
Great Lisbon Earthquake of 1755*

Find them on Amazon at:
https://tinyurl.com/sq6lqzh

Printed
February, 2020